WILDEST DREAMS

THE WILDS OF MONTANA

KRISTEN PROBY

&

Ampersand

Publishing, Inc.

Wildest Dreams

A Wilds of Montana Novel

By

Kristen Proby

WILDEST DREAMS

A Wilds of Montana Novel

Kristen Proby

For Coco Chanel.

LETTER FROM THE AUTHOR

Dear Reader,

I need to take a moment to thank a few people for their help in the research for *Wildest Dreams*, and to tell you a quick story.

First of all, I need to extend my gratitude to David Ossa of Charter Flight Group, who walked me through what kind of plane Ryan would own, was gracious and generous with his knowledge, and just an overall joy to work with. Any mistakes in the story are my own.

In early April of 2024, I was lucky enough to go to Paris for a book event and extend my stay with some friends as a milestone birthday gift to myself. Part of that gift was being able to stay at the Ritz Paris, and it was an absolutely glorious experience. I knew that, for this book, I needed to research a very important suite at the Ritz, and the amazing staff there was happy to give me a tour and answer all of my questions.

I spent over an hour in the Suite Coco Chanel, taking

photos, soaking up the essence of that room, and asking about a million questions about the fashion icon, the Ritz itself, fashion week, and all the incredible things that happen during that time. To say that I was enthralled is an understatement. Like Polly, attending fashion week in Paris is now on my bucket list.

So, I'm extending another huge thank-you to the generous staff at the Ritz Paris for their knowledge, kindness, and hospitality, not only during the hour I was gifted in that suite but during my entire stay. Their attention to detail and luxury is unparalleled.

Of course, I took a couple of liberties for the sake of fiction, but everything in this story about Mademoiselle Coco Chanel is true. I hope you enjoy this piece of the story as much as I enjoyed writing it.

Now, grab yourself your favorite beverage, and let me tell you a story...

xo,

Kristen

PROLOGUE

RYAN

Her thick, red, *fucking amazing* hair is like silk between my fingers where my hand is fisted at the nape of her neck as I plunder her luscious mouth. She tastes like strawberries and champagne and absolute *sin*, and I can't get enough of her.

"Jesus, God, yes," she moans against my lips as I pluck at a nipple. At the rate we're going, we'll make it through the box of condoms before sunrise because I have no intention of sleeping tonight. "It's so *good.*"

I've known her for *years*, have been attracted to her for just as long, and thanks to a few drinks at my brother's wedding and some serious flirtation, I've got her in my bed, naked and writhing beneath me.

"You're so fucking beautiful." Nibbling down her neck, I make my way to her small, round breasts and tug a nipple into my mouth. Polly Allen is petite, at least a foot shorter than me, and she has curves so damn amazing that, once they finished creating her, the gods wept with joy.

My hand glides down her belly, and I slide two fingers inside of her, only to have her grind against me and moan with anticipation.

"You're soaking." I kiss down her belly, needing to taste her. So, I reverse our positions and lie flat on the bed. "Sit on my face."

Polly's green eyes go wide, and then she laughs. "Yeah, right, I'll smother you."

"Not a chance." I hook my arm around her waist and pull her up my body and settle her right over my face, then grab her ass and urge her down over me so I can lick and suck and devour her.

"Oh, my God," she moans, leaning against the dark leather headboard. Her hips move back and forth as she rides my face, and when I push my fingers inside of her again, I feel her already contracting with her impending orgasm.

She comes hard and fast, grinding down over my face, and I lap up every delicious drop of her. When she's finished, I wiggle out from under her, tuck a pillow under her hips to keep her ass in the air, and, once I've protected us both, I tease her with the tip of my cock.

"For fuck's sake, Ryan," she breathes, pushing back, urging me to slam inside of her.

"What?" I fist that glorious hair once more, loving the way it feels in my hand, and lean in to press my lips against her ear. "What do you want, Polly? Use your words."

"I want—" She licks her lips. "I want you to fuck me."

I grin, biting her earlobe. "Good girl."

Taking it easy, I push inside, not wanting to hurt her, but she's so fucking wet she takes me easily, and we both groan with the pleasure of it.

"God, you're snug," I growl and push up to drag my hand down her spine to the small of her back as I push in and out of her. My thumb tickles her tight little pink anus, and she yells out as she comes again, all over me.

It's the most beautiful thing I've ever seen in all of my thirty-three years, and her pussy tightening around me sends me over the edge with her.

I lean in to press my forehead against her back, then kiss her spine, right between her shoulder blades, before I pull out and collapse to the side of her.

Polly's face is buried in a pillow, but she turns to suck in a breath and opens one emerald-green eye to watch me.

"That was fun," she says, her voice still breathless.

"That's one word to describe it."

I'd use life-altering.

"I should go," she says with a frown.

"It's one in the morning." I brush a lock of hair off her cheek and hook it behind her ear. "Where could you possibly need to be at this time of the night?"

"Well, you probably didn't plan on having an overnight guest."

"No, I didn't plan it." I grin and push over to kiss her soft, swollen lips. "It's a happy surprise. You're staying here, Polly. I'm not done with you yet."

She lets out a strangled laugh. "You're trying to kill me."

"But what a way to go."

I WAKE the way I always do: quickly and fully alert. But I don't open my eyes yet. I can smell the sex and Polly's perfume, and I could swear the sound of my name on her lips as she succumbed to that last orgasm still hangs in the air. I grin, remembering how amazing she looked, spread out like a feast before me, and I'm not ashamed to say that I took full advantage.

That couldn't have been more than an hour ago.

I crack open one eye and glance over at my phone on the bedside table, surprised to see that it's already eight a.m. I'm always up by six.

Of course, I don't usually go half a dozen rounds of sex with no sleep in between in one night. I blame Polly.

She's fucking irresistible.

Deciding to snuggle up to her for a few before I make my way downstairs to make her breakfast, I turn over to pull her against me but find an empty bed. Scowling, I run my hand over the sheets and find it already cool.

Maybe she went downstairs looking for coffee and food. I climb out of bed, brush my fingers through my hair as I locate a pair of jeans, put them on, and then go in search of one stunning redhead.

But when I walk downstairs, the house is quiet, and

there's no scent of coffee in the air. I check the rest of the house and then run to the front door and swear ripely when I find that her car is gone.

She fucking left.

CHAPTER ONE
POLLY

It's the first day of glorious summer.

Stepping out of the front door of my shop, Pocket Full of Polly, I take in a long, deep breath. I can smell new leaves and grass in the air, and the birds are chirping with excitement, as if they know it's summer, too. The sun is out, and I don't have to try to remember my damn winter jacket anymore.

In this part of Montana, the seasons literally change like clockwork. We had a small snowstorm just last week, and now it's a warm summer day with just a hint of a cool breeze, and I'm walking down the sidewalk in Bitterroot Valley toward the coffee shop that my friend, Millie Wild, owns.

"Good morning," I announce with a smile as I sashay into Bitterroot Valley Coffee Co. "It's *summer!*"

"Hell to the yes," Millie returns as she smiles back at me from where she's making magic at her ginormous coffee-making contraption behind the counter. "And it's a pretty day. I've had enough gloom and cloud cover to last until...well, next winter."

I laugh and walk to the counter. Every hair on my body stands up as the door opens behind me, and in walks Millie's older brother, Ryan.

The man I've had a crush on since I was old enough to know what that means.

The man who rocked my world last September for an entire night.

The same man who never called me afterward.

"Polly," Ryan says with a wide, happy grin. "It's good to see you."

"Hey, Ryan." He hugs me, and my damn nipples betray me by going instantly hard. "How are you?"

"I'm great." He smiles down at me as he pulls away and stuffs his hands into his pockets. He looks fucking *delicious* in a simple black T-shirt and jeans, and he's wearing his signature baseball cap, backward. "And yourself? Your brother tells me that you've closed the shop for the week."

"I have." I nod and then smile at Millie when she passes me my favorite coffee. I don't even have to order; she just whips it up and keeps a tab for me. "I'm doing some rearranging, replacing old stock with new, and cleaning. I do it every spring before the summer rush starts."

And I freaking *love* it. Touching all the clothes and styling them to look trendy and attractive is my favorite. But freshening the place up, deep cleaning, and showing my business love is also rewarding.

"Mac also mentioned that he'll be helping you today?" Ryan asks as Millie passes him a cup of coffee.

As more customers shuffle in behind us, Ryan and I move off to the side to get out of their way.

"He is," I confirm with a nod. "I have some heavy things that need to be moved, built, and all that good stuff, and Mac's coming to do most of that for me."

"I can help," Ryan offers immediately, and I want to say no. When I'm around him, which isn't often, all I can think about is how good it felt when he gave me some of the best orgasms of my damn life. *But* I'm sure Mac could use an extra pair of hands, and I know from experience that Ryan has the muscles. "I'll bring Jake, too."

"Are you sure?" I shift on my feet, thinking it over. "I can bring in lunch for everyone as a thank-you."

"Are you kidding? Jake will do just about anything for a sandwich. The kid eats anything that isn't tied down."

That makes me laugh. Last winter, Ryan took Jake in after Jake had been brutalized by his foster dad. Earlier this year, Ryan officially adopted the teenager, and I am *so* happy for the two of them. From what I hear, they get along great, and Jake loves working out on Ryan's ranch with the horses and other animals.

"Jake is absolutely welcome to come help. Are you sure you're not too busy? I know you must have your own business to see to."

His lips tip up on one side, and he shrugs a shoulder. "The best part about being the boss is I can make my own hours."

"Well, that's true. I'll be at the shop all day, if you and Jake want to pop in for a while. I'd really appreciate it."

Ryan nods and walks with me to the door. "I'll go kick the kid out of bed. Since school let out for the summer, all he wants to do is sleep after he does his morning chores."

"That sounds pretty normal to me. I'll see you later."

With a wave, I head back to the shop. Is it a bad idea to have Ryan around to help out today? Probably. But I could use the extra hands, and I'm an adult. I can curb my lustful thoughts when it comes to the sexy billionaire cowboy.

Probably.

While Mac loads boxes of new product onto a dolly to bring into the newly cleaned showroom, I'm shifting older stock to clearance racks in the back of the store. Loaded down with about fifty pounds of clothes, I try to lift the hangers onto the tall rack, but I'm just not tall enough.

"It sucks when you're a tiny leprechaun," I mutter to myself.

"Prettiest leprechaun I've ever seen," Ryan says from behind me, startling me. He reaches around me to take the hangers out of my hands and easily lifts them onto the rack. His body presses against mine, and the spicy, woodsy scent of him surrounds me.

I could eat him with a spoon.

"Thanks." I smile up at him as he steps back. "I was too impatient to grab the step stool."

"Now you don't have to." He gestures over to Jake with his head. "The kid and I are here to help. Are you filling these racks with clearance?"

"Yes." I turn to Jake with a smile. "Thanks for this. I know it's probably not how you planned to spend summer vacation."

"It's one day," the handsome teenager says. "And I hear I get a sandwich out of the deal, so it's all good."

With a laugh, I turn back to Ryan. "Mac's in the back, loading up new product to be unboxed. I'll have Jake help me with the rest of the clearance."

"I have my marching orders," Ryan says with a wink, and off he goes to help out my brother.

"I'm so glad you're tall," I say to Jake as I lead him to the racks of clothes that I have sorted by size. "In fact, I think you've grown about six inches in the past year."

"About that..." he confirms. "Ry says it's because of all the food I eat and claims I'm eating him out of house and home, but he can afford it." His grin is a happy one, and that makes *me* happy. It was just last year that I found the boys he was hanging out with shoplifting from my store. I'm so glad that he's turned his life around.

"Things at Ryan's are good, then?"

"The best." He sighs, props his hands on his hips, and looks out the window. "Sometimes I don't know if I deserve everything that he's done for me, you know? It's a lot. Just letting me live with him is enough, but I have the horses, and he bought me a truck for Christmas. Shit, he *adopted* me. Oops, sorry for the shit."

"No problem. I've said it myself." I pass him some more clothes to move. "These can go right behind the others up there. You know, I don't think that a man like Ryan does much of anything that he doesn't *want* to do. And he absolutely wouldn't do it for someone who doesn't deserve it. Powerful men like that are successful for a reason."

Jake turns back to me after placing the clothes on the rack, and we walk back to gather more. "I know. It's so weird to think about how much money he has. Especially because he's just a regular guy. Mostly normal."

I laugh and pass him more clothes and then follow him, loaded down with more of my own, and before long, we've transferred everything to where they need to go.

I'm pleased to realize that there's less left over from last season than I planned for, so I can use more racks for the new stuff.

Ryan and Mac come strolling in, pushing dollies loaded with big boxes of clothes that I can't wait to get my hands on.

"Jesus, clothes are heavy," Mac says with a scowl. "I thought summer clothes were supposed to weigh *less*."

"I can just get *more* in the boxes," I reply. "I have hangers set up over there, with my steamer. I'll get going on that if the three of you want to start putting my new shelves together."

"Power tools," Jake says with a grin. "Manly stuff."

Ryan laughs, and the three of them return to the back, where my big storage room is, to start assembling the furniture. I unlock my phone and turn on my favorite playlist, pairing it to the Bluetooth speakers in the shop, and then set it aside. As Harry Styles starts to sing about watermelon sugar, I dive into boxes, slicing them open with my box cutter, and then I start to hang them on hangers, sort by size, and then steam.

It's a long, laborious process, but I love it. I have four employees who all offered to come in and help today, but they've been here all week, cleaning and sorting, and they've put in long days. So, I told them to take today off, and I'd work on this part alone. It'll take me through the weekend to get it all unpacked, pressed, and set out, but it'll be worth it.

I've just moved on to my fifth box, and Ed Sheeran is crooning about dancing in the dark when I'm suddenly swept up in Ryan's arms, and he dances me around the mostly empty showroom.

I'm laughing when, still singing along, he dips me back and then brings me back up and hugs me.

"I couldn't resist," he says and kisses me on the cheek before pulling away. "We're about ready for the furniture."

"That was fast."

"It's good furniture," he says. "Not particle board that you have to put together piece by piece. Do you want to show me where you want it?"

"Sure." Pleased that he approves of what I chose, I show Ryan where I want each piece, and then he disappears into the back again, and I have to take a deep breath.

Being around that man is...well, it does things to me. And he doesn't seem to be affected *at all.* Which is a bit of a blow to the ego, but oh, well. Before long, the men have everything placed exactly where I want it, and the four of us stand back, admiring it.

"I like the colors," Jake offers. "They're not boring brown."

"I wanted to brighten the space up," I agree. "The only windows are the ones in the front, and dark furniture would make it feel like a cave in here. So, I got pieces that were painted in bright colors. I think it looks great, guys. Thanks. I'll go order those sandwiches."

I take their order and call it in to the deli down the street.

"They'll be here in about twenty minutes."

"What can we do in the meantime?" Ryan asks.

"I have to hang some mirrors in the dressing rooms," Mac says. "You can help me with those heavy fuckers."

"Mac!" I gesture to Jake. "Really? There's a kid here."

"Oh, I've heard it all," Jake assures me. "It's fine. I can help lift a mirror."

"He's a good kid," I say to Ryan when the other two are in the back, measuring for the mirrors.

"Yeah, he is. We've had a few bumps here and there, but he'll be sixteen, and I suspect that's normal."

"I would guess so," I agree with a nod. "Well, I'd better get back to hanging these clothes."

"You know," he continues, not taking the hint at *all*, "you do a lot of avoiding me these days."

I frown down at the pair of white jeans I'm holding. "I don't think that's true."

"At Summer and Chase's wedding last month, you didn't even *look* at me."

"I was busy," I remind him. "I was the maid of honor, and I had a long list of duties."

"Polly."

I stop at the sound of his voice and turn to look at him, raising an eyebrow.

"I don't want things to be weird between us." He reaches out and tucks a stray strand of hair behind my ear.

"You didn't call." I feel my eyes widen. I did *not* mean to say that out loud. "Uh, never mind. That was—"

"You left," he says, interrupting me. "If you wanted me to call, you sent me a mixed message with that move."

I bite my lip, thinking it over, and then let out a gusty sigh, but the other guys return to us, looking smug.

"All done," Mac says and high-fives Jake. The door opens, and Jeannie, the manager of Mama's Deli, walks in, carrying two big brown bags full of food.

"Delivery," she calls out with a smile. "Oh, it's already so *different* in here, Polly. I can't wait to see it when you've finished."

"I reopen Monday morning," I inform her as Mac takes the bags off her hands, and I pass her the cash to cover the order. "I have some new things that I think you're going to love."

"Now I *really* can't wait. I'm so grateful that you carry inclusive sizes for us curvier girls," Jeannie says with a happy smile.

"Every woman is gorgeous and deserves to wear clothes that make her feel confident," I reply. "No matter her size. Definitely come see me next week, and I'll help you shop."

"I can't wait. Have a good day, all of you. I'd better get back."

She hustles out the door, and I turn to find Ryan watching me intently.

"What? Do I have something on my face?"

"No." He shakes his head and takes a bite of his sandwich. "You're a good businesswoman."

Coming from the likes of Ryan Wild, the owner and CEO of Wild Enterprises, a multi-billion-dollar company, that's a *huge* compliment.

"Thanks." I raise my sandwich to tap to his in *cheers*.

God, I'm tired. Down-to-the-marrow-of-my-bones tired.

But I'm also incredibly satisfied with all the work that I got done today.

It's past dark when I get home and shuffle into the bedroom, strip out of the yoga pants and tank that I wore to work today, and put on a loose T-shirt and sweats. Then I pad into the kitchen and pour myself a glass of crisp white wine before walking out back to my little patio.

Mac was here earlier this week and power-washed the patio for me, cleaned up my little patio swing, and got the gas fireplace ready to fire up.

So, I start the fire and sit in the swing, gently rocking back and forth as I take in the fragrant spring air.

The birds have settled down, and now I can hear the buzz of a few insects and the engine of a car as they drive past on the road out front. I can smell someone's grill and the burgers or steak they cooked on it, and it makes my empty stomach grumble.

I haven't eaten anything since the sandwich this afternoon, and that was long ago and far away.

But I'm too tired to put anything together, and the stove in the kitchen isn't working anyway. Who has time for house repairs when they have a business to run? Mac would probably fix it for me, but I keep forgetting to mention it.

I'm hardly ever here, so it seems silly to put that at the top of the priority list.

My phone pings with a text, and I grin when I see Summer's name. She's my best friend and owns Paula's Poseys, the floral shop just across from my own. Someone set her business on fire last fall, and she'll be reopening in a couple of weeks, just in time for wedding season.

Summer: I'm coming to help you tomorrow. You can't say no.

I laugh and sip my wine. As much as I love touching

each piece of clothing myself, with as tired as I am tonight, I know that I *need* the extra hands if I'm going to open by Monday.

Me: Not saying no! I can use your help, and we can gossip and eat chocolate. Win-win. Come in anytime. I'll be there by 8.

I check the time. Shit, eight o'clock is in roughly seven hours, so I'd better to go bed.

But I love it out here on my little patio. I like the sounds and smells of the neighborhood. It feels good to know that although my house is old and small and has *so much* that needs to be fixed up, it's *mine.* I worked hard for it. This little piece of the world belongs to me, and I love it here.

My eyes have started to droop, so I finish my wine and go inside, locking the door behind me, then rinse my wineglass out before setting it on the drainer. I need a shower, so I head off for the bathroom. My bathroom is *tiny,* and it's the only one in the two-bedroom house. The tub always looks dirty, even though I scrub it weekly. The sink needs to be caulked, and the mirror is cracked in the corner.

I didn't do that, so I didn't get the seven years of bad luck from it.

By the time I'm clean, lotioned, and dry, I feel like I'm going to fall over, so I do just that. I'm face down on my pillow, ready to drift off to sleep.

But I'm already excited for tomorrow.

CHAPTER TWO

RYAN

One of the CC TV screens on the wall wakes up, catching my attention. Motion has to have triggered it, and I narrow my eyes, watching closely, but I don't see anything. My property is locked down tight, and I have a security team that discreetly and fiercely protects my home twenty-four seven, so if there *is* anything out there, they'll find it. Most of the time, it's an animal that triggers the cameras, so I'm not particularly worried about it. But once in a while, it's a situation.

It would be nice to be in a position to not need the guards all the time, but this is the downside of what I do and who I am.

I take my glasses off and set them on my desk, then rub my hands over my face and reach for my coffee, scowling when I find the mug empty.

It's two in the morning. I should be asleep, but I spent the day helping Polly at her shop with Mac and

Jake. What I told her is true: I *am* the boss, and I *can* make my own hours, but doing so sets me behind, so I'm catching up tonight.

But I have no regrets.

I had a great time today, and Jake had fun, too. I caught him and Polly laughing and joking around several times, and it made me smile. When Jake first came to live with me last year, he never smiled much. He was too bruised, physically and emotionally, but he's healing, and it fills me with satisfaction to know that this ranch, and maybe being here with *me,* is what has made a difference for the young man.

I cross to the coffeemaker in the wet bar area of my office, pour myself another cup, and then return to my desk. I have another hour of work before I have to take a shower and dress for meetings all day, via Zoom. I'll start at six a.m. with a meeting with my Zurich office, then London and Paris, New York, and finally, San Francisco. I try to schedule these weekly meetings all in one day, but that isn't always possible.

My assistant and right-hand man, Arthur, sends me a message via our inter-office system, and it pops up in the corner of my screen.

Good morning, sir! We have a packed day today. Why are you up so early?

I smirk. Arthur's been with me for eight years, back when I had only three companies to juggle and decided I needed help. He's helped me grow this company into the massive business that it is. The man keeps me organized and schedules and handles pretty much anything I throw at him.

He also hovers like a worried mother hen.

Working, of course. It's early in New York, too. Why are YOU up?

Within seconds, he replies.

Because I'm your loyal and trusted sidekick, who stays three steps ahead of you so I can anticipate your every need, of course.

It makes me laugh, just as he intended, but I also know that it's partly true. Arthur has things to me before I even know that I need them. He's excellent at what he does, and I pay him very well for his loyalty and hard work.

Call me in two hours, before the first meeting. I'll speak with you then.

Yes, sir.

Two hours later, just before my call with Arthur, Jake comes shuffling into my office, his eyes droopy, a crease down his left cheek from his pillow, and his brown hair standing straight up in the back.

"Good morning," I say to him as I adjust my tie.

"Mornin'," he mumbles and rubs his face. Jake isn't a morning person. "Want a bagel and cream cheese? I'm gonna make some."

I grin at him. He always asks if he can do stuff for me. I haven't quite figured out if it's because he feels obligated because of all I do for him, or if it's just who he is as a human.

I suspect it's a bit of both.

"Sure, I'll take one."

He nods, and rather than make his way down to the kitchen, he crosses to my wet bar where I have everything he needs stocked.

I *like* that Jake wants to hang out in here with me, particularly in the mornings. While he makes us breakfast, I move into the connected bathroom to style my hair and make sure my tie is straight before putting on my suit jacket. When I return, there's a bagel with cream cheese and a side of banana waiting for me on my desk.

"Thanks, buddy." I take a bite and eye him. "What do you have on tap for today?"

"Chores this morning," he says around a bite of his own bagel. "I want to spend some extra time with Firefly today. I thought I saw a limp in her back right leg a couple of days ago. I haven't seen it since, but I want to make sure."

My brother, Chase, wasn't kidding when he told me that Jake was excellent with horses. It's why I hired him last summer, and it is one of the best decisions that I've made. It's as though Jake speaks their language.

"Thank you. If anything is going on, you have Dr. Randolph's number."

He nods thoughtfully. "Yeah, I'll call her if there's anything wrong. Then Chase invited me to go fishing over at his place this afternoon, so I thought I'd do that. I figured I could also help them out if they need it. The house is almost done, you know. I can't believe how fast it went up."

I grin at him. My brother decided to go ahead and hire a company—one I helped him choose—to build his new house out on the ranch, where we grew up. Chase's property sits right by a small lake, with excellent views of the mountains, and Jake loves to go out there, sit at the end of the dock, and cast a line out into the water. I love that he enjoys spending time there with my family.

With *our* family now.

"That sounds fun," I reply, finishing my bagel. "Maybe I'll pop over there after my meetings and see how things are coming along."

"It's really nice," Jake informs me. "I mean, it's a lot smaller than this house, but it seems to fit in there, you know?"

"Yeah." I nod and peel the banana. "I get it. I think the design is great, and Summer and Chase will be happy there for a long, long time."

"Why didn't *you* build on the family ranch?" he asks and drops onto my couch, one leg flung over the arm, as if he plans to stay awhile.

I eye the clock. I have about ten minutes until Arthur calls.

"Well, all five of us siblings have a stake in it," I reply. "And technically, we're all supposed to have acreage there. As you know, Remington runs the ranch and owns the biggest share. And he should; he works his ass off out there."

"That's why he and Erin and the kids live in the old farmhouse," Jake says, and I nod.

"Yep. My parents built a small house not too far away from there several years ago when they decided to retire, so Rem moved him and his family into the farmhouse that we grew up in." I take a bite of the banana. "Chase claimed his property there at the lake, and he chose well. It's pretty out there. I'm sure with time, Millie and Brady will pick out a place that suits them, if they want to live at the ranch."

"Brady lives in that really old cabin," Jake reminds me. "Does he want to stay there?"

I snort. "It's fine for now, but it's tiny. If he ever has a family, he'll want something bigger."

"So, what about *you*?" Jake repeats.

I blow out a breath, thinking it over. "I've always been a stubborn ass."

That makes Jake snicker.

"I guess I wanted to do things on my own, in my own way. It wasn't intentional, actually. I knew the old man who owned this property before me, and when he died, his family didn't want to keep it. A fancy hotel guy wanted to scoop it up and turn it into a resort."

Jake scowls. "Gross."

"Yeah, I didn't like the idea either. So, I put in a higher offer and scooped it up. Then, when I saw the original house, well...it was in pretty bad shape. It was going to cost as much to renovate it as it did to just tear it down and start from scratch. Of course, this house is bigger. And maybe a little fancier."

"A *little*?" He raises an eyebrow.

"Okay, a lot fancier. I like it out here, and I also like knowing that I'm only about ten minutes down the road from Wild River Ranch. I can get over there quickly if anyone needs me."

"And they can get *here* if you need them."

I blink at him and nod. "Yeah, I guess you're right."

"Is the river that runs through the south pasture the Wild River?" he asks. "The same one that runs through the other ranch?"

"Yep."

"So, we're still connected to it."

I grin at him. Since losing his own family to a horrible accident almost two years ago, I know that Jake has craved feeling connected and grounded, and I love that he feels that with my family and the deep roots we've planted here.

"Yeah, I guess we are. That's pretty cool."

"Yeah. Why doesn't *this* ranch have a name?"

My computer lights up with the incoming video call from Arthur, but I ignore it.

"I haven't decided what to call it yet. Maybe you and I can hammer that out."

Jake's eyes widen, and then he nods with excitement. "Yeah, I can totally help with that. I'll think about it. Well, I'll go do my thing," he says. "Have a good day at work."

"Thanks." I grin at him and push out of my chair, still ignoring Arthur. Ruffling his hair, I pull Jake in for a quick hug, clap him on the back, and then pull away. He offers me his fist for a tap the way he always does after our breakfasts together, and I bump it with my own. "Have fun today. Call me if you need anything at all. I can pull out of a meeting in a heartbeat."

He flashes that grin of his. "I know. I will. See you later."

After his footsteps fade down the hall, I accept the video call from Arthur.

"Good morning," I say to him. Arthur is about five years older than me, stick thin with the whitest teeth I've ever seen, and perfectly coifed salt-and-pepper hair. The man could probably have been a model if he'd wanted to go that route.

"Good morning, sir," he replies. In all the years he's worked for me, he's never called me Ryan. It's always *sir* or *Mr. Wild*. "First on the docket this morning is Zurich."

My brain is buzzing but in the best way. I'm always energized after speaking with the individual branches and companies, listening to challenges and successes, and brainstorming the best moves for what comes next.

And I absolutely *love* it when they report that we've found new ways to not only make money but to reinvest that money into the communities of each branch.

With a day of successful check-ins behind me, I change out of the suit and into jeans and a T-shirt and drive over to the ranch to see the progress on Chase and Summer's house, and maybe cast a line with Jake.

It's a beautiful summer day, and I'm looking forward to hanging out with my family for a few hours. Maybe I'll take Jake into town for dinner tonight. We can grab burgers or pizza or something.

My mind shifts to Polly, and I wonder if she's remembered to eat today. Maybe I should invite her to join us for dinner. I'd love to see her and talk with her more.

If I'd known that she'd have been open to me calling her all those months ago, I would have that first morning after I found her gone.

I didn't think she wanted to hear from me. So, hearing her say, with frustration heavy in her sweet voice, that I didn't call her, irritated the hell out of me. We need to clear the air there for sure.

Jake sees me come around the corner, and he waves from his place on the dock where he has a line cast, and Summer's sitting next to him, drinking a Coke.

I park in front of Chase's finished shop and climb out of the truck, walking toward the job site that is a hive of activity. I can see that Jake's right. It's almost done. The outside of the single-story house is getting a paint job—white with black trim—and people bustle in and out of the house. I hear someone using a saw inside, so I skirt around the outside to the dock and walk out to join Jake and Summer.

"Hey there," she says with a grin. "I've been kicked out of the house."

"She's a pain in their ass," Jake adds with a shrug. "Those are Chase's words. So, she came out to sit with me."

"I just want to *help*," she stresses. "I'm not allowed to help in my new shop either, because they're finishing things up there, and I'm in the way. I'm in the way *here*. I can't unpack or decorate or do any of the things I'm dying to do in either place. I did, however, help Polly out today, and that kept my mind occupied for a while."

"How did that go?" I ask casually as I reach into the small cooler at Jake's feet and pull out a Coke of my own.

This kid drinks too much sugar.

"It's awesome in there," Summer replies. "We unpacked all the new clothes, got them hung and pressed, and she was fussing with how she wanted things organized, so I left to come out here to help, but then I was kicked out."

"The fact that you were kicked out is really bugging you." I sit next to her and sip my Coke, enjoying the way the cold, bubbly liquid feels on my throat in the sunshine. "Let the professionals do their thing so you *can* do your part. Otherwise, you'll just slow them down."

"That's what they all said," she replies with a sigh. "*Chase* isn't in the way."

"He knows how to use the power tools and stuff," Jake reminds her as he casts a new line. "Did you see the mirrors in the dressing rooms at Polly's? Mac and I hung those."

"Polly said that you and Ryan helped out yesterday," Summer replies, smiling up at Jake. "You did great. And the furniture looks nice, too. It'll be really bright and pretty for summer and easy to decorate for the holidays. It's the facelift that the place needed."

"And how are things going with *your* shop?" I ask, not wanting to bombard her with questions about Polly. "It looks great from the outside."

"It's *so* great," she replies with a grin. "And I'm just relieved that I'll be ready to go for the heart of wedding season. I'm missing the beginning of it, but that couldn't be helped. We should be in full swing by mid-July, and I'm grateful. I was sure I wouldn't be able to open until fall, and that would have been catastrophic. At least the nursery in town was able to make room for me to do weddings and supply the resort until I'm functional again. I've been able to make bouquets and such out of there."

I nod, understanding exactly what she means. Summer probably makes most of her money over the summer, through big events, and that keeps the business afloat through the rest of the year.

"I'm glad it wasn't catastrophic," I reply and turn when I hear footsteps coming down the dock toward us. "Hey, Chase."

"Can I go in?" Summer demands, springing up from her seat. "*Please*?"

"Yeah, the crew is packing it in for the day. You can go in and daydream all you want."

"*Yes.*" She wraps her arms around Chase's neck, plants a big kiss on him, and then runs off, headed for her new house.

"She's excited," Chase says and sets Lily, the French bulldog he's holding, on the dock. "I don't want to get her hopes up too high, but it looks like it'll be finished by the end of next week."

"That's great." I stand and grin at my younger brother. I'm fucking proud of him. He's built exactly the life he wants here in our little town and out here at the ranch.

"There will be a party." He grins and looks back at the house where Summer disappeared. "Because, of course, there will be."

"It'll be fun," I reply and follow his gaze. "It's a hell of a house. I love the wrap-around porch. The view of the sunsets will be fucking amazing."

"We've already sat on it and watched the sunset," he confirms with a nod. "Life is really fucking good, man."

I glance at Jake, whose grin has to be a mile wide as he listens to us. "Yeah, it is great. Hey, when this is all done, I have a project for you."

That grabs Chase's attention. "What kind of project?"

"I want a new table, about three feet by three feet, that I can set up in the corner of my office so Jake and I can have breakfast in there, since we usually eat in there anyway."

Jake's gaze whips around to mine, his eyes wide. "We can sit on the couch or whatever."

"A table would be nicer," I reply with a shrug. "And Chase makes one hell of a nice one. What do you think?"

"I can do that," Chase replies with a nod. "Give me a couple of weeks, and it'll be done."

"No hurry," I assure him.

Yeah, life is fucking great.

CHAPTER THREE
POLLY

"We did *awesome*." Katie, the youngest of my employees at sixteen, props her hands on her hips and grins at the rest of us. All four of my girls insisted on coming in today to help me finish arranging clothes and displays for our reopening tomorrow.

They wouldn't even let me pay them. Well, Melissa didn't seem to like that she was spending her Sunday here without getting paid, but she went along with the others. I assured her that she didn't have to stay, but she insisted that she wanted to, so I dropped it. I think she didn't like the idea of being left out.

All four of them waltzed in at ten this morning with coffees from Millie's place and announced that they'd be helping until it was done. And I was so relieved because I still had *so* much to do.

"It looks so great," Melissa agrees with a smile and points to a nearby rack. "I can't wait to try on that pink dress."

They discuss which clothes they'll be buying for the summer, and I don't butt in or complain at all. I offer a good discount so my employees can buy their clothes here, wear them at work, and when they're not here, too. Word of mouth is a powerful marketing strategy.

"I have to go," Jessica says as she slings her handbag over her shoulder. "I have to get the kids from my piece-of-shit ex and get them dinner. I have to call him a piece-of-shit now because I can't do it in front of the children."

"I have to go, too," my fourth and final employee, Grace, adds. "My brother wants help in the vegetable garden. At least it's light out until almost eleven at night, and we can do chores late."

"Thank you all so much for helping me today." I give them each a big hug. "If it weren't for you, I'd be here well into the night, and now I can get some rest before tomorrow."

"You do a lot for us," Katie says and quickly checks her phone, shooting off a text faster than anyone else I've seen. How do her fingers move like that? "I'm just excited that school's out so I can work more hours. You guys usually get to have all the fun."

"I do believe that Katie is a workaholic," Jessica says with a laugh.

"No," Katie corrects her, shaking her pretty brunette head. "I'm passionate about *fashion*."

"I can't argue with that."

We laugh, and once everyone has gathered their things and taken off, I make one last pass through my place. To say that I'm in love with how it turned out is an understatement.

The clothes are just *so great.* Beautiful fabrics and colors that feel good on the skin. I've tried everything on, and I can say without a doubt that, although every single piece isn't necessarily for *me,* they are well made and will be great for someone. I love that the pieces look and feel luxurious and comfortable, but there is something for every budget.

The new light-colored furniture makes the place look brighter, and Mac came back today to hang some light fixtures that make it look fancy and happy.

Two things I love.

Another delivery came yesterday of a new sideboard piece that I'm using for storage and a place to set out snacks and drinks. For summer, I'll have lemonade and strawberry biscuit cookies that Jackie Harmon makes over at The Sugar Studio. Jackie makes the *best* cookies. It was hard to narrow it down to just one variety.

I go into the back and turn off the lights, make sure the back door is secure and locked, and then I sling my cross-body Louis Vuitton bag on and return to the front of the store to let myself out the glass door and lock it behind me.

I'm going to treat myself to dinner tonight. I called Summer, but she and Chase are busy out at the new house, so it'll just be me tonight.

And that's okay. I'm getting used to my bestie being preoccupied with her man all the time now. When we were both single, it was easy to get together a few times a week, but now I usually see her just a couple of times a month. I miss her, but I'm *so* happy that she's found her soulmate.

In the mood for pizza, I walk down the block to Old Town Pizza. I'll just order something and take it home so that I can sit outside on my little patio and enjoy the evening. I think I even have some white wine that I haven't opened yet.

Pushing inside the older restaurant—it's been here since my parents were kids—I approach the counter and grin at Heather, the owner, as I relish in the scent of garlic and *pizza*.

"Polly." Heather greets me with a smile. "What can I do for you?"

"I think I'll place an order to take home."

I hear the door open behind me, and when I glance back, I see that it's Ryan and Jake, and every molecule in my body is now on high alert.

Why is this man so *potent*?

"Hey, Miss Polly," Jake says with a shy smile.

"Hi, guys." I look back at Ryan, who's watching me with those steady hazel eyes. I know what it's like to have those eyes watch me as I fall apart at the seams. I clear my throat and smile. "How are you two?"

"We're great. Here for dinner. Want to join us?" Ryan asks, and Jake nods in agreement.

"Oh, I was just going to take something home."

"Sit with us," Jake urges me. "Eating alone is bad for the digestion."

I can't help the burst of laughter at that, and Ryan

frowns at the boy. "Where do you come up with this stuff?"

"It's science."

"Right." I nod at Jake. "Totally science. I don't want to crash your party."

"*Please* crash our party," Ryan replies. "Come on, we'll even let you pick the toppings."

"Who could say no to that?" Heather, who's been eavesdropping, asks. "Table for three, then?"

"Table for three," I agree with a nod, and we follow her to a booth by the windows. "Thank you."

"I'll be back in a few to take your orders," Heather replies with a wink, and then she's bustling off again.

"Thanks for including me," I say to the guys across from me as we get settled with our menus.

"How are things at the shop?" Ryan asks, closing his menu and setting it aside.

"Perfect." I smile over at him. I can't hold back, and I do a little dance in my seat. "It's so *beautiful*, and every single thing is officially in place and ready for tomorrow."

"That's great," he replies with a grin. "You work fast."

"My employees came to help today. Not only wouldn't they take no for an answer, but they wouldn't let me pay them, either. They *wanted* to help out, and we had a lot of fun doing it. They're so sweet. I'll do something special for them this week."

"Doesn't Katie LaRoy work for you?" Jake asks.

"Yes, she does." I tilt my head, watching as Jake's cheeks darken. "Are you two friends?"

"Sort of." Jake clears his throat and seems *very* relieved when we're interrupted by Heather.

"Can I take your drink orders?" she asks.

"I'd love a glass of white wine. It doesn't have to be fancy."

"Good, because I don't have fancy, but I do have white wine." Heather winks at me and turns to the guys.

"I'll also have white wine," Jake says, and Ryan and I both gasp, making Jake laugh. "Your faces were priceless. Iced tea, please."

Heather nods and turns to Ryan. "And for you?"

"Just water."

"Okay, be right back."

"I want to talk more about Katie," I say and smirk when Jake frowns. "But first, what do you guys get on your pizza?"

"Everything," Ryan says.

"Even anchovies?" I ask in disgust.

"No, they don't serve them here," Jake says. "But if they did, we would. Because we're men."

"Okay, then."

"But we told you that you could choose," Ryan says, reminding me. "What do *you* get?"

"Everything," I reply and smile. "But not anchovies, even if they did serve them. That's where I draw the line."

"Is that what you *usually* get," Jake wants to know, "or are you just saying that?"

"Hey, Heather," I call out, getting the other woman's

attention. When she looks up and grins, I say, "What's my usual order?"

"Large everything," she replies, and I give her a thumbs-up.

"See? Told you."

Ryan's grinning at me. Just watching me and smiling, and it does things to my lady bits that are not appropriate for being in public. His grin widens, as if he *knows.*

Can the man read minds now?

"I'm going to go get the new high score on the pinball machine," Jake says and scoots out of the booth before walking to the back of the restaurant where the game is.

"I love that he's so sure of himself," Ryan says, watching the boy as he walks away.

"Also, I think he's trying his best to avoid my questions about Katie. He must have a crush on her."

"He hasn't said anything to me, but that doesn't surprise me. Is she a good girl?"

"She's the *best.* She's super smart and gorgeous, but best of all is her work ethic. She's only sixteen, and I swear, she'd quit high school to work full time for me if she thought she could get away with it. She loves the shop." I smile over at him. "So, yeah, she's a good girl."

"That's all I can ask for."

Ryan sips his water, and I rest my chin in my hand, watching him. All the Wild siblings have the most amazing hazel eyes and dark hair. They're all beautiful. But there's something extra special about the man sitting across from me.

"So." He leans forward on his elbows and lowers his voice. There aren't a ton of people in here tonight, but I appreciate Ryan's need for privacy. "You wanted me to call."

Now it's *my* cheeks that darken. I can feel it happening, and I know he can see it because I didn't put on any foundation today.

"I get that leaving when I did and then saying later that I wish you'd called is sending a mixed message," I reply, my voice also low. "And I apologize for that."

"Why did you leave?"

I frown down into my wine, taking a sip for courage. "Because you were sleeping so peacefully, and I didn't want to wake you?"

He narrows his eyes. "Bullshit."

"It's not bullshit; you *did* look peaceful." I set the glass down and shake my head as I try to decide what to say. "I'm pretty sure we said that it was a onetime deal before we even left the wedding reception."

"No, we didn't."

I squint my eyes at him, remembering that night close to a year ago. "I think we did. We were flirting, and you whispered in my ear that you wanted one night with me."

"I said that I wanted to take you home for the night," he says with a scowl. "Not that it would only be for one night."

Frowning, I blink over at him. "Are you sure?"

"I remember every fucking detail about that night as if it were five minutes ago." His jaw tightens, and his shoulders tense. "Are you telling me that you walked out on me because of a misunderstanding?"

"And you didn't call because you thought that I'd bailed." I can't help but laugh. "Well, at least we got that cleared up. We didn't have any problem at all communicating the rest of the night."

Ryan was *excellent* at telling me what he was going to do, what he wanted me to do, and how I made him feel.

It was the sexiest night of my life.

"I'd like to take you out. On a date."

I sober and blink over at him, distracted when I hear Jake yell out, *"Yes! Got it!"*

"You do?"

"Yeah, Polly, I do. What night works for you?"

"I close the shop every night at six." I swallow a sip of wine. "But what about Jake?"

"He's almost sixteen. He doesn't need a babysitter. How about Tuesday night?"

I mentally scan my calendar and then nod. "I'm free Tuesday night."

"Good. I'll pick you up at seven."

Heather makes her way through the dining room with our pies balanced perfectly on the flat of her hands. Jake slides into the booth next to Ryan just as she sets them on the table between us. She gives us plates and silverware and grins. "Be right back with the breadsticks."

"This smells *so good*," Jake says. "I worked up an appetite playing pinball."

I can't help but smile at the teenager as he grabs a slice of pizza and takes a big bite.

"Good?" I ask as I set a slice on my plate.

"It's always good here," he replies before taking another bite.

"He's not wrong." I wink at Ryan and take a bite of my own piece. "Heather never misses."

"God, I love the smell of this place." I inhale deeply as I saunter into The Sugar Studio the next morning to pick up the cookies that I'll set out for customers today. "Jackie, I swear, I gain ten pounds just from walking in here."

"It's worth it," Jackie replies with a wink.

She's a pretty blonde woman with bright blue eyes and a happy smile, and she's always dressed in her white chef's coat. How it stays so pristinely white, I have no idea. Even after she's been in the kitchen for *hours,* she looks fresh as a daisy.

"I have to try one of these." Jackie sets the big tray of strawberry biscuit cookies on the counter, and I pluck one out and take a bite. The cookie melts in my mouth. It has just the right balance of tart and sweet, with a crumbly biscuit, and I close my eyes in delight. "Marry me, Jack."

The other woman giggles and secures the plastic wrap on the end.

"This is a fun summer cookie," she says. "And they're

not messy, so people won't eat them and then make a mess of your pretty clothes."

"Yeah, I thought of asking you to do a s'mores chocolate chip for fall, but no. Too messy. I don't need melted chocolate and marshmallow on everything."

"If you'd like to switch it up now and then, I thought we could do some key lime cookies this summer, too."

"Holy hell, *yes.* That sounds great. Thanks, friend. Add it to my tab, if you don't mind."

"I never mind," she assures me and waves as I walk out of the bakery and down the block to my own shop, where Katie's already inside, hanging pretty blue, pink, and sage-green helium balloons on racks, making the place look extra festive.

"I poured the lemonade into a pretty pitcher," she informs me and gestures to the sideboard, where it's already set out next to a bucket of ice and disposable cups. I arrange some of the cookies on a pink plate and then store the rest down below.

We'll replenish all of this throughout the day.

"Thanks, Katie." I grin over at her and smile at her yellow sundress and brown sandals. She's paired the dress with a brown belt to match the sandals, and her hair is teased into a bun that's anything but messy. "You look extra pretty today."

"Thanks. I'm excited about the big reveal." She joins me behind the checkout counter. "Where do you want me today?"

"Help customers, refold things as they get messed up—all the usual things."

"Sounds fun to me."

The door opens, and I'm thrilled to see that my first customers of the day are my closest friends.

Summer, Erin, Millie, and Abbi hurry in, with excitement written all over their gorgeous faces. All four women are business owners in Bitterroot Valley, and we've become tight, especially over the past year.

"This. Is. Fucking. Amazing." Millie blinks, and her eyes wander across the room, as if she doesn't know where to look first.

"*So* gorgeous," Abbi agrees. "Polly, this bathing suit is adorable, and I *hate* bathing suits."

"Oh, but you have the best curves for it," Katie says, and we all turn to her in surprise. "Sorry, but she does. That suit is made for curves for days, and we have the *best* cover-up to match it."

"She's good. You'd better keep her around," Erin says to me with a grin and pulls me in for a hug. "How are you?"

"I'm relieved that it all got done in time," I confess and can't help but smile as Summer pulls a blue top off of a rack and holds it up to her. "You're our first customers."

"That was on purpose," Summer replies. "First, because we love you and wanted to see everything."

"And second, because we wanted first dibs," Millie finishes for her, making me laugh.

"Well, help yourselves to lemonade and cookies." I gesture to the sideboard. "And if you want to try anything on, go right ahead."

"I'm going to be here for a while," Erin decides, her arms already full of clothes.

"Can I start you a room?" Katie asks her.

"Yes, please."

More women shuffle in. Some are tourists, who have their husbands and kids in tow. The cookies and lemonade are a huge hit, and we're out of both by midafternoon.

I make a mental note to ask Jackie to make six dozen rather than four. Seeing the smiles on the customers' faces is totally worth the expense.

Not to mention, I swear it makes customers more at ease and puts them in the mood to shop. It's the best thing I ever started doing when I opened this store. It's a gesture of friendship.

When we're nearing the end of the business day, Ryan walks into the shop and strides over to me with a big grin.

"What are you up to?" I ask him.

"I ran into Millie," he says. "She told me that she spent a mint in here today because you have the best clothes in western Montana, and she couldn't say no to anything."

"Ha." I smile with satisfaction. "I think I love your sister."

He laughs and reaches out to drag his finger down the edge of my jawline, waking up my nerve endings. "Congratulations, Polly. Sounds like it was a good day."

"It was a *great* day," I confirm. "I already have to reorder some stock. I hope my suppliers aren't sold out."

"Not a bad problem to have." He nods at Katie, who walks out of the back with a few items on hangers. "You must be Katie."

"Hi," she says with a bright smile. She's been here all day, but she's still as bright and fresh as she was this morning. "How can I help?"

"I don't need anything," Ryan replies easily, smiling to put her at ease. "I've just heard good things about you."

Katie glances my way. "Aww, that's sweet. Polly's the *best.* What else do you need today, Poll?"

"That's good for now. You can go on home, Katie. Thank you. You killed it."

"*We* killed it," Katie says with a happy grin before clocking herself out on the computer and then grabbing her stuff to go. "Have a good night! See you Thursday!"

"Bye, Katie."

When she's gone, I grin at Ryan. "See? She's pretty great."

"I like her," he says quietly. "You're beautiful, and I don't want you to take this the wrong way, but you look tired."

"I *am* tired, but in a good way." I lock the front door, flip the sign to *closed,* and walk back to him. "It was a successful day."

"Good. I know our date isn't until tomorrow night, but I think we should celebrate."

"What do you have in mind?"

CHAPTER FOUR

RYAN

I'd intended to take her out to dinner since I was already in town, and I *had* heard from Millie that today was a huge success for Polly.

But she *does* look so fucking tired, so I've had a change of plans.

"Let's get you home," I suggest, and I know it's the right decision when she practically sags in relief. "I'll order something in. Or, if you'd rather not have company, I can wait until tomorrow night to hear about it all."

"You're welcome to join me," she says as she gathers her designer handbag and slings it across her body. "I was just going to have a glass of wine on the patio."

"That sounds really nice."

It really does. I'm curious to see Polly's home, and I'm itching to spend some time alone with her. Sure, a big part of me wants to get her naked again, but it's more than the incredible sex with her. I want to talk with her, *learn* her better.

Polly Allen intrigues me.

I follow her out the front of the shop and wait for her to lock the door. She pauses and takes in a deep breath of summer air.

Grinning, I can't help but reach out and slide the tip of my finger down her cheek, and then down her jawline, where her skin is smooth as silk. "Where are you parked?"

"Oh, I walked."

"Come on." I take her hand and lead her to my truck. "I'll give you a lift. You're dead on your feet."

"I guess I underestimated how exhausted I'd be tonight. I think the whole past week just caught up with me."

"I get it." I hold the door for her, and when she's settled in the seat, I buckle the belt for her, then cross around to the driver's side. "You'll have to give me directions."

"That's right, you've never been to my house." She grins. "I'm over on 4th Street. Not too far from the high school."

With a nod, I put the truck in gear and head off that way. Nothing in Bitterroot Valley is very far away because we're such a small town, and the high school is about eight blocks away.

The sun is still high in the sky, and will be late into the night. We're at that time of year when the days are long and about to get *hot.*

"I'm the little green house," she says, pointing to the right. "You can park in the driveway. My car is in the garage."

With a nod, I pull in and cut the engine. She's not kidding when she says *small.* The lawn is the size of a postage stamp and has recently been mowed. The yard is actually really cute and well-maintained. "This is cute."

"It's a project," she says with a shrug. "But it looks like my neighbor kid came to mow the grass today. I love that kid."

Polly pushes out of the truck, and I follow her to the door. Close up, I can see that the screen door has seen better days, and I don't like that she doesn't have any kind of security at all, aside from the deadbolt.

"I don't have AC," she warns me. "I've had the house closed up, so it shouldn't be too hot, and when the sun starts to go down, I'll open everything up and get a breeze blowing through."

It doesn't surprise me. The house has to be a hundred years old, and most people didn't start adding AC in their new builds until about twenty years ago. Still, it's a little warm when we step inside.

Polly's house is tidy and clean, if a little sparse on the furniture. What she does have is newer and looks comfortable.

"What happened there?" I ask, pointing to the wall in the living room. It's covered in eight swatches of paint.

"I couldn't decide which color I liked the best," she says, wrinkling her nose. "I still can't."

"When did you put the swatches up?"

"Two years ago." She shrugs, and I can't help but chuckle. "There's always another priority to see to, and I'm hardly here anyway. I'm going to take a quick shower. Please make yourself at home."

"I'll order dinner. Take your time."

She smiles over at me, and then she walks down a hallway, and I hear a door close.

I want to follow her and join her in that shower. But I've decided to take things slow with Polly. We already know that the sexual chemistry is off the charts. Keeping my hands to myself is proving to be more of a challenge than I anticipated.

But I don't like that she assumed that I was only interested in fucking her. And now that the dust has started to settle in my private life, I want to see what could happen between us.

Pulling out my phone, I place an order for Italian from Ciao, pleased when they say that the delivery should be here in about thirty minutes, and then I walk into the kitchen and hunt up some wineglasses.

Polly owns exactly *two* of them.

There's a bottle of white in her fridge, so I locate a corkscrew and open the wine. The shower cuts off down the hall, so I pour the wine and take a sip of mine, leaning against the counter and waiting for the gorgeous redhead.

When she walks into the room, I almost say fuck it to my plan of talking and getting to know her and simply fuck her right here on this counter. She's in a black tank top that molds to her curves. No bra. And the little denim shorts she's wearing don't leave much to the imagination. Her wet red hair is up in a knot on top of her head, and she's barefoot.

I want to kiss each and every toe.

"Wine," she says, almost desperately, and reaches for the glass. "Thanks for waiting."

"It's not a problem." I have to clear my throat and cross my arms over my chest so I don't reach for her. "The food should be here soon."

"Want a tour while we wait? It'll take about three minutes."

I laugh and nod. "Hell yes. Show me your home, madam."

"This is the kitchen." She gestures grandly. "The only appliances that work in here are the fridge and microwave. The dishwasher is iffy at best, and the stove gave up the ghost a while ago."

I raise an eyebrow. "Another project?"

"One that I haven't had time for," she confirms and leads me back to the living room. "This is not an open floor plan. I was going to take down that wall that separates the kitchen and living space, but again. Time."

With another shrug, I'm led down the short hallway, and she gestures to the bathroom. "This is my one and only bathroom. But I live here alone, so it works fine for me. Even though it looks dirty, I assure you, it's not."

"It doesn't look dirty," I reply with a frown.

It just looks *old.* The whole place needs a complete overhaul.

"My bedroom," she continues, and I poke my head in.

There are more paint swatches on the wall, and the bed in the center of the room doesn't have a headboard. But it is covered in soft blankets and pillows full of color and looks damn comfortable. "And I converted this smaller bedroom across the hall into a closet."

I follow her and feel my eyebrows climb into my hairline.

"Wow."

She smiles with so much pride and joy that it makes me want to tug her close and hug her.

"I know." She walks inside and stands on the other side of the island, drinks her wine, and gazes around happily. "This is the one project that I refused to put off. I needed a place for my clothes and bags. And shoes. And all of the pretty things."

There are built-in racks and shelves around the room. She has a few bags on display, but there is still a lot of room for more of those. The racks for clothes, however, are practically bursting.

"I *love* clothes," she continues. "Bags. Shoes. Jewelry. Scarves. Fashion is just so wonderful to me."

"You have some blank spaces." I gesture to the shelves she has designated for her bags and watch as she bites her lip and then nods.

"I'm picky," she admits with a laugh. "I want the more luxurious bags. I like labels. So, I save up and buy the bags on my wish list when I can."

"Is there one bag that is *the* bag of all bags that you'd want to own?"

"Duh." She laughs again and sips her wine,

wandering over to pet the leather on a black purse. "I want a black Chanel classic flap, medium, with silver hardware. I'd prefer caviar leather."

"They make leather out of fish eggs?"

That makes her grin, and it's a punch to the gut. Fucking hell, she's beautiful.

"No, it's just a thicker, grainier leather. The lambskin is also gorgeous and feels like butter, but I think it's more fragile, so I'd be afraid of scratching it. Anyway, that's a lot of information about a handbag."

"It interests you," I reply simply.

"My ultimate dream?" she says before taking another sip of her wine. "Buying that bag in Paris, at the original Chanel store on Rue Cambon. In *Coco Chanel's* store, the one she labored in and loved. I'm somewhat of a Coco Chanel history buff."

"Fascinating." Following her out of the closet and back to the living room, I sit next to her and turn to face her on the comfortable couch. "What do you find the most interesting about her?"

Polly narrows her eyes. "She never lived in the apartment above her shop. She entertained there. She *loved* to entertain and would often find ways to trick people into staying longer. I think she was lonely. But she lived just a block away at the Ritz Paris. From her suite, she could see her shop, and that's where she lived for thirty years. The suite still exists to this day, and it's the only room in the whole hotel that is decorated differently because they let her decorate it the way she wanted. From the photos I've seen online, it's beautiful. She was an interesting woman, and I love her bags and clothes."

"Did you study fashion in college?"

The doorbell rings before she can answer, so I collect dinner from the delivery guy, tip him, and when I turn, Polly is standing behind me.

"Let's eat on the patio," she suggests and leads me out back.

I have to blink. It's beautiful out here. There's a swing and several chairs situated around a gas fireplace, and with the click of a button, screens come down, closing us in.

"I had the screens put in last summer," she tells me, "because I hate it when I'm eating and all the flies, bees, and mosquitos decide to join me."

She flips on an overhead fan, and we take our seats next to each other, digging into containers full of food that smell like heaven.

"I haven't been to Ciao yet," she says, choosing lasagna. She adds a piece of bread to her plate and sits back to dig in. After one bite, she closes her eyes and tips her head back, as if in ecstasy. "Oh, my God, I didn't know what I was missing."

That groan hits me right in the dick. She moaned like that when I was inside of her and when I was licking her, and it all comes back in vivid detail.

But I take a sip of wine and sit back with some bowtie pasta with Alfredo sauce and a piece of bread of my own.

"So, what drew you to *this* particular house?" I ask her, trying to keep my libido in check.

"I wanted the project." She rolls her eyes. "Someone should have shaken some sense into me. I thought it sounded fun, but who has the time? My brother helps out a lot. He did the closet and this patio for me."

I can tell where she spends all her time in this house. Out here and in her closet.

Those are the areas she's poured love into. The rest is clean, but an afterthought.

"I like the location," she continues and reaches for her Caesar salad. "And I like the neighborhood. Summer used to live just two blocks over, and we'd hang out at each other's houses in the evening with a glass of wine, chatting. It was nice. I know the neighbors to the left of me. Larry and Denise. They're super sweet people, and they have two teenage boys, Jeremy and Zach. Zach mows my lawn. In the winter, they take care of the snow. They're good kids."

"And the other neighbors?"

"I don't know them as well," she admits and wipes her mouth with a napkin. "They throw block parties in the summer and stuff, but I'm usually at the shop."

"Don't look now, but I think you're a bit of a workaholic, Polly."

She smirks and nods. "Yeah. Guilty. But I love it, so why not? Besides, you're a workaholic, too."

"Totally." I don't even try to deny it. "For the same reasons. I enjoy what I do, and I'm good at it. I've slowed down just a bit since Jake came into the picture and since

I've moved back home permanently. But I still work long hours."

"So, what does slowing down look like for you?"

"Well, instead of working twenty-hour days, I'd say I put in twelve or so. Much to Arthur's dismay."

"Who's Arthur?"

"My assistant. He's a taskmaster."

Her lips tip up into a grin, and then she sets the last of her food aside and sits back, patting her stomach. "I'm so full. That was delicious, thank you."

Her eyes are droopy as she smiles softly over at me.

"I'm going to kick myself out of here," I tell her and begin gathering what remains of our meal. "I'm glad your fridge works so you can keep the leftovers."

"You should take them home to Jake."

"He's having dinner with Rem, Erin, and the kids. Rem had an issue with a horse that he wanted Jake to look at, so Jake is hanging out there for the evening."

"He must be really good with the animals."

"He's excellent," I confirm, pride filling my chest. "He's looking into vet school after he graduates in a couple of years. He wants to be a large animal doctor."

"That's amazing," she says. "He's a far cry from the angry kid that was hanging out with those brats who stole from me last year."

"He's finding his way," I agree, and we walk inside, where Polly stows the food away and then walks with me to the door.

When I'm on the front stoop, she leans on the doorway and smiles softly. "Thanks again."

"I'll see you tomorrow night, for our first official date."

"This wasn't it?"

I shake my head and walk down the steps, impressed that my feet are listening to my brain because I want to stay here and kiss the hell out of her.

"No, ma'am. Because if it was, I'd be kissing you right now."

I wink at her and climb into the truck, loving the way she looks right now, in that skimpy outfit with her hair up, wishing I could stay.

"Taking it slow, Wild," I mutter to myself as I back out of the driveway. "This is one time you need to have patience."

Jake is pulling into the driveway just as I am, and we climb out of our trucks and grin at each other.

"How's the family?" I offer my fist for a bump, which he taps with his own, as we walk into the house through the garage.

"They're good. The kids are cute. They wanted me to give them piggyback rides around the backyard. I'm going to be sore tomorrow." He grins at me, and I can see that he had a great time. "Erin made lemon chicken for dinner."

"You know, I don't think I know what your favorite dinner is." I pull a bottle of water out of the fridge and toss it to him before retrieving my own.

"Food." He shrugs. "I don't really have a favorite. I'll eat anything."

"Pizza? Burgers? Steak?"

"Yes, yes, and yes." He laughs and turns to retreat to his bedroom. "I have some zombies to kill, and Russ is already waiting for me."

"Have fun," I call back.

Jake plays video games online with a couple of friends in the evenings, and I don't mind at all. I'd rather he was here, shooting zombies and talking shit while eating junk food than out and about doing God knows what.

I haven't talked to Jake yet about my seeing Polly. I want to see if it's going to go anywhere before I loop the kid in. If it fizzles, there's no need.

I don't think he'll have an issue with it. He likes Polly.

I make my way through the house and make sure it's locked up tight before I go up to my office to settle in and work for a few hours.

As I pass by Jake's room, I can hear the noise from the game, and Jake yells out, "Haha, you're an idiot, Sheena-WasAMan69. Did you see that? Yeah, man, let's go over there and see if we can get the loot."

I grin. I'm *relieved* that bringing Jake into my home has been so seamless. Almost effortless. Given what he's gone through in the past two years, he deserves to feel safe and happy in his home.

There hasn't been even one day of nasty attitude from him. Even the first time he came out here to work for me, he was sullen and quiet, but he never showed the attitude that Chase warned me about when he asked me to take Jake on.

And I'm happy he's here.

CHAPTER FIVE

POLLY

"I didn't realize until *after* he left that I never even put on a bra," I say to Summer as we set little bouquets of pink roses on the tables at Snow Ghost, the bar at the ski resort where we always hold our monthly Iconic Women's Collective meetings. Today is a lunch meeting. "I was a freaking zombie. My brain was fuzzy from the crazy week, and as he drove off, I realized I wasn't wearing a bra. The girls were just all... out there."

Summer snickers as she places the final bouquet just so. "I bet he was salivating."

"I can never see him again." I prop my hands on my hips. "I have to call off tonight's date."

"Of course, you don't," Summer says, shaking her head. "I highly doubt that you turned Ryan *off* with your post-shower outfit, Polly."

"He probably thinks I'm a first-class tease."

"He probably thinks you're tired." Summer slings her

arm around my shoulders and plants a kiss square on my cheek. "Don't overthink it."

"Do you see who you're talking to? I overthink *everything.* Unless I forget about it entirely. It's one or the other with me, and Ryan is not something I can forget. But thanks."

Before she can reply, other members begin to file in. Millie and Abbi come in together. Today, Abbi has her daughter, Daisy, with her. Erin isn't far behind, and I see that Holly is with her, as well.

"Hi, ladies," I say and smile at the pretty little girls. They're fresh-faced and full of excitement. "What are you up to today?"

"We're businesswomen," Holly replies seriously.

"Yeah, we're opening a lemonade stand, and we want to talk to other women who own stuff," Daisy adds. I see that they're both dressed in cute little white capris, and each girl has on a nice top with sandals. They're in business attire.

"Well, we're happy to have you." I point to a table near the front of the room. "Please, have a seat."

When they bustle over to the table, I turn to the others and grin. "Okay, that's freaking *adorable.*"

"It's summer," Abbi says with a shrug. "I don't want to put Daisy in daycare, and they were excited at the thought of coming to listen today."

"They'll be great," Millie says. "I love that they dressed up."

More and more women file in. I worried that we wouldn't have as much of a turnout for this one because it's a lunch meeting, but it looks like I was wrong because there might be standing room only by the time everyone is seated.

"Hi, everyone," Erin calls out, getting the room's attention. "Please take your seats. There are stools at the bar, as well, and if we need more chairs, we can bring some in. Since this is a lunch meeting and so many of you will have to get back to work, we want to keep today quick."

There's some shuffling as everyone finds a seat, and I'm satisfied to see that there's enough for everyone.

But *just* enough.

"Before our guest speaker begins," Millie says, "I want to remind you all that we're having our summer gala in three weeks, and tickets are on sale on the website. This is the event that men are invited to."

We all chuckle at that. We hold a gala once a season so we can bring our significant others, dress up, and have fun. It's one of our favorite things to do.

"The theme is summer soiree," I put in. "And it's going to be *gorgeous.*"

"But the best part is that this will be the first *official* event at the Wild River Ranch Event Center," Erin says, and the whole place erupts with applause. "I can't wait for everyone to see it."

The new event space out at the Wild ranch is absolutely *stunning.* Erin invited us out there a few weeks ago to see the progress. I can't believe that it started out as an old barn that had collapsed in on itself decades ago, and Erin had the vision to turn that piece of land into a gorgeous place for weddings and other special events.

They're already booked out a year in advance.

"And now, let's get down to the good stuff," Abbi says. "Our speaker this month is no stranger to this area. Most of you know Charlie Lexington. She's the owner of Lexington Luxuries, an event planning service here in Bitterroot Valley. We asked her to speak today because her marketing skills are *genius*, and I, personally, want to pick her brain. Please welcome Charlie."

"It's a good thing that I'm not shy," Charlie says with a wink and takes her place at the front of the room, and the rest of us settle in with drinks and some snacks from the bar to listen, take notes, and ask questions.

Even Holly and Daisy are respectful, sitting quietly and listening to Charlie speak. I think the pretty pink lemonades and grilled cheese sandwiches are helping to keep them occupied.

I *love* these few hours each month spent with so many amazing, intelligent women in business. I've learned so much about bookkeeping, marketing, planning, and strategy. I got the idea for lighter furniture from another member of IWC this past winter.

I look forward to these meetings, and I can't *wait* for the gala coming up.

Just over an hour later, Charlie has wrapped up her presentation, and some of the women are saying their goodbyes as they hustle back to work. Summer and I are always the last to leave because I help her take the bouquets back to her car.

"Take a couple of these for your shop," she offers. "Maybe set them on the refreshment table."

"Oh, that'll be pretty. Thanks, friend."

"Do you have a dress picked out for the gala?" she asks.

"No, but I have a nice selection of summer formal gowns coming in at the end of the week because I know people will need to find something."

"You're a freaking godsend," Summer replies. "We should put something out on social media, letting everyone know."

"Good idea. Well, I have to go overthink my date tonight. I can*not* believe I didn't wear a bra last night."

"Honestly, let that one go," Summer advises. "You have spectacular tits, and I'm sure Ryan didn't mind at all."

"Yeah, okay." I look down at the tits in question. "They are rather nice, aren't they?"

"Spectacular," she repeats with a laugh and gets into her car. "Have fun tonight! Call and tell me about it."

"Bye." I wave her off and slip into my car, start it up, and then frown when the gas light comes on.

I *always* forget to put gas in my car. It's one of those little details that slips my mind. I've never been stranded, at least not yet, but the light always has to come on to remind me.

"At least it's downhill most of the way," I mutter and put the car into gear, headed the short distance back into town. And, it seems there's a first time for everything because despite the short distance into town, and the fact that it's mostly downhill, my car decides to sputter to a stop about a mile from my shop.

A *half* mile from the gas station.

"How long was the light on?" I wonder as I pull my phone out of my purse and call my brother.

"Hey, sis."

"Hi. Um, are you busy right now?"

"Depends on what you need."

I cringe and take in a breath. "Well, I ran out of gas, and I need help."

"You ran out of *gas*? Why didn't you fill up, Poll?"

"I forgot. I'm sorry. If you're busy, I can call roadside assistance."

"We're on the way," he says. "Send me your location."

He hangs up, and I frown down at the phone as I send him the location, and then I stare out the windshield.

"Wait. He said *we're* on the way. Who's we?"

He must not have been far away because before long, he pulls up behind me in his truck. Climbing out of the passenger side is none other than Ryan Wild.

"Fucking hell," I mutter and close my eyes. "I can't catch a break."

Someone knocks on my window, and I roll it down and smile up at Ryan.

"Hey."

"Car trouble?" he asks, his lips twitching. He thinks this is funny. And, I admit, it kind of is.

"Out of gas." I shrug. "I could probably walk back to work from here, but I didn't want to leave my car."

"I have gas," I hear Mac call out from behind me. "Open the tank latch."

Doing as I'm told, I look back up at Ryan. "You didn't have to come with him."

"We were hanging out," Ryan says. "Mac wants to go look at a horse."

"Mac always wants to look at a horse," I reply with a laugh. "That's what he lives for."

"Shut up," Mac replies. "I can hear you. Try the engine."

With just a little finessing, the engine starts.

"You guys are my heroes. I'd better go to the gas station. Have fun checking out the horse."

"I'll see you tonight," Ryan says and taps the roof of my car before stepping back so I can pull away.

I've seen a lot of Ryan Wild lately, and I'm definitely not complaining.

"What do you wear to go on a date with a billionaire?" I wonder out loud as I stand in my closet, clad in only a black bra and panty set that should make Ryan's eyes bug out of his head if we get naked, and stare at my walls of clothes. "Not that Ry is fancy. I mean, sure, he wore a Dior suit to Remington's wedding, but that was a *wedding*. Usually, he's just in jeans and a shirt, nothing crazy."

I shake my head. I'm talking to myself. Maybe I should get a cat so when I talk to myself, I'm actually talking to someone else.

It's summer, so I decide to go with a pretty sage-green flowy dress that accentuates my curves, hides the hips and belly that make me self-conscious, and is *so* comfy. Beige sandals go well and will be perfect if we walk at all. I complete the look with a Gucci crossbody handbag and simple gold earrings.

Casually stylish.

I push my red hair over my shoulder and take in the view in the mirror, turning side to side to see myself from all angles, and decide that this will do just fine.

With a decisive nod, I hang the few dresses and tops that I pulled out to try on back on their hangers and put them away and then hear the doorbell ring as I walk toward the living room.

When I open the door, I can't help but grin at the handsome man standing before me. He's so freaking *tall.* Of course, I'm short, so everyone is tall to me. His dark hair is styled in a short cut, and he's in nice jeans and a blue, short-sleeved button-down, not tucked in, and frankly, he makes me salivate.

"Wow, you look beautiful," he says and slips a bouquet of pink roses out from behind his back. "These are for you."

"Thank you." I bury my nose in the blooms, breathing in deeply, and turn for the kitchen. "Come on back and keep me company while I put these in water. Summer must have told you that these are my favorite."

"No," he replies, and I turn to him in surprise. "I remember that you mentioned at the wedding that you loved these particular flowers in the centerpiece arrangements."

The man pays attention, I'll give him that.

A slow smile spreads over my lips as I turn on the tap and fill a vase with water, then arrange the roses inside of it.

"They're beautiful," I reply, sniffing them once again before I set the vase on my table and turn to him. "I'm ready if you are."

"Let's do this." He reaches out for my hand and then lifts it to his lips, kissing my knuckles and smiling at me over them. Those hazel eyes are full of happiness and promise as he leads me through the house to the front door.

He waits while I lock the door behind me, and when I turn to follow him to his truck, he's frowning.

"What's wrong?"

"Is that the only security you have on the house? Just the deadbolt?"

I look back at the door, up and down the street, and then back to him. "We're in Bitterroot Valley, not New York or LA, Ryan. This is a safe neighborhood."

He nods, but I can tell that he's not particularly satisfied with that answer.

"I leave snacks out for the delivery people during the holidays, and I've never had anyone steal them, not even the neighbor kids. I'm fine, Ryan."

"Okay," he says with a nod and holds the door of the truck open for me. "I believe you."

He winks, and I slip inside, then he rounds the hood and gets in next to me.

"Do you have a lot of security issues at your ranch?" I ask, half joking, but he doesn't smile. He also doesn't start the truck to leave.

Ryan sighs.

"Sometimes," he admits and turns to face me. "I have a gate, cameras, and I have security on staff. Two at a time."

"As in, security *guards*?" I ask him.

"Yes. They don't go out with me or anything, especially when I'm home, but they're on duty at the ranch." He rubs his fingers over his forehead, and I instinctively reach out for his hand. He laces our fingers together. "Sometimes, people suck. Either I make them mad, or they're jealous or just assholes, and they like to make threats. So, I keep the guys on hand, just in case. We've had a couple of false alarms, nothing crazy here."

"Nothing crazy *here*," I repeat, watching him closely. "Where has it been crazy, Ryan?"

"I don't want to scare you off on the first date."

I grin at him and lift his hand so I can press it to my cheek. "I'm not scared."

"Yet," he mutters. "Well, there was one attempt to get into my place in Manhattan. They would have succeeded if not for excellent security in the building, and since he was carrying zip ties, duct tape, chloroform, and a gun in his backpack, we're pretty sure the intent was to kidnap me and demand a payout."

"Jesus." Just the thought of it has my stomach turning. "That's horrible."

"It's rare. I'm not as high profile as Musk, Zuckerberg, Bezos, and the like. I'm not as wealthy as them, either. Yet."

His grin is cocky and sure of himself, and it makes me smile.

"But you will be," I guess.

"I don't need *that* much wealth," he concedes, "but that's not what it's about for me. Anyway, back to the security thing... I'm careful because although I'm *not* as high profile as those guys, there is a level of celebrity status that comes with what I do. People want a piece of it, and they're willing to go to extremes to take it. And some people just hate me for the sake of hating me. I don't really care about that."

"Haters are gonna hate," I reply with a shrug. "I'm glad that you take precautions. But I'm not you. I'm just a small business owner in small-town Montana."

"You're not *just* anything," he says, and with his free hand, drags his fingertips down my jawline. He does that a lot, and it always sends goose bumps down my arms. "I did have one major incident happen around the holidays last year. Actually, it had been going on for a while but came to a head around the holidays. Anyway, I know this is just the first date, but I already know that I don't want it to be the last, and I thought you should be aware. I'll always keep you safe."

"I know." I want to know more about the major incident and decide to ask him about it over dinner. I smile at him, and my stomach growls. "Thanks for sharing that with me. Now, I'm hungry, Mr. Wild."

His smile lights up the whole truck, and he starts the engine and drives us toward the ski resort.

"We're going to Soleil Grill at the resort," he says. "Have you been?"

"Not in a long time, but I *love* French food. We have most of our Iconic Women's Collective meetings at Snow Ghost, the bar up there. It's so beautiful. I know that a lot of locals hated when it was all built, but I think it's gorgeous."

"I do, too," he replies. "I'd like to hear more about your collective."

I grin over at him. "It's one of my favorite subjects."

"Over dinner, then."

He parks the truck under the portico, and a young man rushes over to take the key fob from Ryan and passes him a ticket for the valet.

Once inside, we're escorted to a private table with a view of the mountains that never fails to take my breath away.

"You know, I was born here," I say, ignoring my menu altogether, "but the view never gets old."

He follows my gaze and nods. "I agree. There's nowhere like it in the world."

The waitress arrives with a smile and fills our water glasses. "Hi, I'm Hillary, and I'll be your server this evening. What would you like to drink? We have some excellent wines available."

Ryan looks at me and raises his eyebrow. "Do you mind if I order the wine?"

"Please do."

"We'd like the LaTour 2010 Merlot, please."

She nods, writing it down. "Excellent choice. Do you need time with the menu, or would you like to order an appetizer? I highly recommend the puff pastry wreath with brie."

"Oh, that sounds really good." I grin at her. "Of course, it's cheese, so you're speaking my language."

"I agree," Ryan says. "Let's do that, and we'll check out the rest of the menu."

"Excellent," Hillary replies and bustles off to get our order started.

"Okay," Ryan begins, leaning forward. "Tell me about the Collective."

"I'm sure your sister has told you some," I reply.

"Millie never tells me everything." He shakes his head. "Besides, I want to hear it from *you*."

"Well, it came about because my circle of friends and I are all business owners, and we really just want to lift each other up, help each other, you know?"

He nods and sips his ice water.

"But then we realized that there's a need for a sense of community, a place to learn from each other, whether it's about marketing, strategy, or just simply brainstorming. The meetings are so fun, and we always have a guest speaker to give us food for thought. I got the idea for the light furniture I just bought from someone at a meeting not long ago, and I found someone who is a genius when it comes to branding. I love it."

"It sounds amazing," he agrees, sitting back when Hilary brings the bottle of wine. She uncorks it and does the thing where you pour just a sip into a glass and presents it to Ryan. He sniffs it, then takes a sip, tasting it. "That's great."

I happen to glance at the wine list sitting on the table and about swallow my tongue at the price of this bottle.

Jesus, that's my mortgage payment. For one bottle of wine!

But I don't say a word as my glass is poured, and when he holds his glass up, he grins at me.

"To first dates."

"To first dates," I echo, and we clink our glasses together. This wine is rich and slides down my throat so nicely. I hum in surprise. "Wow, that's amazing."

"I'm glad you like it."

"Me, too, given what you paid for it." I slap my hand over my mouth and stare at him in shock. "Shit, I'm sorry. I didn't mean to say that out loud."

CHAPTER SIX
RYAN

I can't help but chuckle at the complete and utter horror on Polly's face. "It's fine, Polly."

"That was *rude*," she says in a loud whisper, looking around to see if anyone heard her. "And I'm sorry for it."

"It wasn't rude. It was true. It would suck if the wine was crap, given the price. But, it's a good wine."

"Are people always awkward around you?" she wants to know. Jesus, she's hot, sitting across from me in that dress that makes me wonder what's under it. When she licks her plump lips, I want to spend the better part of an evening nibbling and kissing them. Polly's been front and center in all of my sinful fantasies for the last year. "Ryan?"

"Sorry?"

"Do people always say awkward stuff around you? Because of the money? Let's not beat around the bush about it, because I'm curious, and I don't want to feel like I'm walking on eggshells here."

"*Always*? No. And before I go on, I want it known right here and now that you will *not* feel the need to walk on eggshells around me. Ever. Say what you want to say. You won't offend me, Polly. We've known each other for a long time. You're my best friend's sister. There's no need to feel self-conscious about anything."

"Thank you," she says with a smile. "I agree. That's why I asked. So, people aren't weird?"

"I didn't say that." I laugh as the server sets the appetizer on the table and refills our wineglasses. "My family and the people who have known me for years have never treated me differently. I have issues that I need to work through with Remington, but that doesn't really have anything to do with money."

I sip my wine, thinking it over.

"Mostly, people think they can get something for free from me. Family? Yes, absolutely. Gifts are my love language, so I *like* to give. But those who don't know me, don't *care* to know me, and just want a piece of the pie? Fuck that. They're either fired or cut off immediately."

"Does that include women?" She raises an eyebrow and sips her wine. "I've seen the articles and photos of you on red carpets, along with the women on your arm."

"Including women," I confirm, watching her. "My circle is small, and I like it that way. Sure, sometimes things are said because people get nervous. You didn't say what you did out of nerves."

"No, I just don't have a filter."

"Exactly, and that's the way I like it. Does it make you uncomfortable? The wealth?"

She doesn't immediately deny it, and I have to admit that I respect that. She takes a moment, looking out at the mountains, sipping her wine, and then turns those stunning green eyes back to me.

"Uncomfortable? No. I wouldn't say that. I want to make it clear that I'm not on this date with you because of the balance in your checking account. Or whatever accounts billionaires use."

I chuckle at that and stay quiet, letting her speak.

"I'm here because I like you." She shrugs a shoulder and reaches for a piece of pastry with cheese that smells delicious. "And because the sex was off the charts."

I choke on the wine I just sipped, and she grins across from me.

"And now I'm here because of this cheese," she continues, frowning at the piece in her fingers. "Holy Jesus and the apostles, this is incredible. Now, you tell me why you're here."

"Because staying away from you isn't an option."

She stops chewing, and her eyes find mine as she licks her lips.

"Life got busy after the wedding and our incredible fucking night together." I fiddle with the end of a knife on the table, still watching her. "I have Jake, and for a while, he needed my full and undivided attention. So, he got it."

"As he should," she agrees, and I can see by the look on her face that she means every word. It only makes me like her more. "He deserves that."

"Yes, he does. But we're doing well now, and I can't stop thinking about you. That's why I'm here."

"That's a good answer." She gestures to the appetizer. "Eat some of this so I don't inhale it all, please."

I want to inhale *her.* To take her home and lose myself in her. To reacquaint myself with every curve of her body.

But I'll settle for this for now.

"Now I have another question," she says, eyeing me with those gorgeous emerald eyes as she munches on the appetizer.

"Shoot. I'm an open book."

"Tell me more about this *major* security situation you had."

I frown down at the table, the delicious food now tasting like cardboard in my mouth. Suddenly, she reaches across the table and takes my hand in hers, squeezing it. I look up into her eyes, and frankly, I'd tell this woman anything she wants to know.

"Was it really bad?" Her voice is soft, not full of pity, but understanding.

I swallow hard and turn my hand palm up so I can grip hers in return.

"Yeah, it was really bad." I suddenly have a frog in my throat, so I clear it. "I told you about the kidnapping attempt in New York."

She nods, waiting patiently.

"After that, things calmed down for a few months. Then, I found a company that was in financial trouble, and I wanted to buy them out. They weren't keen on selling. In fact, they just wanted me to *invest* and get them out of trouble, but that's not what I wanted in that situation."

"Do you ever do that?" she asks.

"I have in the past, but I knew that if I invested in this case, they'd be right back where they were in less than two years. The owners were shit businessmen. I wanted to take it over because I saw the potential in it."

Just thinking about that time makes my heart start to beat faster, and I reach for my water and take a sip.

"They had no choice but to sell to *someone.* They really didn't want to sell to me, because I turned down the investment offer, but no one else wanted it."

"So, it was a hostile takeover," she surmises, making me smile, despite the anxiety that wants to rise up through my stomach.

"I guess you could call it that," I confirm with a quick nod. "I didn't plan on them taking out a hit on me in retaliation."

Polly gasps, her eyes go wide, and she simply stares at me. "*What?*"

"True story." Jesus, just the thought of it makes me want to sweat. "It was a few months after the buyout was finished, and suddenly, someone else was attempting to break into my condo in Manhattan. Because of the incident before, I had hired my own private security, so they were thwarted."

"They were caught?"

"No." Grimly, I sip my wine. "They got away, but they weren't successful. And they didn't stop trying."

"Jesus Christ," she mutters, still holding onto my hand.

"After about three months of this, I decided it was in everyone's best interest if I moved back to Montana. I'd already built my house, and it was just sitting here, waiting to be lived in. At first, I was stubborn, not wanting to give anyone the satisfaction of running me out of New York, but it became clear that I wasn't safe there."

"Ryan, my God."

I swallow the bile that wants to come up and continue, purging out the rest of it.

"I hadn't been here more than a few months when my team started seeing signs of someone trying to get onto my ranch. We installed cameras and added more men, and right before Christmas—"

I pause and drag my hand down my face.

"It's okay," she says, her eyes full of turmoil. "You don't have to tell me any more."

"No, I'll finish it. They tried to get onto the property by jamming my cameras. And, they succeeded. Thank fuck Jake was with my parents that day because they got into my house."

"No."

"My men apprehended them. I wasn't home. I was in town, actually. I saw *you* that day."

She frowns over at me. "Was that on Christmas Eve?"

"Yes."

"I still have your gloves."

I feel my lips twitch, and my gut loosens as she smiles at me. "You can keep them."

"I plan to; they're warm. So, what happened?"

I blow out a breath and reach for more cheese. "Well, they were arrested. It was a hitman that the other company hired to *teach me a lesson*, as he put it, but it was clear that he'd planned to kill me."

"How do you know?"

I think of the weapons they found on the son of a bitch, the torture implements, and shake my head.

"We just know. I'll leave it at that."

"But he's in jail?"

"For thirty years," I confirm with a nod. "And he sang like a canary, had documented all of the communication between him and those who hired him, and they went to jail, too."

"Thank Christ," she says with a sigh. "I'm so sorry you went through that."

"It was scary," I reply. "And I don't really scare easily. We've beefed up security more because there were rumblings out there that there might have been a second man hired, in case the first failed."

Her eyes widen in alarm. "Ryan—"

"There's been no attempt at anything. We have ears on the ground all over the world," I assure her and lift her hand to my lips, kissing her knuckles. "But we keep an eye on things, just to be sure. I don't want to relax and then get a surprise."

"No, you don't. Now I understand why just the deadbolt on my house gave you pause. But, like I said before, it's sufficient for me."

For now. If we continue on together, I'll have to beef up her home security. I can't let anything happen to her.

"I have some delicious food for you," Hilary announces with a grin, our plates on a big tray, and Polly pulls her hand out of mine as our plates are set before us.

Conversation during our meal is less intense, and I love Polly's quick wit and sense of humor. She makes me laugh like I haven't in years.

"I'm so *full*," she says, but when Hilary returns with the dessert menu, she bites her lip. "Yeah, that crème brûlée is calling my name. Share it with me?"

"Perfect. I'd also like coffee."

"I'd like that, too," Polly agrees, and Hillary bustles off to do her thing. She glances out the window and smiles. "Look at the alpenglow."

The mountains are cast in pink as the sun sets opposite of them. We've been sitting here for several hours, talking and eating and laughing. It's felt like mere minutes with her.

"Chase and Summer are coming out to my ranch on Sunday," I say. "Summer's going to try riding a horse for the first time."

"You're kidding." Polly blinks at me and then busts up laughing. "Oh, to be a fly on the wall."

"Actually, I'd love it if you joined us. They're coming just after lunchtime, but you could come out earlier than that, and I'll give you a tour. I know you've been there before, but—"

"But we didn't really take time for a tour of the house," she says with a wink. "I suppose I can take Sunday off. I'd like that, thank you."

"Don't thank me yet. I'm getting *you* on a horse, too."

She considers that. "It's been a while, but I bet I can still do it."

After settling the check, I take Polly home and walk her to her door.

"Do you want to come in?" she asks.

More than just about anything.

But I lean in and kiss her forehead. "I have to get home."

"Okay." She sighs when I kiss the tip of her nose. "I understand. I'll see you on Sunday."

My hands dive into her hair and fist at the back of her head, and I sink into her, kissing her with all I have. Christ, I've missed the taste of her, the *feel* of her against me.

She whimpers and wraps her arms around my neck, and I pick her up so we're face to face, and I don't have to bend down so damn far to reach her.

She tastes like heaven and smells even better, and when she says my name and pins me in that emerald stare, I almost cave and go in with her.

But then my phone rings, pulling me back to reality.

"I have to get home to Jake," I say regretfully. "That's him, checking in with me."

"I get it," she says, but regret hangs heavily in her voice, and I have to admit that I feel the same way.

"Sunday. I'll see you on Sunday."

She nods as I set her on her feet, and I wait for her to unlock her door. She smiles back at me, and then she's gone. I return to the truck, adjusting myself in my jeans, and call Jake back.

"Hey, buddy, I'm headed home. Where are you?"

"Just got home. Gonna play with Russ for a while. Can you bring pizza?"

I blow out a breath, still trying to settle my nerves. "Sure. I'll bring pizza."

"It's been quiet." Axel is the head of my security, and we meet once a week in my office, so he can update me on any concerns. "I know you want two guys here twenty-four seven, but I don't see a need for it anymore."

"Have you heard that there is *nothing* to worry about?"

Axel shifts on his feet and sighs. "No."

"Then they stay. When that's resolved, we'll cut it down to one on duty at a time. We have the whole ranch covered with cameras, but in the meantime, I want two."

"Yes, sir," Axel replies.

"I'm glad that things have been quiet around here. I'll have guests on the ranch today, and likely often through the summer because my brother's kids will want to come swim, and I'd like to be a little more social. I'm adding Polly Allen to the list of names that have full access to the ranch whenever she wants it."

His eyebrows climb at that. "*Full* access, sir?"

"Yes. Day or night, she's to be passed through immediately. No need to check with me first. Program in her license plate so the gate automatically opens for her."

"I'll see to it right away. Only you and Jake have full access."

My eyes are level on Axel's. "And now Polly." He nods, and before he can argue further, I say, "That's all."

"Sir." He nods and then walks out of the office.

A few moments later, Jake walks in, all sleepy-eyed and rumpled from bed. He's in an oversized T-shirt and gray sweats and pads on bare feet to the kitchenette.

"Bagel?" he asks me.

"How about if I make you a real breakfast?"

That makes him eye me as he scratches his scalp through bed-head hair. "What kind of real breakfast?"

"Eggs, bacon, hash browns. Toast. Protein."

Jake turns to the kitchenette and back to me. "Up here?"

"No, smart ass, in the real kitchen."

"Sure." He turns and walks right back out, and it makes me grin. He's a kid of few words in the morning, but he always finds me so we can have breakfast together.

I shoot a text to Arthur before leaving my office.

Me: I'll be out of the office for the better part of the day. Hold all calls and move any appointments.

Rather than text back, he calls me.

"Wild."

"Sir, you were supposed to meet with Tokyo this afternoon."

"Reschedule it."

"But we rescheduled it last week."

"Do it again," I reply easily. "It's Sunday, and I'm taking some time off."

"Wow," Arthur breathes. "Yes, sir. But we can't miss the next rescheduled meeting with them."

"Fine." The Tokyo issue annoys me. "You won't hear from me until tomorrow morning at six."

He doesn't immediately respond.

"Hello?"

"You're taking the *whole* day off?"

"That's what I said. And I want you to, as well. Go... do whatever it is you do in Manhattan on a Sunday."

"I could go have lunch with Eric," he says. "And then we could go to the farmer's market."

"Go have fun with your husband," I reply. "No work until tomorrow morning. The world won't fall apart. Probably."

"If it does, I'm not getting fired for it."

I grin as I hang up and then make my way down to the kitchen, where Jake's already sitting at the island, drinking coffee—a habit he's picked up since moving in with me—and watching something on his phone.

"I had to talk to Arthur and tell him that I'm taking today off."

"The *whole* day?"

"That's what he said." I pull eggs and bacon out of the fridge. "I could make French toast, if you want some."

"Can I still have all the other junk?" he asks, not looking up from his phone.

"Yeah."

"Okay. Why are you taking the whole day?"

"Today's the day that Chase and Summer are coming out to ride," I remind him.

"I know. I went out this morning and got the girls ready." He always refers to our little herd of horses as *the girls.* "The bridles and saddles are ready, too. I just didn't think you'd take the *whole* day. It won't take that long."

"How do you know?"

"Summer's never ridden before. If she goes too long on a horse, she won't walk for a week."

I smirk and pour milk into the bowl with some eggs, whisking them up. "Polly's coming, too."

"Cool."

He's still staring at the damn phone.

"Would you please put that down while we're talking? What's so interesting?" He doesn't usually do that during our morning meetings, as we started calling our breakfasts together.

"Sorry." He flips it off and turns the phone face down on the countertop. "It's a horse race. So, are you and Polly dating or something?"

"Why do you ask that?"

"Because I'm not stupid. She's nice and pretty, and you said you had dinner last week."

"Yeah, all of that is true. I guess we're dating." I glance up and see that he's watching me with interest.

"What do you want to know about it? You know you can ask me anything."

"Is she going to stay here sometimes?"

"Maybe, but not while *you're* here."

"Good. That's weird." He gets up and circles around the island to help me with the bacon. "Are you going to marry her? And if you do, will you have a prenup? You should. You're loaded, and girls can't be trusted."

"Whoa, there's a lot to unpack here." I laugh and tug the boy in for a hug, then put him in a headlock and ruffle his hair. "So far, we're dating. I like her. It's pretty casual."

For now.

"If and when I marry *anyone*, there will most likely be some kind of legality involved because yeah, I'm loaded. Don't worry, you're in the will."

His head pops up, and he grins at me. "I am? *Nice.* Don't worry, I won't off you or anything just for the money."

"Thanks. That inspires a lot of confidence. And lastly, women *can* be trusted. Look at Grandma Joy and Erin and Summer. Millie. Heck, even Polly. You know Polly, and you like her."

He shrugs a shoulder. "Yeah, I like her. Even when she caught those morons stealing from her, she wasn't a raging bitch or anything."

I raise an eyebrow at him. "Watch the language, kid."

"I'm just saying she wasn't too bad, and I liked helping her at the shop. She's always been decent to me.

And she treats me like a person and not just a kid. So, if she's around some, I guess it would be okay."

"Good. Now, why don't you think women can be trusted?"

And just like every time I want to talk about his past, Jake clams right up.

"So, this horse race," he says, changing the subject. "It's pretty cool."

He tells me about the race, and I finish making breakfast. When we're done eating, we hear Polly's car in the driveway.

"Is Polly early?" he asks me, looking outside to see who it is.

"I told her to come early so we could show her around and stuff."

He eyes me. "I'll go to the barn."

"No way. You'll hang out with us and help me show her around."

"Don't kiss her," he says, shaking his head ruefully. "I don't need to see that. I'm an impressionable child."

I snort. "Right."

The doorbell rings while I'm still filling the dishwasher.

"I'll get it," Jake says and hurries for the door.

I can hear them chatting as he leads her back this way, and as soon as I see her, I want to kiss her like I did the other night. Instead, I smile at her.

"The gate just opened for me," she says with a perplexed frown. "I didn't even have to press the buzzer or anything."

"I told them to let you in whenever you're here. No need to buzz."

"Oh, thanks. This kitchen is impressive. I see you went with white paint. That's probably the smart way to go. You can decorate it with any color you want and change it out with the seasons and stuff."

"We don't really decorate much," Jake says, making me grin.

Polly is nervous.

"Right," she says with a laugh that has Jake frowning. "Of course. Bachelor pad, and all that. Most guys don't change things out with the seasons. Hell, even *I* don't change anything. I've had paint swatches on my walls for two years."

"Don't gag," I whisper to Jake as I pat his shoulder and walk past him and simply pull Polly in for a hug. I tighten my arms around her and feel her shoulders droop in relief. "You're here because I asked you to be. Don't overthink it, okay?"

"Sorry," she whispers with a shaky breath. "I don't know why I'm nervous."

"It's okay. It's just a tour of the house." I pull back from her, smile gently, and trace my fingertips down her jawline, and then I turn to Jake, who's watching us with curiosity. "Where should we start this tour, buddy?"

"Duh." He turns to start out of the room. "In the theater. I want some Milk Duds."

"The kid never stops eating," I inform her as we follow behind him. "We literally just finished breakfast. He's going to break me within a year."

"Nah, he can afford it," Jake says cheerfully and leads us down the hall to the movie theater. "This room rocks."

"Wow," Polly says. "You're right, it's impressive. You even have a popcorn machine in here. And a soda fountain."

"It's legit," Jake agrees. "Sometimes we can get movies that are only playing in the theaters. Ryan has magical powers or something."

I smirk and shake my head. "I just know people. Come on, there's more to see."

We walk through the gym, past several guest suites, and back to the kitchen.

"There's more stuff out here," Jake announces, leading us out back where there's an outdoor kitchen and dining and living space. "And a pool."

"You have a *pool*," Polly says in surprise. "And it's open."

"The guy came last week," Jake says proudly. I love that he's at home here and that he's proud of our place. "There's a hot tub, too. And a fire pit. Ry, is the family still coming next weekend for a pool party?"

"Yep, and we'll do s'mores. You should come, Polly."

"Oh, I don't want to intrude on family time."

"You should totally come," Jake says, nodding. "Everyone is chill. You know them. It's our first party of the season. Ry said I could bring some friends, too, so it's not *just* family."

"Well, thanks. In that case, I'd love to come."

I want to hug him. I love this boy and the fact that

he's so welcoming and genuine. It makes me want to hurt the people who hurt *him* all the more.

"Let's go check out the office," Jake says with a smile and heads back inside.

"He's wonderful," Polly whispers to me as we follow behind. "Just a wonderful kid, Ryan."

"I know."

Once in my office, Jake shows Polly the wet bar and where we usually have breakfast.

"Chase is gonna build us a table so we can eat at it in the morning," he says with a smile and holds his fist out to mine for a bump, and I happily oblige him. "I'm fine on the couch, but I guess Ryan doesn't want me acting like I was born in a barn or something."

"There's nothing wrong with sitting at the table to eat like civilized humans."

"Sure." He rolls his eyes, but he's still smiling. "And that over there is his command center."

I smirk, and Polly grins.

"I love that description," she says. "It fits. Did you buy Antarctica from here or something?"

"Would you like to *own* Antarctica?" I ask her.

"No." She laughs. "I bet some big things have happened in this room. Very cool. Now, I need to see the most important space in the house."

"My video game setup?" Jake asks, rubbing his hands together in anticipation. "Talk about legit."

"Nope, more important than that."

"There *isn't* anything more important than that, lady," he says, making her laugh again.

"I want to see the closet in the owner's suite."

I immediately grin and crook my finger. "Follow me."

"Girls are *weird*," Jake mutters as he follows us.

I can see by the look on her face when we walk inside that it's lackluster.

"You have this *huge* house, with all of these beautiful amenities, and *this* is the closet?"

I look around at the simple shelves and rods for hanging clothes. It's plain and not enormous, but I have that in Manhattan. I don't need a lot of clothes here.

"It's just a closet," Jake says with a shrug. "What's the big deal?"

"I have so much to teach you," I mutter as Polly stares at him in shock.

It occurs to me that when she was here that one and only time, she literally only saw the bedroom, bathroom, and entrance in and out of the house. She didn't even make it to the closet.

She would have, had she not run out on me.

"Have we seen everything?" she asks.

"No," Jake and I say in unison.

"There's still a guesthouse, the garage, and the stables."

"Don't forget the roof," Jake says.

"What happens on the roof?" Polly asks.

"We'll show you."

CHAPTER SEVEN

POLLY

Following behind Ryan on the way up the stairs, I can't help but admire his ass. We're in blue jeans because we'll be on horses today, and his fit snugly and just *perfectly* around his sexy-as-hell butt.

He opens a door and leads me out onto a beautiful balcony that sits on the back of the house, tucked into the gables so it's not really visible from below. But it's also not open to the air.

It's glassed in.

And sitting in the center is the biggest telescope I've ever seen. All chrome and shiny and intimidating.

"You explain it," Jake says. "I have to change and get ready for the others."

He hurries back down the stairs, and Ryan turns to me, watching me with those intense hazel eyes.

"This isn't Jake's jam. It's mine."

"What am I looking at here?"

He tucks his hands into his pockets and looks around.

"This is the most high-powered, state-of-the-art telescope you can get without having to be in an astronomical observatory."

He picks up an iPad and presses a button, and the glass roof opens, and I feel my eyes widen in surprise.

"Whoa."

"The glass is heated, so even in the winter, I can sit in here and study the sky."

"Ryan." I walk around and let my hand graze over beautiful plush orange cushions on chairs arranged for staring out at the view around the house. "This is all just *incredible.*"

"I spend a lot of time out here." He shrugs, but I see the vulnerability in his hazel eyes as he watches me prowl around this amazing space. "Well, as much as I can."

"Do you ever sleep?"

His hands are still tucked into his jeans. "Not much, actually."

I walk to him, unable to stay away, and my hand glides up his chest. Frustrated that I'm so much shorter and can't look him in the eyes well, I step onto an ottoman and grin.

"Hi."

"Hello there," he says. His eyes are full of humor now, but he still hasn't touched me.

"You were really far away."

"I'm right here."

I lick my lips and watch his throat work as he swallows hard. My hands move behind his head, and I lean in for a long, tight hug.

Finally, his arms circle around me, and he returns the embrace, and we stand here like this for a long moment, just soaking each other in. It feels *amazing*.

"Thanks for earlier," I murmur. "For calming me down."

It's a wonder that all it takes to calm my nerves is just one touch from him.

"I want you," he says simply and kisses my cheek. "The wanting you never stops, and it's not just sexual, although there's a lot of that. I like having you here, in my home, in my space."

He pulls back far enough to look me in the eye.

"I'm glad you came today."

"Me, too." I grin, and before I can kiss him, we hear a car making its way down the driveway. "They must be here."

"They can wait." His mouth covers mine, softly at first, and then grows with urgency. He nibbles and urges my lips apart so he can stroke my tongue. One hand moves down to cup my ass and the other to my hair where he makes a fist, and it about makes me beg for more.

I know he loves my hair. He never stops touching it.

But he steps away from me just as Jake bounds up the stairs to join us.

"Isn't it rad?" he asks with a grin. "The others are here, Ry."

"I heard them, thanks. Let's go ride some horses, shall we?"

"Hell yeah," Jake says and hurries off ahead of us.

I lick my lips and still taste Ryan there, and he watches the gesture, then takes a long, deep breath.

"Stay the whole day," he urges me. "We'll come back out here tonight."

"I'd like that."

He takes my hand and kisses my knuckles, links our fingers, and leads me back downstairs. When we walk out the front door to meet Chase and Summer, Summer's eyebrows fly into her hairline in surprise.

"Hey," she says, giving me the look that says *you have to tell me everything that's happening.* "You're here."

"I'm here," I agree with a laugh and hug her close. "I'll tell you later."

"Better," she whispers before pulling away. "Jake, you'd better have my back today. And my ass, because if I fall, I don't want to break it."

"You won't fall," Jake assures her with a smile. "I'm putting you on Lullaby. We named her that because she's slow and goes at her own pace. She's an easy-going girl."

"Thank God," Summer says with a relieved sigh.

"It'll be a quick ride today," Ryan says, "but there are some water bottles and sunscreen down at the stables. Are you guys ready?"

"I have to grab my boots out of my car," I tell him as I hurry over to where I parked. I have cowboy boots for riding, since my brother is a horse fanatic and I never know when he'll put me on one. Summer joins me and stands over me as I sit on the seat and pull off my sneakers.

"What's going on?"

"We had a great date the other night," I reply quickly. "No sex. He invited me to come today, so I said yes, and he had me come early so he could show me around."

"Isn't it a sweet house?"

"That's one word for it."

"What would *you* say?" she asks, tilting her head to the side.

"Intimidating. Huge. Amazing. Glorious."

Summer laughs, and when I get the second boot on, she offers me her hand to pull me to my feet, and I shut the door behind me, not bothering to lock it. With all the security out here, I'd say it's safe.

"Let's join the guys and get me on a horse," Summer says with a bounce in her step. "Chase threatened to do this last year, but time got away from us."

"You'll like it." I loop my arm through hers, enjoying this time together. "It's fun. Are you almost ready for your grand opening at the shop?"

"No," she says, looking so sad. "They had something bad happen with something that I don't know anything about, and now it's going to take about two months longer. Maybe more."

"What?" I frown over at her. "Oh, friend, that is *so* not cool. I'm sorry."

"I know that we need it done right more than anything else, but it was *so close*. Anyway, maybe getting on a horse will take my mind off of it."

"Nice boots," Ryan says, grinning at my feet.

"Thanks. They're a million years old and dirty, so they're perfect for riding a horse."

"Climb in. I'll drive." Jake points to the large side-by-side with a grin.

"I'd rather walk," Chase says, eyeing the boy suspiciously, and it makes Jake laugh. "Also, maybe Montana should rethink their driver's license age laws. Fifteen is too young to be in control of a motor vehicle."

Jake just laughs. "Come on, don't be a chicken."

We climb in, and I'm in the middle of the back seat, between Summer and Ryan, and Jake takes off for the stable. It's not *that* far from the house, but I admit this is faster than walking.

And when we get there, I sigh in delight when I see the horses. Six of them are grazing in the small fenced pasture, and they all come over to see us.

"Hey, baby," Jake croons to a brown-and-white mare. "This is Ladybug, and she's going to be Polly's horse today."

"She's so *pretty*," I breathe and join him to pet her face and talk to her. "Hello, beautiful girl. I get to be your friend today."

Jake smiles and then turns to the others. "Summer's on Lullaby, that white girl there. I'm on Cowboy, and Ryan always rides Firefly. Chase, do you have a preference?"

"I've never ridden Snickers," he says. "I'll take her."

"That leaves Blossom all alone," Ryan says. "I should have had someone else come out to join us."

"Hold that thought," Chase says, holding up a finger as he pulls out his phone and dials a number. "Hey, are you busy? Wanna meet me at Ryan's stable and ride a horse? See you in ten."

He hangs up and grins.

"Who's that?" I ask him.

"Erin. She's on her way. She's been learning to ride with the hands at the ranch, and she needs the practice. The kids are with my parents today."

"Perfect," Summer says with a grin. "What should we do while we wait for her?"

"We'll saddle up," Jake informs her. "And I'm going to teach you that, too."

"I'm ready to learn." Summer follows the teenager into the stable.

"She's excited," I say to Ryan and Chase as we follow behind. "She's going to do great. And Jake is great at this. He should give lessons, work with riders professionally."

"He really is excellent," Chase agrees, and I glance over to find Ryan lost in thought.

I slow my pace, but Chase moves ahead, and Ryan hangs back with me.

"You okay?" he asks me.

"I was just going to ask you the same thing. You suddenly got quiet."

"Not in a bad way." He smiles down at me. "I'm just soaking it all in. You'll love Ladybug."

"I already do." I can't help it. I slip my hand in his and give it a squeeze, and when we walk into the barn, everyone is too enthralled with saddling their horses to notice us. "I can saddle my own."

"Let's do it, then."

Ten minutes later, Erin pulls up and hops out of her SUV. "This is so fun. Thanks for including me."

"We had an extra horse and didn't want to leave her behind," Jake says. "Blossom's a good girl. You'll like her."

"I've met her," Erin says and rubs the horse's nose. "We're friends, aren't we, pretty lady?"

It takes about thirty minutes to get all the horses ready to go, and before we all take off on a ride, Jake takes Summer out in the pasture by herself to show her how to handle Lullaby.

"He's so damn good with them," Erin says softly. "With both the horse and the rider. Those horses have helped heal him, Ryan."

"They've healed each other," Ryan replies.

"I'm doing it!" Summer grins over at us and leans down to pat the horse on the neck. "This is awesome."

"Do you think you could go on a ride with us?" Jake asks her.

"Like this? Yes, just don't get fancy on me."

"Okay, then." Jake laughs and gestures for all of us to follow them. Once mounted up, we're riding two-by-two deeper into the ranch. I can't help but notice all the beautiful wildflowers blooming in the pasture, with the gorgeous mountains rising up into the blue sky in the distance.

"How many acres do you own here?" I ask Ryan, who's riding next to me.

"About five thousand, give or take." He smiles over at me. "You look damn sexy on that horse."

"Thanks." I toss my hair over my shoulder and bat my eyelashes at him. "I like to ride all kinds of things."

"Like?"

"Oh, you know. Horses. Amusement park rides. Ryan Wild."

That has him busting out laughing, and the others look back at us and then go back to their own conversations.

My horse stomps and seems to be unsettled about something in the tall grass.

"Whoa, girl. Whoa. What is it?" I narrow my eyes, looking down, and then immediately turn her closer to Ryan. "Snake."

We make a wide berth around the snake in the grass, and then Ryan looks over at me with admiration in his gaze.

"What?"

"You didn't panic."

"If *I* panic, the horse does, too, and I don't want to end up on the ground with a snake. She was a good girl and warned me, and we figured it out."

"I like that you can handle yourself on a horse," he says.

"I can handle myself just about anywhere."

"I'm going to play games with Russ," Jake says to Ryan after dinner. Once the others left after our ride, we watched a movie in the theater, and then I made the guys salmon for a late dinner. Jake and Ryan just finished the dishes, insisting that because I cooked, I didn't have to clean.

I happily took them up on that offer.

"And," Jake continues, "I'm not coming back out. So, if you kiss or something, I don't have to see it. You did really good today, Polly."

That lights me up inside because I know it's high praise coming from this boy. "Thank you. I had a lot of fun. You're talented with the horses, Jake."

"Yeah, they're my thing. Good night."

He quickly raids the pantry for some chips and cookies, pulls two sodas out of the fridge, and then he's gone upstairs.

"Drink some water, too!" Ryan calls after him. "He asked for a fridge for his room, and I told him no. He has to come out of there sometime to refuel, and I actually like seeing him."

He pulls a bottle of wine out of a wine fridge, snatches two wineglasses from a cabinet, and then gestures for me to follow him up to the rooftop.

The sun is just starting to go down over the mountains, and I take a minute to close my eyes and breathe in the fresh air.

"It's *so* pretty out here, Ryan."

I sit on one side of the outdoor sofa and watch as Ryan opens the wine and pours two glasses, passing me one. There are twinkle lights strung all around the top of the glass, and they're illuminated, casting a warm, pretty glow in the room.

"It's my favorite place in the world," he admits. "Up here, in this place. I love the whole property, but this is the one corner that I don't really share with anyone. Jake comes up once in a while, but it's not as interesting to him."

"Have you always been interested in the stars?" I ask him and then feel my eyes go wide. "Oh, shit, are you going to be one of those billionaires who builds a rocket ship to go into space? Don't be that guy, Ryan."

He laughs and shakes his head. "No. I'm not going to do that. If I want to go to space, I can pay to do it. I didn't always find it interesting. I was in Hawaii a few years ago at the largest and highest observatory in the world, and it just fascinated me. So, like I always do when something sparks my interest, I dove into the science and read up on it as much as I could. There's so much I'll never know because I just don't have the time to learn, but this telescope is great because it has an app that allows me to plug in what I want to see, and it adjusts itself to show it to me. It takes a lot of the guesswork out of it."

"That's cool." I sip my wine and admire the telescope. "Can you see Saturn?"

"I can see past Saturn," he says. "I'll show you when it gets a little darker up here."

"How often do you take quiet days like this?" I sip my wine, lounging back in the soft pillows, watching him.

"No work, no calls, just a little fun on a horse and looking at the stars?"

"I don't know if I ever have. But I like it. I should do it more often. Arthur would have a heart attack."

I laugh with him and slip my feet out of my sneakers so I can tuck them under me. "What did he do today?"

"He mentioned spending it with his husband."

"Good for him. I hope he had as good of a day as we did."

Ryan reaches for my hand. He never goes long without touching me. "I do, too."

He pulls me into his lap and smiles softly down at me, pushing my hair off my cheek. He takes my glass from my hand to set it aside, frames my face, and pulls me in for a sweet kiss.

"You're good at the kissing," I murmur against his lips. "Like, *really* good at it."

"It takes two," he reminds me as his hand roams over my T-shirt, down my side, and under the hem to touch me, skin-on-skin. I feel the goose bumps and he must, too, because his eyes flare as he stares down at me. "You're fucking incredible."

"Aw, shucks."

That makes his lips twitch with humor, and he points up to the sky. "Do you see that bright star?"

I look up, settling against him. "Sure."

"It's not actually a star. It's Venus. It doesn't wink like the other stars do, and it's brighter."

"Okay, show me in the telescope."

I hop off of his lap, and, to my surprise, Ryan pulls

glasses out of a little cubby where the iPad lives and slips them onto his face. Black-rimmed, they make him look even sexier than before, and I would have said that isn't possible.

He taps the screen of the iPad, and the telescope begins to move.

"Have a look," he says, gesturing toward the amazing machine.

I lean in and peek through the viewfinder and feel my breath catch. It's yellowish, with brown stripes, and it glows.

"It's hard to see Venus when it's super dark," Ryan explains. "Because it's so close to us, and the sun is shining on it. So, during twilight, like right now, is the best time to look. Okay, back up."

I do, and he taps the pad again, then nods for me to look once more.

"What is *this*?"

"Jupiter." He's quiet as I take it in. "It's massive and beautiful. It would take just over a year to fly there."

"That's a long road trip," I mutter and pull back to look up with my naked eye. "Can we see the Milky Way in this thing?"

"You can see the Milky Way without anything at all in about an hour," he replies with a grin. "The show is just starting."

"I didn't even bring any popcorn."

"If you want snacks, we can go get some and hunker down for a while. I can show you some amazing things."

"Will you show me while naked?"

He pauses. Blinks. And I laugh.

"I'm kidding, although *that* would be fun. Maybe sometime when Jake's not here."

The next thing I know, my back is pressed to the side of the house, my legs are wrapped around Ryan's waist, and his lips are on mine, hard and demanding.

"We're going to see how quiet you can be," he says against my ear.

"I'm not making any promises."

I've been trying to take things at a slower pace. It pissed me off that Polly thought that all I wanted from her was sex. She's worth more than that.

But damn it, *I want her.* And by the way she's clinging and reacting to me right now, I'd say that feeling is completely reciprocated.

"No sound." I nibble on her lips and set her on her feet long enough to strip her jeans off of her, along with her panties, and I tickle her most intimate lips, satisfied that they're already wet. "Fuck, you're wet."

"Your fault," she breathes and whimpers in the back of her throat as I push one finger inside of her. "Oh, God, Ryan."

"Shh." I cover her mouth with mine again and easily lift her, brace her on the wall, and bury my face in her neck. "I love how small you are. I can just lift you, move you, or throw you wherever I want you."

"Why do *I* have to be quiet but you don't?"

I grin against her skin, then reach down to unfasten my own denim and curse under my breath.

"What's wrong?"

"No condom. Shit."

Polly frames my face in her hands and grins. "I've got the birth control handled."

"There's been no one since you," I tell her and watch as those emerald eyes go wide in surprise. "Are you sure?"

"Ryan," she whispers and bites my lower lip. "Shut up and fuck me already."

I slide so easily inside of her and have to grit my teeth because she's so snug, so fucking *perfect*, and I don't want to ruin this by coming in less than five seconds.

But the long months of being without her, wanting her for so long, and finally having her, won't let me take it slow. I ram into her, hard and quick, and cover her mouth with mine to keep her from calling out.

She quivers in my arms, shudders, and moans long and low when the orgasm moves through her. Like a man possessed, I keep up the pace until I feel my own release pulse through me, and I let go.

She's clinging to me as we recover, out of breath, and when I finally set her on her feet, she lets out a half laugh.

"I'm going to need to visit one of your fifty bathrooms on the way to get snacks."

"Not a problem." She wiggles into her pants, and then I tip her chin up and cover her lips with my own, more softly this time. "Are you okay, sweetheart?"

“Oh, yeah. More than okay.”

I kiss her once more and then open the door for her. “Let’s grab snacks.”

She makes a pit stop in the half bath by the kitchen, and I open the pantry to take stock of what’s inside.

“You have a lot of food in your kitchen.” She grins as she joins me in front of the pantry, and we stare inside. “Like, a *lot.*”

“Jake likes food,” I reply. “And I think the assholes who had him before me withheld food when they punished him.”

She stares up at me, and then her eyes fill with tears. “Are you fucking kidding me?”

“He won’t talk about it,” I continue, shaking my head. “I’ve asked, but he changes the subject. He won’t talk about his biological family, either. I get the feeling that his home life wasn’t stellar even then. I didn’t know his parents well, other than that his dad worked at the ranch for a while before they passed. Remington told me that he didn’t talk about his family much.”

I grab some cookies, Polly snatches up some cheesy crackers, and we make our way back upstairs, not talking about it again until we’re in the observatory and the door is closed.

“I could hear him playing his game when we walked past his room,” she says as she pops a cracker into her mouth. “He was calling someone a sonofabitch.”

“It happens often,” I reply with a laugh. “If he swears in front of me, I discourage it, but he’s a teenage boy, and they all swear. Hell, *I* did. If that’s the worst thing he does, then I don't have much to complain about."

She grins and nibbles that cracker. "You're right. Okay, what kinds of things are you going to show me with your big...telescope?"

I narrow my eyes at her, and she giggles. "You're just full of innuendos tonight."

"Yeah, and it finally got you into my pants, so yay me." She reaches for a cookie. "What took so long, anyway?"

That's Polly. Blunt as fuck and unapologetic about it. I love that about her.

"I've been attempting to be a gentleman."

"Are you about done with that?"

I raise an eyebrow, set the food aside, and crawl over the couch to her, pinning her beneath me. "Did you miss my cock, Pollyanna?"

She snorts, narrows her eyes, and tries to wiggle out from beneath me, but I hold firm.

"My name is *not* Pollyanna. I hate that name. I'm no goodie two-shoes. As evidenced by all the dirty sex we've had."

That makes me pause. "*Dirty* sex?"

"I mean, it hasn't been *clean* sex."

I drag my thumb over her nipple, through her shirt and bra, and feel it pebble beneath my touch, making me grin in satisfaction. "We haven't done one thing that was *dirty*. Hot. Fucking incredible. But not dirty."

"You didn't like that word."

My gaze finds hers, and I hold it steady. "No. I didn't. Because it implies that we did something wrong."

"That's not what I said," she counters and drags her nails down my cheek. "It wasn't *wrong*. Anything that feels that good can't be wrong. It was...not the typical boring missionary sex."

"We'll do that," I reply and kiss her lips. "Whenever you want. Now, I'm not going to push my luck and take you twice when my kid is downstairs. He claims he's in for the night, but—"

"But you never know," she agrees and pushes up to kiss me sweetly. "Tell me more about the sky. I want to learn everything that you know."

"We'll be here a while."

"I have all night."

Before I can reach for the iPad to change the direction of the telescope, my phone rings, and I frown.

"This is security," I mutter and answer. "Wild."

"We have a situation, sir."

"Here, at the house?" I stand and look down at Polly, who's watching me with wide eyes.

"Yes, sir. We just apprehended some kids who were trying to break into the premises. You'll want to come down here."

"Where are you?"

"We have them in the office," Axel replies. "You might want to bring Jake with you."

That gives me pause. "Why?"

"Because he knows these boys."

I sigh and look back at Polly. "I'll be there in ten."

"What's happening?" she asks.

"We have some kids that tried to trespass, and my security detail wants me to bring Jake."

Polly's eyes go sharp and hot with anger. "Why?"

"Because he knows them, apparently. You can wait—"

"I will *not* wait," she insists, hot on my heels as I make my way to the door. "I'll be going with you and Jake."

"If that's what you want, that's fine with me."

I knock on Jake's door and relay the information.

"Russ, I gotta go, man. I'll be back." He shuts down his game, shoves his feet into some shoes, and hurries with us down the stairs and out to my truck.

The security base is on the other side of the property. It's a nice building with two bedrooms, a full kitchen, and a big command center for monitors and computers, and when I walk inside, that's where I find my two men and the two boys who have attitude written all over their faces.

"I'm gonna sue you," the one says, his chin tilted up in defiance. "I'm gonna take everything you've got."

"Okay," I reply and turn to Axel. "What do we have here?"

"These two were caught cutting the fence about five hundred feet down from the main gate," Axel begins, delivering the report as he would if he were still on the police force. "They trespassed onto the property, carrying bags that we now know are full of spray paint and grain filled with poison."

"What the fuck?" Jake exclaims, eyeing the two boys about his age. "Are you *kidding me*?"

"Fuck you," boy one sneers, as the other one, white as a ghost, looks like he'd love it if the floor opened up and swallowed him whole.

"What were you going to do with the poison?" I ask and cross my arms over my chest, eyeing them both with pure anger.

"None of your business."

"What are your names?"

"None of your fucking business," boy one repeats.

"Todd Wells," Jake says, pointing to boy one, "and Steve Taylor."

"You're such a fucking *rat*," Todd says, obviously pissed off.

"Hey!" I shout, getting his attention. "Eyes on me. What were you going to do with the poison? Kill my horses?"

"Like you'd miss them," Todd replies. "You're fucking rich; you can replace them."

"These were the two boys caught shoplifting in my store last year," Polly murmurs behind me. "Ex-associates of Jake's."

"Have the police been called?" I ask Axel, who nods.

"Affirmative, sir. They're on their way."

"Dude, this is stupid," Todd says. "It's just a little paint, and nobody got hurt. It was a prank."

"You're an idiot," Jake shoots off.

"You're a piece of *fuck*," Todd fires back, using his obviously favorite word.

"Dude, just stop," Steve mutters, but Todd doesn't listen.

"You think that just because this asshole adopted you that you're better than us? Bullshit. You're nobody, who comes from shit people, and that makes you shit. You're worthless."

"*Enough!*" I yell and step forward. "You'll keep your mouth shut. Do you hear me?"

"Whatever," Todd snarls as we hear a car pull up outside, and for the first time, a little sliver of fear shows in his young eyes. "I don't care about this. You're all fucked."

An hour later, after the boys have been cuffed and hauled off to jail for the night, I walk into the house with Polly and Jake and sigh.

"I'm sorry," Jake says mournfully.

"What?" I turn to him and scowl. "Why are *you* sorry?"

"It's because of me that they came here," he replies. "If it wasn't for me, it wouldn't have happened."

"You can't control what other people do," Polly reminds him and rubs her hand up and down his back. "And you did the right thing by breaking away from them after the incident at my store. So this is definitely *not* your fault, Jake."

"Feels like it is," he mumbles. "I can't believe they were going to hurt the horses. What kind of sick asshole does that?"

"Hey." I step to him and cup his young face in my hand. "You need to take a breath, buddy. The horses are fine. Nothing happened to them, and the boys are most likely going to juvie for a while."

"They *should*," Jake says. "You don't know half of what they've done and gotten away with. They're no good, and I can't believe I tried to be their friend."

"You were going through a hard time," Polly reminds him. "We all make bad choices when things get rough. You fixed it."

"You fixed it," I echo with a nod. "And now, we move on."

"Are you going to press charges?" Jake asks me, holding my gaze with his.

"Hell yes, I am."

"Good. That's good." He licks his lips and steps back. "I'd better go log back in and tell Russ about it."

"Good night," Polly says, patting his back as he walks past, then she looks over at me when we hear Jake's door close upstairs. "That poor kid."

"He'll be okay," I reply grimly. "I'm sorry that interrupted our star gazing."

She holds her hand out for mine. "We can still go do that. Come on."

"Watch me, Uncle Ryan!" Holly waves enthusiastically from the side of the pool, and when I smile and wave back, she runs and does a cannonball into the water. When she comes up sputtering, she looks for me. "Did you see?"

"I saw," I call back and give her a thumbs-up. "Good job, pumpkin."

The house is a hive of activity. There are plenty of people in the pool, others sitting on chairs and chaise lounges beside it, and even more seated in the outdoor living area, watching and eating and laughing.

It's the most chaos that this house has ever seen, and I love it.

I *love* it.

"Thanks for having me, Mr. Wild." Jake's friend, Russ, nods at me and takes a bite of his cheeseburger. Brady's been at the grill, making everyone lunch for the past hour. "This is legit."

"Glad you could come. And glad I could meet you in person. I was wondering if *'I'm gonna shoot zombies with Russ'* was a real person."

"Totally real," Russ replies with a laugh before he and Jake walk off to have their lunch at a table with Chase and Remington.

Scanning the crowd, I find Polly sitting with Erin, Summer, Millie, and Abbi. The five of them have their heads together, laughing and clearly gossiping about something.

And when I walk over to find out what they're talking about, they clam up and smile at me.

"Hey," Polly says and reaches for my hand. "This is a *great* party."

"I didn't know you had it in you," Millie adds and grins in that *I'm your sister, and I can annoy you if I want to* way she has. "You do know that this will be the epicenter of all family functions all summer now. What with the pool and everything."

"I don't mind," I reply and force a smile. When I glance down at Polly, her eyes are narrowed.

"I'll be back, guys," she says as she stands. "I want to kiss Ryan in private."

"That's disgusting," Millie calls after us as Polly leads me inside.

"Do you really want to make out?" I ask her, pulling her against me. "Because I can oblige you."

"No, I want to know what's wrong."

I frown down at her, but she doesn't back down.

"Seriously, something's on your mind. I just saw you last night, and everything was fine, but now, something's bothering you."

It's been a week since the night in my observatory, and we've managed to see each other every day since. I look forward to my time with her, even if it's just a few stolen moments here and there.

"I really *am* glad that everyone's here and having a good time," I insist evenly, and drag my fingertips down her jawline.

"But?"

"I have to go out of town tomorrow." I sigh and don't mask the frustration in my gut.

"Oh, for how long?"

"A few weeks."

"A few...*weeks*?"

"Yeah. I'm needed in Europe and Asia, so I figured I'd stop in at all of my main properties to make an appearance and take meetings in person. I have to swing by my place in Manhattan first for a few days, and then I'll be traveling pretty much every day."

"But, what about Jake?"

"I thought about taking him, but he insisted on staying with the horses. Brady and Millie will take turns staying here with him. He's mostly fine by himself, but I want an adult here at night. My parents will look in on him. I have a village." I smile at her, touched that her first thought was of my teenager.

"He can call me if he needs anything," she offers.

"Thank you. I appreciate that."

Polly simply walks into my arms and hugs me around the middle, her ear pressed to my chest.

"It sucks that you have to go for so long."

"I'll miss you, too." I kiss her hair and breathe her in. "But the time will go by fast. I heard you tell Millie that business is picking up for you, too."

"It's the crazy season," she confirms with a sigh. "Yeah, I'm busy. And I'm being selfish. I hope you have a productive, safe trip. I'll text you inappropriate messages."

"I'm looking forward to that."

The door slides open behind us, and I glance back to find my mom walking in with an empty pitcher of what was lemonade.

"Oh, excuse me," she says, and the grin spreads wide over her face. "I have to pour more lemonade for the troops."

"I'll help," Polly offers.

"Oh, thank you, dear, but do you mind if I have a conversation with my son?"

Polly laughs and shakes her head. "Not at all. Sounds like you're in trouble." She pats my arm as she heads for the door. "Good luck with that."

She closes the door behind her, and I pat the ache in my chest before turning to my mother, who has a gooey look on her pretty face.

"I know what you're thinking."

"Do you, now?" She clucks her tongue and pours lemonade into the pitcher. "And what is that?"

"That Polly and I make a handsome couple, and you're wondering when you can marry me off."

"That feels a little fast, but sure. When can I marry you off? I like Polly so much. Her mother is in my book club, and she helps out at the food bank with me. Hell, I went to high school with her. I've known her a long time."

"I know," I reply and take the heavy pitcher from her. "Mac is my oldest friend. I know that you know their parents."

"Wouldn't it be fun if they were in-laws?"

I hadn't really thought of that. "Mom, Polly and I are just dating right now. I like her a lot, but no one is talking about marriage."

"You're an idiot." It's said with so much love and a big smile on her face as she pats my cheek. "But, you'll come around. Bring that lemonade outside, will you? The kids want some of it."

I don't remember the last time anyone dared call me

an idiot. Probably Remington, when I told him about my plans to move off the ranch and leave Montana.

And I'm a little disconcerted that the one who called me that is my own *mother.*

"Is that all you wanted to talk to me about?"

Mom grins back at me. "You know your mother so well."

I follow her outside, and there's Remington himself, holding Holly's hand.

"I have to poop," she announces, and I can't help but laugh at her.

"How about if I take you?" Mom offers, and takes Holly's hand, leading her back inside to the bathroom.

"Your kids are the best," I say to Rem, who nods and shuffles his feet. We're alone, with everyone else off talking or swimming or playing games in the grass.

And, despite the fact that I've been home for a full year, Rem is still uncomfortable with me.

"We have to cut this shit out," I say, my voice low. "I need my brother, man. It's been a long-ass time."

"Six years," he says with a nod. "It was six years ago that *I* needed my brother, and he couldn't be bothered."

His eyes meet mine, hot and angry all over again.

"That's not how it was."

"Fuck that," he bites off, shaking his head. "That's *exactly* how it was. My wife died, I had two babies, and I needed you to stay at the ranch for a few weeks."

"You had Mom and Dad, Chase and Brady. Millie."

"I needed *you,*" he bites out. "You were my goddamn best friend, and I needed your help. Instead, you couldn't get out of there fast enough. You showed me that day where your priorities are, and they aren't with your family."

"Rem—"

"No. You can have us all out here, play with my kids, and pretend like you've figured it all out, that you've come home for good, but you'll just leave again, Ry."

"I've been home for a *year*. And in case you missed it, I have a kid of my own now. A ranch with horses and a kid and a goddamn *girlfriend*. I have a life in Bitterroot Valley, so to stand there and accuse me of being ready to bug out at any time is a fucking dick move, and you know it. I *couldn't* stay six years ago. I wanted to, and I felt so fucking guilty—"

"Yeah, so guilty that you just sent *stuff*. Baby stuff, groceries, all kinds of shit. I didn't want that."

"I couldn't give you what you needed in that moment, and I've apologized for it until I'm blue in the goddamn face, Rem. Jesus, I *love* you and those kids, and there isn't much that I wouldn't do for any of you."

"Except stay." His smile is humorless. "You wouldn't fucking stay."

He marches away, past the pool and the games, and out to the trees beyond, obviously walking off the anger that I always seem to bring out in him.

Erin runs off of the patio and follows after him. Rem slips his hand in hers, and they don't say anything as they walk into the treeline.

"It hurts a father's heart," my dad says next to me. I

didn't even feel him join me. "To see his sons at odds, the way you two are."

"I hurt him," I murmur and exhale sharply. "And no matter what I do, I can't seem to fix it."

"Sometimes, all you can do is give it time, son." He lays his hand on my shoulder and gives it a squeeze. "He loves you a lot. The two of you were always so close, only being a year apart, and maybe he expects a little too much from you."

"No, he *should* expect a lot from me. I'm the one who fucked up."

"It was a bad situation," Dad replies. "A sad one. And we've all moved on from it. Remington will let the hurt go sooner or later. Give it some more time."

I nod and look over at my father. All of us boys look so much like him. "Thanks, Dad."

He squeezes my shoulder once more and then walks over to talk to Chase and Brady. Holly and Mom come out of the house, and Holly races up to Chase.

"Let's play chicken in the pool," she announces. "Come on, Uncle Chase, let me get on your shoulders!"

"Who are we playing chicken against?" Chase wants to know.

"Daisy!" Holly says.

Chase looks at Brady. "Put Daisy on your shoulders and get in the pool. We've been given orders."

Daisy claps her hands and eagerly lets Brady lift her into his arms as he wades into the pool. Both men put the girls on their shoulders, and the game starts. The girls try to tug each other off the men's shoulders.

"Daisy's so stinking cute," I hear Millie say to Abbi. "And she likes Brady."

I glance over and see Abbi smile.

"He's a Wild brother," Summer says smugly. "Of *course,* she likes him. They're all hot."

I can't help but smirk as Abbi's cheeks redden.

"I think Abbi likes Brady, too," Millie adds.

Not wanting to eavesdrop and hear about how anyone has a crush on my brother, I return to my place by the pool and sit on the chaise, watching the game in the water.

"Can I sit here?" Polly asks, indicating the tiny square available on my chair.

"Sure." I simply tug her into my lap and kiss her, right here in front of everyone. I can feel their eyes on us, and I don't give a shit.

"Well, that turned out better than I planned," Polly says with a laugh.

"Good." I settle her against me and look around. "I like this. I like it a lot."

"I know." She sighs and leans more heavily against me. "I do, too. It's fun. When you get back from your trip, maybe you can have another party like this for the Fourth."

"Done." I kiss the top of her head. "But only if you promise to come, too."

"Are you kidding? I wouldn't miss it." She frowns up at me. "Speaking of missing things, you won't be here for the IWC summer soiree."

I tip her chin up so I can look her in the eyes. "What's

that?"

"Every season, we put on a formal party so we can invite significant others, and I was actually going to invite *you* today, but you'll be out of town. I mean, it's fine. Maybe I'm being presumptuous to assume that you'd want to go."

It means a lot to her. "I'd want to go. Shit, I'm sorry, sweetheart."

"It's okay. Really."

She's far too understanding. I hate the timing of this trip. I don't want to promise her that I can make it back in time, but I don't want to disappoint her, either.

"I'll try to figure it out."

"Ryan." She cups my cheek and smiles reassuringly. "It's okay. There will be others. Don't sweat it."

I kiss her forehead and then glance at the pool and find Johnny and Holly watching us. They make gagging noises and then laugh hysterically.

And I decide here and now that I'll do everything in my power to wrap this trip up as quickly as possible. I don't want to be away from any of them for long.

"This could have been handled remotely." My voice is cold as I stare at the man sitting across from me on the jet as we fly from Stockholm to Berlin. "Why have I been pulled from my home for three fucking weeks for this shit? So far, in the five days we've been traveling, there hasn't been even one thing that was urgent or warranted my attention in person."

Arthur's expression doesn't waver. "Because you haven't been on-site anywhere since last fall. You *need* to be in your respective offices several times a year. Sir, your people need to see you in person. It helps morale."

I narrow my eyes on him and cross one ankle over the opposite knee.

"You're telling me that *you* decided to send me on this ridiculous tour because it's good for fucking *morale*?"

"Yes, sir."

His throat moves now as he swallows hard, the first indication that he might be regretting his decisions.

"You told me that there were dire situations that required my immediate attention."

"Yes, I did. And I still believe that's true."

I tap my fingertips on my chin and think about the fact that I have a teenager at home alone and a woman whom I'm just starting to make headway with, and rather than being with either of them, I'm in my jet halfway around the world when I don't need to be.

"I'm going to finish this trip in two weeks rather than three," I inform my assistant, "and I'll be working around the clock to fit everything in that you had scheduled. Then I'm going home. If you have a problem with that, I'm quite sure you can find another position somewhere else."

Arthur's eyes just about bug out of his head. "Mr. Wild, you're blowing this out of proportion."

"You *know*," I interrupt him, leaning forward. "You're one of the few people who knows what I went through late last year, what my kid went through, and why it's important to me to be home with him. If I'm needed in London or Dublin or fucking Berlin, that's fine, I'll go, but you will *not* parade me around the world to make an appearance at my own fucking offices because you think it's good for *morale.* I'm in constant contact with my people, and you know it. I expect you to have my back, not decide to be my boss or my goddamn father and dictate how I run my business."

"That's not—"

"That's exactly what you did, Arthur. I won't have it. No, I don't work twenty-hour days anymore, and I'm not going to. I don't *have* to. Are we clear? Because I won't discuss this with you again."

"I understand." He clears his throat and then shakes his head. "You used to be so focused, so *ruthless.*"

"And you think I'm not now?"

"Not like you used to be."

"I'm thirty-four, with an empire that anyone would envy. And now, I have a family and a life outside of that empire, and I won't apologize for that. Nor will I explain myself to *you.* When we land in Berlin, I'm sending you back to Manhattan."

His nostrils flare. "You're firing me?"

"No, I just don't want to continue this trip with you."

"But I have all the information—"

"Send it to me. Yes, I depend on you for a lot, but you're not irreplaceable. It's time you remembered that."

I stand and walk to another seat on my jet, buckle in,

and pull my phone out of my pocket. It's two a.m. in Montana, so not exactly a great time to call Polly, although I'd really love to hear her voice right now.

I've been gone for five days, and it's been fucking frustrating. At every turn, I've been disappointed in Arthur, and the men and women who run each of the offices we've visited have been confused as to why we're there. I hire the right people to make sure that things are handled without me.

I can't be all around the world at once. Nor should I ever have to be.

I miss my ranch, my kid, and my girl, and I have another week of this bullshit. Since I'm already here, I'll finish the trip, but I won't take the leisurely pace that Arthur originally set out for me. I'm going to make sure I get home by that summer soiree that Polly wants me to go to.

I open the photo app on my phone and smile at pictures of Jake with the horses and then feel frustrated that there aren't any pictures of Polly.

I'll change that soon.

"So, what's going on between you and Ryan?" My brother crosses his arms over his chest and leans back against the railing of my parents' back deck while we wait for the steaks to cook on the grill.

"Well, for the past week, not much," I reply and shove my hair over my shoulder. "He's been gone, you know."

"Har har, you're a riot. You know what I mean."

I frown and bite my lip. The truth is, despite my hope that Ryan would be in contact with me often while he's gone, I haven't heard much from him. Between the huge time differences and the work that I assume he's putting in, he must not have time.

"We're dating." I shrug and move to open the lid on the grill, but Mac stops me.

"Let it be," he says without moving. "Don't let all the hot air out. It won't cook evenly. Come on, you can talk to me. It's only a little weird that it's my best friend since I was five and my baby sister."

I wince and then sigh. "You saw us at the party last weekend."

"And when Ryan and I brought gas to your car," he replies.

"So, you don't really *need* me to spell it out for you. We're seeing each other."

"I hope that it goes well because if he hurts you, or *you* hurt *him*, I'm gonna have to do something about it, and that's just weird."

"No one's hurt."

"Yet." Mac sighs and shoves his hand through his hair. "Look, you're both good people with strong work ethics, and I care about you both, but *you're* my sister. Don't make me take sides if it all falls apart."

"I am an adult," I remind him. "I don't need you to swoop in and save me from anyone, even your best friend. I like him, Mac. We have chemistry and...I just like him. And for now, that's good enough."

"Okay."

"I'm surprised you're not trying to warn me off him. You probably know all about his sordid past, and maybe you don't want him with your sister."

Mac considers it, rubbing his hand over his mouth. "I don't think Ry *has* a sordid past. He's too business focused to fuck around with women."

I raise an eyebrow, and Mac rolls his eyes.

"He's no monk," he admits. "He's done his share of dating, but he's not a snake, Poll. I don't think he's left a wake of broken hearts in his past. You're fine. But he's married to his businesses, and he works more than he does anything else."

"Well, that's something we have in common," I reply. "His work ethic doesn't scare me."

"Where's the food?" Dad asks as he steps outside. "Everything else is ready. How are the steaks?"

"I'd say they're about done," Mac replies, our earlier conversation obviously finished, much to my relief. I don't mind talking about Ryan. I've been asked more times than I can count if there's something going on between us, and I've been honest.

I don't know any other way to be, and the man kissed me in front of his *family*, so I'm assuming that it's no secret that we're seeing each other.

But talking about it with my brother is...weird.

Usually, Mac threatens to kill a guy *after* we're done dating.

"Come on, you guys," Mom says, poking her head out the door. "Let's eat. I'm starving."

Once a month, Mac and I come over to the house we grew up in and have dinner with our parents. Although we were raised here, the house doesn't look much like it did when we were young.

My mom loves to change things. There's always a project in the works here, and she's made no secret that it drives her nuts to go to my house and see the paint swatches on the walls with no progress made at all.

Mom and I couldn't be more different.

But I love her to death.

"I have to go wash my hands," I say as I walk through to the hall bathroom and then stop in my tracks. "Uh, Mom? Where did the bathroom go?"

"Oh, I'm sorry, sweetie. I tore that out yesterday. It was time to update it."

"Didn't you just update it three years ago?" Mac asks.

"I *painted* it three years ago," Mom counters. "But it hadn't had a good overhaul since you kids were little. Polly, go use the bathroom off our bedroom."

I hurry through the house, through the bedroom that I don't even recognize, and wash my hands in the en suite, which is also newer and decorated like it belongs in a magazine.

Yep, the apple fell *really* far from the tree.

With a smile, I return to the kitchen and help set the last few things on the table before we sit down to eat.

"So," Dad says as he passes me the twice-baked potatoes. "I hear you're seeing Ryan Wild."

My eyes lock with Mac's across the table. He laughs. I sigh.

Here we go again.

I MISS HIM.

I'm lying on my back, naked as the day I was born, staring up at the ceiling, sweating, and not for any fun reasons. It's moments like these that I question my life choices of not having air conditioning installed in my house. Sure, the hottest part of the summer is short, but it makes for uncomfortable nights.

I have two fans pointed at me, and I'm still too warm.

And it doesn't help at all that I can't stop thinking about a certain billionaire who's currently sitting in an office halfway across the world, probably in a power suit, buying Egypt or something. The vivid picture of it brings a grin to my lips.

I regret not inviting him to be my date at the IWC party earlier than I did. He probably would have still had to go on this trip, but I still wish I'd mentioned it. I won't make him feel guilty about not being able to go with me because it's *just* a party, and he has important things to do. There will be other opportunities to take him as my date. But man, I wish he was going with me.

Since talking about him all evening with my family, Ryan is even more front and center in my mind, and I admit, I miss the hell out of him. I know he's important, and he's busy, but I would give just about anything to hear his voice.

"Screw it," I mutter and reach for my phone. I'll call him. I'll probably get his voicemail, but I don't care. I tap the screen and hold the phone to my ear, and to my utter shock, he answers.

"Polly?"

"Hey," I reply. "I'm sorry, you're probably busy—"

"Never too busy. Hold on one sec." He pulls the phone away from his mouth, but I can still hear him. "I have to take this very important phone call. Everyone, take a break. I'll be in my office."

He's walking. I hear a door shut, and then he's back.

"Are you okay?"

"Yes. I'm sorry, Ryan. This isn't an emergency. I shouldn't have pulled you out of a meeting." Guilt sits heavy in my stomach. I interrupted something important just because I couldn't sleep.

That's ridiculous.

"Don't be sorry," he says with a sigh, and I hear him sit in a chair. "I needed the break and to hear your voice. But it has to be two in the morning there."

"It is," I admit. "I can't sleep. It's too hot in my house, and I'm uncomfortable, and because it's the middle of the night here, and dark, I can admit that I miss you."

"You can only admit that in the middle of the night?" I can hear the smile in his voice, and it makes me relax. Hell, everything about Ryan calms me down. I can already feel my muscles loosening, and I sink down into the mattress, getting cozy.

"Maybe." I chuckle and fling my arm over my head.

"Tell me what you're doing," he says.

"I'm lying in bed, no covers because, like I said, *hot*, staring at the ceiling."

"What are you wearing, sweetheart?"

Fucking hell, I love it when his voice goes all deep and growly like that. "Not a damn thing."

He sighs. "Is that what you always sleep in?"

"Yeah, actually. I guess we've never actually slept through the night together, have we?"

"That's something I plan to rectify at my first opportunity."

"How are you? Don't get me wrong, the flirting is fun, but I want to know how you are, Ryan."

There's that sigh again, and it makes me frown.

"I'm doing just fine. Trying to get through this trip so I can get home, but everything's okay. Don't worry about me, babe."

"You once told me that gifts are your love language; well, worrying about people is mine. It's what I do."

"Good to know. But you don't need to, I promise. So, let's go back to the fact that you're naked."

I chuckle into the phone. "Okay. What else do you want to know about that?"

"I want you to cup your breast and brush over your nipples with your fingertips."

I do as he requests and can't help but sigh as every nerve in my body sits up to pay attention. "Oh, that's nice."

"Mm-hmm." I hear him shift in his chair.

"Did you just unzip your pants?"

"Probably." I can't help but laugh at that. "Drag your fingertips down your belly. Slowly, softly."

"Goose bumps," I whisper with a sigh. "Holy goose bumps, Batman."

"Good. Are your legs spread yet?"

"Is your cock in your hand yet?"

"Way ahead of you."

I bite my lip and let my hand drift farther south.

"Don't touch your pussy," he whispers into my ear. "Touch your thighs. Touch that sexy crease where your leg meets your center."

"You know that makes me crazy." I inhale sharply.

"That's right. Now, just barely brush over your lips. Are you wet for me, Polly?"

"Oh, yeah. That's affirmative."

"I love your sassy fucking mouth." His words make me squirm even more, and I long to push a finger inside of me, but I wait for his instructions. "And your clit? Is it hard?"

"Am I allowed to touch it?"

His breathing has gotten ragged, matching my own.

"You may, yes."

I bite my lip and groan when my fingers skim over that tender flesh. "Yep. Good to go here. Damn, I wish you were here. It's way more fun when you're here in person."

"Soon," he promises. "Now, glide those fingers down through all that wetness and push a finger inside for me."

"God damn, Ry."

"Good girl." His voice is a croon, making me all the crazier. "I want you to make yourself come for me."

"Same." I have to catch my breath and swallow hard, as my hand works between my thighs. "I want you to picture my mouth on you, working you over, and I want to hear you come."

"Fucking hell," he growls as my back bows, and I let the orgasm move through me, not quiet in the least, as my hips jerk with it.

I lie here, out of breath, listening to his labored breathing on the other end of the line.

"Where are you today?" I ask quietly.

"I don't even know my own name right now," he confesses, making me smile. "Tokyo."

"What time is it there?"

"Five in the afternoon."

"Wow." I turn onto my side and pull the sheet up over my hips. "You'll be leaving work soon, right?"

"In a few hours. We have some things to hammer out before we call it a night. I'll have dinner brought in."

"You're a good boss."

My eyes are heavy, so I close them, enjoying the way he sounds on the other end of the line.

"It takes one to know one," he replies, making me smile softly. "Are you sleepy now?"

"Yeah. Sleepy. Miss you."

"Mm-hmm." I must doze, because then I hear him say, "God, I fucking miss you, too, babe."

"Like it when you call me that."

"Babe?"

"Yeah, that."

"Good to know."

I sigh, feeling myself falling asleep.

"Good night, Polly," he says softly into my ear.

"'Night."

CHAPTER TEN
RYAN

Immediately after hanging up the phone, I make a call to Mac and leave a message on his voice mail.

"Hey, it's me. I need the key to your sister's house. I'm about to make a call to have air conditioning installed for her. She's uncomfortable, and that's not okay with me. I'll have the HVAC guys get in touch with you so you can let them inside. It's happening this week. Text me with any issues. And thanks. I owe you."

I hang up, frustrated that it's the middle of the night back home. Even *more* frustrated that I'm not there.

I want nothing more than to curl up around Polly and sleep with her. That conversation is exactly what I'd been needing.

Hearing her voice, her laugh, and the smile through the line is what I needed.

Almost as much as I need to get home.

CHAPTER ELEVEN

POLLY

"Jackie," I call out as I walk into The Sugar Studio and feel my hips gain at least three pounds. "I'm a little early this morning."

"No worries," she calls out from the kitchen. "Give me two minutes. I'm just boxing up your order. These key lime cookies are to die for, if I do say so myself."

At just the mention of the treats, my mouth starts to water.

"Are you coming to the gala on Saturday night?" I ask her as she carries the boxes to me.

"Of course," she replies with a grin. "I'll be in today or tomorrow to shop for a dress. I saw your post on social media that you got some things in."

"I actually have something specific that I think you'll *love.* No pressure, of course." I pass her my credit card so I can pay my tab for the month and then wiggle my eyebrows. "Are you bringing your man?"

"This is *so* not his usual thing," she says with a

chuckle, "but I talked him into it. I had to promise him that he doesn't have to wear a tie, but I *am* getting that man into a sport coat if it's the last thing I do."

"My money's on you," I say with a wink.

"Are you bringing Ryan?" she asks.

"He's out of town." I shrug a shoulder and try to shake off the disappointment that always wants to come when I think of it. "He'll have to miss this one. Maybe next time."

"Well, that's a bummer. Next time for sure," she agrees and passes me back my card.

Once I've signed the receipt, I lift the boxes and smile at Jackie.

"Thanks, friend. See you tomorrow morning for more cookies."

"Have a successful day," she says, waving me off as I push through the door and make my way down the block to my store.

It's an overcast summer day, and I'm pretty sure we'll have thunderstorms this afternoon, which usually brings shoppers inside, so I can't complain about that.

"Good morning," Jessica says as she unlocks the front door for me and steps back so I can walk through. "God, those smell good."

"I know. Jackie is a genius with sugar." I set the boxes on the buffet and start setting out the treats so customers can help themselves. "Did you get those new blouses hung?"

"Yes, ma'am, and the steamer's heating up as we speak. Melissa should be in soon."

"I wonder if I should call Katie in." I prop my hands on my hips and check out my handiwork. "Grace is out of town, but it might be best to have four of us on hand today. I have a hunch that it's going to get busy."

"Probably not a bad idea," Jessica replies as she folds some T-shirts.

With a decisive nod, I pull out my cell and call the teenager.

"'Lo?" she answers. I obviously woke her up. "Polly?"

"Hi, Katie, sorry for waking you up. I was wondering if you might be able to put in a few hours this afternoon. Maybe from noon to five?"

"Sure, I can do that. Thanks, Polly."

"Thank *you*. I'll see you this afternoon."

I hang up, and Jessica grins. "That girl *loves* working here."

"She loves the discount on the clothes," I counter and laugh. "And I can't blame her. I have some online orders that came in overnight, and they need to be filled today, too."

"I can handle that," Jessica offers. "I like filling those, and it doesn't take me long."

"Do you mind seeing to that first thing, before the rush starts?"

"You got it." Jessica passes me the unfolded shirts and moves directly over to the computer to start printing invoices.

I take over the folding and then spend an hour reorganizing and straightening the clothes on the floor, making room for some new stock that should be coming in later this week. The best part about this business is the merchandise is forever changing.

By the time Katie arrives, business is picking up, and I'm helping a tourist find a dress for a wedding she's attending next weekend.

"Thanks for calling me in," Katie says once I get the customer settled in a fitting room. "My plans for today got canceled, so I would have been bored."

"And we don't want that," I reply with a wink. "I appreciate you coming in. I like that skirt."

"Thanks." With a smile, she does a little spin and then stops and clears her throat, looking at someone over my shoulder. "Oh, hi, Jake."

I turn and smile at the teenager and then feel my eyebrows climb when I see that he's holding a bouquet of pink roses.

"Hey, Katie." He nods, and his cheeks darken, and I can't help but smile. "Uh, Polly, Ryan asked me to stop in and bring you these."

He holds the flowers out to me, and I accept them, burying my nose in the blooms, happy that Ryan thought of me.

"How *sweet*," Katie says behind me.

"Yeah, he says he's sorry that he's been quiet and stuff," Jake continues. "He's just been busy. It's nothing personal, you know?"

"I figured that was the case. Thanks, Jake."

"They're from Ryan," he clarifies, and I nod.

"I get it. Still, it was nice of you to stop by with them. How are you doing out there by yourself?" I walk Jake to the front of the shop and step outside with him so we can talk without anyone else listening in.

"I'm not really alone," he says with a laugh, immediately relaxing now that Katie's not within earshot. "Pretty much everyone has been out to stay with me. Even Mac has."

I blink in surprise. "Really? He didn't mention that."

"Yeah, so I can't get a minute of quiet." But the smile doesn't slip from his face.

"You're a popular kid, and everyone enjoys hanging out with you," I remind him. "How *is* Ryan, anyway?"

"Really busy," he says with a sigh. "He manages to call me once a day, but it's only for a few minutes, and then he has to go into another meeting. I think he's in Stockholm right now. Or maybe he's in Germany. Tokyo? I'm losing track, honestly."

"It's a lot of travel." I nod thoughtfully. "Would you ever want to go with him?"

"Maybe on a shorter trip, but not if he's gone for this long. The horses need someone, and they know me. We trust each other."

"That's true." I wish Ryan didn't have two more weeks to go on this trip. I miss him, even though I just spoke with him. "Who's bunking with you tonight?"

"Millie. She's cool, but she wants me to, like, talk to her and stuff, and I just want to play video games with Russ in the evening, you know?"

"You poor thing." I punch him lightly on the shoulder. "Having to have a conversation with a nice lady and everything."

Jake laughs. "Yeah, I know. It's not so bad. Do you need anything?"

I blink at him, surprised. This kid is the *best,* most thoughtful kid I know. "I think I'm good. Do *you* need anything? You can call me anytime, you know."

He nods. "I know. Nah, I'm good, too. It's weird having him gone this long, you know?"

And there it is. He may have a village around to help look after him, but Jake misses Ryan.

I can't blame him. So do I.

"Is this the longest he's been gone since you moved in?"

He nods and looks down at his feet. "Yeah. Back before...after all the bad shit happened, he stuck close. I know he wanted to look out for me, make sure I was okay. But now things are better, and I guess he feels more comfortable with going. He's important and stuff."

But he's important to you, too.

"Hopefully, the next couple of weeks will go by fast, and he'll be back before we know it. Do you mind if I change the subject really quick?"

"Sure."

I look down at the roses and then back up at Jake. "You should ask Katie out, Jake. Like, on a date."

"What? No. No way."

"Why not? She likes you, and I think you like her, too. Why not take her to dinner or a movie or something?"

"She doesn't want to date me," he insists, shaking his head. "We hang out in completely different crowds."

"So? Look, high school may be cliquey, but trust me, life isn't always like that."

"I'm good." He clears his throat. "I should go."

"Hey, I didn't mean to run you off. Forget I said anything. I should probably just mind my own business."

His face softens, and he nudges me with his elbow. "It's okay. But I really do have to go. I'm meeting up with Russ."

I like Russ. I met him at the pool party, and he seemed like a good kid.

"Okay, have fun. Call me if you need anything. And if you don't need anything."

Jake nods and waves as he hurries over to his truck and hops inside.

It's time for me to get back to work, but first, I pull the card out of the roses and read it.

Miss you, babe.

It was good that I brought Katie in today. We were even busier than I expected, which is always a good thing. Of course, that means that I'm exhausted as I head home for the day, walking through the neighborhood toward my little house. It always sounds like a good idea to walk to work, given how many months are under snow, and I won't be able to get the exercise, but I also seem to forget that I have to walk back *home* after work.

And then it's not so much fun.

At least it's not far.

Hopefully, I'm tired enough that the heat won't keep me up half the night again. As much fun as last night was, I don't think I can make a habit of calling Ryan and pulling him out of meetings.

I can't resist lowering my nose to sniff one of the roses in the bouquet that Jake delivered earlier. It was thoughtful of both of them.

When I walk up my sidewalk, I frown at the white piece of paper taped to the outside of my screen door. Peeling it off, I unlock the door and step inside, eyebrows lifting when it's not a hundred degrees in my house.

In fact, it's...*cold.*

I turn on a light and read the note from the door. Skimming to the bottom, I see that it's a note from Ryan, printed off of an email to an HVAC company.

P-

Don't be mad at me, okay? You were uncomfortable last night, and I could remedy that situation. Hopefully, now you can sleep peacefully. Bundle up until I'm with you to keep you warm myself.

-R

"He had air conditioning installed in my house in *one day*?" I shake my head, and, without giving it too much thought, I call him. This time, it does go to voicemail. "Hey, I just got home to your note and a chilly house on this hot summer day. Seriously, Ryan, you didn't have to do that. I appreciate it more than I can say, and honestly, I'm kind of stunned, but you didn't have to. That's not why I called last night. Thanks. Thank you. Okay, I hope you're having a good day, or morning, or whatever time it is there, and I'll talk to you soon. Bye."

I slip the phone into my pocket and then walk over to

the new thermostat on the wall. It's set to sixty-seven degrees, which feels *cold.* So, I up it to seventy and then call my brother.

"Yo," he says into my ear.

"Did you know about this?" I pace down the hallway.

"Which *this* are we talking about?"

"The new AC unit attached to my house that Ryan had put in. *Someone* let them into my house."

"Yeah, I knew. No, I'm not getting in the middle of it. I just do what I'm told. You needed it anyway. It's an oven in that house."

"Should I feel guilty about this?"

"Did you ask him to do it for you?"

"No." I roll my eyes and walk back down the hallway. "I didn't mention it. I did tell him that it was hot in here, but I didn't ask him for anything."

"Then no, you shouldn't feel guilty. Ry likes to do things like this. Just enjoy it."

"I will." I sigh and return to the kitchen and then frown as I sniff. "Uh, Mac?"

"Yeah?"

"It smells like gas in my kitchen."

"*What?* Jesus, get out of that house, Poll. I'm calling the gas company now, and I'm on my way over."

"Okay. It's always something in this place, I swear."

I hang up, grab my purse, and walk out to the sidewalk. When I get there, my phone rings.

"Hello?"

"This is Matt from the gas company. I hear you have an issue in the kitchen?"

"Yeah, I smell gas in there. My stove is gas, but it's been broken, and I haven't used it in a long time."

"Okay, I have someone on their way to you. Are you outside?"

"I am."

"Good, stay out there until my tech gets to you, just to be on the safe side. He should be there in about ten minutes."

"Okay, thanks a lot."

I hang up and sigh. Leave it to me to get a brand-new air-conditioning unit, and on the same day, my house blows up from a gas leak.

That would be my luck.

I turn at the sound of a vehicle approaching and see my brother pull up to the curb and walk over to me, his face grim.

"I'll go in and double-check," he says.

"Smart. I'll be damn embarrassed if the smell was all in my head."

Mac walks inside and, just a few seconds later, comes right back out. "It's there for sure. I wonder what happened."

I shrug just as another truck approaches, and I'm relieved to see that it's the tech with the gas company.

"Hey, folks." He reaches into the truck and comes out with a black box. "I'll go in and measure for gas first, and we'll go from there."

"Thank you."

A few seconds after going into the house, he comes back out, nodding. "Oh, yeah, there's a leak in the kitchen. Looks like the hose behind the stove is leaking. I can cap it off, but then you'll be without a stove."

"It doesn't work anyway," I inform him. "So go ahead and cap it off."

With a nod, he gets to work, and Mac turns to me with a scowl.

"What?"

"I didn't know that the stove didn't work."

"I wasn't ready to replace it," I reply with a shrug. "You already do so much for me; there's no need to rope you into more things that aren't a priority. I rarely eat at home anyway."

"A broken gas stove is dangerous, Polly."

"And now it's being taken care of."

He sighs and digs his fingers into his eye sockets, the way he always does when I irritate the hell out of him.

"You can probably go," I add. "Now that he's here, I'm sure it'll be fine."

"I'll stay."

OKAY, two weeks without Ryan is starting to grate on my nerves, and I still have a week to go until he's home.

"I'm just feeling sorry for myself because he's not coming with me tonight." I shimmy into the white formal dress that I bought just for this occasion. It's short, hitting me just above the knee, has a high neck but is sleeveless, and is complete with a pretty, silver belt that manages to make my waist look small.

I love clothes.

Slipping into strappy silver heels that match the belt, I turn to grab my clutch. It's orange, the only pop of color in my outfit, and I love it. It's my splurge for the month.

Of course, my splurges always have to do with fashion.

My hair is up in a French twist, and as I fasten my silver earrings, the doorbell rings.

"Must be Zach from next door," I mutter as I fasten the second earring and then walk through the house. "I have to pay him for trimming the bushes the other day. Hey, Zach," I begin as I open the door, and then stop short and stare in disbelief.

"Who the fuck is Zach?" Ryan's voice is calm, but his hazel eyes are hard with the question. And oh, my God, he looks *amazing.*

"Ryan." I grab his hand and yank him inside, slam the door, and move in to wrap my arms around him, but he takes one tiny step back, stopping me, the muscle in his jaw ticking with agitation.

"Who's Zach, Polly?"

I frown up at him, and then it dawns on me. He thought I was expecting someone else.

"The neighbor kid," I reply, and can't help but grin when his face relaxes. "I thought he was coming to collect his twenty bucks for trimming the bushes. Instead, I found a super sexy man on my doorstep who appears to be dressed for a party."

He's sexier than sin in a blue sport coat over a white dress shirt open at the collar and darker blue slacks. He has a pink handkerchief in the breast pocket, and he's just...*delicious.*

"Jesus, I missed you," he says and lowers his lips to mine, kissing me like he hasn't seen me in years and missed me every single one of those days.

"You came," I manage, and am mortified to feel tears want to threaten, so I wrap my arms around his neck and hug him, loving the way he simply lifts me off my feet. "You didn't have to, you know."

"Yes, I did. I needed to come *home.* Do we have a second, or do we need to go right away?"

"We can take a second," I reply, not wanting to let go of him, and definitely not ready to share him with a whole bunch of people. "You were a busy man, Ryan. I think you texted me twice after our fun phone call."

"I packed three weeks' worth of meetings and flights into two weeks," he informs me and sits on the couch, setting me in his lap. "I worked pretty much nonstop so I could come home sooner. I missed Jake, the ranch, and *you.*"

"Did you piss everyone off by doing that?"

"I don't give a shit if I did," he says, dragging his fingertips down my jawline. "They work for *me*, not the other way around, and I made it clear to Arthur that he's not to schedule me out of town for more than three days at a time from now on. That's all I'll do."

I blink at him, surprised. "Wow. Well, I know Jake will appreciate that. The kid really missed you."

"I know. I've already been home, and he told me every single thing that happened since I left. It was a long conversation." He grins and leans in to kiss my forehead. "I'll want to hear the same from you, you know."

"Likewise. Do you feel how nice and cool it is in here?"

He kisses my forehead again, and I melt inside. "It's much better. Were you very mad at me?"

"Not mad. Confused, and maybe a little guilty, but not mad. Thank you for it. Did you buy Argentina?"

"Not this time." He smiles at me. "Can I still join you at this party tonight?"

"Are you kidding? Looking the way you do, you'd *better* want to go with me. You'll be my arm candy."

"It's a tough job," he says with a mournful sigh. "But someone has to do it."

"Were you really jealous when I opened the door?"

"I thought I was going to have to kill someone named Zach and call my brothers to help me dispose of the body." His lips firm as his eyes drop to my mouth. "Just because I'm gone for two weeks doesn't mean you get to move on to the next guy."

"You're all I think about." My words are soft, but I see they pack a punch when his eyes flare. "Just you, Ryan. I'm *so* glad you're home. I really missed you. Now, let's go to the party so I can show you off. You look damn hot in that coat. Is it Gucci?"

"How did you know?"

"Fashion is my *job*. Of course, I know."

"I'm *so excited* that this is the first official event at Wild River Ranch Event Center," Polly says, practically bouncing in her seat next to me. My eyes just about bugged out of my head at the sight of her in that little white dress, and I almost pushed her into the house and up against the wall before I heard her say another man's fucking name. Then, all I thought of was homicide. The thought of anyone else putting their hands on this woman is completely unacceptable.

I reach over and rest my hand on her thigh—out of principle.

"It's going to be amazing." She takes my hand in hers and laces our fingers together.

I didn't realize that this was the first event at the family ranch. I knew that the facility was almost finished and that Rem and Erin had done a fantastic job with it. I saw it a couple of months ago, and it already looked great.

As I drive around the corner, the venue comes into view, and pride immediately fills me. What used to be a collapsed, dilapidated barn from a hundred years ago that my siblings and I all played around when we were kids, despite being warned away from it, is now a beautiful, rustic building that seems to blend in with the mountains behind it. It's painted white with black trim, with a long cement walkway leading to the huge sliding door entrance from the parking lot.

"Look at that red carpet," Polly breathes.

Sure enough, there's a red carpet set up on the walkway with a background for photos with the Iconic Women's Collective logo all over it. There's a massive flower arch above the doors. Couples are already gathered, chatting and taking photos, as they make their way inside the building.

"It looks amazing." I park the sexy little Aston Martin that I pulled out of the garage for tonight's event and grin at Polly. "Not as amazing as my sexy-as-fuck date, but it's definitely pretty out here."

"We wanted everyone who comes tonight to feel important."

"I'd say you hit the mark, and we haven't even gone inside yet."

She beams over at me, leans in to kiss me hard and fast, and then reaches for the door handle.

"Whoa, I'll get that." I climb out of the car and walk around to the passenger side, buttoning my jacket as I go. After opening the door, I take Polly's hand and help her to her feet, tuck that hand in my elbow, and escort her down the walkway.

"You're here," Summer calls out with a smile. "Get over here so we can get a founders' photo."

"I'm being summoned," she informs me. Her whole body is vibrating with excitement and anticipation.

"Then you'd better go." I bend down to kiss her cheek, and then she's off to pose for photos with her friends. With my family.

The five of them, Polly, Erin, Summer, Millie, and Abbi, pose for the cameras. Hands are on hips, heads are cocked, and you'd think that they pose for photos for a living.

"They're in their element," Chase says as he and Rem join me.

"Erin's been buzzing about this all week. Hell, all *month*," Rem says with a grin as he watches his wife.

"They should be proud of this," I add. "It's a big fucking deal."

"You got home early," Chase says, clapping me on the shoulder.

"I had to. This is important to Polly, and I missed my teenager. I surprised them both, and they seemed pleased to see me."

"I bet they were," Chase says as we watch our girls finish up with their photo op.

"I hope there's food," Rem says. "I'm starving."

"I have it under good authority that there's a nice steak waiting for us inside," Chase replies as we're waved over to pose with our dates. "Steak from the Wild River Ranch."

"As it should be," I add with a grin.

"I want photos," Polly says as she reaches for my hand, but then her face sobers, and she looks up at me solemnly. "Unless you'd rather not."

"Why wouldn't I?"

"I can't control what goes out to the press on this," she says, pulling me aside so we can talk. "The whole purpose of this is to *get* press, but I don't want you to think that I'm using you or your influence to garner attention for our collective, and—"

I simply lean in and press my lips to hers, and we hear a flurry of shutters from cameras going off around us. I don't give a shit who sees us.

"I'm fine, sweetheart. You're no secret. I'm your arm candy, remember? I'm here to do as I'm told."

"Okay, then," she breathes, then licks her lips and grins. "Let's get photos. More photos, I mean."

We pose for several minutes in front of the red-carpet banners and then move on to give others an opportunity to do the same.

"I don't think we need to be fussed over."

Polly turns at the statement, her brow furrowed. "Jackie Harmon, you get over there and have your photo taken. Oh, my God, you look gorgeous in that gown! I mean, I knew you did when you tried it on the other day, but it's *so* beautiful with your hair and makeup done. And those shoes! Where did you find them? I don't carry those in my shop."

"I went to Missoula with my daughter last weekend," Jackie confesses, her face now glowing under Polly's praise. "Aren't they a great match?"

"They're stunning, and I'm totally jealous. Come on, you and Brandon get over there."

Now, Jackie's all smiles as she poses for photos with her husband.

"You're good with people," I inform Polly as we walk into the venue.

"It's my job, and everything I said to her was true. Sometimes, we just need a little reassurance. Holy Christ on a cracker, it's gorgeous in here."

The two of us pause to take it all in.

The interior of the building is all wood, with huge beams that run the length of the room along the vaulted ceiling. There's a wall of windows that let in plenty of light and gives us the impression that the mountains are knocking, wanting to join us for the party.

Round tables are scattered around the room with light pink tablecloths and flower centerpieces. There's a stage on one end of the space, all set up and ready for a band.

"I didn't realize there would be dancing," I say as Polly and I find our seats.

"Oh, yeah, lots of dancing. The bar your brother made last year is *gorgeous*. Look at that thing."

"Chase is excellent at building things," I agree. "And he still owes me a table. I'll have to nudge him about that."

"Look!" Polly points at the doorway. "London and

Drew Montgomery came! We invited them but weren't sure if they'd be able to make it."

Erin is already hugging her cousin, Drew, and Polly turns to me with happy emerald eyes and a wide grin.

"I love seeing you this happy," I inform her as I drag my fingertips down her jawline.

"I *love* parties like this. Everyone looks great. London's wearing a Louis Vuitton dress, and it's *amazing*."

"So, what you're saying is, you love parties like this for the fashion."

She blinks up at me and then frowns. "Well, yeah. Of course."

"And you've *never* been to fashion week?"

She shrugs a shoulder. "Someday."

Try this year, babe.

"Polly, can I please pick your brain before dinner starts?" a pretty brunette, likely in her forties, asks Polly. "I'm sorry if I'm interrupting."

"Not at all, Elizabeth," Polly replies. "Do you know Ryan Wild?"

"I don't think so," Elizabeth says, shaking her head. "But I just moved to Bitterroot Valley last year, so I'm still meeting people." She smiles and holds her hand out to shake mine, and then she frowns up at me. "Wait. Are you *that* Ryan Wild?"

I cock an eyebrow. "Which one would that be?"

"Yes, he's *that* one," Polly says, laughing. "What can I help you with?"

"Sorry." Elizabeth chuckles and clears her throat.

"It's nice to meet you, Ryan. As you know, Polly, I sell real estate, and it's actually going very well. Better than I'd hoped, being new to an area. Bitterroot Valley is popular right now. But you said something at a meeting not long ago that made me think."

"That could have been anything," Polly says with a laugh.

"You mentioned that we shouldn't spend money on trends to plug our business. That it can be a waste and not profitable."

"Ah, that. Sure. I mean, it depends on the trend, of course, but yeah."

I'm listening raptly, and the change that Polly's entire demeanor takes, from the carefree woman at a party to a fierce businesswoman, is a sight to behold. Both sides of her are alluring as fuck.

"There have been some new trends circulating in my field that seem fun," Elizabeth continues. "But holy shit, the out-of-pocket expense on them is huge, and I don't feel like there's much ROI there, you know? But it's so *pretty*."

"I'm the queen of loving pretty things," Polly says, tapping her chin. "But, Liz, are the pretty things helping your bottom line? Or are people going to buy or sell regardless? Because at the end of the day, I'd want the money in my account so I can buy *myself* something pretty, or simply save the money for something else in my business that will bring in more money on that end."

"You're right," Liz says with a nod. "It's just so tempting to jump on the fun trends."

"But is it a good business decision?" Polly counters. "I'm just playing devil's advocate here. If it's not going to elevate your business or drive income for you in some way, it's not worth it."

"Thank you." Liz exhales and grins at both of us. "I already knew that, deep down. I just needed to hear it."

"Trust your gut," Polly advises. "You'll be great. Have fun tonight."

"Oh, I will. Now, I have to go find my husband. He was talking with someone named Drew Montgomery about football, which means I may never see him again."

Liz walks away, and I bend down to whisper in Polly's ear.

"I want to carry you out of here, find a quiet spot, and fuck you until you can't breathe."

Her green eyes fly up to mine in surprise. "Why? I mean, no complaints here, but what did I do?"

"You're fucking brilliant at your job, Polly. You should be a business advisor."

"I am. That's why we started this collective. For exactly this."

We find our seats at a table with the other four women, and I sit next to my sister. Rem and Erin are across from us, and it seems Abbi, Summer, and Chase are off mingling somewhere.

"Have you thought of taking this outside of Bitterroot Valley?" I ask Polly and Erin.

"Yes," the two women say at the same time.

"We already have some interest in Missoula and

Bozeman," Erin explains. "And I think my cousins are looking into starting up a collective in Seattle."

"We are writing up bylines, trademarking the name and logo, things like that," Polly continues as Erin nods in agreement. "There are legalities and the challenges of making sure that the different branches are led by women with strong ethics and a passion for helping others."

"It would be best if we could sell franchises," Erin says, tapping her chin. "So we're not legally held responsible for every single city that wants to participate."

"I was thinking about that," Millie says as Abbi, Summer, and Chase join us. "I think we could handle most of the branches in Montana, but outside of that, we'd need to sell franchises. There are so many legalities to think about, and this way, we don't have to put in that kind of work. We all have businesses of our own already. It would be a lot to handle."

"You could hire a staff," I suggest, and all eyes turn to me. "If you wanted to keep it in-house, that is."

"We don't generate much money," Abbi reminds me thoughtfully. "Really only enough for the Collective to pay for itself. We sell tickets to the monthly meetings, just to cover the meal and a drink. The speakers donate their time. Even the ticket price for tonight was just enough to cover dinner, the band, decorations, and such. Erin and Remington donated the facility for the night, which is *amazing*, by the way."

"Isn't it great?" Erin asks, all smiles as she leans in to kiss Rem.

"I kind of like where Ryan's going with this," Summer says, tapping her gorgeous white-tipped nails on the table. "We could turn this into a charity situation where we donate to women's causes. We could have online courses, memberships, and things like that so that it could generate enough money to hire a couple of people and to donate to causes that lift up women. That's the whole point of this, after all."

The five women look at each other and then smile.

"We're going to discuss this further," Polly decides. "This week. For now, let's table it and have fun."

"Good plan," Erin replies with a nod.

"I do have one businessy thing to announce," Summer says. "Bitterroot Valley Nursery has been so happy with having cut flowers available in their store while I've been based out of there until my shop is rebuilt that they've asked me to keep a small kiosk there, and Sharla has agreed to manage it. So, I'm officially a chain."

"That's *amazing*," Polly exclaims and jumps up to run over and hug Summer. "You didn't tell me!"

"It was just finalized today," Summer says with a laugh.

"To badass women," Remington says, holding up his glass of whiskey. "I'm kind of afraid of them."

"Here, here," I reply with a laugh. "To badass women."

"I HEARD LAST NIGHT WAS FUN," Jake says the next morning as he and I have breakfast in my office. I'm sitting behind my desk, and Jake is in the chair in front of it. I want that damn table from Chase.

"Where did you hear that?"

"Russ's mom got home while we were still playing last night, and she said it was pretty wicked. She said her husband got to meet Drew Montgomery. You know, the football coach."

"I know Drew," I reply with a smile. "Did her husband mention that he got to meet London Ambrose Montgomery, the owner of that team?"

Jake eyes me and takes a bite of his bagel. "Not that I know of."

"See, that's the problem."

"It's a problem that he likes the football coach?"

"No, it's a problem that he doesn't acknowledge that Drew's wife, who was successful before she met him, was also there, and is an impressive woman, as well. That he wasn't excited to meet *her*."

"I think he just likes football." Jake narrows his eyes. "Wait, is this a lesson about respecting women and stuff?"

"Yeah, kind of. Last night *was* awesome. I was so proud of Millie and Polly and the others because they've built something important. The other women who were there look up to those ladies."

"Why does it have to be just about the girls, though?" Jake asks, nibbling his bagel. "I'm not asking that to be a prick. All I'm saying is, if a bunch of guys formed a club and said that girls aren't allowed to come unless they're specifically invited, women would have a cow. We'd never hear the end of it."

I stare at him for a moment, then I set my bagel down and clear my throat.

"I don't even want to *think* about what they aren't teaching you in school. Did you know that until 1974, a woman couldn't even open a bank account without having a husband or a father with her as a cosigner?"

Jake's brow furrows. "Why?"

"Good question. I don't mean to sound preachy here, but women couldn't even vote in an election until 1920. There are many places in this country where men have clubs that women aren't welcome in. Particularly country clubs, golf clubs, and things like that."

"Rich people clubs," Jake says.

"Some are, yeah. There are also other kinds of clubs that are historically only for men, or *gentlemen's clubs*, as they're called. They happen. They've always happened. Not to mention, let's talk about how women are still *treated* in this country. The way they're ogled, disrespected, hurt. Some men think it's okay to lay their hands on them, to rape them, or mock them."

Jake frowns down at his now-untouched bagel. "Yeah, I know that firsthand."

"I know you do." I reach out and cover Jake's arm with my hand, giving it a squeeze. "I think it's kind of great that Polly and her friends, one of whom is my *sister*, have come together to help other women with their businesses. It's going to bleed over into their home lives, as well. It's going to give those ladies who are in abusive situations the strength to change their lives. To stand up for themselves."

"That's pretty cool," Jake says thoughtfully and then frowns over at me. "Why do some guys think it's okay to beat on girls? To be mean to them and make them feel like shit?"

"Because they can." I sit back and shake my head. "Because women are usually physically weaker, and that seems to make them an easy target."

"It seems to me that guys should help someone who's weaker than them."

"I'm with you, buddy. And that's one of the reasons I love you."

Jake blinks at me, and it occurs to me that this might be the first time I've told him that I love him.

"Oh," he says.

"Jake, I don't just care about you or feel obligated to you. You're here with me because I *love* you. Unconditionally. You're my kid, you know?"

"Yeah." He blinks fast, as if he's fighting off tears. "Yeah, I know. I mean, I guess I know."

He looks over at me and sniffs, and the image of this amazing kid lying in that bed upstairs, broken and hurting because a man who was supposed to protect him beat him forms in my head, and my heart slices as if it were yesterday.

"You're my family, part of a really *big* family." I smile over at him. "And sometimes that family is a pain in the ass."

He nods. "It's pretty great. I never had that before. And when I was younger, when my parents were still alive?"

I go very still. Jake *never* talks to me about his past. "Yeah?"

"It just sucked ass so bad." He swallows hard and wipes at a tear impatiently. "Dad beat my mom up a lot. I think he was taking her to the hospital that day they died because he'd pounded on her that morning, and she was pretty hurt. I went to school because I *had* to get out of there. I wanted to help her, but whenever I tried, I was told not to. By her."

"I suspect she was trying to protect you."

He nods. "I was just a kid, but man, I wanted to kill him. And when they died, I wasn't all that sad. I was kind of relieved, and I thought that made me a bad person."

Shit, I want to cry for this boy and resurrect his parents so I can make them pay for what they put him through.

"And then I had to live with...*them*." He swallows again and shakes his head. "And it was worse. I didn't know it *could* be worse. I hope I'm not like them. That just because I have my bio dad's blood in me, it doesn't mean that I'm like him."

"I'm so sorry, buddy."

His dark eyes find mine again. "But you saved me.

You didn't have to, but you did. And you're *nothing* like those assholes. You're a good person."

"I think I took one look at you and decided that you were *mine.* Like we were supposed to be together all along."

"Maybe we were," he says softly. "I guess what I'm trying to say is, I love you, too. Dad."

I round my desk and pull Jake into my arms, hugging him close.

"You're such a *good* person, Jake. You're nothing like your biological parents, *nothing* like Wally. I promise you that. You're so kind and genuine, and there isn't a violent bone in your body. Unless you're shooting zombies."

"Yeah, I kill those suckers."

He pulls back and grins up at me. He's grown so much since he moved in here. It won't be long until he's about as tall as I am.

"Don't ever wonder if you have your bio father's tendencies inside of you, Jake, because you *don't.* You just couldn't."

"I think I'm more like you, and that makes me happy."

I didn't know that I could feel so much pride from one simple statement. "Me, too."

"So, since, you know, I'm calling you Dad and stuff, you said before that if I decided to, I could take your last name."

I shove my hands into my pockets and nod at him. "Yes, I said that."

"Would—" He licks his lips. "Would that still be possible?"

"You want to be Jake Wild?"

"If it's okay with you."

"Yeah." I smile back at him as a grin spreads over his handsome face. "Yeah, that's more than okay with me."

CHAPTER THIRTEEN
POLLY

The summer is *flying* by. It's already been six weeks since the summer soiree, and the five of us founders of the Collective are already planning the formal party for the fall. It's been the busiest season for Pocket Full of Polly that I've ever had, and being grateful doesn't even begin to cover how I feel.

For the first time since I opened the business, I feel like I'm well into the black when I balance my books, and I don't feel like I have to keep a watchful eye on the bank balance every time I want to order new stock or contemplate hiring more part-time help.

I've even managed to squirrel away a good chunk of money for the Chanel bag I've had my eye on for about a million years.

Ryan has been in and out of town all summer, but true to his word, it's never been for more than a few days at a time. Jake has even gone with him a few times, and

Mac and I took turns seeing to the horses while the guys were gone.

There have been evenings on the patio by the fire, whether at my house or Ryan's, with cold beer on a hot night. Ryan's taken me up to his observatory every chance he gets for meteor showers or just to gaze at the night sky.

It's been a busy, wonderful summer spent with someone that I'm quickly falling in love with.

"Where are you headed off to this evening?" Grace grins at me as she closes out the computer for the night, and I straighten up some T-shirts on a display by the front door.

"I'm having dinner with Ryan," I reply and check the time. "Crap, I'd better go. I'm running late."

"You go," Grace says, shooing me off. "I've got this."

"Are you sure?"

"Of course. We're almost done anyway. Go have fun with that sexy man of yours."

I wink at her as I smooth on some pink lip gloss, drop the tube into my bag, and sling it over my shoulder.

"Thanks, Grace. I appreciate it."

"Have fun."

I lock the door behind me and walk the couple of blocks down to Ciao. The Italian place has become our favorite go-to in town, and tonight, we're meeting up with Drew and London, who are in town, staying at their condo at the resort for the week.

The hostess waves for me to walk to the front of the

line of people waiting for tables and gestures for me to follow her.

"Ryan's already here," she says with a smile. "How are you, Polly?"

"I'm great, thanks."

And it's the truth. Life is damn good these days.

Ryan looks up and sees me coming in, and he climbs to his feet, kisses me in front of everyone, and pulls my seat out for me.

"Hi, friends," I say to Drew and London. "Did I miss anything good?"

"Just this delicious bread," London says, taking a bite of the garlic bread that Ciao is known for. "My God, I could eat an entire basket of this by myself. Actually, I *have* done that."

"Who can blame you?" I ask and smile when I see that Ryan already ordered my favorite red wine. I turn to him and smile. "Thanks."

"My pleasure."

"So, how are things?" I ask London. "How's Caleb? Wait, *where* is Caleb?"

London smiles at the mention of her adorable son, who usually travels with London and Drew. "He's *amazing*, and at almost twelve, he's way too cool to come to dinner with us, so he and Quinn are at the condo, playing video games and eating junk food."

"Thank God for Quinn," Drew says with a laugh. "She seems to be the only one that Caleb thinks is cool these days."

"At least he thinks *someone* is," Ryan says as our waitress strides over to take our order.

Once we've all placed our order for pasta and more pasta with a side of garlic, London sighs and rests her chin on her hand, looking over at the mountains. We're seated outside on the patio tonight because it's so gorgeous out.

"I always miss this place whenever we leave it," London says. "Drew and I have decided to try to come once a month until the season is in full swing."

"I thought it was already in full swing," Ryan says, frowning.

"That's why this is our last visit here for a while," Drew says. "The season officially starts in two weeks, and we're deep into practice and pre-season games, but this was the best time to get away and come over for a few days. It doesn't hurt that it's less than a two-hour flight."

"That's not bad at all," I agree. "Are the condos nice up there? I don't think I've been."

"Honey, they're *gorgeous*," London says with a nod. "You'll have to come up while I'm here, and I'll show you around. There's a club up there that we're members of but never use. I'll add you as a passholder so *someone* gets use of it."

"What kind of club?" I ask and sip my wine.

"There's a little restaurant, a gym, a pool, things like that. It's a little community."

"Like...a country club?"

"Yeah, I guess so," London replies easily. "You should use it."

"That's okay," I reply, shaking my head. "I probably wouldn't have time to go up there."

"Well, it's there if you *do* have time," she says easily.

Good lord, I wouldn't know what to do at a country club. I wouldn't know how to act or who to speak to. I'm just not part of that world like London and Ryan are.

And that's okay.

"Tell me you have some awesome things in the shop for fall," London says, changing the subject as Ryan and Drew talk about football. "I need a couple of new things before I go to Paris for fashion week."

Oh, how I long to go to fashion week. I've wanted to go since I was a kid and read *Vogue* like it was the freaking Bible. Since I met London almost two years ago, she's gone to Paris Fashion Week twice, and each time, she video calls me so I can experience it through her.

"I have some new things, but I'm pretty sure you'll be wearing designer labels for that trip."

"Some." We sit back as our meals are delivered. Once we've been offered fresh pepper and grated cheese, we return to our conversation. "I'll have plenty of designer labels to wear, but sometimes I just want a beautiful piece to layer, or to add, and you always fit the bill for that."

That any woman would want to wear something I carry in my store to freaking *fashion week* is incredible to me.

"Well, I'd love to have you come in. When is it this year?"

"Next weekend," she replies and scoops some pasta into her mouth.

"Please video call me again while you're there," I reply. "You know I live vicariously through you every time you're in Paris."

"Of course, I will. I just wish you'd *come.* The shopping we could do, Polly!"

"Paris is on my bucket list," I admit, and realize that Ryan is listening in. He reaches over and takes my hand in his. "Someday, I'll go and do some serious shopping."

Like when I win the lottery. My business may be doing well, but I'm no luxury fashion house. That's in a stratosphere that I can't even imagine.

London turns to Ryan with a grin. "Tell me you'll talk her into it. Please."

"Seriously, I *can't* go," I say with a laugh and squeeze Ryan's hand. "But I can't wait to hear all about it. Are you staying at the Ritz again?"

"There is nowhere else to stay in Paris," she replies. "I'm telling you, I'm going to get you there, come hell or high water."

I just smile over at her and eat my dinner. I won't argue, but I know that it's highly unlikely because I don't feel comfortable with the idea of letting London pay for me to go, and I certainly can't afford something so extravagant myself.

The rest of the meal is delicious, and the conversation is even better. London's phone pings with a text, and she frowns down at the screen.

"Caleb wants pizza," she tells Drew. "At least he has good timing. I'll put an order in before we leave."

"Jake usually asks for the same," Ryan says, also checking his phone. "But no requests so far tonight."

"How are things with Jake?" Drew asks.

"He's the smartest, best-looking, most well-behaved kid on the planet," Ryan replies with a smug grin.

"And that's exactly what every parent is supposed to think about their child," London says. "I'm glad it's been a good experience for all of you. Do you get along with him well, Polly?"

"I have to admit, I'm kind of in love with that boy." I shrug and then can't hide that my eyes are filling. "He's just the best kid. He's smart and funny, and he's really gentle. When Ryan was out of town for a long stretch, Jake asked *me* if I needed anything. So, yeah, I get along with him well."

Ryan reaches over and rubs his hand over my back in big circles, and London grins in delight.

Just then, Ryan's phone signals a text.

"And there he is. No pizza tonight; he's hanging at Russ's house." Ryan wiggles his eyebrows at me. "Good timing."

"That *is* convenient. I wonder if Grace got the shop closed up okay." I open my bag to fetch my own phone and then frown when it's not there. "Shit. I forgot my phone at the shop."

"We'll stop and get it on our way home," Ryan assures me.

Once the bill is paid, the four of us are on the sidewalk, saying goodbye.

"I'll pop in tomorrow," London promises me as she pulls me in for a hug. "And I'll talk you into coming up to the condo to have a look around. Have a good night, friend."

"You, too. Bye, Drew."

"See you," Drew says as he takes his wife's hand, and they walk away, a hot pizza in hand for Caleb and Quinn.

"I really like them," I say as Ryan and I walk down the block toward my store. "I'm glad they come to visit so often. Sorry that I forgot my phone."

"It's not a problem." He lifts my hand to his lips and kisses my knuckles. "I can wait an extra fifteen minutes to get you to your place and fuck you senseless."

I let out a surprised laugh. "What brought that on?"

"I never *stop* wanting to fuck you senseless," he says, his voice as calm as if he's talking about the weather. "But when you wear little numbers like the one you have on? Game over."

I look down at the black tank dress and frown. "It's just a dress."

"That's not *just* anything." His gaze flicks down the length of me as he licks his lips and then stares straight ahead. "How do you feel about having sex in your store?"

I laugh as I unlock the door, and then every hair on my body stands on end.

"Something isn't right."

We move quickly through the shop, and I scour every nook and cranny, but nothing is out of place.

I check the safe and find the small amount of cash I put in there earlier still there.

"I could swear that I felt like something was off when I opened that door." I prop my hands on my hips and scowl. "But everything seems to be fine. Is the back door locked? I'll check."

"*I'll* check," Ryan says and walks past me. When he returns, his mouth is set in a firm line. "It wasn't locked."

"That must be it." I sigh with relief. "Grace must have forgotten to lock it on her way out. She doesn't normally close, so she probably just overlooked it."

"I guess it's a good thing that you forgot your phone, then," Ryan says as I check my phone, see that I didn't miss anything, and slip it into my purse.

"I knew my forgetful ways would come in handy someday." I grin over at him and then feel my breath hitch.

Christ, he's beautiful, with all that thick, dark hair and hazel eyes that I could just get lost in. He's in a yellow button-down with the shirtsleeves rolled up. His forearms look like they've been sculpted out of marble.

"You make me salivate," I whisper and then raise my gaze to his. A muscle twitches in his jaw. "How do you just go around *looking* like that?"

"Like what?"

"Like"—I gesture up and down as he walks slowly toward me—"*that*. Like you walked out of a damn dream."

His lips twitch as he glides his hands up my arms and frames my face. “I need to get you back to your place so I can show you which one of us walked out of a dream. Spoiler alert: it wasn’t me.”

I chuckle and then moan when he kisses me, and then I break away and lead him by the hand out through the front door.

“I walked to work this morning,” I inform him. “So, we’ll take your truck.”

“No problem.”

Thank all the gods above that it doesn’t take long to get to my house. I want him naked, and I want him *now*.

Impatient, I hurry into the house and turn to him, but when I reach for his shirt, he takes my hands and kisses them.

“We’re always in a hurry,” he murmurs. “It’s always hot and fast and hard, and that’s a damn good time, but sometimes, I want it to be a little slower.”

“I don’t care if it’s fast or slow, as long as it happens soon.”

That makes him laugh, and he easily lifts me into his arms and kisses me as he walks back to the bedroom.

True to his word, he takes his time with me. He slowly peels my dress off of me and lets his gaze roam at his leisure, sending warmth that has nothing to do with the heat of this late summer day spreading through me. He’s on his knees and has me step out of my underwear before he tosses them aside.

“Ryan.”

“What do you need?” he asks me, his voice hushed as

he leans in to kiss my bare stomach. "What do you need, Polly?"

"Just you." And that's the truth. I don't need his money or his connections. I just need *Ryan.*

He rests his forehead against me, and then he nudges me back onto the mattress. As I scoot back, he crawls over me, his eyes full of need and lust, and he drags his lips up my breastbone before covering my mouth with his and kissing me.

His magical hand dances up my inner thigh and, with just one fingertip, touches that most intimate crease where my leg meets my center.

And that touch alone is almost enough to send me over the edge.

"I feel like you haven't touched me in *years.*" I bite my lip when he closes his mouth around a nipple and gives it a little tug. "Even though it was just last night, it's as though it's never enough."

"Because it isn't enough," he says and kisses his way down my belly. He pushes my legs up, his hands planted on the backs of my thighs so I'm spread wide and he can feast on me.

And feast he does.

"Ryan!"

"That's right," he says. "Say my fucking name."

"Ryan." It's a whisper now as my hands dive into his hair and fist there. Jesus, my body is on fire, my control about to evaporate as he licks and nibbles and plunders with that tongue. "Oh, God. Oh, Jesus, I can't."

"You will," he promises me and slips one finger inside

of me. "That's right, baby. You're so fucking amazing, Polly. So fucking gorgeous."

I'm twisting and shuddering on the bed, unable to hold still. The edge is right *there*, and I'm about to fall off of it.

"Ryan."

"Yes. Yes, sweetheart. Go on, baby." He bites the inside of my thigh, then soothes it with his tongue before pulling my clit into his mouth and pulsing, and that's it. I'm a goner.

I cry out with the orgasm, and then all I want in the world is Ryan *inside of me.*

"Need you," I mutter, and when he moves to cover me with his body, I push his shoulder, urging him onto his back.

His eyebrow wings up, but he doesn't argue as he lies back, still fully clothed.

"You're like a present." I go to work on the buttons of his shirt, kissing his skin as I uncover every warm inch of him. "Like the best present *ever.*"

He groans and sinks his hands into my hair. When I've unfastened his jeans, he raises his hips so I can pull them down his legs and toss them onto the floor.

When he's finally naked, his erection standing proud, I crawl up his legs and lick him from root to tip, all the while holding his gaze with my own.

His hazel eyes narrow as his lips part in a silent groan. My fist circles him, pumping him as I suck and lick, and just when I feel him start to pulse, I crawl over him and ease him inside of me and begin to ride.

His hands are planted on my ass, urging me up and down at a pace that satisfies us both. I can't stop moving, clenching on him, and I reach down to circle my clit as I ride him, which sends me into overdrive.

"Ah, hell," he moans, and suddenly, he's lifted me off of him, and I'm on my stomach, ass in the air, and he's inside of me once more, his mouth planted next to my ear. "You're fucking incredible. God, I never stop wanting you."

He's panting, his voice a low growl, and his hand is planted at the small of my back as he plunges in and out of me, faster and faster until we both shatter into a million pieces.

When he eases out of me, I fall into the pillow and don't even care that I can't breathe.

I can die a happy woman now.

But Ryan turns me onto my side and kisses me long and slow.

"Water," I say against his lips. "I need some water."

"As soon as my legs regain feeling, we can go get some."

I grin and kiss him, then swat his butt and climb off of the bed. "Come on. Let's get a drink and then sit out on the swing."

"You need clothes if you're going outside."

I raise an eyebrow. "Says who?"

"Says me." He wraps me in his shirt and buttons it for me. "No one is going to ogle my girl's body but me."

"Did you just say *ogle*?"

He grins and tugs on his jeans but leaves them unfastened as he follows me to the kitchen. I pass him a bottle, and as we drink, I see that he's eyeing the swatches on the wall.

"I'll eventually paint in here."

"Why don't you just let me see to it?"

I frown over at him. "What, in all your spare time?"

That makes him laugh. "I can make some calls."

"Like you did with the air conditioner? You don't have to do that."

"I *know* I don't have to." He reaches out and tucks a strand of my hair behind my ear before dragging his fingers down my jawline. "I don't do much of anything that I don't want to."

"Honestly, paint is the last thing this room needs. The stove isn't even hooked up to anything because I had a gas leak, so we had to cap it off. It's mostly just an ornament now."

His eyes narrow. "You had a gas leak."

"Not long ago, actually. When you were gone, the same day the AC was installed, now that I think about it."

"And you didn't tell me."

I shrug and drink my water. "I had it taken care of right away. I guess I should replace that thing."

"Polly." He sets my water aside and simply pulls me in for a long hug, rocking me back and forth in that way he does that soothes and sets me at ease. It's my favorite thing in the world. "Let me take care of this for you."

"I don't want you to think that I *need* you to do this.

That I want any of your money. Because I don't. Not ever, Ryan."

I feel him smile against the top of my head. "If I thought that, we wouldn't be standing here right now, and you know it. But, babe, I can do this. I can help you with this, and it's something I'd *like* to do."

"Really?" I lean back so I can look up at him and find him grinning down at me. "You *enjoy* home renovation?"

"Actually, yeah."

"Wow. Interesting." I lick my lips. I can still taste him there. "I will never take advantage of you, Ryan."

"Maybe you should, just a little." He laughs when I scowl. "I'm a giver, Polly. I *like* to help, to gift, to make life easier for the people I care about. Don't look now, but that includes you."

Everything in me lights up.

"You're a good man, Ryan Wild."

"Does that mean I can make over your kitchen?"

"Yeah, just don't go crazy, okay?"

"Psh. As if I would."

"This was great," London says with a smile as she passes the reins on Ladybug to Jake and then brushes her dark hair back from her face. "I don't remember the last time I was on a horse. I was probably a kid."

"Can we live here?" Caleb, her son, pats Lullaby's neck lovingly. "It's the best."

"No, but we can visit," Drew replies with a laugh. "And we can help Jake get these ladies cleaned up so they can rest for a while after that ride."

"Can we?" Caleb stares up at Jake hopefully.

"Sure, come on." Jake leads Drew and Caleb into the stables, and I hang back with London.

"I'd like to ask you something."

"Shoot," she says, brushing some grass off of her jeans.

"How do I get an invitation to fashion week in Paris? I know that you can't just show up for that."

"You're right, you can't. Please tell me that you're going to surprise Polly with a trip. I know that she wants to go *so bad*, but she won't let me take her." London props her hand on her hip and looks out at the mountains. "I'd *love* to take her shopping in Paris."

"I'm taking her," I confirm. "Haven't told her that yet. And that's if I can get an invitation."

A slow smile spreads over London's lips. "I know people, Ryan. Hell, *you* probably know people."

"Not in the fashion world," I reply, shaking my head. "Tech? Finance? Automobiles and even sports? Yeah, I have contacts, but not in fashion. That is, except *you*."

"Then you're in luck because I can make that happen for you. Plan on going a few days early so we can shop."

"Are you horning in on my Parisian vacation with my girl?"

"Hell yes, because shopping is important, and I've been *dying* to take her since I met her." She laughs, and we both turn to the stables when we hear Caleb laughing. "I'll email you all the information when I have it. You'll want to call the Ritz right away because they're probably already booked."

"I want the Chanel suite."

Her eyes widen. "That's *definitely* already taken. I have it on good authority that Anna Wintour takes that suite."

She taps her chin thoughtfully, and I push my hand through my hair in agitation.

"You know," London says, "I'll call Anna. She's a

tough old broad, but if I explain the situation, she might give the suite up for another."

"Let's pull out all the stops," I reply with a nod. "I don't give a shit what it costs."

"Obviously, and that's good because it's going to cost a lot. Also, I love that about you. Now, just so you're prepared, Polly will balk. She's proud, and she won't want you to spend the kind of money you're going to drop on this. Because, like I said, it's a lot, and she's not stupid."

"I'm not about to give up my fortune for her or anyone else, London. The money just is what it is, and if I have it and can enjoy it with her, why wouldn't I do that?"

"Hey, I agree." She holds her hands up in surrender. "I'm on your side here. I'm just telling you to be prepared to talk her into the trip of a lifetime. Because she'll *want* it, but she won't want to take it."

"I'll talk her into it," I reply evenly. "And I'll be in touch with you so we can arrange that shopping trip and everything else."

"I'm *so* excited," she says and pulls me to her so she can kiss my cheek.

"Hey, don't make me kill Ryan," Drew says as he and the other guys walk out to join us. "I actually like him."

"No need to worry," London replies with a laugh. "I was just thanking him because Paris is about to be even *more* fun. Now, we should head out. We have a flight back to Seattle to catch."

"We own the plane," Caleb reminds his mom. "They can't leave without us."

"That's a good point," Drew agrees and ruffles the boy's hair. "Thank you both for a fun time. Your ranch is beautiful."

"It was our pleasure," I reply.

"Come back any time," Jake adds and smiles at Caleb. "Whenever you're in town, I'll give you more lessons."

"That's rad," Caleb exclaims and bounces on his toes. "Thanks, Jake. You're the best."

The three of them climb into their SUV and, with a wave, drive away from the stables.

"That was fun," Jake says as we walk back inside to see to the horses. "Caleb's pretty nice, and he catches on fast and respects the animals. I'll work with him."

"He'll love that."

"Hey." Jake picks up a brush and starts brushing Cowboy. "Did I hear that you're taking Polly to Paris?"

I eye my boy as I fill the feeder for Blossom. "I'd like to, yeah. It's something that Polly's always wanted to do. How do you feel about that? I'd be gone for about a week."

"I think it's cool," Jake replies and kisses Cowboy on the cheek. "You've been seeing Polly all summer. I guess it's pretty serious?"

Now I turn and give the teenager my full attention.

"I don't see it ending any time soon, and I like her a lot, so yeah, I'd say it's gotten serious."

He nods. "I like her, too. I know I told you that before, but I've gotten to know her more this summer, and I think she's pretty okay. I suppose you're having sex and stuff."

Now I shove my hands into my pockets, not sure I want to have this conversation with my kid, but also not willing to lie to him.

"We're intimate, yeah, but I'm not using her for that, and it's completely consensual."

"I know," he says and laughs. "I get it. Thanks for not making me listen to it. That's...gross."

"Unless you ask, you'll never know that Polly and I are physical. That's between me and her, *and* I know it's not something you want to be privy to. Nor should you. Jake, how are you? How do you feel about everything? You've been here for more than half a year, and I want to make sure that you're happy."

"I am." He looks over at me now and takes off his gloves. "I have the best home there is. Have you *seen* that house? And these girls?" He waves at the horses, who are busy eating oats. "The difference in my life from last year at this time and now is crazy, and I am completely happy. Plus, I have you and a million aunts and uncles and all the people. What's not to be happy about?"

"I just want to check in now and then to make sure because you're the priority, and I don't want you to forget that."

He grins at me and shrugs a shoulder. "I don't feel ignored or anything, if that's what you're thinking. I don't care if you go on dates and stuff. We hang out a lot, and we always have our breakfast meetings."

"Yeah." I nod and reach out to clap him on the shoulder. "Yeah, we do. Well, I'm glad to hear that we're cool. I feel great about everything. Having you here, having Polly in my life, this ranch, our family. It's all pretty amazing."

"Totally," he agrees. "And you'll have a blast spoiling Polly in Paris. She likes all that girly shi—stuff."

"Nice save."

"I'm going to the rodeo with Brady next weekend. I forgot to mention it to you, but he invited me to go, and I'm curious to see it. Is that cool?"

That surprises me. Brady never lets any of the family see him ride.

"Sure, just be careful, and don't let him get *you* on an animal that intends to throw you off."

Jake nods. "I don't want to ride, but if I'm going to be a vet for horses, there might be times that I have to work at the rodeo, you know?"

I narrow my eyes at him. "I know you have two years of school left, but you're still thinking that's what you want to do?"

"Yeah, I do. I'm looking at Colorado State University in Fort Collins. It's one of the best schools of veterinary medicine in the country."

"Don't you have to get a bachelor's first?" I ask him.

"Yeah. I think I want to stick close to home for that. Maybe the University of Montana in Missoula. That's only like four hours away."

"I just got you here and you're already talking about leaving me."

"Aww, don't cry." Jake grins. "I'll probably come

home to visit once in a while, especially when I put you in the old folks' home."

"I'm going to smack you around for that." I move to chase after him, and Jake laughs and runs away from me. He doesn't look scared in the least, because he knows I'm full of shit.

"It's okay, old-timer. You can't catch me."

"Wanna bet?"

Now I do chase after him, and we run out of the stables and through the pasture to the treeline, in a full-out sprint. I catch up to him, and we tumble to the ground, then roll onto our backs and stare at the blue sky as we try to catch our breath.

"You're pretty fast for an old guy."

"I'm not that old, smartass." I swallow hard, still panting. "I can still catch you."

"Took you long enough." But he's laughing, and then he turns to me, those dark eyes full of humor. "Yeah, I like it here. Dad. Still getting used to saying that."

"Still getting used to hearing it." I grin at him. "But damn if I don't like it."

WITH A SUCCESSFUL MORNING BEHIND ME, I make myself a sandwich and head up to the office to take some meetings and speak with Arthur.

Since our talk on the plane, he's been professional and aloof. Cold. Not disrespectful or untrustworthy, but there's now a rift in our relationship that wasn't there before.

And honestly, I don't care.

I treat him the same as I always have. I *needed* to put him in his place on that trip and remind him that I'm the boss. Not the other way around. I'd rather not have to train a new PA, but I will if I have to.

Just as I sit down at my desk, the phone rings, and I see that it's London.

"Did you even have time to get back to your condo?" I ask her.

"Are you kidding? We're headed to the airport. I wanted to let you know that I got you that invite to fashion week, via Dior, which is at the top of Polly's favorite fashion houses, *and* I spoke with Anna. You owe me, Wild. Big time."

I lean back in my chair and look out the window, watching Jake drive the side-by-side back to the house. "It's all set, then?"

"All set in spades. Give me your travel itinerary when you know it, and I'll get appointments set up for shopping at the fashion houses before the shows start. Polly will want to be dressed to the nines. Then, we'll have appointments after the shows to buy what was shown for the new season. It's so freaking awesome, Ryan."

"I'll email you when I have things ironed out."

"You'll want to call the Ritz right away," she continues. "They know it's you that's taking the suite, but just to be sure."

"I'll call as soon as we hang up," I assure her. "Thanks again."

"Thank *you*. You just made Paris even better than usual, and that's saying a lot. Oh, and I talked Drew into joining us, so double dates in France are on the docket."

I laugh and shake my head. "Even better. Have a safe flight."

"Talk later."

She hangs up, and I immediately call the Ritz and make the arrangements for the suite, and also give them Arthur's name so he can make further plans for me directly with the hotel.

With that settled, I call the man himself.

"Hello, sir," he says stiffly.

"Good afternoon, Arthur. I want to let you know that I'll be out of the office all of next week. Actually, make that ten days."

He's quiet for a moment. "You're taking a *vacation*?"

"Sort of." I explain my plans for Paris, and when I'm finished, I can hear him clapping his hands.

"This is fabulous," he says. "Leave the details to me. I'll be in contact with the hotel to make sure there are extra touches in place."

"I appreciate it. Now, how much do I have to work over the next four days to make sure I'm uninterrupted during this impromptu getaway?"

"You can sleep on the plane."

AND NOW, for the most challenging piece of this plan.

I've been working around the clock for the past twenty-four hours, and I'm picking Polly up to take her on a date. I'm as nervous as a teenager who just got his license and is picking up the girl he's had a crush on the whole school year.

It's ridiculous. Jake even gave me a pep talk on my way out the door.

I knock on her door and wait for her to answer, and when she does, she gifts me with one of her bright, amazing smiles.

"Hey," she says and steps back to let me inside.

"I'm sorry I'm late." I pull her to me and kiss her long and slow, my fingers running through her amazing, thick red hair. "Work has been crazy."

"We didn't have to do this tonight." She cups my cheek and narrows her eyes. "You're exhausted. Ryan, you need some rest."

"I'm fine." I take her hand and kiss her palm. "Really, it's nothing I haven't done before. But how do you feel about staying in tonight?"

"I'm all for it. I was actually craving a burger from The Wolf Den. What do you say we order in delivery?"

"I say you're a goddess, and I'll offer you all I have in exchange for that burger."

She smirks and reaches for her phone. "No need to get that dramatic over a burger. I'll hook us up."

She places the order, and then we curl up on the couch together, Polly tucked into my side and resting her head on my chest.

"How are *you*?" I ask her.

"I'm also a little tired. It's been busy at the shop. Things will start slowing down a bit now that summer is almost over."

"Are you fully staffed right now?"

"Yeah." She frowns up at me. "Why do you ask?"

"I have a surprise for you, but I have to tell you a couple of days early so you can make arrangements of your own because you also own a business." I drag my fingertips down her jawline. "We're going to Paris, babe."

She blinks and then frowns. "Excuse me?"

"You. Me. Paris. We leave in two days."

She stands and paces the living room, still scowling. "Ryan, I can't just up and go to Paris."

"Why not?" I stand, as well, and shove my hands into my pockets. "You own the business, and you have people who can handle the shop. You don't have kids or pets, so why can't you go?"

"Because." She flings her hands in the air. "Because I can't *afford* to, okay? Is that what you want to hear? I can't afford to go to Paris. Trust me, I wish I could, and maybe if I can save up over the next year, I can go next fall, but—"

"You *can* afford to." My voice is level again. I want to pull her to me, but I know she needs to walk off the energy. "Because you're not paying for it. I am."

"No." She shakes her head and paces around the living room. "Absolutely not."

"Give me one good reason why not."

"Because I will *not* take advantage of you like that."

"I said one *good* reason," I counter. "Polly, you're not taking advantage of shit. I'm having to talk you into it. It's all set up. Everything. All you have to do is pack, and don't do much of that because you'll be shopping for some new things with London."

That stops her in her tracks, and she stares at me with wide, emerald eyes.

"*London* is in on this?"

"Yeah, and she's actually really excited about it. She's like a kid at Christmas. She kissed me and everything."

"I feel like an idiot." She drops her face into her hands and sighs as she lowers herself onto the couch.

"What? Why?"

"I feel like a complete charity case."

"Whoa."

"I feel like—"

"Unless you follow that up with *loved and cared for*, you're going to want to stop right there. Stop it, Polly." I squat before her and pull her hands away from her face, kiss them, and hold on to them tightly. "I'm taking you because I want to. I *want* to."

"But—"

"No buts. And yes, London knows because I needed her help with a few things, and she's thrilled to shop with you and show you everything there is to see at this thing. She knows more about it than me and has more contacts. Of course, I'd ask her for help so I can make it special for you."

"I can't afford—"

"Hey." I pull her to me now. She's so damn short, so I sit and plant her on my lap and hook her hair behind her ear. "I don't want you to think about the money for another second. Don't, babe. This is my gift to you."

"I guess my birthday *is* coming up." She nibbles on her lip.

"If that's what you want to call this, fine. But it's not for your birthday. It's just because. I'd love to show you Paris and see it through your eyes. Hell, I've never been to fashion week, and maybe I should see what all the fuss is about. London talked Drew into coming, so there will be more testosterone there. Apparently, double dates are in our future, and that's cool with me because we like them."

She smiles, just a little, but her eyes are still uncertain. "You're sure this isn't too much?"

"It's absolutely *not* too much." If I tell her that I'll never even feel the loss in my account, it'll just freak her out, so I keep that to myself. "Let me do this for you. For *us*. Hell, this will be the first vacation I've taken in...ever."

"Ever? Jesus, Ryan, that's crazy. Just don't go overboard," she says, like she did when she agreed to let me make over her kitchen. "I know you didn't stick to your word about that with my kitchen."

"I don't know what you're talking about."

"I know about the top-of-the-line appliances," she informs me, narrowing her eyes, but there is humor there.

"You need quality appliances," I counter and plant a kiss on her chin. "You know you want to go."

"More than just about anything," she admits, not bothering to deny it.

She straddles me now, and her smile turns...*naughty.*

"I think I'll show you how much I appreciate you." She bites my lower lip.

"Fuck yes. Show me, babe."

But before we can get naked, the doorbell rings, signaling that our food is here, and Polly shimmies off of my lap and hurries to the door. She pays the delivery kid with cash and then motions for me to follow her through the kitchen and out to the patio in the backyard.

She lowers the screens, and we sit side by side on the swing, to-go boxes of burgers and fries on our laps.

"Is that why you've been working so much?" she asks as she chews on a fry. "Because you're going to be out of the office for so long?"

"Yeah, I'm trying to get ahead so I can take the time off." I don't want her to think that it's a hardship for me to do this with her, so I shrug and take a bite of my burger.

"Will you still be behind when you get home? And don't lie to me, Wild."

"Behind? Not much. I'm the boss, remember?"

"I know from experience that just because you're the boss, it doesn't mean that your workload isn't massive. In fact, the bigger the boss, the more work you have." She leans over to kiss my shoulder. "So, thank you."

"You're welcome."

"What about Jake?"

I love that my kid is never far from her mind. "He's

cool with it. More than, actually. He'll have the village looking out for him. He encouraged me to take you."

"Yeah, I love him," she says, and hearing those words warms me, even if it *is* in reference to my teenager.

"He's a lovable kid."

"So, we leave in *two* days?"

"That's right."

"What time does the flight leave?"

"Whenever we want it to." Polly pauses in wiping her mouth and stares at me. "We're taking my jet, so we choose the flight time."

"You're kidding."

"No, ma'am. It's the most convenient and, I have to admit, it's quite comfortable. You'll like it."

"I'll like it." She giggles and shakes her head. "Yeah, I'm pretty sure I'm going to like it. Jesus, what is this life?"

"It's a damn good one."

"Yeah." She sighs and then pops a fry into her mouth. "It is that."

"THERE ARE a million groceries in this house, and your gas tank is full, but I put a grand in your bank account, in case you need anything."

"You put a *grand* in my account?" Jake echoes with a laugh. "Jeez, you're only going for a week, Dad."

"Could be ten days," I remind him. "And I want to make sure you have plenty of spending money."

"Well, that should be plenty," he says, shaking his head. "You do know that I hardly go anywhere, right? I'm pretty much a homebody."

"Yeah, well, you're covered for emergencies." I don't know why I'm so nervous about leaving him alone this time. It's not the first time, and it probably won't be the last. "Millie's coming to stay for the first few nights."

"I know. She already texted me."

There's a knock on the door, and Jake and I frown at each other.

"Are you expecting anyone?"

"Yeah, right," he says, rolling his eyes as we both walk to the front door and open it to find Chase standing there with a grin.

"I have your table," he announces proudly. "But I need both of you to help me muscle it inside."

"*Nice,*" Jake exclaims and runs down the stairs to Chase's truck.

"This thing is heavy," I say as we lift it out of the bed of the truck. Chase is right: It does take all three of us to do it.

"Pure maple," Chase says. "This table will never wear out. You'll be able to pass it down to your grandkids."

"It's really nice," Jake says as we make our way up the stairs with it and set it in the office, right where I envisioned that it would go in my head. "But we don't have chairs."

"Follow me." I lead the men out to my detached garage, and there are four chairs waiting for us. "I bought these weeks ago so we'd be ready for the table."

Jake takes two of them and immediately heads back to the house, and Chase and I follow with one chair each.

"He's excited," Chase murmurs to me.

"Breakfast is our favorite time of day," I reply. "And he likes that I wanted a special table for it. And that *you* built it? Well, that's extra cool to him."

We find Jake already in the office, his chairs placed at the table, and Chase and I add ours, and then the three of us step back and admire our handiwork.

"This is fucking legit," Jake says. "Sorry for the language, but it *is*."

"Yeah, it is," I agree and ruffle his hair. "You did an awesome job, Chase. Thank you."

"It was my pleasure," he replies. "Did I see suitcases downstairs?"

"You just caught me." I lead them back down to the foyer. "I'm headed out to Paris for a week or so with Polly."

"Well, aren't you fancy?" Chase grins and then eyes Jake. "Who's taking care of your child?"

"I'm not a child," Jake insists, which is exactly what Chase wanted him to do. "Millie's coming tonight."

"Call me if you need anything," Chase tells him. "Summer and I are ten minutes away. Is the security detail staying here, or are they with you, Ry?"

"They're staying, and a different detail will be with us. Everything should be good here, but I'm glad you're close by."

"Why don't you come out for dinner tomorrow?"

Chase asks Jake. "We'll do some fishing off of the dock afterward."

"Cool," Jake says with a shrug, but the smile on his face tells me that he's happy to be invited. "Just let me know what time, and I'll be there."

"I'll double-check with the wife and text you," Chase replies and then turns to me. "Have fun."

"Thanks. I plan to. And thanks again for the table. It's really great, man."

"You're welcome." With a wave, he's off, and I turn back to Jake.

"Don't be eating at that table without me."

"No way. We'll do it together when you get back." He offers me his fist for a fist bump, which I happily oblige, and then I pull him in for a quick hug.

"You're sure you're okay with this?"

"Dude, why are you so weird about this one? You've been gone before, you know."

"Yeah, but that was work, and this is fun, and you're my kid, so I have dad guilt for leaving you behind when I'm going on a freaking vacation. Do you want to go with us?"

Jake's eyebrows climb into his hairline. "Aww, that's so sweet. You're gonna miss me. But do I want to go shopping in Paris? No thanks. That sounds horrible to me. No offense. Besides, you guys can be all gooey and gross without a kid hanging around. Go have fun."

"I'll take you wherever you want to go. You and I can take a trip."

He blinks at me. "Honestly? I'm fine here. Maybe we

can take a hiking trip up to Glacier or something later, but I'm not worried about it. Like I said, go have fun. Be safe."

He wiggles his eyebrows at me, and I laugh and ruffle his hair before grabbing my suitcases to load into the truck.

Jake helps me, and before long, I'm headed over to Polly's to pick her up and take her to the airport.

Yeah, it's going to be damn fun.

CHAPTER FIFTEEN

POLLY

"This is insane, you know." I wipe my mouth with the cloth napkin given to me by the ridiculously efficient flight attendant. We're an hour into this flight, and I've been served an appetizer and a main course that I would find in a fancy restaurant. And don't even get me started on how incredible this plane is. "I was nervous when you mentioned a private plane because I pictured a tiny little thing with tons of turbulence carrying me over the ocean."

Ryan grins across from me. There's a beautiful marble table between us, covered with a white tablecloth and a spread of food laid out for us to pick and choose what we want. The roasted chicken with carrots and potatoes is delicious. "I prefer to travel in a more comfortable setting."

I let my eyes roam over the cabin of this jet. "How many can this seat?"

"Thirteen comfortably," he replies and takes a bite of

chicken. "And I like that I barely have to duck down to walk through."

"And what kind of jet is this?"

He smiles again, almost smugly. "It's a Gulfstream, G650ER, if you want to get technical. We can fly from Montana to Paris without having to stop for fuel."

"You're kidding."

"No, ma'am. I'm not."

The leather on the seats is just...*butter.* The wood paneling gleams, and there are televisions set out for entertainment, boasting Netflix, Passionflix, and other streaming services to choose from.

There's even a king-sized bed in the back, already made up for us with the softest, fluffiest blankets I've ever seen. I have a feeling I'll be joining the mile-high club today, and just the thought of it has my stomach clenching in anticipation.

"You look a little overwhelmed, and we haven't even gotten there yet," he says, setting his fork on his empty plate.

"I mean, have you seen this plane?" His grin is quick, and I can't help but think about how damn handsome he is.

I also don't want to think about how many women he's had sex with in that bed.

"What?" he asks.

"What what?" I counter.

"Something just went through that sexy brain of yours. I saw it in your eyes."

"I have no idea what you're talking about." I sip my

water and try to act nonchalant, but he narrows his eyes and reaches over to drag his fingertips down my jawline in that way he does that makes me all gooey.

"Bullshit," he says softly. "Don't lie to me, babe. We're far past that."

"I am not lying—" I stop and exhale. "Jealousy isn't something I'm particularly comfortable with, and I know it's not an attractive trait, and I don't want to tell you what I was thinking."

"Okay, that's honest." He doesn't take his eyes off mine. "And now I have to know what it was."

I chuckle, shake my head, and look out at the clouds skimming by beneath us. "That bed back there looks comfortable."

"Look at me."

His voice is still mild but also leaves no room for argument, and I turn my gaze back to his.

"I was just thinking that I don't want to know how many women you've taken on a trip and fucked in that bed. See? Not terribly attractive."

Without answering me, Ryan presses the call button for the flight attendant, and within seconds, he's standing beside Ryan's chair.

"We're finished here," Ryan says. "And I'd like to be left in private until an hour before we land, then we'll have breakfast and coffee."

"Of course, Mr. Wild." The attendant nods and takes our plates away. "Give me five minutes to clean this up, and I'll be out of your way."

We sit in silence, watching each other as he bustles back and forth, cleaning our meal. He sets out four bottles of water and assures Ryan that all he has to do is buzz for him in case we need anything, and then he goes to a private little room and closes the door.

"He has his own room?" I ask in surprise.

"I value privacy," Ryan returns and stands, reaches for my hand and pulls me up next to him, then leads me back to the bedroom. "We left in the afternoon so we can sleep through the night and arrive in Paris in the morning, local time, and start our day. It's the best way to avoid horrible jet lag."

"Okay." I don't like that he's suddenly a little cold toward me, as if my earlier statement irritated him. I also don't like that he didn't address it at all. "Look, I'm sorry if I upset you, but you told me not to lie, and—"

Suddenly, Ryan lifts me off my feet and onto my back on the bed, and he's covering me with his long, lean body and kissing the hell out of me.

"No one," he says against my lips. "I've had *no one* on this plane. I use it for business, and if I wanted to fuck someone, I did that somewhere else. Not here. Only you, Polly."

I swallow hard and plunge my fingers into the thick, dark hair at the back of his head.

"Why did I make you mad?"

"Not mad." He rubs his nose against mine. "It frustrates me that you'd think of me with someone else when all I can think about is *you*."

He kisses me again before I can reply. His hands roam over me, and I'm instantly swept up in him. His lips journey down my body, leaving wet kisses as he uncovers my skin while shedding my clothes. I want his skin under my touch, so I tug at his shirt, pulling it over his head. We're a tangle of arms and hands as we undress each other, and then we're naked and pressed together as he kisses me some more.

Ryan's mouth might be my favorite thing in the world.

"Can't get enough of you," he groans against my breastbone. "I can't fucking stop *thinking* about you, and when I have you with me, under me, against me, it's almost not enough."

"I know." I fist my fingers in his hair and urge him up so I can kiss his sexy lips. "I know, Ryan."

"And my name on your sexy mouth is almost my undoing."

He takes my lips again as his hand journeys down my side, over my hip, and between my legs, where he playfully tickles my lips.

"You're fucking soaked."

"Do you expect to be able to say things like you just did, kiss me the way you do, and it *not* have an effect on me?" I smile at him and then sigh when one of his fingers sinks inside of me. "It always feels so damn *good.*"

With one hand circling my throat—not pushing, just resting—Ryan presses himself inside of me, and we both moan with the pleasure of it.

"There's *no one* but you," he says as he starts to move.

I raise my legs higher on his hips and drag my nails down his back as he picks up the pace. When my neck arches, his teeth latch on to the skin under my ear, and then he growls, "You're fucking *everything.*"

I've never felt so cherished as I do when I'm with this man. His words send me over the edge into oblivion. I don't hold back the loud cry, and I clench around him as the orgasm moves through me.

With two final thrusts, Ryan loses control, emptying himself into me.

After we take a minute to catch our breath, Ryan kisses my shoulder, then my lips, and then climbs from the bed and walks into a bathroom bigger than the one in my house. I hear the water running, and then he returns with a hot washcloth and proceeds to clean me up.

"You're the sexiest woman I've ever seen." He says it as simply as if he's talking about the weather.

And I snort laugh because literally no one has ever said that to me in my life.

"I don't find it particularly funny." His hazel eyes climb to mine as he tosses the cloth aside and pulls the covers back on the bed, and we climb inside to get cozy. We lie on our sides, facing each other, and I tuck my hand under my cheek.

"I mean, thank you for the compliment, but, Ryan... I've seen the women you've dated in the past. Or, at least the women you've been photographed with."

"And?"

"I'm not a tall, leggy blonde."

"No, you're a petite, curvy redhead with the most gorgeous emerald-green eyes in the world. And speaking of your hair." He reaches out to drag his fingers through it. "Do you know that when we were together that first night, I was obsessed with your hair? I couldn't get enough of it. I still can't. In addition to all the outside beauty," he continues, "you're smart and funny. You help others. You're generous with your time and your business. For fuck's sake, you buy your customers cookies."

"That's just good business sense." I'm practically glowing from the inside out at his praise.

"Like I said, you're smart."

"I do have faults, you know."

He raises an eyebrow. "And those are?"

"I'm forgetful. I suspect that when we get to the hotel, I'll discover that I left something at home that I need."

"You have your passport, right?"

"I'm not *that* forgetful."

"Then anything else can be replaced. What else is wrong with you?"

That makes me snicker. "I'm pretty stubborn."

"I noticed."

I laugh again, and he grins at me. "God, I love your smile, Ryan Wild."

He pulls me closer to him and kisses my forehead.

"Wanna know a secret?" I ask him in a whisper.

"I want to know *all* your secrets."

"I think you're incredible," I reply, feeling safe here in this cozy bed, in the dark, so high up in the sky. "I've been proud of you for *years* because you were my brother's best friend. I've seen how you help people. Sure, you're rich. I don't even want to know how much this plane cost."

"About sixty million," he says with a shrug, and my eyes just about bug out of my head.

"Fucking hell, Ryan."

"But back to what you were saying."

I swallow hard and lick my lips again. "Jesus, I can't even wrap my head around that. Anyway, I know that you're generous, and you're so damn intelligent. You're amazing with your son, and you have a fabulous family. And don't even get me started on how freaking handsome you are."

"No, go on. Tell me how hot I am."

I laugh and lean in to quickly kiss him. "Also, you're so humble."

"I really am."

"I guess I'm saying that the sentiment is reciprocated here. I think you're incredible, too."

His eyes sober as he drags his fingertips down my cheek. "Thanks, babe. We should sleep for a few hours."

"I could sleep." I move into him, rest my cheek on his chest, and take a deep breath. "You know you've now ruined me for all other travel. How am I supposed to book a commercial flight after this?"

He chuckles and kisses the top of my head. "You don't need to book any commercial flights. Go to sleep, beautiful girl."

With a sigh, I feel myself falling into sleep with the sound of his heart under my ear.

"Welcome home." The bellman at the Ritz tips his hat to me as Ryan, with his hand in mine, leads me through the doors of the hotel, up the stairs, and through the revolving door into the lobby. His security team met us at the airport and followed us to the hotel. Now, two big, burly men with earpieces in their ears, wearing suits, follow us inside.

I take a second to soak it in. The floors are marble, with blue and gold rugs that line the long hallway down to what I assume are the restaurants. There are three steps up to the right that lead to the concierge desk, and the reception desks are just around the corner.

Ryan quickly handles the check-in, and we're escorted to the nearby elevator and up to the second floor, then down a hallway to a double door with the words *Suite Coco Chanel* written on the right-hand side.

My wide eyes look up to find Ryan smiling down at me.

"No way."

"Right this way, mademoiselle," the man says as he unlocks the door and escorts us inside, me at the front. The security detail stays behind in the hallway. "You have the whole suite, which includes two bedrooms and two bathrooms. Everything is as you requested, Mr. Wild."

He shows us where the phones are, opens the drapes, and gives us information, but the blood is rushing through my ears.

Ryan booked us the *Coco Chanel* suite during fashion week. I'm staying in her freaking suite.

"Can I ask you some questions?" I ask before he can bustle out.

"Of course. What can I help you with?"

"Is this her original suite?"

"No," he replies with a soft smile. "Her original apartment was on the sixth floor, on the other side of the hotel, where she could look out at her shop. It was moved in 2012 during our renovations, and, as you can see, I think it has the best view in all of Paris. That is the Plaza Vendome."

"It's a beautiful view," I agree as I look out at the square with people bustling about, cars driving by, and a very tall copper statue of Napoleon Bonaparte. "Is anything in here original to her?"

"Yes, the folding screens at the end of this room," he says, gesturing to them, and I notice that Ryan is hanging back, his hands stuffed in his pockets, listening to us. "There were six originally, and two of them are here. I believe the other four remain in her apartment above the shop on Rue Cambon. And although these are not her original rooms, they are decorated the way she had them, and that camel-colored couch is an exact replica of her sofa."

I nod, taking it all in. "Thank you for the information."

"Of course, that's what I'm here for. If you wish to have any other tours or have questions, don't hesitate to ask."

I nod at him. Ryan follows him out, and, I'm assuming, tips him.

I cross to the windows and stare out at the view below. Louis Vuitton is on the corner to the right, with Dior next to them. On the left is Cartier, and across the street is Van Cleef and Arpels.

The fashion on this street is overwhelming and exciting all at the same time.

I hear the bellman deliver our luggage, and then Ryan murmurs something to his security guy before he shuts the door again, and we're alone. I can smell the spectacular display of pink roses that sit on the table beside the couch.

I feel Ryan approach me from behind, and he takes my shoulders in his hands and bends down to kiss my neck.

"Talk to me," he whispers. "You're tense, and I can't read you."

"You didn't have to do this." I turn in his arms and stare up at him as I cup his cheek, which is rough with stubble. He did all of this for *me.* "We don't need a two-bedroom suite this week."

"Yes, we do," he counters. "We'll be in the master, and the other room will be your dressing room. I have it under good authority that we'll have a lot of clothes and bags and shoes and I don't even know what else delivered here."

I'm struck dumb as I stare up at him.

"For what?"

Ryan laughs and kisses my forehead. "For *you*, silly. Now, are you hungry? London and Drew don't get in for a couple of hours yet, and I know you and London have some appointments later this afternoon for shopping. But before that, we should grab something to eat."

"I don't even know." I look around and still can't believe that I'm in the Coco Chanel suite. "You're right, I'm keyed up. Maybe we should talk, and I'll calm down. These flowers are pretty."

"I had them brought in," he says with a frown as I wander away from him. "Why are you nervous, babe?"

"I didn't expect all of this." I sweep my arm, indicating the room around us. "I thought we'd just be in a regular suite."

"There are no *regular* suites in this hotel," he says with a grin. "And I knew you'd love this, so I made it happen."

"Who did you have to sweet talk to give it up?" I roll my eyes when he simply shrugs a shoulder. "I may be naïve when it comes to this stuff, but even *I* know that this suite had to have been booked out for someone important in the fashion industry."

"Anna Wintour."

I stare at him, and then I have to sit down because I feel like I'm going to pass out.

"You took this room from *Anna Wintour*, the editor-in-chief of *Vogue* magazine? Are you fucking kidding me?"

"She was fine with taking another suite," he replies simply, as if it's no big deal.

"Sure. Of course, she was." I shake my head and stand, then circle behind the gorgeous couch, running my hand along the back of it. Then I move to the side of the room to look at the photos of Chanel herself. Some were taken in her original apartment at the Ritz. "I can't believe I'm here. I probably owe you all kinds of sexual favors for this."

"You don't owe me anything."

I turn to find him standing across the room, his hands still in his pockets, watching me with cool eyes. His voice is full of insult, and it makes my heart hurt. I don't want to hurt his feelings.

"You're angry."

"I'm...fine. I'll do or say whatever you need me to in order to make you comfortable."

I realize that I'm being ridiculous. I need to loosen up and *enjoy* this opportunity of a lifetime. Just because it's something that I wouldn't normally be able to afford doesn't mean that I shouldn't enjoy the gift that it is.

So, I smile and run across the room and launch myself into Ryan's arms, wrap my arms around his neck, and kiss him with all I've got.

"Thank you," I say against his lips, enjoying the way his hands are planted on the globes of my ass and the way his muscles bunch under my hands. "Thank you *so much* for all of this. It's amazing and wonderful and a dream come true, and I'm so grateful."

"You're welcome. And this smile is way better than the frown from a second ago."

"I think I'm just overwhelmed," I admit, and rest my forehead against his. "That's all. We're in the *Coco Chanel* suite, Ryan."

"Yes, we are."

"That's fucking amazing."

"I'M HERE, and I'm ready to shop," London announces when she waltzes into our room a couple of hours later. Ryan and I ordered room service and took showers, then enjoyed a quick walk around the hotel to get our bearings and look around. It was exactly what I needed to refresh and fight off the jet lag.

When London texted and said that they'd arrived, we came back to meet them at our room.

"Welcome to my humble abode," I say with a wide grin. "Look at where I'm staying!"

"I know," London says with a little squeal and then does a happy dance before pulling me in for a big hug. "Holy shitballs, Batman."

"Nice digs," Drew says as he walks in behind her, looking handsome in a white button-down shirt and dark blue jeans.

"Which suite are you in?" I ask them.

"The Hemingway Suite," Drew replies. "And it's ridiculous. Not this big, but it's fancy as shit."

I grin at him. "I don't know if you've noticed, but I think every room in this place is fancy as shit."

"You'd be right," London counters, and then high-fives Ryan. "We pulled it off. Okay, you two, show me everything. I've never stayed in this room."

It takes us thirty minutes to walk around and ooh and aah over every little detail. We speculate and gossip and talk about the icon herself until we're both a couple of giggling idiots.

It's the best day ever.

"We have shopping appointments," London says, checking her watch. "In thirty minutes."

"So, we're shopping *before* the shows?" I ask her as we sit on the iconic couch.

"Yes, because while you always look stylish and put together, you'll want some ready-to-wear pieces from the fashion houses to wear to the shows. *Then*, when it's all said and done, we'll shop again for the new stuff. It really doesn't suck."

I do a mental inventory of my bank account and just about break out into a sweat.

There's just no way that I can shop like this and still pay my bills.

"Don't overthink it," London advises, her voice low as the guys have a conversation in another part of the suite. "This is Ryan's treat, Poll. I'm not footing any of the bill, so you don't have to be uncomfortable."

"I'm not exactly comfortable with *him* footing the bill."

"I'm going to give you a piece of unsolicited advice,"

she says and pushes her dark hair behind her ear. "Ryan wants to do this for you. For the both of you. He wants you to get whatever you want, to really experience every minute of this trip. Take him up on it, Polly. He can afford it, and it's all his idea. It's a gift."

"I know." I nod and take a long, deep breath. "I know it is, but I'm not used to any of this. And maybe I wonder if it's possible to get used to it."

"He's worked hard for his money," she counters. "Damn hard. He's generous with charities and causes and gives away more money than he keeps. You wouldn't be with an unethical man."

"I'm not saying that."

"And you work hard, too," she continues. "You work your ass off, and you're good at your job. Consider this a work event, Polly. You'll be networking and getting ideas for your shop. Even if you don't carry luxury labels, the entire fashion industry takes its cues from these brands. The colors, the cuts, the styles. It all trickles down."

"You're right about that."

"So, it's for work. And maybe a little for fun." She winks at me, covers my hand with hers to give it a reassuring squeeze, and then stands. "Now, we have an appointment across the street there at Louis Vuitton."

"And we don't want to be late," I agree as butterflies set up residence in my stomach. "Let's go do some damage."

"Are you ladies headed out?" Drew asks as he draws London in for a sweet kiss.

"Hell yes, we are," London replies with a grin.

“The boutique has my card on file,” Ryan informs me as he also pulls me in to kiss me. “Get whatever you want. Don’t look at price tags and freak yourself out.”

“Ryan—”

He covers my lips with his. “Don’t freak yourself out,” he repeats. “And have fun.”

“Thank you.” I cup his cheek and smile up at him. “I already *am* having fun.”

CHAPTER SIXTEEN

RYAN

"I actually have work," Drew tells me after the girls have left. "I think I'll head back to our suite for a while and hammer some of it out."

"I can get on board with that," I agree. "I have some things to see to myself. I'll see you at dinner."

"See you," Drew replies and lets himself out of the suite.

I open my computer and am in the middle of replying to an email when there's a knock on my door.

With a frown, I set the computer aside to open the door to find both of my security details here.

"We have a situation," Mark, the head of my European team, says.

"Come in." I step back, glad that Polly isn't here for this. When both men are inside, I close the door and turn to them. "What's going on?"

"We got word that Claudia Dubois is here in Paris," Mark replies.

I narrow my eyes on him, not thrilled, but also not surprised. "She's a runway model. Of course she's in Paris."

"This isn't ideal, sir," Mark says with a sigh. "I can find out which shows she's working and make sure you and Polly don't attend those."

"Fuck that." I push my hands through my hair, frustrated. "I'm not about to let the likes of *Claudia Dubois* intimidate me or keep Polly from experiencing anything she fucking well pleases on this trip."

"We know she's unstable," Mark says with a shrug. "And could very likely make a scene."

"Then she makes a scene." I brush it off. "It'll be her own reputation she hurts, and I don't give a rat's ass. Just make sure that Polly isn't hurt in any way."

"Understood," Mark says with a nod. "One of us will be nearby twenty-four seven. I'll have a man outside this door, and we will go with you when you're on the move, just in case."

"Is someone on Polly now, while they're shopping?"

"Affirmative. She didn't bat an eye. She must assume it's normal for you to have detail at all times."

"Good. If she asks, I'll tell her it's the norm. Keep her safe. She's the *only* priority."

"Sir, I hate to disagree with you, but *you're* our priority."

"Fuck that. I can protect myself. If anything happens to Polly, I'll have your heads."

Mark nods, understanding in his eyes, and then the two men leave.

Two hours later, Polly and London return, carrying shopping bags with smiles on their faces.

"We're back," Polly announces and holds up a sack and a garment bag. "I got some loot."

London frowns down at the floor, but Polly doesn't notice. She hurries over to me and offers me her lips, which I happily kiss, before she steps away again.

"I have to run to the ladies' room," she announces before rushing off.

"What's up?" I ask London. "It doesn't look like she got much."

"She didn't," London confirms. "She looked at a lot of beautiful things, but she just wouldn't take the plunge. She ended up with a nice blouse and a scarf."

I blink at her and scowl. "That's it?"

"Yep." London sighs. "I know there were bags and shoes she was practically salivating over. And when we went to Dior, there was a dress that would have been divine on her—*was* divine on her because I talked her into trying it on. But when she saw the price, she declined it."

"Fuck," I mutter and drag my hand down my face. "Okay. I'll take her tomorrow."

"You'll have better luck with her," London says. "And maybe she's tired. It's a long travel day, jet lag, and all that jazz."

"You're right." I nod as Polly walks out of the bathroom.

"I'm hungry," she announces. "When's dinner?"

"We have reservations in," I check my watch, "fifteen minutes. You two are just in time."

"Should I change?" Polly asks.

"You look great," London assures her. "No need to change."

"Good." Polly's shoulders fall in relief. I can see the fatigue in her face. I would rather stay in, have room service, make love to her, and then sleep. But I know that she wants to spend time with our friends, too. Polly smiles at me. "Let's go eat."

"Now this is a breakfast," Polly says the next morning after room service has set up the table and left us alone. "Are those chocolate croissants?"

"Yes." I grin as I pour her coffee, add the cream and sugar she likes, and deliver it to her in bed. Then I put the croissant, some berries, and yogurt on a plate and bring it to her, as well.

"This china is *gorgeous*," she says, holding the cup up so she can check it out. "So dainty and sweet."

"I believe they sell it," I reply and take a bite of my own croissant. "If you ever want some for yourself."

"I'll enjoy it here," she says and bites into her pastry. She moans and closes her eyes, not unlike the way she did when I was inside of her less than an hour ago. "Jesus, the food here is so *good*."

"French food is amazing," I agree. "Do you want

some scrambled eggs? Bacon? They brought a little of everything."

"Bacon," she agrees. "And more coffee. So, what are we doing today? I don't think that any of the shows or parties start until tomorrow."

I refresh our drinks and food and then decide to bring the whole table closer to the bed.

"We're shopping. Just you and me."

That makes her eyes light up. "We are? I'd like that."

"Didn't you have fun with London yesterday?" I pass her the coffee, and she takes a sip and then frowns down into her cup. "You can tell me; I'm a vault."

That makes her smile, and she leans over to kiss my shoulder.

"I know. It's not that I didn't have fun. I did. London knows so much about the brands, and she already knows the sales associates in the stores, so it's nice to already have a contact there."

"Okay." I watch her face as she seems to choose her words carefully.

"I love the blouse I got," she continues. "And yes, there were some other things that caught my eye."

"But?"

"But I want to go to Chanel," she says and cringes. "And I didn't want to sound difficult because I know she made those appointments for us. I *love* the ready-to-wear clothes at Chanel. And yes, there were some things at Dior that I liked, but I didn't want to spend the money there until I'd seen what Chanel has to offer first, because I don't want to go crazy until after the shows when I can buy the new seasons' stuff. Does that make sense?"

It all starts to make perfect sense, and I sigh in relief. She's not freaking out about the money; she's trying to be thoughtful and mindful of her choices.

And I can respect that.

"I get it. I'll arrange for an appointment at Chanel first thing so you can choose what you want, and then we'll make our way back to Dior so you can pick up anything else you'd like."

"Thanks." She grins, obviously excited about that idea.

"What about jewelry?"

She blinks. "What about it?"

"Well, I'd like to buy you some. Cartier, Van Cleef and Arpels, Chopard...is there anything you prefer, or should we go to all of them? They're right here, so it's not out of the way."

She's staring at me with those green eyes, and then she bites her lip.

"All of those are amazing brands." Her voice is soft, and it makes me smile.

"Do you have a preference?"

"Not really."

"Then we'll go to all of them." I take a bite of bacon. "We're going to shop until we drop today. We'd better hydrate."

Polly laughs and then shakes her head. "Why does this feel like a *Pretty Woman* moment?"

"In what way?"

"You know...the rich guy takes the poor girl shopping on Rodeo Drive."

I shake my head, not particularly liking that comparison. "I'm just a man crazy about a woman who likes to shop, and I want to spoil her senseless. Plus, we're not on Rodeo Drive. We're in Paris."

Polly's shoulders shimmy with excitement.

"We're *totally* in Paris. I can be ready to go in less than an hour."

"Then I'll start making those appointments."

By the time she comes out of the bathroom, looking fucking amazing in a black dress that I know she got at her shop, her thick hair swept up in a high ponytail, and her makeup perfect, I've managed to secure a full day of appointments.

And, just as she wanted, we're starting at Chanel.

"Holy shit," Polly whispers as we come down to the lobby and see all the paparazzi gathered around the front of the Ritz. "What's going on?"

"It's fashion week," I remind her. "They're hoping to catch glimpses of celebrities."

"Well, I'm about to disappoint them," she replies as we walk outside.

The shutters immediately start to go off, and someone calls out to me.

"Mr. Wild, can you pose for us, please?"

I shake my head as security flanks us, and we set off down the block, over to the Chanel store.

"This is insane," Polly breathes. "I know I keep using that word, and it could get annoying, but I don't have any other words for it. We're going to the *original* store?"

"Yep, the one on Rue Cambon."

"I might cry," she says and squeezes my hand, practically skipping with her excitement. "You've been warned."

"So noted." I lift her hand to my lips as we walk into the store. We're immediately greeted by the sales associate that's been assigned to us and shown into a room upstairs where we can shop privately.

"It's such a pleasure to meet you. I am Stephan, and I'll be with you today." She smiles at Polly. "What is it that you would like to see?"

"Clothes," Polly says immediately. "Particularly dresses. I have shows and dinners and maybe a party or two to go to while I'm here, and I'd like to dress mainly in Chanel, if possible."

"I'm quite sure we can make that happen," Stephan says with a wink. "You can leave your things in here—it's secure—and come with me. We'll pick some items out for you to try on, and I have some things in the back that I think will be beautiful that I'll pull for you."

Polly turns to me, all smiles and practically glowing. "She has things in the back."

I laugh, happy that my girl is having fun, and I hang back, watching as Polly and Stephan discuss clothing and the colors that Polly's interested in. Before I know it, we're back in our private room with champagne on hand, and Polly's in the dressing room, changing.

By the time we leave, she's bought three dresses, a coat, two bags, and three pairs of shoes. The color is high in her cheeks when we walk out of the boutique; all of her packages were sent ahead to the hotel, where they'll be waiting for us.

"Okay, that was fun," she says and takes my hand in hers. "That green dress—"

"Is fucking incredible," I finish for her. "Now we're off to Dior."

"Oh, I think I have plenty—"

I turn to her, right here on the sidewalk, and kiss the hell out of her, and when I pull back from her, I brush my thumb along her lower lip.

"You'll have everything you want," I reply, leaving no room for argument. "London said there is a dress there that suits you."

"It's a nice dress," Polly concedes.

"Then it's yours. Let's go."

Watching her shop, interact with the sales associates, try on things, and get excited about the things that make her happy is like crack to me. I'd buy her everything in the store, if that's what she wanted.

We make our way through the jewelry stores, where she chooses pieces that are tasteful and beautiful on her, and when we finally make our way back into our suite, all of her finds are waiting on the table in the main sitting room.

"Ryan," she says as she stands before the small mountain of boxes and bags.

"Yes, babe?"

"This was quite possibly the best day of my life." She turns to me, and I'm stunned to see tears in her eyes.

"Hey, don't cry."

She shakes her head as I scoop her into my arms, sit on the couch, and settle her in my lap. I use my thumb to wipe away the tears running down her cheeks.

"Talk to me, babe."

"I've dreamed of shopping like that since I was a teenager," she says as her chin wobbles with emotion. "And it's always been just that: a dream. And that's okay. But today, this whole week, you made it happen for real. I can never pay you back for that."

"Ah, sweetheart." I kiss her cheek and then her lips and brush her hair back from her face. "I already told you, you don't owe me anything. I had a fantastic day, too."

"I think you actually did," she says with a watery laugh. "You got excited about stuff and smiled a lot. You never looked bored once."

"I wasn't bored. Watching you shop is sexy. And there's a particular pair of heels from Dior that I'd like you to wear later with nothing else on."

She raises an eyebrow. "I know the ones you're thinking of, and I assure you, that can absolutely happen."

"Good." I kiss her softly, but she wraps her arms around my neck and hugs me tightly.

"Thank you."

"You're welcome, babe. I have a question."

"I'll tell you anything."

"There was a bag at Chanel that you wouldn't let me buy for you. You paid for it. Why was that so important to you?"

"I've saved for that bag for years," she admits. "I *wanted* to buy it for myself. I worked hard for it, and it might have come a little earlier than I'd planned or saved for, but I'm in Paris, in Coco's original store, and they had my dream bag. I *had* to buy it."

"I'm glad you did." I brush her hair off her neck. "I know you're going to want to show London all of your new things."

"I will," she says, but doesn't make a move to get up. "But this is nice, especially after all the hustle and bustle of today. The quiet, being here in your arms, is exactly where I want to be and what I want to do right now."

"I can get behind that." I sigh and kiss the crown of her head.

"Have you talked with Jake?" she asks me.

"I was texting with him earlier," I confirm. "He's probably asleep now, or just waking up to take care of the horses."

"Is he okay?"

"He's great. Told me to stop pestering him and to pay attention to *you*."

Her head comes up at that, and she laughs. "He did not."

"He did. He's glad that we're having a good time."

She smiles and settles against me once more. "When is Jake's birthday? We should get him something while we're here."

"He turns sixteen in December."

"We definitely need to get him something fun. There are some hip fashion places here in Europe that are popular that the kids can't get back home. I'll find him some things."

"The fact that you're thinking about my kid when we're on vacation together is incredibly sexy, you know."

"I like him a lot," she murmurs. "I have a soft spot for him."

"Me, too." I skim my hand down her back, then back up again, and plunge my hand into her amazing hair. "We have a couple of hours before dinner."

"Really? What should we do?"

She grins as I lift her and carry her toward the bedroom.

"I have some ideas."

"My shoes are back there," she says, pointing over my shoulder toward the room we just left.

"Later," I reply. "You can wear them for me later. Right now, I just want *you*."

She sighs as I undress her, and when we're both naked and sweaty, panting and humming from an intense orgasm, I pull her to me and kiss her long and deep.

I'm in love with her. I feel it in every fiber of my being. And I want to tell her exactly how I feel.

But before I can, my phone rings, and it's Jake's ringtone.

"Sorry, babe."

"It's okay. Talk to him."

I kiss her nose and then roll over to get my phone. "Hey, buddy."

"Dad?" I immediately sit up, every muscle on high alert.

"Are you hurt? What's wrong?"

"I'm okay." He sniffs on the other end of the line. "Dad, we lost Blossom. I had to call Dr. Randolph, and she came right away, but she couldn't save Blossom."

"Whoa, take a deep breath, buddy. I'm right here. Deep breath. What happened?"

"She—" He sniffs again as I pull a T-shirt over my head and push the button for FaceTime, and Jake accepts it. "Hi."

"Hey. It's going to be okay. I'm not mad at you. You didn't do anything wrong."

Jake starts to cry again, and it tears at my heart.

"She had colic," he says when he can catch his breath. "When I went out there this morning, she was in pain. I could tell, so I called Dr. Randolph, and she came. Mac was here, and I called him, too, and he came to help me. I wasn't by myself."

"Good." I nod, feeling so fucking guilty that *I'm* not there. "That's good."

"She was in pain, and there wasn't anything we could do for her, Dad. So, I held her head and kissed her and stuff while Dr. Randolph put her down. Dad, she was in pain all night, by herself. I wasn't there to help her."

"You didn't know." I shake my head and wish I could hug him to calm him down. "You couldn't have known, buddy. It's not your fault, and you were with her in the end, when she was hurting and scared. That's important."

"We should go back," Polly says, and I glance up to see that she's dressed and has tears of her own. "You should be there with him."

"No," Jake says and wipes his eyes. "Don't come home. I'm okay. The other horses are okay, too. Dr. Randolph checked everyone to make sure. It was just a freak thing, that's all. Mac's here, and Aunt Millie's coming out, too. She said Grandma and Grandpa might come with her. I have lots of people."

"Can I please have the phone?" Polly asks, holding her hand out for it.

I oblige her, and she stares down at Jake.

"You are more important than this trip," she tells him, leaving no room for argument. "If you want your dad home, you just say the word, and we'll be on the plane. Be honest, Jake."

"Really," he insists. "I'm doing better now. I'm just sad, but coming home doesn't bring Blossom back. I just wanted to talk to you guys, you know?"

"Of course, I know, and that's why I'm telling you that we'll come home if you need us."

"No." I can see him shake his head adamantly. "I'll call Dad if I change my mind, but I'll be okay."

Polly narrows her eyes on him, and it seems she's satisfied with what she sees because she nods.

"Okay, then. I'm sorry, Jake. I really am. Here's your dad."

“Polly’s kind of bossy,” Jake says with a half smile when I come back into view. “It’s kind of scary.”

I laugh and give him a shrug. “I think you’re right. Call me if you need me, day or night. Promise?”

“I promise,” he says with a sigh. “Thanks. I feel better.”

“Good. Go take a nap, or kill some zombies.”

“That’s a great idea,” he says. “I’ll kill some zombies. Have fun. See you later.”

With that, he’s gone, and I look over at the woman who just finished sending me straight into complete and unconditional love with her.

“I’m sorry that I intervened, I just—”

I cover her mouth with mine and kiss her long and slow, and when I pull back and look down at her, those green eyes are round, and her plump, swollen lips are parted.

“You were looking out for Jake, and I appreciate it.”

“I guess so.” She covers her lips with her fingers. “I’m glad you didn’t hate it.”

I laugh and pull her to me and lie down on the bed with her. “No, I didn’t hate it. I’m damn grateful for you and the way you care about my kid. Now, let’s nap, babe.”

“That sounds nice.”

"How is everything at home?"

I glance up from my phone and smile at Ryan, who's fastening cuff links on his shirt. He's so tall, so freaking handsome with his tanned skin against that white shirt that it makes me melt inside.

And he might be the only man I've ever known in my life to use cuff links.

"It's good." I smile and finish the text I'm sending off to my staff. "They assure me that everything is fine at the shop. The new apple tart cookies are a hit for fall."

I tuck my phone into my small handbag and then stand to cross over to him to tie his tie. I have to stand on an ottoman to reach him comfortably, and it makes him smirk. Ryan watches me with those amazing hazel eyes as I work the silk in my hands.

"It's been an incredible week," I say with a happy sigh. We've been to at least two or three shows a day, dinners, and parties, and I've met people that I've read about in fashion magazines or seen on TV. London has been incredible about sticking close by so she can make introductions and start conversations. I haven't felt out of place even once.

I even had the opportunity to thank Anna Wintour for the suite, and I didn't stutter when I spoke with her.

"I'm glad you've enjoyed it," he says and runs his hand up and down my arm. "It's not quite over yet."

"Ryan, you don't have to buy me anything else. I know that tomorrow is the buying day, but seriously, you've already done so much, and I'm *fine.* Hell, I'm way more than fine. I'm fabulous."

I smooth my hand down the tied tie, and he leans in to press his lips to my forehead.

"You don't have to buy anything that you don't like." I start to protest, but he presses his finger to my lips. "Let the houses flirt with you, Polly. See what they offer. *Enjoy* the experience, and only take what you love."

I move in and wrap my arms around him, holding him close. He immediately engulfs me in his embrace, and we stand here like this for just a moment.

There isn't anything in the world like being in Ryan's arms.

And I want to tell him that taking what I love means simply taking *him.*

"You've spoiled me rotten this week."

"That was the goal." I feel him smile against my hair. "Have I mentioned today how fucking gorgeous you are?"

I chuckle and pull back so I can smile up at him. "Probably once or twice."

"This green dress," he says, letting his gaze roam down my body, "should be illegal."

"I saved it for the last day," I agree and step off of the ottoman and then turn a circle for him. "The silk feels like heaven, and I admit, I think my boobs look pretty good in it."

"Spectacular," he agrees, his eyes hot with lust. "We're meeting London and Drew downstairs in ten. Otherwise, I'd show you just how much I appreciate that dress. Are you ready to go?"

"Yep, I just have to put on some lipstick." I cross to the bathroom and smooth it over my lips, step into my shoes, and buckle the ankle straps, and then I return to Ryan, who's waiting patiently for me. "Not only did I save the best dress for last, but the show I want to see the most is also last."

"Chanel," he says with a grin and kisses me softly before opening the door for me. "I admit, I'm interested to see what they have on tap, as well."

We ride the elevator down to the lobby and then meet Drew and London, who are already waiting for us.

"Holy shit, Poll," London says. "You look like you should be walking the runway."

I laugh and shake my head at her. "You're sweet, and you look fabulous, too. That pink jumpsuit is to die for."

"And it doesn't hurt that it's comfortable," she says with a wink. "Let's go drool over some pretty clothes, shall we?"

“Oh, we shall.”

Ryan takes my hand as we walk out the revolving door and into an onslaught of flashing cameras.

“Wait,” he says, frowning down at my feet. “Your strap is unbuckled.”

Right here, in front of everyone, he kneels before me and fastens the strap and then presses his lips to my bare calf before standing and taking my hand once more. My entire system is on high alert, so in tune with him that I want to hurry back to our suite and make love to him all night long.

But I’ll have to settle on knowing that I can do exactly that when we return later.

“I didn’t want you to trip.”

My heart is hammering, and the paps are yelling questions, but all I can see is Ryan’s smile as he leads me out to the car, waiting for us.

“Well, that was sexy,” London says when she’s sitting across from us. “And will look *fabulous* in the photos they were snapping.”

My heart is still working overtime. It *was* the sexiest thing ever.

TODAY WENT BY *FAST*. The Chanel show was amazing, and I know I’ll have a hard time saying no to anything offered to me tomorrow.

We’ve been at a party for the past hour, and I have to admit, I’m starting to feel partied out. It’s a lot of the same faces and the same conversations, and with our time in Paris growing short, I'd honestly rather spend some time with Ryan alone.

"Your martini, madam," the waiter says as he passes me my drink. "And someone asked me to deliver this."

He passes me a napkin, gives me a slight bow, and then he walks away.

I turn to Ryan, but he's busy chatting with someone I don't recognize, so I open the folded napkin and feel my cheeks flush.

Stay away from him.

That's it. No signature. Just those four words.

"What's that?"

I glance up to see Ryan frowning as he reads over my shoulder.

"The waiter said someone asked him to deliver this to me. People are weird, Ryan. Unless you have a confession to make."

He actually laughs and shakes his head. "No. Let's chalk it up to the weird thing because you're absolutely *not* staying away from me. If they even mean *me*."

"Maybe they mean Drew."

Ryan grins again. "They could mean anyone. Do you want to get something to eat?"

"Actually, would it be wrong to tell you that I'd like to get out of here and spend some time alone with *you*? We could get room service or take a walk and find a café somewhere...I don't care. I'm just ready for a little quiet. This has been a lot for this small-town girl."

His eyes warm, and he leans in to press his lips to my ear.

"I'd love nothing more. Come on. Let's get out of here."

He taps the screen of his phone to, I assume, call the car, and we turn to London and Drew to let them know that we're taking off.

"I don't blame you," London says with a wink. "Go have some downtime. We're not staying much longer, either."

"I'm jealous," Drew says and then grins at me. "I'm ready to go, too. See you later."

We're headed toward the door when suddenly, a woman wraps herself around Ryan.

"Well, hello, lover. I was so *surprised* when I saw you in the audience today, and you didn't even call to tell me you'd be in town." Her lips tip down in a pout, making me roll my eyes. "What a magical surprise, baby."

She moves in to kiss him, and I decide that I've had about enough.

"I'd hate to get blood on this brand-new dress, but it might be worth it."

Ryan takes the woman by the shoulders and pushes her off of him.

"Who is *this* tiny thing?" she asks, wrinkling her nose like she's just smelled something from the garbage.

"I can be your worst nightmare," I reply with a toothy smile. "Especially if you don't stop trying to touch my man."

"Have a good evening, Claudia," Ryan says as he

wraps his arm around me, and we turn for the door once more.

"Are you fucking kidding me?" Claudia shrieks. "Fuck you, Ryan! You're a bad lay!"

Without looking back, we climb into the waiting car, and when the door is closed, I take a deep breath.

"Well." I let it out slowly. "That was fun."

"I'm sorry," he says, but I hold a hand up, stopping him.

"You fucked Claudia Dubois?" I turn in the seat and stare at him.

"Years ago," he confirms without hesitation. "Then I realized she's loony tunes, and I cut that off real quick."

I shake my head and right myself in the seat. I'm not mad at him. It's not his fault at all. Mostly, I'm...amused. I can't hold the giggle back that escapes my lips.

"Did you just *laugh*?" he asks me.

I can't reply. All I can do is laugh some more. I laugh so hard that my sides ache and my cheeks get sore.

When we pull up to the Ritz, the door opens for me, and I step out to more flashing bulbs, but I can't stop laughing. Ryan hurries around the car to take my hand, and we walk inside and to the elevator.

I've just started to calm down when I look up in the mirror on the back of the elevator door and my eyes lock with Ryan's, and then the giggles start all over again.

He doesn't speak when the elevator opens or when we walk to our suite.

But once we're inside, as he's taking off his jacket, he

says, "Does the idea of me with another woman amuse you that much?"

"No." I shake my head and press my hand to my chest, willing myself to calm down. "No, I wanted to rip her heart out through her throat."

He lifts an eyebrow. "Well then."

"It was the look on your face." Thinking about it makes me giggle some more. "You were so shocked, so *worried.* And she was clinging to you like you were a tree and she was about to fall into a rushing river. And then you confirmed that you'd slept with her, and I had this image go through my head."

I can't keep talking. I have to sit on the couch so I don't fall over, and I laugh some more. Finally, it all slows down, and I swallow hard.

"Sorry, but it *was* funny. And she was so offended that you didn't defend her."

"She was?"

"Hell yes, she was. I could see it all over her face. She actually believed that you'd come to Paris to surprise her. *Lover.*"

"Don't call me that." He points at me and shakes his head. "*Never* call me that. I slept with her *once* and took her on two dates, and she wouldn't stop calling me that afterward. It's the main reason I broke it off."

"But she said it in a really sophisticated French accent," I remind him, and he pins me in an agitated glare that makes me snort. "Okay, I'll stop."

"You handled yourself well," he says.

"Is this going to happen whenever we travel?" I

counter. “Do I have to be on guard for scorned lov—partners?” I ask, correcting myself when his eyes narrow. “Like, have there been *legions* of them?”

“No.” Ryan scowls and shoves his hands into his pockets. “And fuck her for doing that. You don’t have anything to worry about.”

“Oh, I know I don’t have to worry about other women. I’m not jealous. I’m just wondering if they’re going to accost us wherever we go so I can sharpen my nails and brush up on my sarcasm.”

Ryan stalks toward me and pulls me to my feet, then lifts me in his arms and takes off for the bedroom.

“No. And now, I’m going to show you what this dress does to me.”

“Nice change of topic.”

“I thought so.”

“It’s just so *beautiful* here,” I say with a happy sigh as Ryan and I walk through a gorgeous park with tall trees and flowers planted along the walking paths that lead to the Louvre museum. I love that so much of this area is walkable and safe.

Ryan and I decided to take a walk to find dinner, and I’m glad we did. We’ve been in Paris for a week now, and I’ve barely seen it.

“It’s a pretty city,” he agrees and glances down at me. “Should I buy an apartment here? And then we can come whenever you want?”

I laugh at that, but then I notice that he's not kidding. "No, you don't need to buy an apartment. There are hotels, you know."

"I'm just saying, if you want to come often, we could have a home base here."

I shake my head and step around a mud puddle. "There are moments when I'm reminded just how different we are, economically speaking. I'm happy to visit once in a while, but not enough to where we need an apartment. Besides, we have lives in Montana that aren't easy to be gone from for long. Speaking of, how's Jake? Have you talked to him today?"

"No, we were too busy."

With a frown, I pull my phone out of my jeans pocket —it feels damn good to be casual—and dial the teenager's number.

"Hey, Polly," he says into the phone.

"Hey yourself. We haven't heard from you today, so I'm checking in. How are you?"

"I'm okay. There's not a whole lot going on, actually."

"How's school?"

Ryan raises an eyebrow, and I smile at him.

"School is dumb, but it's fine, I guess. Mac says that I can't skip, even though Dad's gone, which is pretty lame if you ask me. Football's going good, though."

I was surprised, in a good way, when Ryan told me that Jake had decided to go out for the football team.

"Mac would be right, kiddo." I laugh and then glance at Ryan. "Do you want to chat with your dad?"

"Yeah, I probably should. When do you guys come back?"

"In just a couple of days. We have a full day tomorrow, and then we fly out the next day."

"Okay, cool. I guess I'll talk to the old man."

I pass my phone to Ryan and listen to the banter between the two men. It sounds like Jake is trying to get out of going to school on Monday, since we'll be home by then, and Ryan is having none of it.

"Okay, I'll see you soon. Call if you need anything. Yep. Love you, buddy. Bye."

Ryan passes me back my phone.

"He sounds good," I say.

"He's ready for me to get back," he replies. "I can hear it in his voice, but he'd never say that. He's not the guilt trip type, you know?"

"We can just go, Ry. I told you, I don't need to buy anything tomorrow. I have so much new stuff, I don't know what to do with myself."

"It's just one day," he says and points to a place with a view of the Louvre called Café Marly. "Let's eat there."

"I'm in."

We cross the street and walk up the stairs to request a table, and before long, we're seated outside on a patio with a view of one of the glass pyramids of The Louvre.

"Seriously," I begin once we've ordered and have fresh bread and butter on the table. "Let's go home tomorrow. Or *tonight*."

"I'm not cheating you out of the best part of the week," he insists. "Polly, those fashion houses have appointments to bring their stuff to *you*, in our suite, where they'll set up in that second bedroom and offer you a bunch of cool, new things. I want you to have that. You're not missing it."

"And it does sound fabulous," I admit with a grin. "Let's compromise. We'll do fashion stuff in the morning and leave later in the afternoon when it's all finished. Let's do both."

Ryan takes a bite of his bread and watches me. "Are you sure?"

"Absolutely. As fabulous as all of this is, I'm ready to go home to our lives. I promise."

"Then I can live with the compromise," he says and passes me a buttered piece of bread. "Thank you."

"No. Thank *you*, Ryan. For all of it. I'll never forget it."

CHAPTER EIGHTEEN

RYAN

I'm supposed to be working.

We're headed home after a long day of fashion houses wooing my girl, showing her new items and offering them all to her, and Polly trying things on and taking her time to ponder what she truly wanted for her closet.

The little worry lines between her eyebrows were adorable as she considered, then finally decided on several items from each house.

She didn't go crazy, and I like to think that's because she was being practical, not because she was worried about spending my money.

When all was said and done, I even walked away with some new shoes, some shirts, and a jacket. I think Polly slipped a belt in there somewhere, too.

I think she had more fun shopping for *me* than she did for herself.

And, of course, rather than work like I'm supposed to, I'm sitting here at the desk on this plane, watching Polly sleep twenty feet away from me. She curled up on the bed not long after we ate and has been out cold ever since. Her deep red hair fans out behind her, and her hands are curled up under her chin as she lies on her side and dreams.

I want to wrap myself behind her and join her, but it's time that I pay attention to my work, so I sigh, take my glasses off to rub my eyes, then replace them and open my email.

Jesus, there are over a thousand unread files.

So, I dial Arthur's number.

"Sir?" He sounds surprised. "I wasn't expecting you until tomorrow. Is everything okay?"

"Yes, everything's fine. We're headed back to Montana, and I just opened my email. Arthur, there are more than a thousand unread messages. I'm going to need some help."

"I can do that," he says immediately. "But before we continue, may I just ask, did you and Polly enjoy yourselves in Paris?"

I glance over to where Polly rests and feel my heart go to mush. "Yeah. We had a great time."

"Good. Listen, sir—"

"How long have we worked together, Arthur?"

He's silent for a moment, and then, "About a dozen years, I suppose."

"Don't you think it's time you called me *Ryan*?"

I hear him clear his throat on the other end. "Perhaps, once we reach fifteen years. Now then, I owe you an apology."

I frown. "You do?"

"Yes, sir, for the way I behaved a couple of months ago, during your trip. I said some things on the plane that were unacceptable and out of line."

"Yes, you did."

"Well, I apologize for that. If you need to back off from work, that's none of my business."

"No, it's not. Look, Arthur, thanks for the apology. We've worked together for a long time, and I know that my life is shifting a bit. I have a child and a woman and a home that I actually love. And while I *do* care deeply about Wild Enterprises, there will be times that it's not my first and only priority."

"I understand," he says, and from the tone of his voice, I can tell that he really does understand. "And, for what it's worth, I'm happy for you. Now, aside from the email, how can I help?"

I run down a few more things that Arthur can see to while we're in the air, and after we hang up, I take a sip of water.

"You know," Polly says softly from the bed, her still-sleepy eyes blinking lazily, "I always find you *very* attractive, but I have to admit, the billionaire boss might be my favorite."

I tip up an eyebrow and grin at her. "Is that so?"

"Yeah. You've got your shirtsleeves rolled up, and it's well-known that forearm muscles are to die for. You're wearing those sexy glasses, and your hair is kind of messed up from running your fingers through it. You have this serious look on your face as you stare at the computer, and add to it, you're riding in this fancy plane that you *own*, and yeah...hot billionaire boss."

"It's such a relief to me that you approve."

She smirks but doesn't move to join me, and suddenly, the twenty feet between us feels way too distant.

"Why don't you wear them all the time?" Polly asks when I take my glasses off and set them aside.

"Because I don't *need* them all the time."

Standing up from the desk, I stride closer to my girl. Lifting the covers off the bed, I feel both of my eyebrows climb into my hairline. "Why didn't I know that you were naked under here?"

"You didn't ask." She grins and bites the tip of her tongue between her teeth as I begin to shed my own clothes. Her gaze rakes down my body, heat filling those emerald eyes as my pants slide down my hips and pool around my ankles.

She licks her lips and rolls onto her back in invitation, making me grin.

"Lift your arms over your head, and press your palms to the wall above you."

Those eyes flare with excitement, and she does as she's told, watching me as I cross my arms over my chest and take her in. Her soft skin is smooth, her pink nipples puckering under my perusal. Her slightly rounded belly is kissable and just freaking *beautiful*, leading to that magical place between her legs.

Polly bites her lip and starts to move her hands, and I pin her in a hard stare.

"I didn't say you could move."

"Oh, I like it when bossy Ryan takes over."

I want to laugh at that, but I firm my jaw, gazing down at her sternly.

"Spread your pretty legs."

Without hesitation, she complies, bending her legs at the knees and spreading herself open for my enjoyment. She's pink there, too, and already wet as fuck.

Jesus, I want her. I never *stop* wanting her.

"You're every goddamn fantasy I've ever had in my life, Polly."

Her eyes widen in surprise, and finally, I can't stand it anymore. I *have* to touch her. I cover her with my own body and push my hand into that thick, gorgeous red hair and fist it there, loving the way her curves fit under me. I can never get enough.

"Do you feel better after your nap?" I ask against her lips.

"I don't know...how *do* I feel?" She grins and moves suggestively beneath me, making my cock harden and my pulse quicken even more than before.

"You always feel like fucking heaven," I growl, and, unable to resist her, I urge her leg up over my hip, opening her up to me. "You're soft and smooth, and you smell so fucking good."

She sighs and lifts her hips in invitation, but rather than slide inside of her, I kiss her lips softly, then bite her chin.

"Keep your hands above you. Understand?"

She nods, but I shake my head.

"Use your words, beautiful girl."

"I understand."

"Good girl." I kiss down her neck, to one of her breasts, and lave the nipple before suckling it into my mouth. Suddenly, her fingers are in my hair, and I pull back out of reach and glare down at her. "Do as I say or this ends."

"You don't have to be quite *so* bossy," she pouts, but when I simply lift an eyebrow, she huffs out a breath and presses her hands to the wall above her.

"This is what you get when I'm in work mode. If you move again," I continue as I resume kissing down her body, "I'll spank your delicious ass."

"You would *not*."

I stare up at her and nibble her navel. "You know that I would."

She bites her lip, but her hands don't move as I move lower still, and when I cover her clit with my lips, her hips jerk, but those hands stay put.

"There we go," I croon and settle myself here, between her legs, her pussy laid out before me like a fucking feast.

At first, I taunt her. Little licks, tiny nibbles, slight brushes with the tips of my fingers here and there, making her squirm and moan.

But she doesn't move her hands.

Finally, I give in and push one finger inside of her as I lap and kiss, more deeply now, giving her what I know she wants. She sighs contentedly, and if I'm not mistaken, she whispers, "*Finally*," making me grin.

I work her over with my mouth and fingers until she's practically snarling with the need to come.

"Not yet," I warn her.

"Please," she begs with a whimper as her legs move restlessly, and her chest heaves, pushing those gorgeous tits up into the air. "Please, Ryan. Oh, God."

"You're fucking gorgeous," I growl as I kiss up her body. I reach up and take her hands in mine, kiss them, and smile down at her. "Good girl."

"You're killing me."

I slip inside of her, and her mouth opens in a wide O, her eyes on mine with pure pleasure. Jesus, I could lose myself in those emerald orbs.

"It's never the same," she says, frowning as I begin to move and fist my hand in that glorious fucking hair. "Just when I think I know what to expect when it comes to sex with you, it changes and shifts and freaking turns into something I never expected."

"I know." I cover her mouth and kiss her, moving slow and steady in and out, making love to her more sweetly than I have before. She consumes me. Every minute of every goddamn day, Polly completely consumes my every thought, my every need.

I drag my hand down her side, over her hip, and down her thigh, then lift it higher against me. Her eyes widen, and her breath comes harder.

"This," I whisper against her lips as I move, pushing deeply into her and loving the little sounds she makes in the back of her throat. “This is mine, babe.”

My hand fists in her hair again, and I pull, exposing more of her neck to my lips.

“Ah, shit,” she groans, and I feel her pulse around my cock, like the seconds on a clock, *tick tick ticking* with every second, but she’s ready to come apart.

“Mine,” I repeat and feel her hovering so close to the edge of reason. I want to push her off, to send her into the stratosphere, so I push inside of her and grind against her clit, and she comes undone, crying out my name as she falls over that delicious edge.

“That’s right,” I mutter, satisfied and ready to follow her. “That’s fucking right.”

Later, as we fly toward home, I wrap Polly in my arms and kiss her hair softly. She sighs in sleep, and I want to wake her to tell her I love her so much that my heart might burst with it.

That I can’t do this life without her.

Not anymore.

Never again.

But I let her sleep and close my eyes, falling asleep with her.

“You’re staying at my place tonight,” I inform her as I drive us away from the small airport just outside of Bitterroot Valley.

“Oh, it’s no big deal—”

"It's a very big deal." I take her hand and kiss her knuckles. "I want you with me for tonight. It's two in the morning, and we can curl up in my bed and rest, even if we don't sleep. I want you nearby."

I cast her a look in the darkness of my truck, and she smiles softly at me.

"Okay, I'd like that. We can go back to real life tomorrow."

"I don't know if you've noticed, but this *is* real life."

"It feels like something out of my wildest dreams," she murmurs with a small laugh and settles back against the soft leather. "Have I thanked you for the past week or so?"

"Only about seventy times."

"Seventy-one, then." She kisses *my* hand now. "Thank you, Ryan Wild, for the best week of my life."

Her sweet words fill me with happiness. "It was absolutely my pleasure. We'll do it again next year."

She laughs now and shakes her head.

"Let me recover from *this* year before we start planning the next one. I'll have to add a new closet on to my house for everything we bought."

If I have my way, she won't need to. I'll be building her a closet at *my* house, where she belongs.

I turn onto my road, and the gate slides open smoothly. Everything here seems quiet, and I note that Brady's truck is in the driveway as I pull into the garage and park next to Jake's vehicle.

"I'm going to let Jake know I'm home," I inform Polly as she hops out of the truck. "And probably send Brady on his way, too. I'll meet you upstairs. Make yourself at home."

"I think I'll hop in the shower, if that's okay with you."

"Whatever you need, babe." I wink at her and kiss her softly before I open the door to the mudroom and let her precede me inside.

Polly makes her way up the stairs to my suite of rooms, and I break off to the guest room, where Brady's bunked.

I knock on the door and open it quietly.

"It's just me," I say softly. "I'm home early. You're welcome to stay, or you can head on out if you want."

"I'll sleep here," he says, his voice raspy. "Everything good?"

"Had a great time," I confirm. "Thanks for helping Jake out."

"Love the kid," he says simply and falls back onto the bed. "I'll head out around six."

"Sleep well," I reply and back out of his room, shutting the door behind me.

Next, I make my way to my kid's room. It smells like old pizza and stale socks when I walk inside, and it occurs to me that I missed that more than I realized.

"Brady?" Jake asks with a scowl.

"It's me," I say and sit on the side of his bed, folding him into my arms for a hug. "I wanted to let you know that I'm home a little early."

"I'm glad you're home," he says against my shoulder. "You can tell me about it later. What time is it?"

"Two," I reply and ruffle his hair. "Go back to sleep, and take the morning off. I've got the horses today."

"Won't argue," Jake says and flops back onto the bed, instantly asleep. I grin and watch him for a moment, sleeping in the moonlight.

He's such a handsome kid. In the past year that I've known him, he's grown from a boy into a young man. His features are squaring off, less round and child-like. But there's still so much kid in him.

I'm glad that I have a couple more years with him before he goes off to college.

Once inside my room, with the door behind me, I can hear the shower running in the bathroom. As I sit on the side of the bed and sigh with the contentment of being home, I realize that nothing is better than this.

"THIS IS SO *LOVELY*," Polly says the next morning as we sit at the brand-new table in my office, eating bagels with cream cheese and fruit with a side of bacon that I found in the fridge. It was already cooked; I just had to warm it up in the microwave. "Chase did an amazing job on this table."

"I love it," I agree, wondering where in the hell my kid is. I told him to sleep in, but I thought he'd be up by now. I'm eager to have him in here with us.

"How were the horses?" Polly asks as she pops a grape into her mouth.

"Everyone seems fine. It's weird not having Blossom

out there," I admit with a sigh. "And I feel bad that Jake was the one who had to handle that."

"He did a great job," she reminds me just as the boy himself fills the doorway of my office.

"Uh, hi," he says with a frown, looking from Polly to me. "I didn't think we were breaking that in yet."

"It's the first day." I stand and gesture to a chair. "Sit. Eat with us. Did you stock the bacon in the fridge? Excellent and delicious idea. I've decided you get your brilliance from me."

"Yeah." He clears his throat, still not smiling and not sitting. He glances at Polly, then looks over at me and shrugs. "I think I'll just grab something downstairs. I'm gonna go find Russ and goof off for a while."

"Jake—"

"Welcome home," he says, already rushing down the hall before I can say any more.

"Well, shit," Polly says, tears in her eyes. "I think we hurt his feelings."

"Why?" I scowl at her and then look at the empty door again. "For fuck's sake, it's just breakfast."

"At the *new* table, for the first time, after you've been gone for more than a week, Ryan. He was excited to share this with you, and instead, it was *me* sharing it with you."

"That's stupid."

"No, it's not stupid." She stands and crosses to me, taking my hand in hers. "He's just found his comfort zone here, and now I'm taking up space in it. Maybe I should stay away for a while—"

"Fuck that." I turn on her and frame her face in my hands. "You're *not* staying away."

"Why are you so angry?" She frowns up at me, and I take a second to breathe in and calm down. I *hate* the look of betrayal on Jake's face, and I hate that I'm the one who put it there. She's right, I fucked this up.

"I'm not angry." I sigh and tip my forehead against hers. "And I'm the one who fucked up. I didn't mention that you were here last night when I told him I was home. I ambushed him."

"Go talk to him," she suggests and starts to clear what's left of our breakfast from the table. "I'm going to head home. Wait. I don't have a car."

"Take the Aston Martin."

She laughs and shakes her head. "Right. I can call Summer—"

"Just take the car," I repeat. "Seriously, it's not a big deal."

"Fashion Week, private jets, an Aston Martin...all part of my normal life now." She laughs and rises up on her tiptoes to kiss my cheek. "Okay, thanks. Just call me later."

"Count on it."

Polly leaves, and I text Jake to find out where he is.

Me: Did you already leave? Polly just went home, and I'd like to talk to you.

The bubble jumps as he types out a response.

Jake: Made it to Russ's. We're going fishing out at Chase and Summer's house. Be there all day, unless you need me for chores?

I shake my head and feel frustrated because I want to hang out with my kid.

Me: No chores for you today. Take the day off. But we need to talk. Mind if I join you in a bit?

Jake: Not enough bait. But it's a free country.

If the kid was trying to hurt my feelings in return, he did a good job of it. I grab my hat and keys and hurry out to my truck and drive over to the family ranch. When I pull up to a stop at Chase's house, Jake and Russ haven't arrived quite yet.

"Hey," Chase says as he comes outside. "Heard you were back. Did you have fun?"

"Yeah, it was a great trip. How's everything on the home front?"

"Not much going on, actually. Jake texted and asked if he and Russ could come out to fish."

"Yeah, he told me, and I came out to meet him. Need to have a talk."

My brother's eyes narrow. "Is he in trouble?"

"No, we just had a misunderstanding, and I need to apologize. Where's Summer?"

"At her new shop," he says, shoving his hands into his pockets. "She got the go-ahead to move everything in and get it decorated, and I was kicked out. She said she can handle it without me."

"The rebuild took much longer than she thought it would. And turnabout is fair play."

Chase frowns at me. "Huh?"

"You kicked her out of her own house while you were building it."

Chase laughs and glances down at his boots. "Son of a bitch, I hadn't thought of that. Yeah, she's turned the tables on me. She's got her girls down there helping. Should be open next week, finally. She wasn't happy that she had to spend the entire wedding season working out of the nursery when she was supposed to be in her shop months ago."

"Why the holdup?"

"They ran into issues, of course. I warned her that construction is almost never on time, but I was sorry to see that I was right. She did do a good job of keeping the crew in line."

"Good for her." I nod, and then we turn when we hear a truck coming up the driveway. "There they are."

Jake parks next to me, and he and Russ hop out and fetch their poles out of the back.

"Hey, Uncle Chase," Jake says with a nod. "Thanks for letting us fish."

"You never have to ask," Chase reminds him. "Just come on out whenever. Hey, Russ."

"Hi, Mr. Wild," Russ says and then turns to me. "Hey."

"Hello. Jake, I'd like a word."

"Fish aren't going to catch themselves," Jake begins, but before he can breeze past me, I catch his elbow and pull him with me over to the wraparound porch that looks out over the lake.

"Have a seat." I gesture to one of the outdoor chairs, and Jake lowers into it. "Jake, I'm sorry."

That has his head coming up in surprise. "What?"

"I'm sorry," I repeat. "Why did you think I wanted to talk to you?"

"I figured you were going to make *me* apologize for being rude."

"You weren't rude." I frown down at the deck. "You weren't super happy, but you weren't rude. I'm the one who owes you an apology. I didn't mention to you that Polly slept at our place last night, and then you walked into the two of us having breakfast at our spot."

Jake's throat works as he swallows hard, obviously fighting to keep his emotions in check.

"It's fine."

"No, it's not fine, buddy. You and I agreed that we'd test that table out together."

"It's just a table."

"Jake."

His lip wobbles at that single word, and I feel like a complete asshole.

"I don't know why I'm even acting this way," he says and brushes angrily at a tear on his cheek. "It's just a stupid table."

"I missed you, too," I say softly. "And right before you came in, I told Polly that I was excited for you to join us. I'm sorry that you were taken off guard. I didn't mean to do that to you."

"I know." He blows out a breath and wipes his eyes again. "I guess it surprised me, that's all. I figured we'd have our first breakfast at the table today, but instead, Polly got to do that, and maybe I'm just being pushed out of the way."

I gape at him. "*What*? Pushed out of what way?"

"I'm probably a pain in the ass," he continues. "I mean, sure, it was fine when it was just the two of us and everything, but now you'll want to be with her. I get it. She's nice. I'll be eighteen soon, and then I'll be out of your way, so—"

"Stop. Fucking. Talking."

I'm so damn *frustrated* that I have to stand and pace the goddamn porch.

"I don't even know where this is coming from. You were all for the trip to Paris. Everything seemed fine until you came to my office this morning."

"I *am* fine," he says stubbornly.

"You're *not* being pushed out of the way," I insist, my hands balled into fists. "I told you before, you're my kid. *My boy.* I love you, no matter what, even when you're being an idiot."

"Hey!"

"You're my family. Yeah, I have the hots for a woman, and I plan to spend some time with her. Hell, a *lot* of time with her, but that doesn't mean that I wouldn't want you around. If anything, Polly will be joining the two of us."

"Ew."

"Don't be gross." I point my finger at him, and he grins at me. "You know what I mean. Now you *are* being rude. Neither Polly nor myself have ever given you *any* reason to think that we don't want you around. Hell, Polly asked about you every day, and when I said I hadn't talked to you, she called you herself."

"I know. That was kind of nice."

"Then why would you think that we'd want to push you out?"

"Because you'll want to be together, and maybe you'll get married and have your own *real* kids, and I'll just be a third wheel. You did something nice for me, and I'm grateful, but I'm not your real kid, and—"

I pinch the bridge of my nose and decide right this minute that Jake needs a counselor. But before I can make that happen, I simply reach out to take his hand, but he flinches as if I'd hit him.

"Whoa," I murmur and frown.

Jake licks his lips.

"Come here." I pull him to his feet and tug him against me. "*Never* in this or any other lifetime is there a moment when I would lay hands on you; do you hear me?"

He nods against me.

"You are my boy, and I am *not* any of the people you've ever been with before. I'm here to protect you and to love you, and that does not include ever striking you. I'm not even mad at you. I'm concerned, and I want to make sure you're okay."

"I don't think I'm okay," he whispers against me. "I know you don't want to hit me. I know that I'm safe with you. I don't know why I did that."

"Habit," I reply grimly and take him by the shoulders so I can look him in the eye. "We're going to get some help. For both of us."

"Like, a *therapist*?"

"A therapist."

"I don't want to do that. The horses are my therapy."

"Just a session or two," I reply. "Just to work some stuff out. Because, Jake, I'm never going to intentionally hurt you, physically *or* emotionally. I'm very sorry for this morning, and I know Polly is, too. She cried."

"She *cried*?" He looks mortified at that and pushes his hand through his hair. Shit, the kid needs a haircut. "Damn it, I didn't mean to make her cry."

"She cares about you almost as much as I do. So, the next time we hurt your feelings, you need to stay and tell us so. Tell us *off*. But give us the chance to make it right."

He sniffs, wipes his nose on the sleeve of his green flannel shirt, and nods. "Yeah, okay. It hurt my feelings when you were eating breakfast at our table."

"I figured that out." I grin at him ruefully. "I'm damn sorry, Jake."

"Okay," he says and clears his throat. "Can I still fish with Russ, or should I go apologize to Polly?"

"You could text her," I suggest and clap him on the shoulder. "Go fish. Russ doesn't look like he knows what he's doing."

"He's shit at casting," Jake says with a grin. "Okay, I'll text her. Thanks, Dad."

"You're welcome."

Jake hurries off to help Russ with his casting, and Chase joins me on the porch.

"Being a father is fucking hard," I say as we watch the boys.

"That's what I hear," he says, shoving his hands into his pockets. It's a beautiful fall day, blue skies and warm, although I can feel the hint of cooler weather in the air. "You get it figured out?"

"Looks like it. For now, anyway. He expects me to drop him for the next good thing, and when I wanted to pat his shoulder, he flinched, like I'd fucking *hit* him."

"Damn," Chase whispers. "Those assholes did a number on that poor kid."

"His bio parents did, too," I say softly, sure that Jake can't hear. "He hasn't had much good in his young life."

"Then, we'll keep giving him the good," Chase says, and I'm grateful for my brother and the knowledge that my family has accepted Jake to be one of theirs. "Until that's what he's used to."

CHAPTER NINETEEN
POLLY

"I think this is what driving like the proverbial granny is like," I mutter to myself as I pull onto the highway, scared to death that I'm going to do something to hurt Ryan's gorgeous car.

I'm as bad as old Mrs. Wilburn, the lady who drives twenty-five miles per hour on this highway.

With my lip gripped in my teeth, I press the accelerator and feel my eyes bug out when the sexy little car picks up speed and *wants* to get me a speeding ticket.

Careful not to go too far over the limit, I make my way into town, loving the way the powerful vehicle handles, and wonder if I could borrow this more often.

Then I shake my head. It's too much responsibility. If something happened to this thing, I could never replace it.

It's a beautiful Saturday morning as I coast into Bitterroot Valley. My first instinct is to swing by the shop, but then I shake my head.

"You planned to stay away until Tuesday," I remind myself. "The least you can do is give it until Monday to jump back in."

But I do let myself drive by real quick to take a peek of the outside. I like the new display in the window, and everything looks fine from here, so I sigh in relief and continue on to my house.

I notice that the grass has been freshly mowed when I pull into the driveway, and I make a mental note to pay my neighbor boy later today.

I grab my purse and am sure to lock the car when I close the driver's door and head inside. After unlocking the door, I push inside and stop cold, blinking slowly.

All of my packages from Paris, along with my luggage, are sitting neatly in my living room, waiting for me.

"Who the hell delivered those?" I wonder out loud and make another mental note to ask Ryan exactly that when I talk to him later.

I will admit, though, that it's nice to have them here already, and I can unpack and sort and stow away everything when I'm ready to. I can't *wait* to admire all my new clothes and bags and shoes.

"Was it a dream?" I murmur, and then look over at the bags from Dior, Chanel, Louis Vuitton, and Hermès and decide that it was *very* real.

With a happy sigh, I turn to go back to my bedroom and then pause once more when I realize that the living room is now open to the kitchen, and it's *finished.*

The entire renovation is done, and my brand-new

kitchen, which looks like it came out of a freaking magazine, is decorated and looks like it's been this way for years.

"What in the actual hell?" I mutter as my feet slowly carry me toward the new space. First of all, I love that it's now open to the other room. It feels so much bigger, and the tones of cream and sage green, with pops of pink here and there, are just so...*pretty*.

The lower cabinets are painted that lovely green, with the uppers cream, and the countertop is a gorgeous white marble. The appliances are top-of-the-line stainless steel, and even the light fixture is new.

"How did they manage to do all of this in a week?" I wonder as I stand here, just on the other side of the island, and turn a circle, taking it all in. There's no sign that any construction took place at all.

How?

I mean, sure, he's wealthy, but how did Ryan pull this off?

I shake my head in wonder and then step around the amazing new island to open cupboards and explore. My old dishes are there, but there are some new ones mixed in, too. New small appliances, and I realize there's a door that wasn't there before.

Upon opening it, I find a freaking *pantry*.

"Is he a wizard?" I turn again in awe. He managed to have a pantry added on, and my house isn't that big.

I cross my arms over my chest and turn so I can see the whole space, the kitchen and living room, and when I see all the bags and boxes from our trip, my heart starts to beat faster.

This is a *lot.*

Add in the air conditioning he had installed not long ago, and Ryan Wild has spent a shit ton of money on me.

I frown and tap my finger to my lips.

"I wonder how much the trip cost." I cross to my carry-on bag and pull my laptop out, open it, and find the website for the Ritz Paris, then price out what the *Suite Coco Chanel* costs each night.

"Holy fucking shit." I cough, practically pee my pants, and have to back away from the computer.

It's suddenly hard to breathe in here, so I grab my purse and walk outside, but frown at the Aston Martin, which is blocking my garage.

I don't want to drive that.

So, I set off on foot toward downtown. I need to see Summer. She texted me the other day and said that she's at her shop pretty much twenty-four seven as she gets ready to reopen, so I figure she's probably there already this morning.

Even if she's not, I need to clear my head.

Bitterroot Valley is beautiful any time of year, but I especially love it in the fall. The leaves have started to change color, and some are even falling to the ground.

I rub my arms, wishing for a sweater, and then sigh.

Of course, I forgot it at home. I forget everything.

But it's not long before I'm turning down Main Street and knocking on the door of Paula's Poseys. Summer comes around from a back room, smiles, and hurries over to unlock the door for me.

"You're home!" She wraps me in her arms and holds on tight. "I'm *so* glad you're home."

"Me, too, actually," I reply. "I know I'm interrupting and you're busy, but—"

"Get in here." Summer yanks me by the hand, pulls me into the shop, and locks the door behind us, setting an alarm. Her husband, Chase, is a stickler when it comes to alarm systems. "I want to know *everything*. Did you bring your new stuff to show me? Where is it?"

"At home," I reply with a laugh. "It's too much to bring to you. You'll have to come over later, and I'll unpack it all and show you as I put it away."

"Wow." Summer wiggles her eyebrows. "*Score*. I can't wait to see. Did you have a magical time?"

"Yes." Of that, I'm certain. "We had a great time, and Paris is amazing. It was everything I'd ever hoped for."

"Aww." She sighs happily. "You're going to make me cry."

Suddenly, Summer's dog, Lily, saunters out of the back and hurries over to me to get some pets.

"Hello, beautiful girl." I squat so I can give Lily attention, and the French bulldog happily licks at my face. "I missed you, too. Yes, I did. Are you a good girl?"

"Did you have all the French sex?" Summer inquires.

"Oh, yeah. Lots of that." I laugh and stand, and Lily finds her dog bed, curls up, and immediately begins to snore. "Those Wild men...the orgasms are *intense*."

"I know." Summer winks at me. "And bless them for

it. Tell me *everything*. I want to know about the shows and the parties and the celebrities you met! Oh, and don't forget to fill me in on the story of this."

She opens up her phone and turns it to face me, and there's a photo of Ryan and me. I'm in the green dress, and he's kneeling next to me. He had just fastened the strap of my shoe, and his lips are planted on my calf. My red lips are tipped up in a half smile as I gaze down at him.

My stomach clenches. I have to frame that picture.

"That might be the sexiest photo I've ever seen," Summer continues and fans her face.

"Will you send this to me?"

"Of course." She taps the screen again, and then my phone dings in my pocket. "There you go. Now, spill it."

"I will. I promise. I'll tell you every single detail, and I'll use all the dirty words—"

"Because you're my person."

"But I need some advice first."

"Oh." She blinks and then frowns as she *really* looks at me. "You're a little pale. Are you okay?"

"I'm...confused."

I lean on her new countertop and drop my head in my hands. Tears threaten, and before I can ask, there's a tissue under my nose.

"Come on, tell me what's going on. Was he mean to you? I'll kick his ass. He's my brother-in-law, and I love him, but that doesn't mean I won't kick his ass."

I laugh through the tears and shake my head. "No, he wasn't mean at all. The opposite, actually. Summer, he's just so...*generous.* I looked up how much it costs to stay in that suite per night, and I *know* they increase the price during fashion week. That alone was in the six figures. He bought me *everything* I wanted. If I looked at it, he signaled for the sales associate to put it aside for me."

"Atta boy, Ryan," she says smugly, but I shake my head.

"Then I came home just a bit ago, and my entire kitchen renovation is *done.* Completely finished, and it wasn't a minor thing, Summer. It was a big project, and he managed to make sure that it was done by the time I got home. It's even decorated, and there are new dishes and stuff in the cabinets."

"Wow," she says, blinking in surprise now. "It took me three months longer than I was contracted for to get this place done."

"I know! So, how did he do that?"

"Honey, I don't think you quite understand just how rich Ryan is. I don't think there's much out there that he can't make happen."

"Isn't that weird? It's weird, right?"

I pace away from her now, on a roll.

"He had the AC installed in one day. And then this with my kitchen. And when I got home, all of my luggage and bags and boxes from Paris were in the middle of my living room, waiting for me. *Who* did that, Summer?"

"Mac has a key to your house," she reminds me. "Ryan probably texted him and asked him to unlock the house so everything could be delivered. It's not magic. He's not some kind of wizard."

"I think he is." I let out a deep breath. "And this morning, we hurt Jake's feelings. We didn't mean to, but we were having breakfast at the new table, and when Jake walked in, his face was just crestfallen, Summer. That was supposed to be a special thing for the two of them, and there I was, horning in on it. I felt *so guilty*. They're just hitting their stride together, and they don't need me messing it all up for them."

"Wait, are you telling me that you don't want to be with Ryan?"

"No." I shake my head and then sigh, feeling tears coming again. "This jet lag is stupid."

"Oh, honey." Summer hurries around the counter to pull me in for a hug. "You're overwhelmed; that's what this is. And I get it, that's a lot, even if it *is* all good stuff. Except the part about Jake. That sucks."

"I feel so guilty," I admit out loud for the first time. "I feel guilty that I'm pulling some of Ryan's attention away from Jake because that kid *deserves* every bit of Ryan's attention, Summer."

"I know he does."

"I should have known better." I pull away from her and dab at my eyes. "I *knew* that they hadn't used it yet. I knew. But I was in this haze of hangover from the best trip of my life and all the amazing sexy time and how good I feel when I'm at Ryan's house, or just with him at all, and I was thoughtless."

"Uh, Polly? You were simply human. You'd just traveled a long way, it was morning, and you wanted breakfast. Cut yourself some slack."

"You didn't see his face."

"That's fair. I didn't. Okay, you need to chat with Jake. What else do you feel guilty about?"

"Make that guilty *and* ungrateful," I say as I wipe my hand down my face and lower myself into a new chair in the corner of the store. "You put chairs in here?"

"For the brides," she confirms. "When they come in for consults."

"Oh, smart. Love that. Good idea. Anyway, he dropped too much money on me. Not just on Paris, but on my house, too. It's too much, Summer. We're just dating. We're not engaged or married, or anything like that."

"But you're exclusive, right?"

"Well, yeah. I mean, we haven't said the words, *we're exclusive*, but we're not seeing anyone else. And exclusivity doesn't mean that he should drop hundreds of thousands of dollars on me."

"Okay, I'm going to be real with you here," she says with a sigh. "I've said it before, and I'll say it again. I don't think you really understand just how wealthy that man is. Polly, he's not simply rich. He's filthy rich. The filthiest rich there is. What he's spent on you? It's pocket change for him. He'll never miss it."

"I—"

"Whoa." She puts up a hand, stopping me. "I love that you don't want to take advantage of him, but you're not, Polly. Ryan is a generous guy. He paid for a good portion of our house."

I feel my eyes go wide. "What? Why?"

"That's between Chase and Ryan, but I think part of it was as simple as because he loves his little brother and wanted to buy him a house." Summer shrugs. "I don't know. I wasn't there for that conversation. He's generous, and he *likes* to give like that."

I worry my bottom lip with my teeth. "He did tell me that his love language is gifts."

"He didn't lie," she confirms. "He's not trying to impress you or buy you. He just wants to give you nice things. And he *can*. It's actually really romantic."

"And really overwhelming."

"Do you hate the kitchen? Did he overstep and approve something that you don't like?"

"Are you kidding? It's beautiful. It probably doubled my property value."

Summer laughs. "I can't wait to see it. It's okay to get spoiled. You're not a jerk about it or anything."

"I guess." I sigh, feeling marginally better. "But maybe I should take a few days and keep a little distance. Let Jake and Ryan settle back in and smooth those ruffled feathers."

"I don't know that I agree, but you know them better than me."

My phone pings with another text, and I pull it out to check it.

"This is from Jake," I say, surprised.

Jake: Sorry I was a big jerk. I'm glad you're back and had fun. Dad didn't make me send this.

I laugh and show it to Summer, who grins at me. "I think those boys like you, my friend."

"Yeah, I think they do. Okay, I feel better. Have you been over to my shop lately?"

Suddenly, Summer looks guilty.

"What aren't you telling me?"

"I promised I wouldn't say anything until you were back."

"I'm back now, so spill it."

"Well...oh, hell." Summer shakes her head. "Grace quit while you were gone and left the others in a bit of a bind. They've been working extra shifts to cover, but it's been rough being down two people, you know? I actually went in and helped one afternoon, but I don't really know what I'm doing."

"Holy fucking *shit!*" I can't believe this! "Why didn't anyone tell me? I would have come home."

"That's exactly why no one told you," she says. "Because although it's been tight, they've done it and will continue to do so until you're back to work."

"Which will be *today.*" I check my watch and want to cry. "Shit, that's in an hour. I'd better get home and change so I'm not late."

"Do you think it'll really matter if you're a few minutes late, given that you're not even supposed to be there today?"

"You know what I mean." I hurry to her and hug her close. "Thanks for the advice. I think that I panicked."

"Understandable. Don't get in a wreck on your way home."

"I'm on foot. I don't have my car because I took Ryan's Aston Martin home this morning, and it was blocking my garage with my car inside, so I just walked."

Summer smirks. "Oh, you took the Aston Martin."

"Shut up." I turn and walk away, pausing while she unlocks the door for me. "See you later!"

"Good luck!"

RYAN: *I'm headed to town for a bit. I can pick up the car, if you'd like?*

I grin as I rush out of my house, changed and ready to go to the shop for the day, coffee in hand.

I sit in the car and get situated and then return his text.

Me: Yes! Please take this car back before I do something horrible to it. I'm too clumsy to be responsible for it. I'm headed to work, so you can pick it up in front of the shop.

I sip my coffee and wait while that little bubble bounces as he replies.

Ryan: You're not clumsy, but I'll pick it up at the shop. Why are you working? Thought you were taking a few more days?

Me: Seems there were some issues while I was away, so I need to go in. My vacation is over. I guess that's what happens when you're the boss. I hope you are able to take today off!

More bouncing bubbles, and then,

Ryan: I'm sorry to hear that. I'll pop my head in when I get there. See you soon!

With that settled, I start the car and drive the short

distance downtown, parking in front of my store. When I reach for my coffee, it slips in my hand, the lid pops off, and half of it spills all over this amazing vehicle, drowning my phone.

"You have *got* to be fucking kidding me!" I groan, paralyzed. What do I do first?

I decide that first, I say *fuck* about seven more times, and then I whip my shirt over my head—there's no time to run in for towels—and sop up most of the coffee.

My phone won't even turn on at this point, so I think it might have given up the ghost. I look around, make sure no one is looking this way, and then I rush into the shop. They opened twenty minutes ago, so the door is unlocked.

"I'll be right there," Melissa calls out from the back, and I frown. Melissa *and* Jessica should be here until Katie gets here after school.

I rush over and pull a green T-shirt in my size off of the table and yank it over my head, then pair it with a cute, white button-down shirt to go over it.

I've just finished tucking the tee into my jeans when Melissa comes around the corner, and her face immediately goes white as snow.

"Oh." Her mouth bobs open and closed. "Hi, uh, Polly. Welcome back."

"Thanks." For the first time since walking in here, I look around and feel my anger from earlier fill me up all over again. "Melissa?"

"Yes?"

"What in the actual fuck?"

"I know it's a little messy, and I planned to have it cleaned up before you got back, but with Grace quitting —oh, she quit, by the way—and now Jessica's out, too—"

"Why is Jessica out?"

"Her dad died." Melissa cringes and then shrugs. "She's taking leave until after the funeral next week. So, it's just been Katie and me figuring things out—"

I hold up a hand, stopping her from saying any more.

Suddenly, the bell above the door dings, and I turn to find Ryan striding in, looking fresh and perfect, with no sign of jet lag anywhere to be found.

"Hey, babe," he says with a grin and leans in to kiss me. When he pulls back, his eyes narrow. "That bad?"

"Yeah, I think so. Listen, about your car." I wince and feel close to tears, but suck them in. I'm *so* mad and embarrassed and tired. "I spilled my coffee inside, and I sopped up most of the mess, but it's going to need a detail. I'm *so sorry*, Ryan. I *told* you that I'm not to be trusted with nice things."

"Stop," he says and drags his fingertips down my jawline. I want to lean into him. I want to go home with him and cuddle up on the couch and just *be*. "It was an accident, which could happen to anyone. I'll take care of it."

He's totally calm, as if the fact that I spilled coffee all over that incredible leather interior doesn't bother him at all.

"That's it?"

"What did you expect? That I'd scream at you?" he

asks and shakes his head. “It happens, no biggie. I’ll call you later.”

He kisses me once more, and then he’s gone, and I didn’t even get the chance to tell him that I think my phone was a casualty in the Polly versus Coffee war.

With a sigh, I turn back to Melissa, who’s managed to pull herself together. Something doesn’t feel right here, and I’m determined to get to the bottom of it. I have a feeling that I have some long days ahead of me.

“Come on,” I say with a weary sigh. “We have work to do.”

CHAPTER TWENTY
RYAN

"Poor Polly," Mom says, shaking her head, after I just told everyone about how my girl accidentally spilled her coffee in my car. We're all out at Remington and Erin's place for family dinner, and I've been giving everyone a quick rundown of what happened when we were in Paris and after we got home. "I bet she was beside herself."

"I felt bad for her," I agree, and take a sip of my beer. "I assured her that it was fine, and it's been cleaned since then, but she was pretty upset. Personally, I kind of thought it was funny."

"It's just a car," Holly speaks up. "I spill stuff all the time, and my mom and dad always say that it can be cleaned up."

"That's right," Erin says and leans over to kiss Holly on the head. "Sometimes, things get spilled. No biggie. But the important thing is that you two had a fabulous time. I haven't seen Polly since you got back."

"I did," Summer volunteers. "Briefly. She was...tired."

Summer stares down at her plate and starts shoveling in the food, as if she already regrets saying as much as she did, and now it's my life's mission to find out what's going on.

I haven't heard from Polly at all over the past few days since I picked up the car. She's not returning my calls or texts, and it's driving me fucking crazy.

"When's your next home game, Jake?" Brady asks my kid, who sits up tall and smiles like a loon.

"This Friday," he says. "It would be cool if you guys wanted to come."

"We'll all be there," my dad replies and winks at Jake. "You'll have the loudest cheering section BVHS has ever seen."

"Legit," Jake says with a wide smile. "I'm starting this week and everything."

"Because you're brilliantly talented," Millie says. "And they'd be stupid not to start you."

"Well, duh." Jake grins at my sister, and I want to hug her to thank her for being so awesome to my boy.

They're all amazing with him.

"Hey, Jake," Johnny says, "can we go out back and toss the ball after dinner?"

"Me, too!" Holly insists.

"Sure," Jake says. "I could use some practice anyway."

The kids, excited at the prospect of playing outside after dinner, hurry through their meal, and when we're all done eating, are excused from the table.

"I'll call you in for dessert in a bit," Erin calls after them as the back door slams behind them. "I love Jake. He's so good with the kids."

"He's good at a lot of things," I reply with a nod.

"Then why do you keep leaving him here to fend for himself?" Remington counters, speaking for the first time.

"Rem—" Mom starts, but I lift my hand and hold my gaze on my older brother's.

"What in the hell are you talking about?"

"Someone has to go stay with your *amazing* kid constantly because you're out of town. Can't be bothered to stay home and take care of your responsibilities. Which is pretty typical for you, but now you have someone else to take care of."

"You're out of line," Brady begins, and I shake my head.

"Does my kid look like he's low on attention or confidence or love?" I ask Remington and feel the proverbial knife twist in my back the way it always does whenever Rem decides to take some shots at me. Which is pretty much always.

The rest of the table has quieted, their gazes moving between us.

"I think he deserves better," Rem replies. "Sure, you can give him all the money in the world and a nice house, but you're never here. When you are here, you're in your office."

"You don't know what I do or when because you don't fucking talk to me," I counter. "I'm the villain in your story, end of. I spend a *lot* of freaking time with Jake. Besides, it feels pretty hypocritical for you to throw this in my face when it wasn't all that long ago that your kids spent more time with Mom than they did with you because you were too busy running a goddamn ranch."

"Don't fucking start—" Rem's voice has raised when Dad stands and slams his hands on the table.

"Enough!" His face is red as he stares at both of us, disappointment written all over his face. "I've had it up to my goddamn eyeballs with the two of you swiping at each other. I don't care how old you are, I won't have it. You're both excellent fathers, both run good, loving homes, and you'll shut your mouths on the subject."

"I love my kid," I say, my voice calm again. "More than anything. If you have a problem with the way I parent him, you can come to me in *private*, and we'll have a conversation."

Rem's eyes narrow on me, but he doesn't say anything in reply, and finally, Erin stands and says, "Who wants some pie?"

"I do," Millie says. "Let me help you cut it."

"I'll open a bottle of wine," Mom says as Summer stands to join them. "God knows I need it."

When the women are out of the room, Brady sighs loudly. Chase shakes his head.

Dad continues to glare at us.

"I've told you," I begin, speaking to Rem, "that I'm *sorry* for what went down after Holly was born. I didn't handle it well, and I wasn't there for you the way you needed me to be, and I can't go back and change it. I would pay every goddamn penny I own if I could."

Rem smirks, but I keep talking.

"I regret it every day. It's the *only* thing in my life that I regret. But I can't fix it. All I can do is continue to apologize, even though you won't accept it, and be here. I have a life here, and I'm not going anywhere."

"Unless the mood strikes, and you get on your fancy plane."

"I have a job." My voice is weary now. "And that takes me away for a few days at a time. And yeah, I took a vacation, for the first time in my adult life, with a woman that means a lot to me. Jake understands. The family has helped me immensely."

"He hasn't done anything wrong," Chase says, speaking up. "And just like you, he's doing the best that he can."

"We all are," Brady puts in. "And if you think there's even one of us who minds helping out, or who wouldn't do the same for you, you're an idiot."

Rem sighs and drags his hand down his face. "I apologize for saying what I did in front of others."

And that's the only apology I'm going to get.

"Fine."

Dad sits as the girls return and set dessert on the table, and I can hear Erin calling out the back door for the kids to come in and get their share.

When we're finished eating, Summer and I offer to clean up the kitchen since we didn't help cook, and I take on the task of rinsing dishes and passing them to Summer to be placed in the dishwasher.

“I haven’t heard from her in days.”

Summer sighs. She doesn’t have to ask who I’m talking about. Polly is her best friend, and we both know it.

“She walked into a mess when she got home.”

“She said something about that.” I pass her a salad bowl. “But she hasn’t even texted back. You said something at the table about her being tired, but you were going to say something else.”

She blows out a breath and leans on the counter. “Ryan, Polly is like a sister to me. I can’t betray her confidence.”

“I’m not asking you to. I just want to know that she’s okay.”

“She is. I will say that she was a little overwhelmed on that first morning, and she *was* tired from the jet lag, and she wanted to talk. She didn’t say anything bad.”

That, at least, sets my mind at ease.

“Just give her a few days to catch her breath.”

I nod, and then Remington walks into the kitchen, and Summer frowns.

“Okay, I’m not going to lie. You two and all of your shit make me uncomfortable, so Remington can help with the dishes.”

She wipes her hands on a towel, and then she’s gone.

“Way to scare the women,” I say and return to rinsing dishes. “Did you come in here to tell me that I never should have adopted him? That he'd be better off without me?"

"Jesus." Rem blows out a breath and shuts the dishwasher, paces away and back again. "I didn't mean any of that."

"That's what it sounded like."

"I shouldn't have said it, okay? Jake *is* great, and we all love him."

"I know." I turn to look at him now. "I know you do. You treat him as if he's been here since he was born, and I'm grateful. He *loves* being part of this family. He asked if he could change his last name to ours."

That makes Rem pause. He blinks and shoves his hands into his pockets.

"Do you have a problem with that?"

"No! Fuck no. He *should* have our name because he *is* ours. Jesus, Ry."

"What? Why wouldn't I assume that you'd think that? You can't stand me, and we both know it."

"No, I—"

"So, I won't come to dinners anymore. I'll send Jake and make up excuses about work."

"No. Damn it—"

"I love you." I turn to him, and now it's time for me to shove *my* hands into my pockets because I don't know what else to do with them. "You've always been my best friend, until...well, until. I didn't know what to do, and I didn't feel like I had a choice."

"You did—"

"I know that now. But six years ago? I didn't. I'm

sorry. I hate that one decision lost me my big brother. But I can't have you resenting my kid for it. One of these days, you'll slip and say something in front of him, and he already carries enough baggage from a past that he didn't ask for. I won't ever have you making him feel insecure about this family, Rem. So, I'll stay away because that's what makes you the most comfortable."

"For fuck's sake."

"Looks like you're doing the dishes by yourself."

I walk out of the kitchen and smile at Jake, who looks my way. I see that Chase, Summer, and Brady have already left, so it won't be weird when I suggest to Jake that we follow suit.

"You ready, buddy?"

"Sure. I have homework. Which is stupid."

"I hate homework, too," Johnny says with a knowing nod. That boy has started idolizing Jake, and I think that's pretty damn cute.

"Everything okay?" Jake asks when we're in the truck and headed back to the ranch.

"Sure, why wouldn't it be?"

"It seemed kind of tense when we came in for dessert."

I shake my head and silently curse my brother. "Nah, it's all good. Thanks for humoring the little ones."

"They're okay," he says. "Hey, are you sure it's okay that you have to take on the afternoon chores now that I'm doing football? I could quit and go back to handling it."

"Are you implying that I'm not as good as you at taking care of my own horses?"

I glance over in time to see him grin. "Yeah. Because I *am* better than you, old man. But for real, you're busy."

"So are you, kid. It's fine. Besides, football will be over before we know it, so I say you just have fun. I like doing the afternoon chores."

"You do?"

"Sure. It gets me out of my office and into the barn, and just like you, the horses are my therapy, so it's all good."

"Does that mean we don't have to go to *real* therapy?" There's hope in his voice, but I shake my head.

"No way. We're going next week."

"Well, damn."

"Hey, baby girl," I croon to Lullaby and lean in to kiss her nose. I wasn't lying to Jake. I *do* love being out with the horses. I have since I was a kid. My dad and Rem always called me the horse whisperer.

So, I take my time mucking out their stalls, filling their water troughs and feed bags, and then because I'm not ready to go inside, I take a turn with each of the horses, brushing them down and checking them over to make sure there aren't any injuries or insects causing trouble.

Ladybug nuzzles my shoulder, asking for extra pets

and maybe an apple. I just happen to have one, so I offer it to her, and she happily munches away.

"You're just a precious girl, aren't you?" I pet her neck and kiss her cheek. "You've been good for our boy. Jake sure loves you."

Her head comes around at the sound of his name, and I smile.

"Yeah, you love him, too, don't you? All of you do. I think you've helped each other heal from some shit that no one should have to deal with."

I brush her back, enjoying the feel of her hair under my palm.

When the horses are cared for, I pull my phone out of my back pocket to check it and then swear when there's nothing from Polly.

It's been five days without even one word from her. Summer advised me to let her catch her breath, but I'll be damned if I'll let her ghost me.

If she's decided that a relationship with me isn't what she wants after all, well, she can damn well say it to my face.

Grimly, I make my way back to the house. It's starting to get dark, and Jake should be home from practice soon. He'll want dinner and to tell me all about his day and about how excited he is for tomorrow night's game. So, there's no time now to go find Polly and figure out what's going on.

I'll go to her store tomorrow morning, right after she opens, to have a talk with her.

When I get to the house, I see Mom's SUV parked in

the driveway, and I pick up the pace, waving when she steps out of the vehicle.

"I was just going to call you to see if you were home," she says with a smile. "I guess I should have done that before I drove over here, but it didn't occur to me."

"I was finishing up at the barn. You have good timing. Come on in."

"Okay. I brought you and Jake dinner. I just have to get it out of the back seat."

"I can do that." She opens the back door, and I fetch a big insulated bag and raise an eyebrow at her. "How many are we feeding?"

"You'll have leftovers for tomorrow," she says with a laugh. "I made some clam chowder and fresh bread. There's salad, too."

"Sounds delicious. Thank you."

I follow her into the house and then to the kitchen, and Mom sits on a stool by the island as I unpack dinner and set the pot on the stove to heat it up.

"Jake's not home yet?"

"No, ma'am. He should be on his way soon, though. What's on your mind?"

"What's going on with you and Polly Allen?"

I pause and look at her in surprise. "Excuse me?"

"I know you're both adults, and I think it's wonderful because I've always loved that girl, but I'd like to know. I assume it's serious, since you flew her across the world and bought her a bunch of fancy things."

"It's serious on my part," I confirm. "But I haven't talked to her much lately. She's been busy."

"Are you going to marry her?"

I frown and cross my arms over my chest. "I was not expecting this conversation today."

"I know. I would have asked at family dinner, but unlike your older brother, I don't like putting my children in the hot seat in front of an audience." She smiles widely. "So? Marriage? Babies? I'm not getting any younger, you know."

"Mom."

"What?" She simply holds my gaze, not ashamed by this line of questioning in the least. I think I get my gumption from her.

"I don't feel comfortable telling you that I love her when I haven't even told *her* that yet."

Now Mom's face goes all mushy. "Oh, that's sweet. And what are you waiting for?"

Good question.

I turn on the burner under the chowder and then face her. "You know, not everyone falls in love in the span of a weekend and ends up married just a couple of months after that."

"I was lucky," she agrees with a nod. "But you've known Polly a long time. Her brother is your best friend. It's not like you started out as strangers. Is the sex bad?"

"Mom!" I toss my head back and laugh, and she smiles back at me. "I'm *not* having that conversation with you."

"I think Jake would be an excellent brother."

"I think you're rushing things." I walk around the island to her and kiss her temple. "I love you, Mom."

"I love you, too, my sweet boy. I'm sorry that Remington is so hard on you. You don't deserve that."

"He would say that I do."

"You mark my words: If *anyone* else in the world spoke to you the way he does, he'd punch them out."

"Probably."

She rests her head against my chest and hugs me close. My mom has always given the best hugs.

"I hope you two work it out." She sighs just as Jake comes in and sees us.

"Whoa, what's wrong? Gram? What's going on?"

"Nothing, buddy." I smile at him as Mom pulls away from me and walks over to fold Jake in her arms for a big hug.

"I just wanted to see two of my favorite men and bring them some dinner."

"Do I smell clam chowder?" Jake's eyes brighten at the idea.

"You do," she confirms.

"That's legit. You're the best gram ever."

"I do my best."

CHAPTER TWENTY-ONE

POLLY

I haven't seen Ryan in a week.

It's been the fastest week of my life because all I've done is work, pretty much every waking minute of the day. With both Grace and Jessica gone, it's been almost impossible to stay on top of things, and I'm sticking close to Melissa because I was right not to trust her. After getting a second set of eyes on things, I'm finally able to prove what I suspected was going on.

And I know that Ryan's been just as busy. He's got to be buried in work and has the ranch to see to. Jake is playing football in school, so they've had a lot going on. I'm definitely going to the game tonight, no matter what. I'll close the shop early if I have to.

"Are you still mad at me?" Melissa asks as I walk into Pocket Full of Polly with my arms full of apple tart cookies, fresh from Jackie's bakery.

"I'm not happy," I reply and immediately walk over to the sideboard, where I set the cookies out on display for customers. “I get that you wanted me to have fun without worrying, but this is my *business.* This is my livelihood. I have a right to know every single thing that happens, no matter where in the world I happen to be.”

“You’re right,” Melissa says, holding up her hands. “I made the wrong call, especially after Jessica had to be gone for bereavement. I should have at least told you what was up but that I was handling it.”

“But you *weren’t* handling it, Melissa,” I counter and turn to her, my arms crossed over my chest, more than ready to have this conversation and get this woman out of my shop. “This place was a *mess* when I came in on Saturday. There were piles of clothes that needed to be folded and hung up, the floor was filthy, and even more clothes were left in fitting rooms. Don’t even get me started on the fact that you didn’t even close out the till at the end of the day.”

“I couldn’t stay twenty-four seven,” she says and rolls her eyes. “Even *I* have to sleep, Polly.”

“We weren’t *that* busy. Summer is over, and the bulk of the tourists left with it. How is it that you were so slammed that you couldn’t run a vacuum over the floor or hang up product?”

“Oh, so you abandon your business and then question the way it’s managed when you’re gone?”

“THAT’S MY WHOLE GODDAMN JOB, MELISSA!” I can’t believe I just yelled like that, but now I’m fucking *furious.*

“I don’t need to stand here and be yelled at like this. I might just quit.”

"You don't have to. You're fired." Holy shit, that felt good.

Her jaw drops. "You can't fire me."

"Oh, trust me, yes, I can. And I just did. You did a pissy job of looking after my business while I was gone. I spoke with Katie last night."

Now her face goes sheet white.

"She told me that Grace quit because you were a complete bully and a jerk to her about changing the shifts that *I* laid out before I left. I also know that you threatened Katie if she told me. Well, she did, and she doesn't care that you know, because Katie has balls. *Katie,* the sixteen-year-old, is the one I trust. I also know that you stole money and product from me while I was gone, and I'll be pressing charges."

"You can't prove—"

"Yes, I *can* prove it, Melissa. We took in a combined total of over twelve hundred dollars in cash sales in the week that I was gone, but not *one* red cent was deposited into the bank account. There were no deposits made in the night drop the way there was supposed to be."

"Maybe that was Katie," she says, but she won't look me in the eye.

"Both *you* and Katie signed off on the slips at the end of the day," I reply, watching her closely. "And I find that weird because you didn't actually close out the computer at the end of the day, so you were messing with numbers there. But I left *you* in charge of making those nightly deposits."

She licks her lips, still not looking at me.

"Leave the key on the counter, get your things, and get the fuck out of my place."

With her face blazing red now, she turns on her heel and marches into the back room. I stay close, wanting to watch her every move, but she simply takes the key off her key ring and drops it onto the floor—classy—and then stomps out of the shop.

This means that I'm down to just me and Katie, and Katie only works after school and on Saturdays, so I have to hire someone new soon.

"That was fucking hot."

I whirl, my heart thumping, and I'm shocked to see Ryan standing next to a table of T-shirts, his arms folded over his impressive chest.

"Holy shit, Ryan." I cover my mouth and take a deep breath. "You scared the shit out of me."

"I came in when you were screaming at that former employee," he says. "I have to say, watching *you* in boss mode is pretty damn arousing."

I shake my head and sigh. "She fucked up."

"Big time. I miss you, babe."

Without another word, I walk to him and into his arms. He hugs me close and rocks us back and forth, and for the first time in a week, my system settles.

"I miss you, too."

"I thought maybe you were avoiding me."

I tilt my head back so I can look up—way up—at him. "No, it's a shit show around here, as you can plainly see. There have been some long days. And maybe I was giving you and Jake a little time to settle back in."

"We're settled." He cups my face in his hands and leans in to rest his lips on mine. "I told you before that you wouldn't stay away."

"I'm not doing that," I assure him and step back so I can pace a little. "I admit, after I got home on Saturday, I had a minor case of being overwhelmed, and it took me a minute to settle. Okay, maybe I'm still figuring it out. You've done too much, Ryan."

"You don't like the kitchen? The photos are great, but if you don't like it, I'll have—"

"What's not to like?" I interrupt. "It's freaking amazing. But I told you not to go overboard."

He simply smiles at me, and I can't help but laugh.

"Anyway, just as I was getting the being overwhelmed thing under control, I found out about what was happening here, without my knowledge, and I went into full-blown boss bitch mode."

"You didn't answer my calls."

"My phone died."

"And you didn't charge it for a week?"

"No, it *died* when I spilled the coffee in your beautiful car—just let me know what I owe you for the detail—and I haven't had time to replace it. And *no.*" I point at him and narrow my eyes. "You're not going to have one brought to me."

"Why not? I can have one here in about thirty minutes. Also, you don't owe me anything for the car."

"I can order the phone myself." I'm not even going to argue with him over what it cost to clean that gorgeous car.

"You just told me you don't have time." Now those hazel eyes narrow, and he looks irritated. "Polly, if you've decided that—"

"Stop." I shake my head and push my fingers through my hair in agitation. "Don't even finish that thought because it's *not true.* I haven't changed my mind about you, and I won't have you say those words out loud. I know I messed up this week, and you didn't deserve that, but that bitch basically tried to make me go out of business. Even if that wasn't her real intent, that's the way it would have gone if she'd stayed in charge another day. You understand business. So, rest assured, I'll get online today and order a new phone. It'll be here tomorrow."

"So, what's wrong with me having it delivered to you *today*? I can take that off of your plate, Polly."

"I can do this," I insist and hear the stubbornness in my own voice. "I can handle it. But I do need to thank you for the kitchen."

"No, you don't."

"Yes, I do. Thank you for the kitchen. I've barely been home long enough to look at it, but it's seriously beautiful, and I probably don't deserve it."

"Of course, you deserve it. I'm glad you like it. Did you get everything unpacked from the trip?"

"Only the bare necessities from my luggage." I sigh and feel close to tears *yet again* and make myself rein it in. *What is with all the waterworks lately?* "I think between the jet lag and coming into what I did here at the shop, I've just been too tired. I got home last night around ten and immediately went to sleep, and then I was up and back at it at seven this morning. How about you? Are you all caught up on work?"

"Not even close." He smiles now, and I feel some of the tension between us melt away. "But since I haven't been able to reach you, I decided to come find you and make sure you were okay."

"I'm sorry." I return to him and hug him once more, practically clinging to him. "I really am. I'm not ghosting you or anything. I'm just getting a grip on some stuff. But Jake's game is tonight, and I'm absolutely going to that."

"I'll save you a seat in the Wild section," he says before kissing the top of my head. "Right next to me."

"That sounds like a fun section."

"It's the best, complete with grandparents, kids with missing teeth, and a bunch of men who will yell at the coaches *and* the refs a whole bunch."

"That's my kind of party. Thanks. I'll be there."

"I can't wait." He kisses me, his hands framing my face, and I give myself over to him, enjoying the way he feels. God, I've missed him even more than I realized.

Suddenly, the bell dings over the door.

"Well, maybe I should come back."

"Hi, Mom," I say without looking away from Ryan. She said she'd be stopping by first thing to shop for some dresses. "Come on in."

"I was just about to go," Ryan says as he backs away and then smiles over at my mom. "It's always good to see you, Mrs. Allen."

"Hello, Ryan. How are you and your sweet boy doing?"

"We're great, thank you. Mac mentioned that he took Jake over to your house for dinner one night while we were gone."

"I just love that kiddo," Mom says with a warm smile. "He's welcome at our home anytime. I hope that next time you'll come with him."

"I'd like that."

Am I wrong, or did my mom just invite my boyfriend over for dinner?

"Let's make it for next Sunday," Mom continues, and I can't help but smirk. Yep, that's my mom for you.

"I think that works for us," Ryan agrees. "Thanks for the invitation. What can we bring?"

"Just yourselves. How does pot roast sound?"

"Like my favorite. I'll see you then." He smiles down at me now. "Don't work too hard today, babe. I'll see you later."

He brushes his fingertips down my jawline, and then he's off, and my mom sighs after him.

"I've always liked Ryan," she says. "It would be great if he was an official member of the family."

"Whoa." I hold up a hand and shake my head. "We're barely dating, so let's not get ahead of ourselves."

"He took you to Paris and remodeled your house," she reminds me as she admires a purple dress that is all wrong for her. "I'd say it goes past *barely* anything, but I will say that Ryan's mom, Joy, and I had lunch last week, and the two of us couldn't be happier."

"Did you two already plan the wedding?" Mom's head whips around, her eyes full of joyful hope, and I roll my eyes. "I'm being sarcastic, Mom. He didn't pop the question or anything."

"Well, what's he waiting for? That's what I want to know. Anyway, I really need a dress for this book club party we're having next weekend."

"I think I have just the thing."

For thirty minutes, I help Mom pick out some things to try on, and when she's tucked in the dressing room, I open my computer to order my new phone. Ryan's right. I need to take care of it right away, and I'm impressed that no one has shown up to magically hand one over since he left.

After placing my order, I check my email and frown. There's a new message from *Unknown Sender*, no actual name, and when I open it, it simply says:

I warned you.

"Darling, I think I found the one!"

"I'll be right there!"

Something tells me not to delete this. Instead, I just close the computer and go see which one Mom has decided on.

She does a quick twirl in the rust-colored dress, making the fabric swirl around her legs, and I grin. That's the one I would have chosen, too.

"I love it," I tell her. "You'll be the best dressed one there."

"I think so, too. I'll take it."

While she changes back into her other clothes, I take a minute to call Grace and see if she'd be willing to come back to work.

"Hello?" Grace says.

"Hi, Grace, it's Polly."

"Hi, Polly," she replies softly.

"Hey, I hear that things went *really* sideways while I was gone, and I wanted to reach out to you and apologize. I didn't know that Melissa would behave the way she did while I was gone, and I'm sorry that she made you feel so uncomfortable that you felt that you had to quit."

Grace sighs on the other end of the line. "It's not your fault—"

"Yes, it is my fault. I own this place, and it's up to me to make sure that everyone feels safe while they're at work. I'm sorry that you didn't feel that. I want you to know that Melissa was fired this morning, and I sincerely hope that you'll consider coming back to work for me. I'll pay you your regular salary for the week you lost."

She's silent for a moment. "Gosh, Polly, I would, but I already accepted another job, and I started yesterday."

I close my eyes in disappointment. *Damn you, Melissa!*

"I understand," I reply. "I'll still be sending you a check for the hours you lost last week, and I hope you accept my apology."

"Of course, I do," she says. "I appreciate it, Polly. Take care."

"You, too. Good luck with the new job."

I hang up and blow out a long, gusty breath, just as my mom comes out of the dressing room. I ring her up, giving her the deep family discount, and once she's paid, we decide to walk down to Bitterroot Valley Coffee Co. to get a latte.

"I'll just flip the sign," I tell her, flipping it to *closed*, and lock the door. "I think it's going to be slow today, so this is great."

"What a treat," Mom agrees, lacing her arm through mine, and we walk arm-in-arm down the block. "In all seriousness, I hope you had a good trip. I haven't even heard about it yet."

"I'm sorry, I've been slammed, but yes, we had a really good time. I'll show you my new goodies soon. And you have to swing by to see the kitchen."

"Oh, I saw it," she says with a sly smile. "You know I can't stay away from a rehab. They did an amazing job."

"I swear, it was done by Disney woodland creatures and a fairy godmother, it happened so fast."

"You're not far off the mark," she says with a laugh. "Hey, honey, I heard the call you were on, a few minutes ago. I know you're understaffed right now."

I sigh and shake my head. "Right before you got there, I had to fire Melissa. She was stealing from me while I was gone. So, it's just Katie and me until I find someone."

"I'd like to be that someone," Mom says, shocking the hell out of me. "I have free hours every week, and I can come help you until you find some permanent help."

I stop on the sidewalk and blink over at her, immensely grateful. "Are you sure? Mom, you don't have to—"

"I'm sure," she assures me and links her arm with

mine once more. "I want to help. I'll come train with you this afternoon."

"You have no idea how much I appreciate this." I trust my mom more than just about anyone, and until she retired late last year, she worked in a service job for twenty years. She's *great* with people. "Thank you."

"You're welcome," she says as we walk into the coffee shop.

"You're a piece of work," I hear Millie say, but she's laughing and actually *smiling* at Holden Lexington, who's leaning on the counter, smiling back at her.

"I just call it like I see it."

"Well, you need glasses."

Millie looks over at us and clears her throat, pastes a scowl on her face, and squares her shoulders.

"Do you want coffee or not?" she asks Holden.

"Just the house blend," he says, that smile never wavering. I have to admit, Holden Lexington is *hot* with a capital H, all tall and dark, with that chiseled jawline and muscles for days.

It's too bad that the Lexingtons and the Wilds have been rival families for the past hundred years. They're obviously hot for each other; you can tell by the body language when we walked in, and I've seen Holden bring her flowers or just gaze at her longingly when he thinks no one's looking.

Of course, when someone *is* looking, they bicker like cats and dogs.

Millie pours the coffee, then sets it on the counter for him.

“That’s five dollars.”

Holden lifts an eyebrow. “For *drip coffee?*”

“Inflation is a bitch,” she says with a fake smile as Holden passes her a twenty.

“Keep it,” he says as he pushes away from the counter and walks toward the door. “Ladies.”

“Hey, Holden,” I reply with a smile. “Have a good day.”

“Off to a good start.” He winks at me, and then he’s off.

“Why do they fight it?” Mom whispers.

“You know why,” I whisper back, and then turn to Millie. “Hey, I need a latte, stat.”

THE GAME STARTED thirty minutes ago, and I’m *so mad* that I missed the beginning, but I’m going, and I’ll see Jake after so he knows I was there.

He texted me this afternoon to make sure I’d come see him play, and I assured him I would.

I will *not* break that promise.

I rushed home from work and changed my clothes, stuffed a granola bar down my throat, and now I’m jogging the block and a half to the football field. There are moments like this that I’m grateful that I live so close to the high school. It’s an easy trek, and I don’t have to drive and find parking at the field.

A bright red sports car drives past slowly, and I frown. I’ve never seen that car before. They must not know exactly where they're going. I shrug and keep on walking, and I can hear the music from the pep band and the cheers of the crowd. Friday nights haven't changed a bit in Bitterroot Valley over the past century. The town loves its football team.

To my surprise, the same sports car makes the corner in front of me, still moving slowly.

"I wonder what they're looking for," I wonder out loud. But then, they press on the accelerator and zoom off down the street. "Idiot."

The lights are shining as I approach the tall fence that borders our small field. I pay the volunteer to get in, and then my eyes scan the home bleachers to find the Wild family.

"Polly!" I look up at the sound of my name and see all of them waving at me. I happily wave back and make my way up the bleachers.

Man, there are a lot of them up here. Rem and Erin with their two kids. Brady, Chase, and Summer. Of course, Millie and Ryan are here, and Mac's sitting next to Ryan. Abbi even came, and she's sitting next to Erin, with Daisy sitting next to Holly.

The whole gang's here, and I'm thrilled to be a part of it.

Ryan, with his hazel eyes full of happiness, pats the seat between him and his mom, and I plop down and lean into him as he wraps his arm around me and hugs me.

"Hey, sorry I'm late."

"You're fine, things are just getting going," he says and kisses the top of my head. "You okay?"

"Yeah, just rushed, that's all. Seems to be the story of my life lately, but my mom is going to fill in at the shop for a while, and I trained her this afternoon."

"Did I just hear you say that your mom is helping out at your adorable shop?" Joy asks me with a smile.

"Yes, ma'am. I'm severely shorthanded, and she's a godsend."

"Well, I'd love to work there, too," Joy says. "Can I put in an application?"

I blink at her, stunned.

"You want to work at my dress shop?"

"Yes, that sounds wonderful. I can help out until you hire a permanent staff, at least. Your mom and I can get you through this transition, honey." She pats my knee, and I feel tears threaten.

Again.

Jesus, I'm just an emotional wreck lately.

"I would *love* that. Oh, my gosh, thank you. Can you come in tomorrow morning for some training, or is that too soon?"

"I'll be there." She pats me again, and then we turn our attention to the field.

"It's going to work out," Ryan murmurs in my ear and kisses me once more. "You've got this."

I take a deep breath, let it out slowly, and silently agree with him. Things are looking up.

"Okay, what position is Jake playing?"

"He's number twenty-seven," Ryan says, pointing out

to the field. Our boys are wearing green jerseys with gold numbers. "He's a wide receiver."

"Wow, that's impressive."

"He already caught one," Johnny says, practically vibrating in his seat. "And then he got tackled. It was so cool!"

"Tackled?" I look up at Ryan. "I don't like that. They'd better not hurt my boy. I'll kick some ass."

"Easy, tiger," Ryan says with a laugh.

The game is fun. We yell and cheer, and by halftime, the bulldogs are up by ten. When the buzzer sounds, signaling the halftime break, Brady stands and smiles at Abbi.

"Wanna go to the concession stand with me and get snacks?" he asks her.

"Oh, my god, snacks are my love language," she says, standing. "Plus, my butt needs a break from these bleachers. What does everyone want?"

Summer and Chase decide to go with them, to help carry everyone's orders, and I stand to stretch my legs. I'm used to standing all day, so sitting for this long makes my legs cramp up.

"You're the perfect height," Ryan says, pulling me between his legs and wrapping his arms around my waist. I'm not that much taller than him, and he's still sitting down. "I'm really glad you came."

"Me, too. I needed this." I wrap my arms around his neck and hug him. "How was the rest of your day?"

"Productive." He lets me go when I pull away and take my seat next to him. "When is your next day off?"

"I decided to be closed on Monday," I reply. "I need the break, and that's usually a slow day anyway. I want to put my goodies away from Paris and admire my kitchen the way it *should* be admired."

"You definitely need to do that," he agrees.

"How about if you and Jake come for dinner? Wait, you come earlier than that, any time you're free, and we'll have Jake meet us at my place for dinner."

"We'd love that."

Brady, Abbi, and the others arrive with their arms full of goodies, and Abbi passes me my popcorn.

"Thanks," I reply with a grin and watch as Brady glances down to check out Abbi's butt.

Well, well, well.

"I got a hotdog!" Daisy grins adoringly up at Brady. "Thank you."

"You're welcome." Brady boops her on the nose, making Daisy laugh, and halftime is over.

"Here we go, dogs!" I yell as our guys take the field. We get the ball first.

The quarterback snaps the ball and jogs back. Jake's open, so the ball is passed to him. He catches it and runs for the end zone.

We all rush to our feet, yelling and cheering as Jake makes the touchdown. He runs back to his teammates and jumps into them in celebration.

"That's my boy!" Ryan yells, pointing. "That's my kid."

In the next play, our team intercepts the ball,

prompting more elation and cheering, and then Jake takes the field once more.

This time, he's open again, but when he catches the ball, he's immediately tackled.

Hard.

When the other boy stands, Jake doesn't get up with him, and I cover my mouth with my hands, my eyes glued to Jake.

"Get up," I whisper. "Oh, Jesus, get up, baby."

"He's okay," Joy says, taking my hand in hers reassuringly, and I cling to her as Ryan rubs a big circle on my back.

"I need him to get up."

Finally, I see Jake nod, and someone offers him a hand and helps him to his feet. The crowd applauds as Jake walks to the sidelines. He waves up at us, and I breathe a huge sigh of relief.

"Thank Christ," I mutter.

"It's always nerve-wracking watching the boys you love get beat up on the field," Joy says with a knowing smile. "But they're tough."

"I'm gonna hunt that kid's mom down and have words with her."

Ryan laughs out loud and kisses my head. "I don't think that's necessary, but I like the thought."

When the game is over, we've won by twelve points, and everyone pours onto the field to congratulate our team.

Jake comes right over to us, hugs his dad and grandparents, and then he sees me and grins. He marches over and picks me up right off of my feet and hugs me.

"You came," he says.

"Of course, I came. A very important player invited me himself."

He grins widely. "Did you see that touchdown?"

"Yes, and I also saw that tackle. Took ten years off of my life."

"Just knocked the wind out of me," he says with a negligent shrug. "No big. Hey, Dad, is it okay if Russ and a few of the others come out to our place to watch movies and stuff tonight? We have the best house."

Ryan grins with pride. "Sure, bring whoever you want. Be sure to tell them that their parents can call me if they want to."

"Awesome, thanks." Jake grins. "Can we maybe order pizza?"

"I'll handle it," Ryan assures him. "You deserve it after that game."

"Best day *ever*," Jake says as he gives the rest of the family hugs, takes the time to put Holly up on his shoulders, and then Daisy when the little girl doesn't want to be left out, and then he jogs off to join his friends.

"I guess you're hosting a party tonight," I say with a laugh.

"I don't mind. He deserves it."

"Yeah, he definitely does."

"We'll come help," Brady says, indicating himself and Mac. "You'll need it."

"I appreciate it," Ryan agrees and turns to me. "I want to see you soon."

"Oh, don't worry about that. You will."

CHAPTER TWENTY-TWO
RYAN

"I have two rules," I inform the twenty or so teenagers who have gathered at my home after the game. They're sitting in the theater seats in the movie room, and I'm standing down front.

"Let us have 'em," Russ calls out.

"One, there will be no drinking alcohol in my house. If I catch any of you doing that, I'll call your parents right away. I'm a cool dad, but I'm not *that* cool."

Jake snickers at that.

"What's the second rule?" someone asks.

"You have to eat all the food in that kitchen. The pizza, the snacks, the sodas. Because I don't want leftovers."

"You got it, Mr. Wild," someone else calls out. "Thanks for letting us hang here. Is it okay if some of us sleep in here?"

"Have you called your parents? Do they know where you are?"

Several of the boys nod enthusiastically. I'm glad that they didn't bring any girlfriends tonight. I didn't want to have to referee teenage sex in my house.

Christ, I'll never be ready for that.

"If your parents know you're safe and that you're here, I don't care if you sleep over."

"*Yes.*"

"Legit."

"Let's watch the movie!"

I grin at Jake, and he smiles back, and then I make my way out of the room to leave them to it. Brady and Mac are waiting for me outside on the outdoor patio, where there's a fire crackling.

With a Coke in my hand—I'm not going to break my own rule tonight—I open the glass door and step out to join them.

"You have owls," Brady says with a grin. "They've been hooting for the past twenty minutes."

"That's cool." I sip my Coke and sit on the couch, stretching my legs out in front of me, and one of the owls hoots. "I wonder if they're a mating pair."

"Owls mate for life," Mac informs us.

"Thanks for that info, Steve Irwin," Brady says, making me laugh, and Mac tosses a pillow at him, hitting him in the head.

"What's up with you and Abbi?" I ask my brother, who immediately sobers and leans on the throw pillow.

"Absolutely nothing."

"Didn't look like nothing," Mac adds.

"We bought popcorn and hotdogs," Brady says with a scowl. "So what?"

"You're awfully defensive for someone who has nothing going on with the hot single mom," I reply and sip my Coke.

"Abbi *is* hot," Mac agrees. "Nice curves on that one. Good hair. I'll bet she's fun—"

"Okay, shut the fuck up," Brady grumbles and reaches over to snatch my Coke out of my hand, taking a sip. "Why can't we have beer again?"

"Because it's a bad influence on those teenage boys in there."

"Fuck." Brady scowls and stares out into the darkness. "I don't know her, okay? I mean, I barely do. She comes around with Erin and the other girls, and her kid is cute. That's all I know."

"Is that all you *want* to know?" I ask him, and my brother continues to scowl.

"She has a kid."

"So?" Mac and I ask at the same time.

"You already said she's cute, and you're good with the kid," I add.

"It just adds a level of responsibility. Sure, I'd like to take her to bed. She's...well, she's every man's fucking wet dream, but she's a mom, and you don't fuck around with that."

"At least you know that much," Mac says with a shrug. "Maybe you want more than to fuck around."

"No time for that," Brady replies, shaking his head. "I'm practically married to the rodeo. When I'm not there, I'm working the ranch, and I eek out a few minutes here and there to see the family. That's it. A woman takes too much time."

I think of Polly and all the time that I've missed with her this past week.

"Sometimes, you *want* to give them your time."

"I know, and that's what I'm saying. I don't have it to give. So, it's not even worth talking about. Are you seeing anyone, Mac?"

"Fuck no," my best friend says, shaking his head. "No time for that shit." Brady and I both bust up laughing at that answer.

"Hell, I don't necessarily have time," I reply and drag my hand down my face. "And the past week, there has been *no* time together because of her business, but sometimes you have to just make it the priority. I want to see her. So, I get up at two in the morning to work, or I don't go to sleep at all."

"You don't *sleep*?" Brady demands.

"If that's what it takes."

"Never thought I'd see the day," Brady says, shaking his head.

"Be careful what you say next," Mac warns him. "He's dating my *sister*."

"That's right." Brady laughs again. "Well, that's kind of cool. At least you know you like her family."

"True. I do."

"And you wish she was here instead of us," Mac guesses. I simply grin at him, and he busts up laughing. "Totally cock blocked you there."

"It's not like I would have sex with her with twenty kids in my house," I point out, and Mac scowls.

"I like to think that you *don't* have sex. You just play gin rummy or something."

"You go on thinking that. It's absolutely *not* true, but if it helps you sleep at night, you stick with it."

"Damn," Mac grumbles.

"Is it good?" Brady asks with a grin. "The gin rummy?"

"Best gin rummy I've ever had."

"Okay, I'm outta here," Mac announces and abruptly stands. "We've crossed a line."

"Like you've never played gin rummy," I call after him as he walks away, around the house toward his truck in the driveway.

"Fuck off," he calls back, and Brady and I dissolve into laughter again.

"That was fun," Brady decides after a minute.

"It was too easy," I add.

"Is it going to get weird between you and Mac if things progress with Polly?"

"I hope not." I frown. "So far, things have been normal. I just won't talk about boning his sister every chance I get."

"Good plan. You don't want him to punch you out."

"So, you're really *not* going to ask Abbi out?"

"No." He sighs deeply. "I'm not. End of."

"Okay." I hold my hands up, palms out, as if in surrender. "I'll drop it."

"How's your security situation been? I know there were issues for a while."

"I had a meeting with the team this morning. It's been mostly quiet for months now, so we're going to lighten up on things a bit, at least here at the house. One man on duty at a time. With the cameras and everything, I'm comfortable with that."

"Good. I'm glad to hear that things are calming down. People are just weird, man."

"You're not kidding."

"I think I'll head home. I have a ride tomorrow afternoon, and I should probably get some sleep."

"I wish you'd let us come watch you," I reply and hear the frustration in my voice. Brady has ridden bulls for *years*. He competes nationally and makes good money doing it.

But he won't let the family come watch him.

"No," he says, shaking his head. "And you know why."

"Seriously, Brady, nothing's going to happen to you. You're safe, and you're good."

"If something *did* happen, I don't need my family watching me die in that arena. It's nonnegotiable."

"You invited Jake a few weeks ago."

He shrugs. "I wanted him to see how they handle the animals, but when it was my time to ride, I made him leave."

I frown. Jake didn't tell me that part.

"We're proud of you," I tell him as we both stand. "All

of us are. And if you'd let us, we'd be up in those stands, cheering, just like we did for Jake tonight."

"I know." He nods and pats my shoulder. "I know you would. But I can't risk it. Besides, this way, I'm not distracted by whoever's in the stands. I can just do my job and focus on the bull. Eight seconds of work, no distractions."

"You're fucking badass. You know that, right?"

"Of course, I know that." He grins, and I walk him around the house to his truck. "Call me if you need me."

"Same goes." We always say the same thing, even if we don't plan on needing each other.

It's just what brothers do.

After I wave him off, I walk into the house and up to my observatory.

I won't be sleeping tonight. Not because I have kids here, but because I can just tell that it's going to be a night that I'm awake, so I open the glass roof, grab my glasses and iPad from the storage cubby, and bring the screen to life.

It's a good night to look at the sky.

CHAPTER TWENTY-THREE

POLLY

I can't sleep.

I *want* to sleep, and I absolutely should be out cold by now because it's after midnight and I've been working myself ragged, but I just can't drift off. There's nothing wrong. The house is peaceful, and I'm tired, but I miss Ryan.

That's what it boils down to. I simply miss him.

And that's stupid because he's less than ten miles away.

So, I peel back the covers on the bed and walk across the hall to the closet where I pull on some cute burnt orange cropped sweats that I recently indulged in, along with a matching sweatshirt. I pull my hair up into a high ponytail and slip my feet into some white sneakers, then I grab my purse and keys and pull out of my garage.

On the way down the street, I see the tiny red Mercedes sports car I saw earlier parked about two blocks away and smile.

They must have found where they needed to be.

It's a gorgeous night, the sky full of stars, as I drive out of Bitterroot Valley to Ryan's ranch. I don't even pass by any other cars, it's so quiet in town tonight. Of course, I avoid downtown. The bars would be hopping.

Unless I'm with my girlfriends, I've never really been much of a bar hopper.

The gate to Ryan's place glides open as I approach, and I drive through, down the windy driveway, to his beautiful, big house. There are several vehicles parked out front, and I grin at the thought of all those teenage boys inside, enjoying themselves with Jake.

This house *should* be the hub for the teenager and his friends. It's perfect for it, with the movie room, the game room, and all the free space for them to hang out.

I do notice that Mac and Brady's vehicles are *not* here, so Ryan is inside without another adult, and that makes me happy. I can't wait to see him.

I don't bother to lock my car and walk up the stairs to the door, surprised that it's not locked, but then remember that Ryan probably wants the kids to be able to come and go freely. I walk through and don't find him in the kitchen or on the back patio. He's not in his suite of rooms, and then it hits me: He's up on the roof.

With a grin, I climb the stairs and open the door, and when I poke my head out, I see Ryan standing by the telescope, his glasses on and holding his iPad.

"I don't want to startle you," I say softly.

He doesn't jump, but he turns his head to look at me, and a slow smile spreads over his face as he sets his iPad aside, pulls his glasses off, and walks over to me.

"Well, this is a good surprise." He pulls me against him and wraps his arms around me. "Are you okay?"

I love that he's always checking in with me, making sure that I'm fine.

"I'm fine, I couldn't sleep, and I wanted *you.* Just to be with you. I guess I'm needy."

He chuckles and kisses the top of my head before tipping my chin up so he can slant his lips over mine and kiss me soft and slow, making my toes curl in my white sneakers.

He smiles down at me when he pulls back, and I glance over at the telescope. "What are you looking at tonight?"

"Well, if my calculations are right, in about twenty minutes, I'll be looking at the northern lights."

I feel my eyebrows climb. "You're kidding. Really?"

"You're just in time," he confirms and gestures for me to sit on the super comfy couch. He picks up the iPad again before sitting next to me, taps the screen, and I hear the door lock.

"You can lock the door *on your iPad*?"

"Handy, isn't it?" He leans forward to set it on the coffee table, then pulls me into his arms and kisses me again. "I've fucking missed you this week. It was *torture.* I'm usually a patient man, but I hated that you didn't reply to me and that I couldn't see you."

"I'm sorry. I hated it, too, especially because I'd grown so used to being with you all the time, but the week flew by, and before I knew it, six days without you had passed, and, well...if you hadn't come to the shop, I would have found you. I missed you every minute." His hand drifts up under the hem of my sweatshirt, and when he discovers that I'm not wearing a bra, he groans. "I didn't really do that on purpose. I just threw some clothes on so I could come over here."

"I'm glad you did. If I didn't have a gaggle of kids here, I would have come to you. It was great having you next to me at the game, but torture at the same time because I haven't touched you in a week, and I wanted you to myself."

I grin as I toe off my shoes and tug his T-shirt up his torso. He obliges me, pulling it over his head, and I run my fingertips over his smooth, warm skin.

"I love your body," I whisper as I gently caress him. "So strong, so confident. Even though you're so much bigger than me, we seem to fit together well."

"Like you were made for me," he says, watching me with happy hazel eyes as he lets my hand roam over him patiently. "You're so damn beautiful, babe."

I love that he thinks so.

He undresses me so slowly, so patiently, I can't help but wonder what in the hell he's waiting for because it's been a *week*, and I can't wait to strip this man down and get him inside of me.

But when I hurry, he just kisses me and slows me down again.

"You're killing me," I whisper against his lips.

"I'm savoring you," he whispers in return. "Every inch of you. You're such a gift, Polly."

God, he can make my heart stutter with just a couple of words. With just a look, a simple touch.

When I'm naked and laid out before him on the cushions of the couch, the night sky bright above us, Ryan kisses down my neck, between my breasts, over my belly, and then spreads my legs wide so he can kiss me in the most intimate of places.

I arch my back, push my fingers into his hair, and revel in the cool air as it swirls over my bare skin while Ryan does delicious things to me.

"Open your eyes," he says. "And look up."

I do as he says and gasp.

Above us, the sky is alive, dancing with greens and reds, as if moving with the beat of my heart.

I glance down at him, and Ryan smiles at me and then licks me, and I can't help but watch the sky as he takes me up over that glorious peak of release.

Finally, he pushes out of his jeans, and I reach down to grasp onto him as he covers me. He pushes inside of me, and we both sigh in relief, in absolute pleasure, and he fists his hand in my hair as he kisses me again.

"So beautiful," he says against my lips as he starts to move. "So fucking *mine*."

Yes. I'm his. Every bit of me, everything I am, is his. I feel so connected to him in every way; there's no way that I could ever be for anyone else.

It's only Ryan Wild.

"Let me straddle you. I want you to see, too."

He moves swiftly, never pulling out of me, as he sits on the couch, and, with my knees planted on either side of his hips, I set the pace now, rocking and moving on him. He tips his head back on the cushion and glances up, and that magnificent mouth smiles.

"Jesus, this is incredible." He looks at me with so much love in those hazel eyes, it almost drowns me. "Go over, babe. Come on."

"Together." I tip my forehead to his, tightening around him, and his fingertips dig into the globes of my ass deliciously. "With me."

And we do. The climax rocks through us with heat and a power I've never experienced before.

As I catch my breath, with Ryan still seated inside of me, I can't resist looking up again at the dancing lights, sighing in happiness.

"Ryan," I whisper, in awe of this whole night. "It's amazing."

"I love you."

My gaze whips down to his in surprise, and he drags his fingertips down my jawline.

"You do?"

"More than anything." He looks so...*calm* about it, and he cups my cheek and pulls me to him so he can kiss the hell out of me.

"God, I love you, too," I whisper when I come up for air. "For a million reasons. The fact that you love the sky so much is only one of them."

He lifts me off of him and then grabs his T-shirt to wipe us off, and once I'm back in my clothes and he's in his jeans, we cuddle up to watch the show above us. Ryan's fingers are in my hair, combing and stroking, and my eyes are getting heavy.

"I think I might finally be sleepy," I murmur.

"The show is almost finished," he says and kisses my temple. "Do you want to go to bed or stay up here?"

"We should probably go to bed. Or I should go home. I don't want Jake and his friends to see—"

"See what? Two people in a healthy, loving relationship? Fuck that. Besides, you *are* home, Polly."

I frown up at him, but his gaze doesn't waver. "I mean, we *just* said the L word, Ry. I'm not sure I should move in on the same day."

He chuckles and shakes his head. "It doesn't have to be today. I'm patient. But I've felt like you belong here since that first time you came to the ranch."

I sigh and look up at the fading lights. "I do love it here. But I love my little house, too. And you *just* remodeled my kitchen."

"Keep the house," he says. "Rent it out, or use it as a guesthouse. Whatever you want."

"A guesthouse," I murmur, considering. "Not a bad idea."

Suddenly, I'm flat on my back again, and Ryan is staring down at me intently. "Does this mean you're moving in here? I need the words, babe. Spell it out for me."

I caress his cheek, loving the scruff there. I look into his gorgeous eyes and feel the night swirling around us.

The sound of owls call nearby, and I *love* the smell of the woods out here on this ranch.

"First, will Jake be okay with it? Ryan, you're *just* hitting your stride together, and I don't want to fuck that up for you two."

"I will talk to him," he promises me. "We won't ambush him. But he adores you, and I can't imagine him saying no. He's a sweet kid."

"I know he is, and I love him so much. When he didn't get up on the field tonight, my heart stopped. Okay, if Jake doesn't freak out about it, I think the answer is yes. Are we crazy?"

"Crazy in love," he says with a grin, and I groan.

"That's so cheesy."

"I don't give a fuck." He kisses me, harder this time. "I love you to distraction."

"I love you, too."

It's been another busy week, full of training my mom and Joy on all the ins and outs of my shop, but they're doing great, and Katie adores them. Finally, I feel like things are back on track there, and I've been able to relax a bit.

I've decided that I won't press charges against Melissa, but only because a court case would cost more than the cash I lost.

I've been able to see Ryan every night. We haven't started moving my things over yet because he says he wants to have some rooms added onto the house so I can have the closet of my dreams, which is silly to me because there are already a plethora of rooms that I can turn into a dressing room, but he insists that it should be part of the main suite, and who am I to argue? I've learned that Ryan loves this kind of thing, and he's excited.

Besides, it gives us a little more time to talk to Jake. I want to make sure that he's okay with all of this before we move even *one* thing over. Moving slowly works great for me.

I'm bustling about the shop, ready to head out for a couple of hours, when the shop phone rings.

"Pocket Full of Polly, how can I help you?"

"May I please speak with Polly?"

"This is she." I balance the phone with my shoulder as I go through some mail.

"Hi, Polly, this is Willa Hull. I own Dress You Up in Cunningham Falls, and I'm calling for a reference for an applicant."

I frown as I lean on the counter. Cunningham Falls is a cute ski town five hours from here. "Okay, I can help with that. Who's the applicant?"

"Melissa Foss," she says, and I can't reply for a moment. "Polly?"

"Sorry, I'm just taken aback. I fired Melissa only a week ago. Did she move up there?"

"Not yet. She said she's considering a move up this way but that she wanted to secure a job before she made the change. If you fired her, I assume you don't want to give her a good recommendation?"

"No," I confirm firmly. "I absolutely do *not*. She stole from me, Willa."

"Wow. You can prove it?"

"Yes, ma'am. I wouldn't trust her at all, and I do not recommend you hire her."

"Well, I'm glad I called. Looks like it'll be a hard pass on Melissa. Thank you for your time."

"You're welcome."

I hang up and feel like punching something. How does Melissa have the freaking *balls* to list me as someone who might give her a positive recommendation?

Before I can grab my purse to head out, the door opens and in walks Jessica.

"Jess," I say in surprise. "Did you get the message I left, offering my condolences? I didn't want to intrude too much, but I wanted to touch base."

"Yeah," she says, swallowing hard and looking guilty. "I got it. Listen, Polly, my dad didn't die."

I blink at her in surprise. "Excuse me?"

"I made it up." Tears spring to her eyes, and I can feel my mom and Joy pause in hanging dresses across the store to listen in. "It's just...Melissa was *so awful*, Polly. She wasn't just a bully, she was abusive to all of us, and I couldn't take it, but I didn't want to quit because I love this job."

She sniffs, and I feel angry all over again.

"I feel awful for leaving Katie alone with her," she continues, "but that girl has spine. Whenever Melissa got mean with her, Katie would tell her to go fuck herself. I want to be that girl when I grow up."

"Me, too," I mutter, taking this all in.

"I know that I lied, and I'm sorry, but I just couldn't do it. So, if that means that I'm fired, I understand, but I needed to come in and tell you the truth."

"I appreciate that." I sigh, suddenly feeling nauseous, which has been happening a lot lately. "You're not fired, Jessica. The truth is, I *need* you, and I think you do a good job."

She sighs in relief.

"However, if you lie like that again, you will no longer have a position here."

"I understand," she says immediately. "I would *never* do that under normal circumstances. Does...does Melissa still work here?"

"No."

"Thank God." She smiles at me. "Thank you. Thank you *so much*. When do you want me to come in?"

"Tomorrow. You can open with me."

"That's perfect," she says, nodding. "I'll see you then."

After she leaves, I take a look around. Jeez, a lot has happened already today, and it isn't even lunchtime.

"Okay, you guys have everything under control?" I ask as Mom and Joy giggle over folding T-shirts. "I'm headed over to the Iconic Women's Collective meeting if you're okay here."

"Oh, honey, we're great. Besides, Katie will be here in a couple of hours, too. Don't you worry about a thing." Mom smiles over at me and folds a red T-shirt.

"Thanks. I'm so happy you two are having fun."

"Are you kidding? This is the *best* job," Joy replies with a wink.

The phone rings, but when I pick it up, no one answers on the other end. "Pocket Full of Polly, can I help you? Hello? Annoying." I hang up and blow out a breath. That's the third time that's happened this week.

I go into the back and grab my new Chanel bag, then I have to stop by the bathroom.

I've been feeling so queasy the last few days. I haven't actually thrown up, but man, am I nauseous. I haven't been eating much because nothing sounds good, but maybe I'm just hungry.

I'll be sure to eat something at today's lunch.

With my tummy settled for now, I walk out to my car and scowl at the note tucked under the windshield wiper.

You're going to regret this.

It's a handwritten note, and if I'm not mistaken, it looks like Melissa's writing. She must have already heard from Willa and isn't taking the news well.

With a roll of my eyes, I tuck the note into my bag and drive up to the resort, where we'll be having lunch at Snow Ghost. When I arrive, I see that most of the attendees are already here, and I'm surprised to see that even London is here, too.

"You're in town!" I hug her close, so happy to see her. "But isn't it football season?"

"Yes, but I carved out a day away so I could come to this. I love these meetings, and it's a nice break from the city. Caleb came with me and convinced me that he's old enough to stay at the condo by himself. Since I'm so close by, I decided to give it a go. I'm nervous as hell."

"He'll be great," I assure her. "Besides, you're only a three-minute walk away."

"That's what I figured," she says with a laugh and frowns when I clutch my stomach. "Hey, you okay?"

"I think I might throw up." I cover my mouth with my hand and rush off for the bathroom. The yogurt I managed to choke down this morning comes back up, and I take a minute to breathe deeply and rinse my mouth before returning to the others.

But when I walk out of the restroom, not only is London waiting for me, but Summer, Millie, Abbi, Erin, and even Doctor Roni Masters are all frowning at me.

"Uh, guys, I'm fine."

"Didn't sound like it from here," Millie says.

"How long have you been nauseated?" Roni asks.

"A few days." I shrug a shoulder. "I probably have a little bug or something. I don't have a fever, though, so I'm fine."

"We're going to go start the meeting," Abbi says and reaches out to pat my shoulder. "Talk to Roni for a sec, just to be sure."

"I'll stay here," London assures the others. "Go get started, and we'll be right behind you."

"They're making a fuss about nothing," I inform Roni as she touches my forehead. "See? No fever. I'm totally *fine.*"

"Let's go back into the restroom, where there's privacy," Roni suggests, and the three of us move inside. Once the door is closed, she turns back to me, just as Summer slips inside with us.

"Bestie," Summer says with a shrug. "Can't stay away."

London loops her arm around Summer's shoulders, and they stay back, listening.

"I'm really okay," I insist, feeling silly now that so much attention is being aimed my way. "It comes and goes."

"Polly," Roni says, "is it possible that you could be pregnant?"

"No." My answer is immediate, and I shake my head emphatically. "I'm on the pill. I may be a forgetful person, but I *always* take my pill. I have an alarm set and everything, just to make sure."

"While the pill is usually reliable, it's not 100 percent. Are you sure you didn't forget it?" Roni asks.

"No, I'm sure." I shake my head, but Summer's eyes narrow. "What?"

"What about in Paris?" she suggests. "Were you on schedule in Paris?"

"Yes. My alarm went off at nine p.m. every day."

"Wait," London holds up a hand. "There's a time change, Polly. Did you account for that?"

I open my mouth and then close it again.

"And to be clear," Roni adds, "you have it set as an *alarm*, not in your health app? The health app updates with the time differences."

"I didn't even know that I *have* a health app." I blink

at the three women, and my heart starts to thump hard in my chest. "Oh, Jesus. Oh, God."

I have to lean back against the counter as Summer rushes over and puts an arm around me.

"It's getting stuffy in here," I say, struggling to breathe.

"I'll get some water," London volunteers, leaving the bathroom.

"Okay, I need you to take long, slow breaths. I don't want you to pass out," Roni says, breathing the way she wants me to, but my mind is whirling. *Could* I be pregnant? Oh, God, I'm not ready for that. Things are so good right now. I don't want to mess it all up.

"It's okay," Summer assures me. "Polly, everything is okay. Whether you're pregnant or not, you've got this."

"Not part of the plan," I mutter and hang my head in my hands. "It's so new, Summer. It's too soon."

"Hey, Ryan cares about you."

"I *know* that," I reply as London walks in with water. "We already told each other we love each other, and he's asked me to move in."

"Congratulations," London says with a wide smile as I sip the water. "That's excellent news. Of course, anyone with eyeballs can see that he's completely smitten with you."

"But a baby? We just said the L word last week. It's too new, you guys."

"Whoa," Roni says, "slow down. You're sending yourself into a panic attack, and we don't even know for sure if you *are* pregnant. I suggest you go take an at-home test. They're very accurate, and if you're having symptoms, you'll get an accurate reading. Do that first and then take the next step."

"She's right," Summer says. "Let's go. We'll take a test."

"We have the meeting."

"I'll make your excuses," London says. "It'll be fine, and they'll understand. I'll just say that you're under the weather and Summer left to help you. It's really okay. You'll go crazy if you wait to take the test."

"She's right," Summer agrees.

And I know that I could never sit through this whole lunch with my mind whirling, wondering if I'm *pregnant.*

"Okay," I agree. "I'll swing through the pharmacy. Meet at my house?"

"Let's do it," Summer says with a nod.

Less than an hour later, I'm staring down at two lines on a white stick.

"Well, fuck me."

"He did, and he has super sperm because you're pregnant even while on the pill."

I feel my eyes fill with tears as I look up at Summer, and she rushes over to pull me in for a hug.

"Oh, honey, don't cry."

"I've been crying nonstop for the past week," I reply and accept the offered tissue. "Shit, he's going to think I'm trapping him for his money."

"Oh, for fuck's sake," she says, rolling her eyes. "Ryan isn't stupid. You're in love, you're hot for each other, and these things happen. He's not going to think you're trapping him."

"Everyone else in town will."

"Stop it. No, they won't. Besides, who gives a shit if they do? He *loves* you. He already said that before a baby was even a consideration, so I know that it's soon, but, Polly, you could do far worse than being in love with a very wealthy man whose mission in life is to make sure your every whim is seen to."

Well, when she puts it like that...

"Okay, maybe it won't be that bad, but..."

"No buts. Go find that man, tell him about this baby, and figure it out together."

I blink at her, wipe my nose, and sigh. "You really think it'll be okay?"

"I do. I know Ryan. He's not going to disappoint you with this, friend."

"Okay. I'm going out there now, before I lose my courage."

"Excellent idea. Call me later."

I have no idea how I'm going to bring up the subject with Ryan, but I figure I'll wing it when I get there.

I pull out of my driveway and head down the street. The red Mercedes is still parked down the block. I wonder if they moved in? After I pass them, I see them pull onto the street behind me, and then I don't pay them any attention at all as I feel dread fill my chest.

Poor Jake. I don't want him to feel bullied into sharing his dad with me and a new baby. I'm already about to interrupt his life, and I feel bad enough about *that.* Add on a baby, and that's a lot of disruption for a kid who's lived with chaos most of his life.

I turn onto the highway, headed out of town, and suddenly, something hits me from behind.

With a gasp, I look in the rearview mirror and see the red Mercedes.

"What the fuck?"

They ram me again and then zoom up beside me and side-swipe me, pushing me off the highway altogether. I scream as my SUV plummets into the ditch and then head-first into a tree.

I'm dizzy, looking around, and see that the tiny car also hit a tree, and whoever is driving isn't moving.

Oh, God. I have to call for help. But I'm so dizzy.

I'm so...dizzy.

CHAPTER TWENTY-FOUR

JAKE WILD

I can't *believe* I forgot my practice bag at home this morning. I had to drive all the way out to the ranch to fetch it after school and then all the way back to town for practice. We don't have a game tonight; instead, it's tomorrow, so I can't miss this practice. If I do, I won't get to play tomorrow, and I love playing too much to have to sit out.

Aside from Dad and the ranch, football is the best thing in my life right now.

I don't really mind the drive in and out of town every day. I *love* my truck, and driving it is totally legit, so it's all good.

I'm almost to town when I see Polly's car, and I can't help but smile. I sure love her. I wonder when Dad's going to figure out that he does, too, and finally ask her to marry him. Just when I raise my hand to wave, a red car zooms up next to her and pushes Polly off the road.

I check the mirror before slamming on my brakes and flip around to rush over to Polly.

Oh, God. Oh, God. Oh, God.

She can't be hurt. What the fuck did that idiot do that for? Oh, shit, she has to be okay.

As I push out of my truck, I call 9-1-1.

"I just saw an accident," I begin. "Two cars."

I give all the details and whip the door of Polly's car open.

"She's unconscious," I say, feeling fear and panic rising in me. "Oh, shit, she's unconscious. Help!"

"Okay, it's okay. Feel her neck. Is there a pulse?"

I press my fingers to Polly's neck and almost cry in relief.

"Yeah, there is. Yeah."

"Good. I have an ambulance on the way. How is the person in the other car?"

"They're looking around," I reply with a scowl. "It's a woman, and she's looking around."

"Stay there until the first responders arrive."

"I'm not leaving." I hang up and immediately dial my dad's number.

"Hey, buddy, did you forget something else?"

"It's Polly." I lick my lips. "It's bad, Dad."

"Where are you?" His voice is hard now, like he gets when something is really serious, and I can hear him running through the house.

"Close to town. I saw the car hit her. She's not awake. She has blood on her head."

"I'm on my way. Did you call 9-1-1?"

"Yeah, I called them first. They're coming."

"Okay, you stay with her, Jake. I'll be there in five."

He hangs up, and I take a breath. God, this is what happened to my parents. This is how *they* died.

But I didn't have to see it.

"Polly," I say gently and squat beside her. I don't want to move her in case she hurt her neck. They told us in health class to never move someone in an accident. "Hey, I'm here with you, okay? You're kind of beat up, but you'll be okay. Dad's coming, and the ambulance will be here soon."

Tears spring to my eyes when I hear the sirens coming.

"Hear that? They're coming now. We'll go to the hospital. I'll go with you. I won't leave you alone, okay?"

"Jake?"

"Polly!" I take her hand when she reaches for me. "Hey, I'm here."

"Dizzy," she says. "What happened?"

"That crazy bitch ran you off the road." I glance over and see that she hasn't gotten out of her car yet, and I'm not going to her. I won't leave Polly. "I saw it all happen. She did it on purpose."

"Why?"

"I don't know. Hey, don't cry." Tears are running down her cheeks. "Does it hurt?"

"A little." She clears her throat and squeezes my hand. "I'm okay. I'll be okay. Thank you for staying with me. I love you, Jake. It's going to be fine."

Now I can't control *my* tears. It's probably just adrenaline or something. Finally, the ambulance screeches to a stop behind us, and people come running up to us while others go to the other lady.

"This is Polly Allen," I inform them. "She says she's dizzy."

"Looks like you have a knot on your head," one of the EMTs says. "Does anything else hurt?"

"My knee," she says. "I think I hit it."

"No neck pain?"

"Headache," she says. "Dizzy. Is Jake still here?"

"I'm here," I say and take her hand again. "I'm going with her."

"Are you family?" someone asks.

"She's my mom," I lie easily, not willing to be away from her, and it makes me feel good when Polly smiles and doesn't tell them that I lied.

Just as we're loaded up into the ambulance, I see my dad's truck come screeching up, and he's out of it in a flash, running towards us.

"Wait," I say before they can shut the doors. "I'm going with her! She's okay."

"I'll be right behind you," he says as the doors close, and we take off for the hospital.

"Do you have any medical conditions?" the EMT asks Polly, who's still holding on to my hand. She's on a flat board with her head strapped down, in case her neck is hurt. Her eyes move to me, and she licks her lips.

"I'm going to tell them something that you need to keep between us, okay, Jake?"

"Sure, okay." I nod at her. Hell, I'll do whatever she wants right now.

"I'm pregnant."

"Holy shit." I was *not* expecting that.

"Jake—"

"I won't tell," I insist. "But does Dad know?"

"I was on my way to talk to him," she says, as tears spill out of her eyes. She can't move, so I wipe them away for her.

"Hey, it's okay. You can tell him. Holy shit, I'm gonna be a big brother! Oh, God, we're having a baby!"

She squeezes my hand so tight, and she starts to cry more, and that makes me cry, too, even though I don't want the other guy to see it and think that I'm a baby.

But I kind of don't care.

"It's okay, sweetie," Polly says. "I'm so sorry."

"Sorry? Why? We're having a baby!"

"You're not mad?"

"No!" God, why would I be mad? I like kids. I always wanted a family of my own, a *real* family, and I have it. It's the coolest ever. "It's going to be really hard not to tell Dad, so you have to tell him fast, though."

"How are you feeling, Polly?" the EMT asks. "Still dizzy?"

"No, not as bad. Just the headache now."

"That's a good sign," he says with a kind smile and winks at me, and it makes me feel a little better.

I look out the back window, but I don't see my dad's truck. I frown, wondering where he is when we pull into the hospital.

"Okay, let's get you checked out."

We're whisked inside, but Polly doesn't let go of my hand, and it feels good that she wants me with her.

We're going to have a baby.

The ambulance pulls away, and I rush back to my truck, but before I can close the door, I hear someone screaming my name.

"*RYAN!* Oh, Ryan, I knew you would come for me."

I spin and stare, not believing what I'm seeing.

"*Claudia*?"

"Oh, Ryan." She throws herself into my arms, sobbing on my shoulder. "I knew you'd come."

"What in the hell are you doing in *Montana,* of all places?"

"I came, of course," she says, frowning. "I knew, when you were at my show in Paris, that you wanted me. So, I came. I had to get rid of that annoying little gnat that was attached to you, but I came. And now we can be together."

Jesus fucking Christ.

"Ry?"

I turn at the sound of my brother's voice.

"Chase, get her off of me," I say grimly, wanting nothing more than to follow that ambulance and find out if Polly's okay.

"What? No!" Claudia's gorgeous face turns mutinous as Chase pulls her away. "Ryan, what are you doing?"

"I'm pretty sure she caused the accident," I say to Chase, ignoring Claudia altogether. I'm so fucking *pissed* that I'm afraid I'll do something stupid, like punch her. "Jake will confirm. He saw it all."

"That rental is in a Claudia DuBois's name."

"That's her," I reply wearily. "I'll fill you in later, but I need to get to the hospital. I don't know how badly Polly's hurt."

"What are you talking about?" Claudia demands, her blue eyes wild as she screams. "*I'm* the one you love. We're getting married! We're together, lover. Why are you acting like this?"

Chase's lips twitch, and I sigh. "I'll punch you in the face," I say to him, and he laughs.

"Don't worry, we'll take care of her. I'll want to talk to all three of you, but I'll come to the hospital after we have this wrapped up."

I nod and don't even give Claudia a glance as I walk to my truck and take off to the hospital.

I knew that Claudia wasn't...right. Based on what I knew of her a couple of years ago, I figured that she most likely had some mental health issues. Hell, she basically stalked me for the better part of a year, and I was *not* pleased when we ran into her in Paris, but I'd hoped that enough time had passed that she would be mellow about it.

Apparently not.

The fact that she ran the love of my life off the road and tried to kill her means that I have zero sympathy for Claudia, and I'll make sure that Polly will be pressing charges against her.

Right now, my only focus is Polly and making sure that Jake is okay.

"Polly Allen," I say immediately when I get to the emergency room. "She was just brought in."

"Let me check," the receptionist says and calls back. "I have someone here for Polly. Is she okay to have another visitor? Okay, I'll send him back." She hangs up the phone and says to me, "Room seven."

Before the words are even out of her mouth, I'm rushing through the door that she just buzzed open, looking for room seven, and brush the curtain aside as I step inside.

"Dad," Jake says quietly. "She's sleeping again. She has a mild concussion, and we're waiting to see what the X-ray says about her knee."

I simply pull Jake into my arms and hug him close. "Thank you for being here with her."

"Sure, it's no big deal."

"It's a huge deal." I bump my forehead against his, and then I take Polly's hand and sit next to her. When Jake starts to leave, I frown up at him. "Where are you going?"

"Well, um, I'm gonna find something to eat."

With that, he hurries off, and I feel Polly squeeze my hand.

"Hey," I say and kiss her knuckles. I hate that she has the beginnings of a black eye and a bandage on her head, near her hairline. "How are you feeling?"

"I'm okay," she says. "They gave me something for the headache. Bump on the head, and we're pretty sure the knee is just sprained."

Relief rushes through me. Jesus, it could have been so much worse.

"Who was in that car?" she asks with a frown. "Was it Melissa?"

"Melissa? No," I frown over at her. "Why would it be her?"

"I didn't give her a positive reference for a job." She swallows hard, as if her mouth is dry. "She's mad. Left a threatening note on my car."

I kiss her hand again and make a mental note to have Chase look into Melissa.

"No, it was Claudia DuBois."

Polly frowns and blinks at me. "*What*?"

"I know, it's unbelievable."

"Ryan, I've seen that car all over town. It's been driving through my neighborhood for a week and was parked down the street from my house. I've seen it drive by the shop. I figured a neighbor got a new car." She tries to sit up straight, obviously agitated, and I lean in to kiss her cheek.

"Hey, easy, babe. I don't want you to get upset."

"Too late," she mutters and closes her eyes. "I wish I had more energy. I want to pace."

"Stay still. Claudia's mentally ill," I tell her. "I told you that I dated her, very briefly, a couple of years ago. Well, after I broke it off, she stalked me for a while. She'd go underground and then pop up, surprising me, showing up in random places all over the world. She's smart. She was obsessed with me, or, I guess, the idea of me. I'd already upped my security presence because of the other situation, so she didn't really worry me much. But I alerted the police, and she stopped contacting me and showing up in the same places I would be. I thought she'd moved on."

"And then we saw her in Paris, and she caused that huge scene."

"Yes."

"And you didn't say anything to me about all of this, even though you told me that you'd been with her."

I sigh again and rest my forehead on the back of her hand. "I thought it was over. It had been over for a while. I was absolutely *not* expecting her to decide to hurt you, Polly, or I would have had my men take care of it."

"I feel like this might be something we should have anticipated," she says with a frown. "If she was that unhinged before, it makes sense, Ryan."

"Fuck." I push my hand through my hair and stand to pace myself.

"Hey, no fair, I can't do that."

"I'm sorry," I say and look down at her, so small and frail looking in that bed. "You're right, I should have figured she would try something, and I didn't think of it because I've been too focused on you and Jake and this incredible life we're building. I *should* have thought of it. I'm smarter than that."

"Yeah, you are. But your security team should have thought of it, too."

I stop and nod. "You're right. That's their job. I suspect after Claudia is charged with attempted murder, assault, stalking, and any other charges we can bring against her, we won't have to worry about her anymore."

Polly takes a deep breath, lets it out, and her bottom lip starts to quiver.

"Ah, baby."

I rush back over to her and pull her against me.

"I'm so sorry, my love. I'm *so sorry.*"

"It's not your fault," she says with a sniff. "I'm extra emotional these days, and maybe the past hour is catching up with me. But we have to talk, Ry."

"I'm right here."

She starts to speak, but the doctor comes in with a smile.

"Good news," he says as he puts films on a light board and turns it on. "No break. Looks like you just wrenched the knee, so you'll need ice and some ibuprofen for that. Oh, wait," he consults the chart, "you'll want to stay away from ibuprofen if you can. Let's stick with Tylenol, but if that doesn't help, you *can* take a small dose of the other, but not after twenty weeks. I'll write that down for you."

I frown. Twenty weeks of what? She'll have knee pain for that long? I'm no doctor, but that doesn't sound right.

"Let me get some discharge instructions printed for you, and you can go home," he says. "Take it easy, and be sure to see your doctor as soon as possible."

"Thank you," Polly says as he leaves the room. She turns to me, and her green eyes suddenly look guarded. "I have to tell you something."

"Okay."

She blows out a breath and then bites her lower lip.

"Hey, it's okay. What's up?"

"Oh, Jesus, this is harder than I thought."

I narrow my eyes on her. "Polly, I'm going to need you to say what you need to say, please."

"I'm pregnant."

I blink rapidly and feel all the blood drain from my face as she stares up at me.

"You're *pregnant*?"

"Yeah. I literally *just* found out this afternoon, and I was on my way out to the ranch to talk to you when the accident happened. I wasn't keeping it from you, Ryan. I promise."

"Okay." I nod and take this in.

"I suspect it happened in Paris," she continues. "I screwed up the timing of my pill because of the time change, and even missing it by like eight hours appears to be enough for your superhuman sperm to do their thing."

I shove my hands into my pockets as I watch her face. I can't tell how she's feeling.

"Say something," she finally says.

"How do you feel about this?" I ask her.

"I'm not thrilled," she admits and then closes her eyes. "And I feel guilty about that. But, Ryan, we're just starting, and I'm still building a business, and it's just really bad timing. And by the look on your face, you're not exactly elated about it."

"I'm actually really happy," I reply, "but I need to know what you feel. Let's get you out of here and home, and then we can talk."

"Okay." She licks her lips and nods just as Jake comes strolling in with Chase right behind him.

"Do you need to ask her questions right now?" I ask him, shoving my hands into my pockets. "Or can you talk to her tomorrow?"

"I'm not here for that," he says, shaking his head. "I'll do a formal interview tomorrow. I wanted to stop in to make sure Polly's okay."

I smile at my brother and then down at the love of my life, lying in that bed.

"I'm going to be okay," she assures him. "Thank you for stopping by."

"That's what brothers do," he says, clapping me on the shoulder. "It's what *family* does. You call any one of us if you need anything."

"Thank you," I tell him. "Will you call the others?"

"Already done," he says. "They'll be checking in with you later. I'm headed out on another call. You get better."

"I'll do my best," Polly says with a smile as Chase leaves.

"Did you guys...talk?" Jake asks.

"He knows," Polly assures him, and Jake offers me his fist for a bump.

"Isn't it cool? We're having a baby. I'm gonna be a brother. Sorry that I found out first, but the EMT asked in the ambulance, and I was there. I swore I wouldn't say anything, though. It's gonna be totally cool. Did they spring us? Can we go home?"

I lock eyes with Polly, who's grinning from ear to ear.

She may be conflicted, but it's clear that she loves Jake and the fact that they shared a secret, even for a little while.

"Yeah, we can go," I tell him and then turn to Polly. "I'd like to take you to the ranch."

"I'd like to go to the ranch," she replies and holds her hand out for mine, which I immediately take and kiss her knuckles. "Thank you."

"We're going to figure everything out," I assure her.

"I'm going down to the stables," Jake says later, after we get Polly situated on the couch with an ice pack on her knee. "Do the afternoon chores."

"Oh, Jake," Polly says with a frown. "Did you miss practice?"

"It's okay," he says with a shrug. "No big."

"You'll have to sit out of the game tomorrow," she says. "Oh, shit, I'm sorry."

"Seriously, it's okay," he assures her, then smiles. "I had to stay with you. It was way more important."

Then he's off, and I finish making sure Polly is comfortable and lay a cool pack on her forehead.

"I'm going to run outside for a second. I'll be right back. Are you okay?"

"I'm fine," she assures me and lifts her chin so I will kiss her lips. "Thank you."

"Christ, I could have lost you today." I can't resist pressing my lips to her cheek as every worst nightmare runs through my mind.

"You didn't." She cups my face in her hand and smiles up at me with so much love, it takes my breath away. "I'm right here, and I'm not going anywhere."

"Good. I'll be back before you know it. There's something I have to do."

I texted Axel a few minutes ago and asked him to meet me by the garage. I don't want to do this in the house where Polly could hear me.

Axel is waiting for me when I approach.

"What in the ever-loving *fuck* am I paying you for?" I want to punch him in the face, so I stop twenty feet away, where he's out of reach.

"Mr. Wild, we had no reason to think that Claudia would come here."

"She's been erratic in the past," I remind him. "Why wouldn't you have kept eyes on her after the incident in Paris?"

He blows out a breath and hooks his thumbs in his pockets. "It didn't occur to us."

"And it almost killed Polly!" I've never been so fucking livid. "The entire security detail is on notice. If any one of you so much as *sneezes* wrong, you're out of here. This was a mistake that will not be tolerated."

"Sir."

I can see the anger radiating off him, and it only fuels my own.

"Do you have a problem with that?"

"No, sir."

"Then explain to me why you look pissed off right now."

"Because you're right." His hard eyes find mine. "We fucked up. *I* fucked up. I know better, and I should have anticipated it. If you want my resignation, I'll give it to you."

I pause, watching him.

"Ten minutes ago, I would have taken it."

He doesn't flinch.

"Don't you *ever* fuck up like that again."

"No, sir."

I'm on my way back to the house when my phone rings, and I see that it's Remington on the screen.

"Hey."

"How is she?" he immediately asks.

"She's going to be fine," I reply, emotion running through me. Jesus, I've never felt like falling apart the way I do right now. "It was scary, but she's okay."

"Good. I'm glad to hear that. Do you need anything?"

This. This is all I've needed from Rem for the past six years. "I can't think of anything off the top of my head."

He's quiet for a heartbeat, and then, "I'm not good at apologies. You know that."

I swallow hard and sit on the steps that lead up to my front door. "Yeah, none of us are."

"You've apologized," he disagrees. "And I've been a jerk about it. I'm not sorry about the way I reacted back then. My feelings weren't wrong."

"I get that."

"But I'm tired of being pissed off at you, and I miss you. So, I'm sorry for not working things out before this."

I clear my throat, glad that no one is around to see the tears fill my eyes.

"Thanks for that."

"And if you need *anything*, we're just a few minutes away."

I nod, even though he can't see me. "I appreciate it."

"Okay, then."

"Rem." There's a pause on the other end of the line, waiting for me. "I'm really *so* sorry."

"I know. We're okay, little brother. Call if you need me."

"Same goes."

We hang up, and I drop my head into my hands and let the onslaught of emotion hit me.

Relief that she's okay.

Anger at my security team.

Love for my family.

Anticipation for a new baby.

It's been a lot for one day.

Climbing the stairs, I let myself into the house and

walk into the living room, where Polly's lounging on the couch, looking at something on her phone. She sets it down on her lap when she sees me coming, and I sit on the table across from Polly and lean my elbows on my knees.

"Let's talk, babe." Every time I think about the fact that she's pregnant, I get butterflies, and I want to get excited, but until I know exactly what Polly's feeling, I don't want to show it. I don't want to influence her.

"Are *you* okay?" she asks. "You look shaken."

"It's been one hell of a day," I reply with a rueful smile. "I'm going to be fine. I just want to hear what's going on in your gorgeous mind."

"Do you want more children?" she asks me, reaching for my hand. "We've never talked about it."

"Yeah, I do." If it means having them with Polly, I'll have a dozen more. "I like kids, and I've discovered that I'm kind of good at being a dad."

"You're an *excellent* dad," she says with a soft smile. "I don't have any question about that."

"What about you? Do *you* want kids?" I'm watching every emotion cross her beautiful face. There's hope and fear and then hope again.

"Yes. Definitely. But I wasn't planning on it happening *now*. I've worked really hard on my business, and I love the IWC."

"No one said anything about you giving those things up."

"But my attention will be split," she says.

"Erin and Abbi do it. London does it. And I hate to be

the one to point this out to you, but I'm here, too. I have no intention of giving up my businesses, either. We have families, and we can hire help if we need it."

She bites her lip and nods. "I guess that's true."

"Hey." I lean in closer and drag my fingertips down her jawline. "Be brutally honest with me. What has you hesitating? Do you want to end the pregnancy?"

"No," she says immediately, and my shoulders drop with relief. "Okay, I'm just going to purge out everything that's running through my head."

"Great. I'd love for you to do that."

"I feel so *guilty*," she says, surprising me. "I assured you that I had the birth control covered, and I *did*. I do. I can be really forgetful, but never when it comes to that. I have alarms set. I would *never* be irresponsible when it comes to that."

"I know you wouldn't."

"But when we went to Paris, my alarms got screwy because of the time change. I didn't even think of it, and I feel so stupid because I *should* have thought of it. It makes total sense. And now, I'm pregnant, and I don't want you to think that I'm trying to trap you or that I'm some kind of gold-digging asshole, and I know people are going to talk, and that makes me so mad. I don't *like* surprises like this. Having a family isn't something that should sneak up on you. We should have had the chance to do it on our own terms, when *we* were ready."

She swipes at tears, and it just about rips my heart out of my chest.

"And you're so stoic about it. Jake was *excited*. He isn't

mad at all that I'm bringing another baby into the family, and it's going to take your attention away from him. He took it really well, but you haven't even cracked a smile, and I'm afraid that you think I'm a gold digger and that you want me to end the pregnancy, but I don't want to do that. I'm just confused, and if you were excited, I think I'd get more excited. But I just found out *today,* and I'm totally freaking out."

"Breathe." I kiss her forehead as she takes a deep breath. "Honey, I *am* excited. I'm fucking thrilled, but I've been trying to keep that in check because I can see that you have conflicting emotions about this, and I'm trying to support you."

"Okay, but show me that you're happy."

I laugh and kiss her, framing her face and breathing her in, relieved that she's safe and whole and here with me.

"I love you," I tell her, feeling a little panic when her eyes fill again. "I told you that the other night, and I've told you every day since."

"I love you, too," she whispers.

"This doesn't change that. Not at all. If anything, I love you *more.* Babe, I intend to build a life with you. That's what I meant when I said move in here with us. We're starting a life together, and now that includes someone new."

"Yeah, I guess so." She sniffs and takes another breath, readjusting the ice on her knee. "I wish we had more time together before this happened."

"We're going to have time," I assure her. "This baby

isn't an imposition. No more than Jake would be. Sure, it's quicker than we thought, but we just pivot, babe. I live my life pivoting, and it's going pretty well for me so far."

She smiles at me, those beautiful green eyes *finally* full of happiness and hope. "We're having a baby, Ryan Wild."

"It's a good thing I built a big house." I kiss her softly. "We have lots of space for a dozen babies."

"A *dozen*." She laughs and drags her hand down my chest. "Let's start with one and see how that goes."

"I can live with that." I pull my fingertips down her jawline. "You are every wildest dream I've ever had come true. As long as we're together, we'll figure everything else out."

"You say some really sweet things, you know."

"It's the truth."

"I have an idea," Jake says as he walks into the room and then stops short. "Whoops. I'll come back after you're done sucking face."

"We're done," Polly says with a laugh. "What's your idea?"

"Well, a while back, Dad and I were talking about what we should call this ranch, since it doesn't have a name yet."

"You said you'd think about it," I reply, remembering. "What did you come up with?"

Jake clears his throat and licks his lips, suddenly nervous. "Maybe it's stupid."

"Not stupid," I reply. "Let's hear it."

He shoves his hands into his pockets. “Rising Hope Ranch. Because some of us came here to heal but found love instead. Found hope.”

“Even me,” I murmur and look over at Polly. “What do you think of that?”

“Me?”

“Yeah, you,” Jake says. “I mean, you’re gonna live here, too. And you get two votes because there’s two of you.”

“First, I vote that Jake is in charge of always telling me that I get two votes,” Polly says, making us laugh. “And second, yeah. I think that’s beautiful, Jake. What a great name.”

“It’s settled then.” I grin at my boy. “Rising Hope Ranch.”

“Sounds like home to me,” Jake says before rushing off to raid the kitchen, and I turn to Polly, who’s smiling over at me.

“Sounds like home,” she agrees softly.

Two Months Later...

"How long is she going to jail for?" Millie asks as we put cookies from Jackie's bakery on a platter. Ryan and I are hosting a party at our house today, and everyone thinks it's just a pre-holiday thing. They don't know that we're going to announce that we're pregnant.

I'm *so* excited.

"Ten years," I reply.

"Not long enough," Erin says, scowling. "She should *never* get out."

"I don't make those rules," I reply and finish with the cookies. Ryan and I didn't attend Claudia's trial, but our attorney kept us informed every day of what was happening, and since she pled guilty, it wasn't a long one.

"I *love* your closet," Summer says as she samples a cookie. "Seriously, Ryan is *good* at hiring people for renovations. And, given that he added about five thousand square feet to this already massive house, it happened really quickly."

"Ryan may claim to be patient, but he gets things done fast," I agree with a laugh, just as the man himself walks into the kitchen.

"What is going on in here?" he asks. "Everyone's here."

"We're just talking," Abbi tells him. "Getting dessert ready."

"We're good to go," I assure him, kiss him quickly, and then carry a tray to the living room, where our parents, siblings, and friends are all gathered, laughing and having a good time. Even London and Drew have flown in for this, and Caleb is hanging out with the kids.

Jake has Russ here. He wanted his best friend to hear the news with everyone else, and we had no problem with that. And Katie finally asked *Jake* out on a date about a month ago, and they've been seeing each other ever since. She's here, too, sitting with the guys.

"Mommy!" Daisy says, running over to Abbi. "I asked Brady to be my date for the father-daughter dance, and he said yes! He's taking me!"

"Oh, uh..." Abbi smiles, but I can see the uncertainty in her eyes as she looks up at Brady, who is *blushing*. I've never seen that man blush before. "You don't have to—"

"Yes, he does," Daisy insists. "He said he would."

"I'm happy to go," Brady says and smiles sweetly at the little girl. "Thank you for inviting me."

"You're welcome. I'm going to wear a pretty dress."

"I can't wait." Brady winks at her and then smiles at Abbi, who looks a little flummoxed. I swear, they've been dancing around each other for months.

I wish they'd just go out on a date, for fuck's sake.

"Hey, Polly, do you mind coming outside for just a minute?" Ryan asks me, and suddenly, everyone in the room is smiling. He wraps a coat around my shoulders, leading me to the glass doors off of the kitchen.

"What's...going on?"

"I just have to speak to you alone really quick," he says, taking my hand and leading me outside.

It's already been a snowy season. We must have three feet on the ground, and it's not even *officially* winter quite yet.

Ryan closes the door behind us, takes my hand, and guides me on a freshly shoveled path that leads to a clearing under a big evergreen tree, where candles hang in glass mason jars from the limbs above, casting everything in a pretty, yellow glow.

When we get closer, I see that there are pink rose petals on the ground, and my heart starts to pick up speed.

"Ryan."

"I'm excited to *finally* tell our families and friends about our little secret," he begins as we slowly walk closer to the candles. "But first, I have to admit that we've been keeping a secret from *you*. I've wanted to do this since that night on the roof when I told you that I loved you for the first time."

I turn and gaze up at him, my heart already so full

I'm surprised it can hold all the love I feel for this amazing man.

"I worried that it might scare you off, so I decided to wait. I feel like saying the words *I love you* just isn't enough to fully convey how I feel about you. It's not big enough. Not bold enough. I thought I had everything I needed before you came into my life. I'm a wealthy man, and I have a gorgeous kid and a great family, and then you came into the picture and knocked me on my ass."

I grin, loving this beautiful speech. I wish I was recording it because I'm full of so much excitement right now that I'm afraid I'll forget something.

"You are funny and sweet and so fucking smart. Much smarter than me."

"Well, yeah."

He grins down at me. "Nothing's better than being with you. You make me a better person. You make me *want* to be a better person, Polly. I am committed to making sure that every day is the best day of your life. We will have adventures and fights and fun and struggles."

"And makeup sex."

"That's a given." He clears his throat and lowers to one knee, pulling something out of his pocket as he does.

In his fingers is a beautiful oval diamond the size of a baby's fist, glinting in the candlelight.

"I love you, and I'm asking you here and now if you'll do me the honor of being my wife. Marry me, babe."

I sit on his knee so I can kiss the hell out of him, and then I tip my forehead to his.

"Yes. A million times, yes."

He slips the ring onto my finger, and I stare down at it in awe.

"I'm going to be terrified to wear this in public. I'll probably get mugged for it."

"We have security," he says before kissing me again.

When we walk into the house, everyone stands and cheers, and someone offers me a flute of champagne, but I shake my head and look up at my fiancé.

"Tell them," he says as Jake moves over to stand on the other side of me.

With my men surrounding me, I smile at our loved ones as they quiet, wondering what's going on.

"We have another surprise for you," I begin, and feel Jake shift in excitement. I look up at him and grin. "You tell them, buddy."

"Me?"

"Someone tell us," Chase calls out.

"We're having a baby," Jake says. "Well, *she's* having it. You know what I mean."

The room erupts in more applause, and we're all surrounded by hugs and love. I'm a little surprised when Remington embraces Ryan and says, "I'm proud of you. You're a damn good father. I'm sorry for being an asshole."

Ryan blinks, nods, and then hugs Remington back, and it brings tears to my eyes.

"Thank *God* everyone knows and I don't have to keep it a secret anymore," Summer says as she hugs me. "I'm so happy for you, friend."

"Thank you." I hug her back. "Holy shit, we have to plan a wedding."

"Hell yes, we do."

"Wait!" Ryan calls out, quieting the room once more. "We have another announcement!"

"Shit, you've been busy," Brady says with a laugh.

"You're not kidding," Ryan replies and pulls Jake to his side. "As of last week, Jake is officially Jacob Remington Wild. It even says so on his birth certificate."

My eyes fly to Remington, whose throat works with emotion.

"You're *kidding*," Joy says, clapping her hands. "Well, isn't this just one of the best days of our lives?"

"I'm a Wild," Jake says, his hands in the air. "And it's *legit*."

We all laugh, and there are more hugs passed around, more excitement and love.

I overhear my dad asking Jake how he feels about the new baby coming.

"It's the best," Jake says in reply. "I finally get to be a big brother."

I glance down at the flashy ring on my finger, then to where Ryan is talking with Remington and Brady, and over to where Jake, Katie, and Russ are laughing. I take in my girlfriends, laughing and chatting, and all the kids, playing and running around.

It's a busy, chaotic, amazing life.

And it's mine.

EPILOGUE
BRADY WILD

We stayed late into the night, talking and celebrating Ryan and Polly and their family. No one left before ten, and the bulk of us stayed past midnight.

I'm damn happy for them.

I've just finished helping pick up empty glasses and plates and stacked them in the kitchen. Ryan called in a service to come tomorrow to give everything a deep clean.

"Come on, baby, I need you to wake up. You know that Mommy can't carry you anymore."

I frown and turn the corner at the sound of Abbi's voice. Daisy is fast asleep on the couch, her little hands under her cheek, and Abbi looks tired and flustered.

"I'll carry her out," I offer, and Abbi glances up in surprise.

"Oh, it's okay. I'll wake her up."

"No need. She had a busy evening." I scoop the little

girl up and cradle her against my chest. "We're ready when you are. No rush, though."

"Let me just grab our coats," she says and hurries to the entry closet. She wraps her red winter coat around herself, and with Daisy's jacket draped on her arm, she nods. "Okay, I'm good."

We wave to Ryan and Polly, and then I follow Abbi out to her SUV, with the little girl still sleeping peacefully against me.

I ease Daisy into her booster seat in the back and gently close the door.

"There you go."

"You really didn't have to," Abbi insists. "She'll have to wake up when I get her home anyway. I'm pretty strong and have never had an issue carrying her, but I swear she's grown so much since school started in September, and I just can't do it anymore."

"I'll follow you home."

Abbi frowns. "Oh, you don't have to do that. Really, we'll be fine."

"The roads are icy tonight," I reply, unsure why I can't just let it go. They manage without me every damn day. "I'd like to make sure you get home okay."

"I have a feeling that fighting with you is a waste of time."

I smile at her, and she rolls her eyes, climbing into the driver's seat.

"I'll be behind you," I inform her before closing her door. I wouldn't usually drive back into town. I live out at Wild River Ranch, so I'm going the opposite way, but there's something about those two girls that pulls at me.

With Daisy, it's easy. She's cute as a freaking button. When she asked me to escort her to the dance, it was an easy yes.

And, I admit, Abbi is hot as hell. She's a curvy woman, with a body that I'd love to get my hands on. My mouth. Hell, every part of me. She has plump lips that I want to sink into and kiss for days. I want my hands in her thick, blonde hair.

I shift in my seat and will my cock to calm the fuck down. Just because I want her doesn't mean that I get her, tonight or any other night.

Abbi lives in a cute townhouse in a good neighborhood in Bitterroot Valley, and she pulls into her driveway and cuts the ignition.

I park at the curb and join her at her SUV, open the back door, and see that Daisy's still sleeping away.

"She won't wake up until tomorrow," Abbi says, smiling softly. "She's always been a good sleeper."

I pick the little girl up and follow Abbi into the townhouse, up the stairs to Daisy's room, and help her quickly change Daisy into pajamas before I pull the covers over her and kiss her forehead.

I notice that the townhouse is clean and decorated nicely and that Abbi's bed is made as I pass by her bedroom.

I'd like to pull her in there and mess that bed up.

"Thanks," Abbi says as we go downstairs. "Would

you like anything? Something to drink? I have some hot chocolate, if you'd like."

Yeah, I want to stay. I want to stay all night.

Which is why I have to go.

"Thanks, but I'd better head home."

"Right." She nods and looks a little embarrassed.

"I'll see you Friday."

She frowns up at me.

"The dance."

"Right. The dance. You have a date with my daughter." She laughs and shoves her fingers through her hair. "I'll see you then."

"Abbi—"

What? What am I supposed to say next? I'm sorry I'm an asshat who can never get serious with a woman? That would be stupid.

Instead, I sigh and head for the door.

"Good night," I say as I turn the nob.

"Good night, Brady."

My name on her lips is a punch to the gut, and I get out of there as fast as possible. What was I thinking, following them home like this? Going into their home?

It's too fucking tempting.

I'd better just stay the fuck away.

But I promised Daisy that I'd take her to that dance. So, I'll do that, and *then* I'll stay away.

It's what's best for everyone.

Are you interested in reading Drew and London Montgomery's story? You can read all about them in The Stand-In, available now in Kindle Unlimited!

https://www.kristenprobyauthor.com/the-standin

Turn the page for a preview of On the Wild Side, Brady and Abbi's story!

https://www.kristenprobyauthor.com/on-the-wild-side

ON THE WILD SIDE PREVIEW

Prologue

Abbi

Five Years Ago

"What am I supposed to do without you?" I can't stop the tears that fall onto my cheeks. Nate has been in and out of sleep, and they tell me that he'll likely slip into a coma soon, so I should say everything that I want to say now, while he can still hear me.

He's on a ventilator, but he's watching me with those big, brown eyes, and his hand tightens on mine.

"I'm so sorry this happened," I continue and lean in to kiss his cheek. "It's not fair. It's not right."

He squeezes me again, comforting me.

Nate is the *sweetest* man on the planet. He's good and generous, and he doesn't deserve this.

"I'll take care of Daisy. Don't worry about us. I promise we'll be okay."

His eyes suddenly look panicked, and I brush my fingers through his hair, doing my best to calm him.

"I won't let her near our baby, Nathan. I will *not.*" He blinks, and I can see that he wants to talk, but he can't.

"I know," I continue. "We already talked about this, and everything is in place, so she can't touch us. I'll make sure of it. And I'll make sure that she always knows you. She's still so little."

Not even two years. Nate didn't even have two whole years with his daughter before he caught pneumonia that devolved into a systemic infection, causing his organs to fail.

He isn't going to get better. He isn't going to leave this hospital.

And I want to wail at the injustice of it.

"I love you." His eyes droop, and I can see that he's so, so tired. "Thank you for five wonderful years. Thank you for being my best friend and such an awesome dad to our baby girl."

He squeezes my hand once more, and then he's asleep again, and all I can do is lay my head on the bed next to him and cry.

Chapter One

Brady

"Come on, girls, it's going to be a bitch of a winter." I crack my whip and maneuver my horse in the snowy pasture, herding our cattle to a meadow closer to the barn, where we can keep an eye on these ladies during the coldest months of the year. Winter in Bitterroot Valley, Montana is a bitch, and it's only early December. We've already seen record snowfall this year, which tells us that it's going to be a long, cold winter.

And we need to make sure these girls make it through calving season in a few months.

"Storm's moving in," my oldest brother, Remington, yells out to me, and I tip my head back to look up at the sky. The wind has picked up, and the clouds have dropped and grown darker.

"Fuck," I mutter and crack the whip again before I call back to him. "We'll be down this hill in an hour!"

"Let's hope the blizzard holds out that long," Lucky, our senior ranch hand, replies. He's got to be ninety if he's a day. I swear, there's never been a time when Lucky wasn't old as fuck. And no one on this ranch knows what they're doing better than him.

Which is saying something, because my family has owned this land for well over a hundred years. My father, leading us all up ahead, passed the reins on to Remington a few years ago. Ranching, *cattle* ranching, is in our blood. It's who we are.

It's what we do.

But shit, I think Lucky worked for my *grandfather* once upon a time.

I wonder if he's a goddamn vampire.

When we're about a mile from the pasture that the cattle will spend the winter in, the snow starts to blow harder. None of us, the humans or the animals, want to be out here in this, but it reinforces that it's the right time to move the herd.

We might not be able to get to them in a few days, and they'll have a better chance of survival if we can watch them.

With our heads down and our minds on the work, we get everyone safely into the fenced field in less than the hour that I predicted.

"I'll get the water," Bruiser, another of our men, shouts as he swings off his horse and hurries to the troughs to fill them with fresh drinking water for our cows.

Despite the troughs being heated to keep them from freezing, we'll have to come out here several times a day to break up ice that'll form on the top.

Montana is fucking brutal.

But damn if I don't love her.

We work as a team to spread hay, and when everyone is settled into their new home, we lead the horses into the barn so they can warm up and rest. We all put in one hell of a day.

I take my time with my boy, Blackjack, giving him apples and brushing him well before I settle his blanket on his back and kiss his cheek.

"You did great today, boy." He nudges my shoulder, and I grin. "Yeah, we both did, huh? Good boy. I'll see you in the mornin'. You get some rest."

I kiss him once more and then close the door of his stable behind me as I walk out with the others.

"Want to come in for dinner?" Remington asks me.

"You could join us, too, if you want," Bruiser adds. We have a house here for the hands to live in, and they make some damn good food.

I usually eat at either my brother's, or with the hands, but I shake my head.

"Thanks, guys, but I have a date tonight."

My brother turns and frowns at me. I don't usually date at all, and I would never announce it to anyone, so the look on his face makes me laugh.

"I'm taking Daisy to the father/daughter dance at her school."

"Shit, that's right," Rem says, dragging his hand down his face. "I have to take Holly to that. I'd better go get cleaned up."

"Me, too."

"Have fun," Lucky says with a wave. "I'm gonna go put some chili on the stove."

The other two men walk in the direction of the bunkhouse, and I walk with Rem out to his truck.

"I guess I'll see you there," I say with a wink.

"I hate these things," Rem complains with a sigh. "I *love* my girl, but I hate dances."

"Come on, it's only a couple of hours." I laugh again and head over to my 4Runner. "See you later."

With a wave, I hop into the vehicle and drive the couple of miles over to the old cabin that I live in here on the Wild River Ranch. It's the oldest dwelling on the property, and it could use some updating, but it suits me fine. I've lived in the tiny two-bedroom, one-bathroom cabin for almost a decade, and I haven't needed anything more.

Besides, I really only sleep here. I'm always working the ranch or riding a bull. There's no time for anything else.

But when Daisy asked me to take her to her little dance, the night that my brother Ryan proposed to Polly, I couldn't say no. She reminds me of Snow White, with her dark hair and deep brown eyes. She's the cutest little thing, and she was so...earnest when she asked.

Only an asshole would have turned her down.

Besides, I *like* the kid. She hangs out with Holly all the time, and Daisy's mom, Abbi, is always with my sisters, since they started up their women in business group. And that part, the part where Abbi's always around? That's harder to swallow.

Because she's fucking beautiful. I want to have my way with her, and nothing good can come of that, so I have to keep my distance.

"Good job doing that," I mutter as I finish in the shower and towel off. "Taking her kid somewhere is definitely the way to stay away from the mom."

I shake my head in disgust as I get dressed. I'm wearing a goddamn *suit* tonight. I usually only do that for weddings and funerals.

And yet, here I am, the consummate bachelor, taking a little girl to her dance.

My phone pings with a text, and I see that it's Abbi.

Abbi: Hey! The snow is really coming down here. We understand if you don't want to brave the roads to come all the way into town from the ranch tonight. It might not be safe.

I smirk. I've been driving into town from this ranch for half my life. Sure, I'll take it easy, but it's nothing I can't handle.

Me: I'll be there in an hour.

The bubble bounces, then stops for several seconds before it comes back, as if she doesn't know what to say.

Abbi: Okay, we will see you soon. Please be careful.

After I tie my purple tie—Daisy was sure to let me know that she'd be wearing her favorite color, *purple*, to the dance—I grab my black Stetson and head out. Of course, I have a stop to make before I get to Abbi's place.

Abbi was right; the roads into town are a bitch. I have to slow way down because it's hard to see through the blowing snow, but I reach Bitterroot Valley without a mishap.

And just before my sister-in-law, Summer, closes her flower shop for the day.

"I just caught you." I grin at Summer as I walk into her store. "Sorry, the roads were shit. Hey, Chase."

My brother, Chase, is standing by the counter, obviously waiting for his wife.

"It's bad enough that I'm taking Summer home with me, and we'll get her car tomorrow," Chase says.

"Good idea. That bend at Half Moon is icy. Be careful."

"Will do," Chase says with a nod.

"I have your flowers ready," Summer says with a big grin and hurries into the big walk-in refrigerator where she keeps the flowers. She returns with a clear plastic box holding a corsage of purple roses, and a bouquet of pink and orange flowers whose name is completely lost on me.

"Nice," Chase says with a grin. "All of that for Daisy?"

"Fuck off," I warn him, but my brother's smile only grows. "I can't take flowers to one and not the other."

"Right, 'cause that would be rude," Chase says, and Summer rolls her eyes.

"Be nice to your brother," she tells her husband. "He's doing a really fun, cute thing for that little girl."

"Yeah," I agree, making Chase laugh.

"It *is* nice of you," he concedes. "And you look... spiffy."

"I don't want to have to punch you and get blood all over my outfit."

"I'm in uniform," he points out. "I don't want to have to arrest you for assaulting an officer."

I smirk and pay Summer for the flowers.

"Be careful out there," I call out to them as I walk to the door.

"Have fun," Summer calls back.

Abbi lives in a little neighborhood of townhomes on the edge of town. It's a newer area, with a park for Daisy and nice sidewalks and trees. It's a good part of town, which makes me feel good because I know that they're safe.

And I don't even want to *think* about why that's something I worry about.

I pull into the driveway of Abbi's end unit and cut the engine, and with the flowers in hand, I make my way to the door, which is immediately opened by Daisy, who is currently jumping up and down in her ruffly purple dress.

"You're here! You're here!"

"Well, hello there, princess." I wink at her and step inside when Abbi gestures, keeping most of the cold outside. When the door is closed, I offer Abbi her bouquet of flowers, and her gorgeous eyes soften. "For you."

"You didn't have to do that." But she buries her nose in a bloom and fusses over them. "Thank you."

"And for my *gorgeous* date, we have this." I present the box, and Daisy frowns down at it.

"What is it?"

"A corsage," Abbi says with a laugh. "Come on, let me set these in the kitchen, and we'll get the corsage on you, baby."

"Okay." Daisy takes my hand and leads me into the kitchen. I like this townhome, with its open floor plan. This floor is just the kitchen and living room, with a door out to the garage, and another that I assume is a half bath.

The bedrooms are upstairs.

"You look handsome," Daisy says with a bright smile.

"And your tie matches my dress!"

"I heard a rumor that you'd be wearing purple."

Daisy giggles. "I told you, silly."

"Oh, yeah, that's right. Well, your dress is super pretty, and your hair is all curly."

"Mommy did it," she says shyly, gently touching the curls that fall around her shoulders.

"Here, I know how to do this, thanks to prom about a million years ago," Abbi says as she takes the corsage out of the box and slips the wristband around Daisy's wrist, tightening it to fit.

"This way," Daisy says, "it's easier for me to sniff them."

She does and then closes her eyes, as if it's the best thing she's ever smelled.

"Good?" Abbi asks.

"I'm gonna smell them all night. Can we go now?"

"Pictures first," Abbi says, grabbing her phone. "Here, stand by the fireplace."

We pose for photos. In some, I'm holding Daisy's hand. In others, I'm squatting next to her, and she has her arms around my neck.

It all makes me wonder where her father is. Who would willingly miss out on something this great?

Before long, we're on our way to the school where the dance is being held. Daisy's in the backseat of my 4Runner, chatting away.

The kid never shuts up, but it's kind of cute.

"Robert is nice," she says, "but he has red hair."

"Do you not like red hair?"

I glance in the rearview and see her frown, thinking it over. “I do. Polly has red hair, and I like her.”

“Okay, so what’s wrong with his red hair?”

“It’s just...I can’t say because Mom says it’s mean.”

I frown back at her. “You’re not a mean girl.”

“*I know.* Okay, if I tell you, you can’t tell Mom I said.”

“Cross my heart.”

“What does that mean?”

I grin as I pull into the parking lot.

“It means that I promise not to tell.”

“Okay. So, I don’t like Robert’s hair because it looks like spaghetti sauce.”

I wait, positive that there’s more to this story, but she doesn’t say anything else. So, I pull into a parking spot and cut the engine, unbuckle my seatbelt and turn to look at the little girl.

“*That’s* why you don’t like him?”

“I don’t like spaghetti.” She leans her head back in despair. “We had to play duck, duck, goose the other day in the gym, and I didn’t want to touch his hair.”

“Because it looks like spaghetti.”

She nods solemnly.

“And what don’t you like about spaghetti?” Now I’m starting to wonder if *I’ll* ever eat it again.

“It looks like Robert’s hair,” she says, and I can’t help but laugh.

“Well, sweetie, I think of all the things in the world, this isn’t so bad. You don’t have to touch his hair *or* eat spaghetti.”

“Okay. Let’s go in!”

I learned a few things during the dance.

One, little girls will dance forever if given the chance, and they give zero shits about silly things like keeping their shoes on or if anyone cares what they look like.

Two, my brother may have moaned and groaned about going to this thing, but he indulged the hell out of Holly all evening and never once frowned or complained.

Three, Robert's hair does, indeed, look like spaghetti sauce.

And four, I am completely smitten with a little girl.

Of course, I already knew number four. I've had a soft spot for Daisy since the first time I met her, so I'm glad that I came tonight.

"I'll see you tomorrow," I say to Remington, keeping my voice down. We're each holding a little girl, and both of them are passed out cold. "They danced until they dropped."

Rem grins and waves before we go our separate ways to our trucks. I ease Daisy into her booster seat and then drive the five minutes to her house.

The snow hasn't stopped falling. If anything, it's only started falling harder, which means the drive home will be an adventure.

Daisy doesn't even stir when I lift her out of the truck and walk up to the door, where Abbi must be watching because she opens it when I approach.

"I saw your lights," she says and smiles at her daughter. "She must have had fun."

"I've only seen more dancing on *Footloose*," I confirm, making her chuckle. "I'll carry her up."

"Thanks." Abbi gestures up the stairs. I know which bedroom is Daisy's because I helped them home a couple of weeks ago after Ryan and Polly's engagement party.

It doesn't take us long to have Daisy in her pajamas and tucked into bed, and I follow Abbi back downstairs.

"Are you sure it's safe for you to drive home?" Abbi asks with a frown as she nibbles on her bottom lip. "It's snowed another foot since you picked her up."

I sigh and shoot my brother, Chase, a text. "Let me check with Chase."

Me: How nasty are *the roads?*

Almost immediately, he replies.

Chase: Rem just texted. He barely made it home without going off the road. It's a shitshow out there.

I show her the response, and she cringes.

"Stay here," she says, and my whole body reacts. "I have a guest room upstairs, and I'd feel better if I knew that you were safe. The storm should pass by morning."

"Abbi, you don't have to—"

"Am I that repulsive?" she demands, her hands on her hips now. "I know I'm not a skinny woman, and I'm a mom, but I'm only suggesting you stay here, where it's safe. You don't have to worry about me getting naked and trying to have my wicked way with you when my daughter is twelve feet away."

Her eyes go wide, and she covers her mouth with her hand.

"Oh, God," she whispers.

"Number one," I begin, and immediately move in, sliding my hand over her hip. "You're every fucking fantasy I've ever had, so don't *ever* say that shit about yourself again. Got it?"

She's watching me intently as she nods, and her hand falls from her face.

"Number two." I lick my lips as my gaze slips down to her mouth. "I want to kiss you. I won't take it further. I know Daisy's right here, but fuck me, I want to kiss you."

She doesn't pull away.

My hold tightens on her hip, and I cup her jaw with my free hand as my mouth descends to hers, and I nibble. I take my time tasting her before I sink in and *take.* She moans deep in her throat as she moves closer to me, and her hand dives into the hair at the nape of my neck, and I am completely lost to her.

Fuck me, I've wanted this for *months.* I have no business doing it. None whatsoever, but I'll be damned if I can stop.

Finally, though, I loosen my hold on her, and she pulls away, just out of my reach. She's breathing hard. Her blue eyes are on fire as she watches me, and her blonde hair is the perfect halo of light around her, illuminated by the firelight.

"Every goddamn fantasy," I repeat before swallowing hard. "And your curves? Jesus Christ, Abbi, your curves are enough to kill a man."

She giggles, pushes her hands through her hair, and turns away from me, pacing.

"You'll sleep here," she insists. "Because I don't want to worry about you getting home safely."

"Yes, ma'am." I shove my hands into my pockets so I

don't reach for her again. "I have a bag in my truck with necessities."

She lifts an eyebrow, and I grin.

"I get pretty messy at the rodeo. It pays to have extra things on hand."

"Ah. Makes sense. Go grab it."

With a nod, I hurry outside, through the falling snow, and retrieve the bag from the back seat. When I return inside, the lights are off, and Abbi's waiting to escort me upstairs.

Her ass sways back and forth as she climbs the steps ahead of me, and I have to swallow hard and think about something other than burying my face between her legs.

"You're in here," she says, gesturing to the fourth door on this floor. "You'll have to share a bathroom with Daisy."

"No problem." I grin and walk inside, setting my bag on the queen-sized bed. "I appreciate it."

"You're welcome. I'm making pancakes for breakfast, in case you want to stay in the morning."

"Just for me?"

She laughs softly and shakes her head. "No. We have pancakes every Sunday. Goodnight, Brady."

"'Night, Abs."

She bites her lip and flushes, as if she wants to say something else, but she decides against it and closes the door behind her.

When I'm alone, I blow out a breath and shake my head. I shouldn't have kissed her, no matter how badly I wanted to. But damn it, hearing her say that she wasn't attractive to me was fucking ridiculous. Does the woman not know how damn hot she is?

I guess not.

And I was happy to remind her.

But this can't become a habit because I can never commit to her, and she's a *mother.* You don't fuck around with that. She deserves so much more than I can give her.

You can get more information for On the Wild Side here:

https://www.kristenprobyauthor.com/on-the-wild-side

NEWSLETTER SIGN UP

I hope you enjoyed reading this story as much as I enjoyed writing it! For upcoming book news, be sure to join my newsletter! I promise I will only send you news-filled mail, and none of the spam. You can sign up here:

https://mailchi.mp/kristenproby.com/newsletter-sign-up

ALSO BY KRISTEN PROBY:

Other Books by Kristen Proby

The Wilds of Montana Series

Wild for You - Remington & Erin

Chasing Wild - Chase & Summer

Get more information on the series here: https://www.kristenprobyauthor.com/the-wilds-of-montana

Single in Seattle Series

The Secret - Vaughn & Olivia

The Scandal - Gray & Stella

The Score - Ike & Sophie

The Setup - Keaton & Sidney

The Stand-In - Drew & London

Check out the full series here: https://www.kristenprobyauthor.com/single-in-seattle

Huckleberry Bay Series

Lighthouse Way
Fernhill Lane
Chapel Bend
Cherry Lane

The With Me In Seattle Series

Come Away With Me - Luke & Natalie
Under The Mistletoe With Me - Isaac & Stacy
Fight With Me - Nate & Jules
Play With Me - Will & Meg
Rock With Me - Leo & Sam
Safe With Me - Caleb & Brynna
Tied With Me - Matt & Nic
Breathe With Me - Mark & Meredith
Forever With Me - Dominic & Alecia
Stay With Me - Wyatt & Amelia
Indulge With Me
Love With Me - Jace & Joy
Dance With Me Levi & Starla
You Belong With Me - Archer & Elena
Dream With Me - Kane & Anastasia
Imagine With Me - Shawn & Lexi
Escape With Me - Keegan & Isabella
Flirt With Me - Hunter & Maeve
Take a Chance With Me - Cameron & Maggie

Check out the full series here: https://www.

kristenprobyauthor.com/with-me-in-seattle

The Big Sky Universe

Love Under the Big Sky

Loving Cara

Seducing Lauren

Falling for Jillian

Saving Grace

The Big Sky

Charming Hannah

Kissing Jenna

Waiting for Willa

Soaring With Fallon

Big Sky Royal

Enchanting Sebastian

Enticing Liam

Taunting Callum

Heroes of Big Sky

Honor

Courage

Shelter

Check out the full Big Sky universe here: https://www.kristenprobyauthor.com/under-the-big-sky

Bayou Magic

Shadows

Spells

Serendipity

Check out the full series here: https://www.kristenprobyauthor.com/bayou-magic

The Curse of the Blood Moon Series

Hallows End

Cauldrons Call

Salems Song

The Romancing Manhattan Series

All the Way

All it Takes

After All

Check out the full series here: https://www.kristenprobyauthor.com/romancing-manhattan

The Boudreaux Series

Easy Love

Easy Charm

Easy Melody

Easy Kisses

Easy Magic

Easy Fortune

Easy Nights

Check out the full series here: https://www.kristenprobyauthor.com/boudreaux

The Fusion Series

Listen to Me
Close to You
Blush for Me
The Beauty of Us
Savor You

Check out the full series here: https://www.kristenprobyauthor.com/fusion

From 1001 Dark Nights

Easy With You
Easy For Keeps
No Reservations
Tempting Brooke
Wonder With Me
Shine With Me
Change With Me
The Scramble
Cherry Lane

Kristen Proby's Crossover Collection

Soaring with Fallon, A Big Sky Novel

Wicked Force: A Wicked Horse Vegas/Big Sky Novella
By Sawyer Bennett

All Stars Fall: A Seaside Pictures/Big Sky Novella
By Rachel Van Dyken

Hold On: A Play On/Big Sky Novella
By Samantha Young

Worth Fighting For: A Warrior Fight Club/Big Sky Novella
By Laura Kaye

Crazy Imperfect Love: A Dirty Dicks/Big Sky Novella
By K.L. Grayson

Nothing Without You: A Forever Yours/Big Sky Novella
By Monica Murphy

Check out the entire Crossover Collection here:
https://www.kristenprobyauthor.com/kristen-proby-crossover-collection

ABOUT THE AUTHOR

Kristen Proby has published more than sixty titles, many of which have hit the USA Today, New York Times and Wall Street Journal Bestsellers lists.

Kristen and her husband, John, make their home in her hometown of Whitefish, Montana with their two cats and dog.

Made in the USA
Middletown, DE
05 August 2024